A World on Fire

Michelle Ray

A World on Fire © 2019 Michelle Ray

www.michelleraybooks.com

ISBN: 978-1790-659-31-9

Cover image: *Destiny* (1900) by John William Waterhouse. Public Domain

ALSO BY MICHELLE RAY

Falling for Hamlet

Mac/Beth

Much Ado About Something

To Jonathan for his inspiration & research
To Lauren for years of reading & suggestions
To Jews everywhere who question & persevere

Excerpt of Edict of Expulsion of the Jews 1492

...and we knew that the true remedy for all these injuries and inconveniences was to prohibit all interaction between the said Jews and Christians and banish them from all our kingdoms...where it appears that they have done the greatest injury.... Because every day it is found and appears that the said Jews increase in continuing their evil and wicked purpose wherever they live and congregate, and so that there will not be any place where they further offend our holy faith.

...Therefore, we ... resolve to order the said Jews and Jewesses of our kingdoms to depart and never to return or come back to them or to any of them.

Given in our city of Granada, the XXXI day of the month of March, the year of the birth of our lord Jesus Christ one thousand four hundred and ninety-two years.

I, the King [Ferdinand], I the Queen [Isabella]

CHAPTER 1

Lisbon, 1497

Dearest Béa,

*There can be no man who loves more than
I, nor one more anxious to come home from
his travels.*

Beatríz closed her eyes and imagined Yusef whispering his beautiful words in her ear, speaking so close his breath might tickle her neck. Smiling, she shivered, and then looked back at the paper, disintegrating from being folded and unfolded so often.

*Tripoli is wondrous, and I would share it
with you if I could —*

"E-hem."

Beatríz startled out of her dream.

Her sister, Reyna, was standing in the doorway of their bedroom, her face solemn. "I have news of Yusef."

Beatríz's stomach dropped. "Tell me," she whispered, the paper trembling in her hands. Thoughts of shipwrecks and plagues and pirates whirled in her mind, horrible possibilities always for a man at sea.

Reyna's face cracked into a smile. "He's here."

Beatríz blinked, unable to hear past her fears. "What?"

Reyna's smile widened. "Yusef has returned. He is waiting for you downstairs."

Heat, then cold, raced up and down Beatríz's body. A joke? Her sister had made a joke about something bad befalling Yusef? If she had not wanted to get to him so much, she would have slapped Reyna.

Beatríz threw the letter aside, racing down the dark, narrow stairway. Reyna nearly tripped on her skirts as she followed, giggling.

Beatríz's step hitched when she saw Yusef – his thick, dark hair, his confident stance, and the medallion she had given him dangling over the rich fabric of his doublet. Her father was finishing an amusing story, and Yusef's laugh bounced off the walls of the stone entryway. It ceased when he caught sight of her. He beamed and reached out his arms, and she ran down the steps, launching herself into his embrace. Without letting her feet touch the ground, he spun her around and kissed her firmly on the mouth. Beatríz felt a thousand stars explode in her.

Beatríz's father cleared his throat, so Yusef put her down and Beatríz moved a step away, though they kept their fingers laced together. Yusef winked at her, and she squeezed his hand tighter in her own. There was nothing more perfect than this moment, this simple holding of his hand. Of having him here beside her.

When Yusef was away, she forced herself to feel nothing to avoid the ache of his absence. But now it felt as if his touch was cracking the ice that encased her heart. She could hardly keep from leaping at him again, though, with her father standing there, she knew she had to behave.

"When did you arrive?" she asked.

"Only this afternoon," Yusef replied, his piercing gray eyes studying her face. He reached out and twirled dark strands of her hair around his fingers, and Beatríz wanted nothing more than to kiss those fingers. Every inch of her felt alive and desirous of his touch. She knew she was supposed to keep her face a mask, for propriety's sake, but was finding it impossible to do.

"Would you stay for supper?" Beatríz's father asked, angling his body so that the couple could see him.

Yusef untangled his hand from Beatríz's hair. "No. I only came to say hello. My mother has whipped the servants into a frenzy preparing a feast for my return. I find the fuss foolish, but it makes my mother happy."

Beatríz's father nodded. "Well, keeping the women of a house happy is always important."

"Indeed," replied Yusef. Then Yusef reached out for Beatríz's hand again. His rough palms made her esteem him all the more, for his wealth was not simply gained through talk, but earned with hard work. His hand was sweaty and shaking slightly, and she realized he was working hard to control his feelings, as well. "Speaking of making women happy, I know Beatríz loves to visit the port. Might I take her there for a short walk?"

Her father nodded slowly. "Short," he said, looking directly at Beatríz, the brief word laden with warning.

Beatríz linked her arm through Yusef's and headed for the heavy wooden doors of her home, catching sight of Reyna who mouthed, "Lucky."

Beatríz did feel lucky. She had her betrothed back, a man whom she was not being forced to marry, but someone she truly loved. Someone who loved her for who she was and not just the money her parents could offer for a dowry.

"Go on," said her father, "before your mother finds out." Beatríz's mother was always more protective, furious that her father did not more closely guard their "investment." Being referred to as such irritated Beatríz, though she knew that was precisely what her training in music, writing, painting, embroidery, and on and on had been for: to marry into one of the most prominent Jewish families of Lisbon.

"Yusef is a respectable young man," her father would remind her mother, "and his family needs us as much as we need them. Besides, Yusef would not compromise her."

Beatríz and Yusef's hurried around the corner. As they made their way downhill, Yusef held Beatríz's arm for support. The seven hills of Lisbon provided for spectacular views of the endless sea, but also made for treacherous walking for a young lady. They slowed their pace as they entered the nearest square, and Beatríz took a deep breath as she always did when she found herself in an open space. The streets where Beatríz spent most of her time were narrow enough that the sun never shone fully on them. But the squares – ah, the squares – were where Beatríz could fill her lungs and enjoy the light.

They passed a stall selling nuts, and Yusef bought almonds, holding out his palm for her to take a few. Another chance for skin to touch skin. She held his gaze as she laid one on her tongue and rolled it around in her mouth. With a crunch, she turned to the next stall of dried herbs and leaned over to sniff the mound of rosemary. Some women she knew grew rosemary in window boxes, but her mother thought it too base, so Beatríz could only enjoy these sensory pleasures at the market.

They strolled on, and Yusef reached into the water of the fountain children were splashing in. He scooped up water and splashed his face with it, then shook like a dog, droplets hitting her, making her laugh. Then he stopped laughing and his face filled with a familiar desire.

Beatríz knew she had to distract him. "What is that crisscrossed circle design?" she asked, pointing at the sculpture in the middle of the fountain.

He threw her a sidelong glance and smirked. "An armillary sphere, a navigation tool. Many Portuguese artists work nautical symbols into their designs because of our —"

"Prowess at sea," Beatríz finished. He knew she knew. This game, this endless game of getting close and backing off. It had to end.

Beatríz pulled at his hand. "The port," she said.

"You are determined," he replied, raising his thick eyebrows.

"I never get down there," she reminded him. He slipped his hand around her waist and walked her out the other side of the square. "You know my father rarely lets me come to the boats with him anymore, and my mother never wants me to leave the house. What is so interesting about needlework and visiting, I'll never understand. Mamá's friends are dull compared to the harbor. The spices that are carried off the boats — cinnamon and cloves, galingale and cubeb! And all of the languages one can hear – Remember when we heard that man speak Greek? And the fabrics! Oh, the silks and—"

"Why do you care about that? As Jews we are not allowed to wear silk."

"Well I do like to *look* at the things that I cannot *have*," she said meaningfully, and Yusef tucked his lips between his teeth to keep in a laugh.

Sometimes she wondered if she ought to convert to Christianity like some of her friends had back in Toledo. Life would be easier, she supposed. She could wear what she wanted, eat what she wanted, and cease to be a curiosity or an object of hatred. And yet, Judaism was all she knew. She could not profess to have any deep faith, wondering what God really was and what she was supposed to think or feel when she thought of Him. But she believed in *Kavannah* – that God knew of the intent in her heart to be a good person, a good daughter, and hopefully soon, a good wife and mother. She followed Jewish customs of dress and prayer and cooking and therefore *was* a Jew. How could she cease to be herself? It was not something she wanted, no matter the dangers.

They made their way outside the city gates and through the Alfama, the old Muslim section of the city that rested against the sea. Here the buildings were so close that in most spots, three people could scarcely walk shoulder to shoulder through the streets. Despite the light color of the buildings, most walkways were dim, for they were shrouded in shadows morning to night.

Beatríz stopped as they came through the final arch leading to the water and she saw ships of all sorts dotting the blue beyond. There were fragile *barcas* with their fixed square sails, dozens of simple fishing boats loaded down with nets, and the *leudo* with their tapered hulls and single masts. There were even *caravels* – multi-masted ships with pointed sails that could actually cross the ocean. A rumor was spreading that a man by the name of Vasco da Gama would soon lead a fleet of four *caravels* in an attempt to find a route to India. He might be in the harbor at that very moment.

"So terribly beautiful," she said. Overwhelmed by the view, she closed her eyes and breathed in the scent of the sea.

Yusef kissed her gently behind the ear, letting his lips linger as he whispered, "*You* are terribly beautiful." Then he kissed her again, and she was both filled with peace and tingling with anticipation.

Her heart beat much quicker and she wrapped her arms around him, forgetting that they were where others might see, forgetting that she ought to show restraint.

Sailors catcalled at them, and Beatríz buried her face in his chest from embarrassment.

"Forget that Jew," one of the sailors called out. "I'll show you what a real lover is like."

Spying the flag of the Catholic monarchs on the ship, Beatríz felt as if she had stepped out of a warm bath only to have her towel ripped away. She understood every word the man said, for she had lived in Toledo until five years ago when she, like all Jews, was forced to leave her beloved *Sepharad,* the name Jews had given the Spanish kingdoms for over a thousand years. Unlike her parents, Beatríz now hated the land that had thrown her people out, and seeing the flag only made the sailor's words sting all the more.

"I've never had a Jewish girl before," called out another sailor, "but I hear their trenches are deeper and wetter." He licked his lips at this, making her stomach turn.

"If the Portuguese king decides to expel them, too, I'll

take the girl and protect her," shouted the first, his gestures profane.

"She'll need protection from *you*. Remember what you did to that last girl?" a third added. The sailors' guttural laughs sent a chill down Beatríz's spine.

Yusef moved sharply toward the men, but Beatríz grabbed his cape. He turned and looked in her pleading eyes.

With a quiet, determined voice Beatríz asked, "Shall we keep walking?"

He looked at the men again, absently tugging at the red fabric six-pointed star sewn on his cape, and she was keenly aware of the one on her own cloak. They hated being forced to wear the stars, for there was danger enough without showing the world so plainly that they were Jews. But it was the law.

She pulled Yusef farther down the waterway. "You've not told me the most interesting part of your trip." She had to concentrate on keeping her steps steady as they moved away from the sailors. One sign that her legs had gone to jelly and he would insist on bringing her home. When he did not answer, she squeezed his hand. "Tell me of Venice."

"There were canals." He grimaced and looked over his shoulder.

She put her hand on his cheek to bring his gaze back to her own. "That could not have been the most interesting part. Four months you were gone! You know I want to hear about your journeys so that when I go with you someday, I will not be so surprised by what I see."

He stopped. "You will never come with me," he said, his jaw set.

"But we used to say —"

"It does not matter what we once said. We were young

and naïve. You saw those men. I could never bring you out onto the seas. Do you know what happens to women out there?" When Beatríz shook her head, he looked back at the men once again and snarled. "No, you stay here where I know you are safe."

They walked in silence as the bustle around them continued, her heart plummeting. Separated over and over? Being stuck in one house in one city forever? Disappointment dampened the sounds of the water slapping at the walkway, ships knocking against their moorings, men shouting orders and grunting under heavy loads.

Yusef felt her step slow and stopped to face her. "Béa," he said quietly. She loved the way 'Bay-ah' whispered off of his tongue, not like the way her mother said her full name, as if the Z could slice her open. "Béa, my love, we shall have a fine life together. You will see."

She nodded and smiled, trying to think about his returns rather than his departures. He turned and led her under another archway and they wended their way back toward her house in silence.

Before allowing her to go inside, he said, "I have one more thing to tell you."

His grim expression made Beatríz's stomach flip.

"My father has been preparing a new shipment. I have to leave again. In seven days' time."

Beatríz gasped. "Seven –" She could not bring herself to finish.

"This last trip was . . . I came home with nothing. All of that work and –" Yusef narrowed his eyes at the sea. "The captain took everything. Every coin. Every crate. He said I could give it to him or be stabbed and thrown overboard."

"He would not –"

"He would have, Béa. I told you, there is much to this business.... Much I did not believe myself. Much I knew but thought to keep from you. But I want you to know the truth. I do not want you to be ignorant like most wives."

Beatríz nodded, then argued. "My father's money is surely enough to –"

Yusef shook his head. "Your father does not have the money he has promised my family for your *nedunya*. He is attempting to collect on old debts in Toledo, but his cousin has been imprisoned."

Beatríz winced. As a *converso*, Noám had been allowed to remain in Toledo. After converting, he went to church regularly, had his children baptized, appeared to be a good Christian. But he must have been pretending and been caught, or had a business rival turn him in as a "false Christian." Either way, her father had no one to continue collecting on the debts, his primary source of income.

"We can still marry, Yusef. This is love. Not business."

"Our fathers have a contract. You know that, Béa. They must each come to our marriage with what was promised in the *Erusin*." When she opened her mouth to argue, he put a finger against her lips. Seeing her anger flash, he removed his finger but stopped her with a kiss.

Beatríz backed away, not wanting to be placated or silenced. "Contracts. Shipments. I tire of it. Most of my friends are married and have children, friends with far less income, and yet we are still waiting! I am nineteen already and –"

"It will happen, but first I have to go back out and find a port that is safe."

The word 'safe' caught her attention. "What do you mean?"

"The world is on fire, Béa. It grows worse and worse. In truth, I hardly know where to sail." Beatríz's eyes widened, and he added, "Nothing you need to worry about. I will be safe."

She shook her head. "You cannot tell me that your life was threatened by a captain, say, 'The world is on fire,' and expect me not to worry. What is happening?"

Yusef kicked at the cobblestones, clearly questioning whether it wise to have said anything at all. "Civil wars. Land wars. Religious wars. It seems everyone wants to kill each other. All I want is to gather goods and come home to you."

"Do not go."

"This is how I make my money. This is my business. I cannot stop because of fear. My father expects me to trade in Messina this time. I must leave now or I will not be able to go this year. If I do not get enough money, then how will we marry?"

"How will we marry if you are dead?"

He laughed.

"It is not funny!" she raged. A neighbor leaned out of her window to hear the argument, so Beatríz lowered her voice. Quiet or not, she would not give up. "And what if we are expelled from Portugal in your absence?"

"Béa, this is another matter we must discuss," he said, his voice low, his face pleading. "If it happens, would you be willing to travel with my parents instead of your own?"

She hesitated.

"Béa, say that you will." His words were sharp and urgent.

She reached out, stroking the soft fabric of his doublet. "I doubt that such a thing will —"

"My family is sure the expulsion will happen. They have already begun contacting friends and relatives. If you stay with my parents, I will know places to look for you."

"I can leave word for you of where we are going…. *If* we have to go, that is."

Yusef frowned. "If things grow worse, I cannot be certain of crossing the sea twice. My first duty will be to bring the goods to my father wherever he is. If you are there already, we can marry without delay."

It made sense, yet she had to ask, "If I am separated from my parents, how would my father pay my dowry?"

"If we are expelled . . . arrangements will have to be made. Say you will go with my family. Please, Béa, I cannot leave with this uncertainty hanging over my head."

Beatríz thought. She could not fathom being forced out of her home again. But if she had to consider it, she wanted to believe that she would begin her life anew with Yusef as quickly as possible wherever they landed. And if everyone scattered around the Mediterranean, it could be months or years before she and Yusef could reach each other. She would follow his family.

"If your parents are in agreement –" she began.

"They are."

Beatríz was taken aback, but said, "Then I will travel with them."

He smiled, relief smoothing the creases in his brow. "Shall I speak to your father and mother?"

"Let me," she said. Though it would be more traditional to let him, she knew she could manage her parents better than anyone.

"Promise me one thing, though," she said, and he pressed her hand against his heart. "Tell me everything. Tell me what is happening in Lisbon, in Italy, everywhere. I need to understand the world. Your world."

Yusef pulled her into his arms. "Of course. Shall I begin explaining on our way to Juan's house tonight?"

"He is having a card party?" she asked with some excitement.

"You will come?"

She nodded, and as he began to kiss her, the door swung open and her mother stood in stern-faced welcome.

"Until tonight," she said, pushing Yusef away. She smiled a little and went inside.

CHAPTER 2

Don Vidal,

In the name of God.

I am afraid I cannot offer to house you here in Venice. We took in my wife's brother's family some months ago. I have asked a few of my friends, men you might remember from our travels, but none have a place for you, either. I will inquire more widely in the coming weeks, and will write again if I have news.

May God have mercy on you.

- Don Manuel

Beatríz stood reading the letter addressed to her father. It had been lying open in the hallway and the first line caught her eye. It seemed that Yusef was right and her father was planning their escape.

She entered his sitting room holding the letter, checking to be sure her mother was nowhere nearby, and held it out to him. When concern furrowed his brow, she said, "I admit I read it, and I am not surprised by the news. Yusef explained that we might need to leave."

Her father sat back in his chair, turning the letter over and over. "Yusef tells you of such things? Only men need to concern themselves with —"

"Women are also forced to leave their homes, Papá," she interrupted. "It does concern me very much, and yes, Yusef and I speak of such things *together*."

"Unorthodox." He rose and escorted her to the door. "Yusef might treat you like a man, but that is not how I run my house. Neither your mother nor Reyna should hear of these matters. Not yet. Reyna will ask too many questions and your mother . . . well, I do not need her to take to her bed when nothing is certain. You can manage to keep quiet?"

"Of course," she said as he opened the door and guided her out. She turned to face him. "Papá, there is a matter I need to discuss with you. It is about my *dowr—*"

"Not now, my dear. I am busy," he said and closed the door.

She stood a moment facing the dark wood, considering whether to knock again. Instead she straightened up and went to ready herself for the card party.

"Yusef is waiting!" called her father, but Beatríz stood staring at herself in the mirror hoping her gown was appropriate and flattering. Turning side to side, she scowled, trying to forget her mother's reprimand earlier in the evening that she looked too informal and of questionable morals in her favorite burgundy velvet gown.

Clothing had always been a source of dispute in their home. Her mother preferred dark colors and *verdugada* — a skirt stiffened with reeds set in casings. Something about its structure seemed to match her rigid, often dour, personality. Yet Beatríz, and therefore Reyna, liked the richest, boldest colors they could afford to buy and a more flowing style, which offered freedom of movement. To her mother's horror, Beatríz chose to have the sleeves of her *camicia* puffing through the spots between the ribbons tying her sleeves to her bodice. An exposed undergarment was the fashion, and her mother had given in once she saw the best young ladies dressed in this "distasteful" fashion, but she still clucked her tongue and commented under her breath.

Beatríz put on two necklaces, the thicker one tight against her throat and the thin chain hanging down her bodice. Both were gifts from Yusef. She sat twisting the chain around her fingers watching Reyna fuss over earrings, then shoes, and then back to her hair. Yusef had told Beatríz of the Venetian women who wore their hair loose and frizzy, which sounded far easier than the elaborate braids and twists Beatríz had created.

Impatient to go, Beatríz finally refused to spend another moment waiting and threatened to leave without her. Reyna shrieked and threw her hairpins high in the air, which made Beatríz laugh. Still chuckling, she grabbed Reyna by the sleeve and led her out of their room.

"Do not stay out past midnight," their father instructed. He leaned in and whispered, "Go before your mother comes and says ten o'clock."

Beatríz kissed her father on the cheek, and Reyna yanked his beard. He shook his head smiling and opened the door for them, even though a servant stood by for just that purpose. He felt that doing things on his own every so often was good for a man of his stature.

"Oh, my necklace!" shouted Reyna, who ran back up the stairs. Beatríz and Yusef laughed as her father rolled his eyes, and the couple stepped out into the salty evening air to wait.

Yusef touched Beatríz's earring.

"I wore these just for you," she said smiling, thinking of how the rubies had glimmered when she had held them up to the window earlier that day. They were the most lavish gift he had ever brought back for her, and she always tried to wear them when he was in Lisbon. His frown made her stop paying attention to how lovely his fingers felt on her neck. "You do not like them anymore?"

He shook his head. "I do. I . . . When I was in Italy this time, there was a new law declaring that no Christian women can wear earrings."

Beatríz tilted her head. "The Italians are an odd people. Why ever not?"

"Because they have declared earrings to be a sign of concupiscence."

"Well, love," Beatríz said, lacing her fingers through his, "if we are ever forced to move there, I will turn these into a ring or a necklace."

Yusef shook his head and held her hand more firmly. "No. If we ever move there, you would be *forced* to wear earrings. The other part of the law is that Jewish women must wear them."

Beatríz narrowed her eyes. "So that they are seen like prostitutes."

"Béa, what are we going to do if we must leave here? How can I protect you?"

"It is not your responsibility to protect me."

"It is my only responsibility."

She pulled him to her and stared into his worried eyes.

17

Standing on her toes she kissed one of his stubbly cheeks, then the other. Putting her cheek against his, she whispered, "Yusef, I –"

Reyna burst out onto the street, and Yusef and Beatríz moved away from one another. He sighed and Beatríz winked then put her arm through his. As they walked Reyna chattered incessantly, excited beyond her usual high level by the prospect of a night out, something that she, as the baby sister, was rarely allowed.

Several miscarriages had left a five-year gap between Reyna and Beatríz, and the stillbirths that followed had made her, as the last child, even more precious to her parents. As such, even at fourteen, Reyna was babied by her parents and ignored by her oldest siblings. Beatríz, who was closest to Reyna, tried to be patient at times like this. She listened to Reyna for a while, but lost interest in Reyna's speculations about who might have the most intricate embroidery on her gown. Beatríz tightened her arm against Yusef's and turned her mind to a night two years earlier when her brothers had taken her to a card game like the one they were about to attend.

The crowd had been young and boisterous. Juan, a newly married friend of her brother, Solomon, loved to host dinner parties and card games, and encouraged his friends to bring friends. Juan's wife enjoyed entertaining as much as he, and always kept the door open and the wine flowing. The rules that guided behavior in their daily lives were forgotten once inside, making these gatherings especially entertaining and alluring.

Beatríz begged Solomon to let her go to these weekly parties. Solomon and Beatríz were close in age and similar in temperament, and they were the closest of the siblings.

Solomon was the one who held her when she wept at being forced out of Toledo and offered a hand as they scrabbled the craggy mountains into Portugal. And she was the one whom he told of his esteem for the girl who became his wife, and he asked Beatríz what a girl might want if he wanted to woo her. Solomon and Beatríz were often reprimanded at meals for snickering and for throwing meaning-laden glances when their parents discussed her future. Solomon understood how much she loved to escape their house, and when Yusef was attending the card games, Solomon knew Beatríz would not accept a "no."

That night two years prior, Beatríz had sat beside Yusef for hours watching a game that she did not yet fully understand. Desperate for diversion, she had slid onto Yusef's lap as he played a hand, hoping to distract him enough that he would lose. Indeed, it worked. He had thrown his cards into the middle of the table with mock exasperation, took Beatríz to the window seat, and had placed her back on his lap. Yusef and Beatríz had whispered for a while and watched the others joke and throw more money onto the pile.

Suddenly, Juan's wife had begun dancing around in an attempt to get Juan's opponent, Francisco, to look away long enough for Juan to steal back some coins. Francisco had thrown himself across the coins to protect his loot while calling for Juan's wife to continue her provocative dance. The crowd cheered him on.

Beatríz had thrown back her head to laugh and Yusef had kissed her neck. She let him cover every inch of her throat with *besos* before lowering her chin to return the favor.

No sooner had her lips scratched his stubble than Beatríz had felt herself being jerked away. She stumbled on her dress as her oldest brother, Yakob, dragged her into an alcove. She had not even realized he was at the party.

"What in God's name do you think you are doing?" her brother had asked.

"Kissing my future husband," she had snapped, pulling her arm out of Yakob's grip.

He had grabbed it harder and she felt his fingers digging into her flesh as he had done so often when they were younger, just to be cruel. "You are ruining our family's reputation."

"With a kiss?"

"A whore's kiss."

"You are disgusting," Beatríz had hissed. Beatríz hated Yakob and was sick of his warnings. It reminded her of when she was eleven and Yakob had held her down and rubbed soap in her eyes for looking at a boy. Now she was promised to Yusef, and touching was acceptable at a card party. "Our own father trusts me more," she said. "I will not be ruled by you." Then, defiantly, she had marched over to a dumbfounded Yusef, taken his face in her hands and kissed him once more.

Yakob seized her braid and tossed her to the ground. Beatríz screamed with fury as much as from the pain. When she righted herself, Yakob smacked her across the face. Beatríz stood for a moment breathing hard, nostrils flared. She noticed silence in the room. Aware that everyone was waiting for her next action, and determined not to appear weak, she shoved Yakob as hard as he could, but it was not enough. He raised his hand high and slapped her so hard lights flashed in her eyes. She felt Yusef charge at Yakob, but Solomon stepped between them. Solomon nudged Yakob away, slipped his arm through Beatríz's, and hurried her out the door. Looking over her shoulder, Beatríz saw everyone staring, all mirth having dissipated the moment Yakob had laid hands on her. A friend was holding a shouting Yusef back as Yakob strolled across the room, chin jutting out, to get more wine.

Solomon whispered fiercely as they walked. "The only thing you have to offer in this world is your purity."

"You sound like Yakob."

"He is not always wrong. Be smart."

"I have done nothing," Beatríz argued as her brother led her out into the night air."

"I saw that kiss. Everyone did. It was *not* nothing."

Beatríz was determined not to cry, despite the rage and fear that brought a lump to her throat. Yakob could have confronted her any number of ways, but he always went out of his way to humiliate her. If she had not already hated him for a thousand offenses – making comments about her to his friends, pinching her back and arms as she walked by, laughing when her monthly courses came – she certainly would have hated him for this one. Focusing on her rage allowed her to keep from thinking about facing her father. Worse was wondering if Yusef would be ashamed of her behavior and decide that he did not want her after all.

Yusef, however, was not deterred, and had showed his commitment to her and their *Erusin* by calling on her the next afternoon. Simply drinking port and speaking with her mother about the weather was enough to tell everyone in the community that no family squabbles would keep him from her, and that he did, indeed, like her kisses.

Yakob had told her parents what had transpired, and her parents had kept her away from such gatherings for nearly a year. But after much begging and promising, as well as their growing confidence in Yusef's commitment, her father had agreed to let her out again.

In the time that had passed since that disastrous card game, trust had grown further and Reyna had matured enough to be considered a companion. But, as Beatríz had once been forced to beg for an invitation, so Reyna had to beg. Beatríz gave in often enough to placate her sister, but not always. Sometimes she wanted her attention to be wholly on Yusef and not to have to worry about her little sister's mischief.

Beatríz was now freer at card games because Yakob's wife let it be know that she thought the gatherings improper and would no longer tolerate his attending. So Beatríz was especially relaxed as they entered Juan's home. The crowd was loud as always. The married women stood off to the side while the betrothed girls stayed close to their men.

Yusef and Beatríz sat next to each other, only half paying attention to the card game. Beatríz lost her money within an hour and Yusef offered her a few coins, but she did not care to lose any more. She leaned on him and closed her eyes, listening to the yelling and laughing around her. Tired though she was, having him home was so rare that she wanted to soak in every moment.

"I will give you these coins to play, but only if you agree to marry me," a man said to someone.

A girl laughed and replied, "All right."

The voice was Reyna's. Beatríz's eyes popped open. Her sister was coyly taking a coin and throwing it down on the table. The young man next to her was Moises, a scraggly bearded youth whose doublet hung loosely on his thin frame. Moises tickled Reyna and she swatted his hands away.

"Ladies and gentlemen," he said in a voice as booming as

he could muster. "I have finally found a bride."

The crowd cheered for a moment, and then Francisco called out, "You'll never get her family to agree."

"She took the token," someone called out. "It's sealed."

"Moises, are you so desperate you need to trap a child into marriage?" Francisco teased, and when Moises simply smiled and shrugged, Francisco asked, "Who's playing the next hand?"

Everyone went back to the game and the matter seemed forgotten, but Beatríz could not help but consider what she had just witnessed. Her sister knew that accepting a gift from a man in response to a proposal meant engagement. In fact, she and Reyna had been warned constantly in their youth about taking objects from men, any man at all. Girls had been trapped into marriage by total strangers with nothing more significant than a cloak given to ward off the cold. Only when she saw Moises move across the room and begin talking to a cluster of married ladies did Beatríz relax.

The next morning, Beatríz was called to the sitting room. Despite the walls being washed white, the low dark ceiling made it dim no matter how strong the sun shone outside, so it took her a moment to see Moises in the room. She had to grab the doorknob to steady herself once she spotted Reyna in a corner crying. Then she saw her mother glaring and her father stood with his mouth agape.

"Beatríz," Moises said as he bowed stiffly. He turned to her parents and announced, "So I leave you. I will bring my parents tomorrow to discuss the details."

Reyna wailed.

Moises bowed again and brushed past Beatríz.

Beatríz caught him by the elbow and hissed, "What are

23

you playing at? Why are you here?"

He smirked and said with equal quiet but more joy, "This is no game. And you know why. You were there." He peeled her fingers off of his arm and said loudly, "What a joy it will be when we are family, eh, Beatríz?"

"Leave at once, Moises," she growled.

As soon as the heavy front door banged shut, Beatríz's father shouted, "Did you know about this? The engagement?"

"There was no – It was a joke," she said firmly.

"That boy does not seem to think so!" her mother shouted, twisting her lace-trimmed handkerchief between her hands.

"He says he gave your sister a gift and she said she would marry him," he father said.

"Coins to play a hand. Everyone laughed and no more mention was made."

"So she accepted?" he asked, his face going slack.

Beatríz shook her head. "The coins. Not the proposal."

"That is not what we were told."

Beatríz threw up her hands. "This is absurd. You must fight it."

"Of course we will fight it!" raged her father. "That worthless son of a canon maker will not be a part of this family!"

Reyna wailed again in the corner. The sound caused Beatríz to lose her breath and her place in the conversation.

"And how do you plan to fight it?" asked her mother. "It is done. She is betrothed." The word 'betrothed' rang sorrowfully against the walls.

Beatríz regained herself and began to pace. "I cannot understand this. I thought such agreements were outlawed."

Her father threw his hat onto the table — a prized possession carved in the style of the Moors, with interlinked swirls and eight sided stars. "Nonsense. If we were in Salonika, perhaps your sister would have a chance. Given the problems it has caused here, I cannot believe the rule stands. But you know as well as I that no decision against these proposals has been made. Not yet. Not here."

"Of course not," her mother said, her lips curling against her teeth. "Lisbon is barely civilized."

"Mother, please," groaned Beatríz. For spite, she asked, "Would it be different in your precious Toledo?" She was sick to death of her mother going on about Toledo. Toledo. Toledo. For as long as Beatríz could remember, they had lived there in dread and had left in fear and frustration. Though it still had been hard to leave all she knew, she never wanted to go back. Not ever. Lisbon was her home, and she wished her mother could feel the same.

Before her mother could answer, Beatríz's father interceded. "Insolent girl, *kiddushim* are binding here. What does it matter that rules of betrothal would be no different in Castile?"

Reyna slid to the floor, and, though they all fell silent, no one went to her aid.

"Beatríz, go and get your brothers," her father commanded.

She hesitated. "I will go to Solomon, but not to Yakob."

"This is your fault. You will do as we say!" shouted her mother.

"My fault? How?"

"You were to look after her."

"It happened so fast. Was I to keep her from speaking all together?"

"Yes."

Beatríz looked at her irrational mother and chose to say nothing more. She turned and went out the door, bracing herself for the conversations to come.

Beatríz nearly knocked into Yusef as she hurried out of her home. His smile faded as he took in her face, lined with worry. When she told him the trouble, he held her by the shoulders and said, "It cannot be taken seriously."

"And yet it is."

"The room was full. Anyone could say what really happened."

"Yes, the room *was* full. And anyone could say what she said and what she took."

Yusef nodded grimly, but offered, "The rabbis will rule against it."

"It depends which rabbi each asks."

"And who pays more."

She pursed her lips. "They blame me."

"Oh Béa," he said as he pulled her into an embrace.

"I could not have expected anything different." She let him hold her for a moment more and then reluctantly backed away. "I should go. I've got to bring the news to my delightful siblings."

"Would you like me to speak with your brothers?"

It was wrong to allow him to, especially when she had been ordered to do so herself, but she had no desire to do as she was asked just then.

She nodded and stood on her toes, pressing her lips against his slowly, then harder, her limbs liquefying as his fingers pressed against her back. He stepped back and nodded at a neighbor who was leaning far out of her window to watch the couple.

Beatríz's eyes met the woman's and she saw the look of disapproval. "If you do not like it, Dona Samuela, why do you always watch?" Beatríz asked before heading the opposite direction from Yusef.

Beatríz's older sister still had to be faced. Beatríz was escorted to the formal receiving room, where Astruga was sitting in a high backed chair with hoof feet. The solid back of dark-brown stamped Cordova leather added to the imperiousness with which Astruga always presented herself. Her hair was pulled into a severe bun and topped by a black caplet, and her dark eyes remained narrow throughout their conversation.

After Beatríz explained what occurred, she noticed a slight smile creep across Astruga's lips. Beatríz went hot all over and, with barely contained outrage, said, "You are taking pleasure in this."

Astruga lifted her chin and puffed out her chest, raking her fingers along the brass nails that studded her chair. "You girls have grown up – if I dare use that phrase – to be silly and careless. Yes, I admit to finding some satisfaction that my predictions have come true. Since we arrived in Lisbon, I have been warning Mamá and Papá that you needed looking after, much as I was looked after back in Toledo."

Beatríz took a step forward, forgetting the reverential distance she was meant to keep. "You complained that you were practically a prisoner in our home. I remember you carrying on about it –"

"And yet it worked!" shouted Astruga, rising to her feet. "Did I ever bring shame upon my family? Did I ever do anything that would cause Papá to run about –"

"You never had the chance!"

"Precisely. And you ought not to have been given one, either. So, yes, I take pleasure in watching all of you suffer – you silly girls *and* our parents who have grown careless, even neglectful. Since coming to Lisbon, Mamá has been so busy thinking about the home she lost, and Papá has been so busy trying to replace it for her, that they have forgotten the importance of thinking about one's family."

At that moment, a nursemaid came in with Astruga's newest baby, and Astruga waved her away. "I am busy!" she shouted at the skinny girl who appeared weighed down by the infant.

Beatríz rocked on her heels, and would have laughed at the irony if her sister had had a sense of humor.

"Go. This is not my affair."

Beatríz stormed onto the street.

As she entered her home, she spotted her younger sister slumped on the stairs. Reyna put out her arms, beckoning Beatríz to her side. Voices were rising and falling from behind the doors of the receiving room, and Beatríz knew that the argument would continue for a while, so she sat on the steps, wrapping an arm around her sister.

"Do not fret, love. Moises might not be so hateful."

"He eats with his mouth open and snorts when he laughs. Ugh. You have seen how his eyes squint when he thinks. If he thinks at all. I cannot imagine having to look at that for the rest of my life."

"Father will fix it. He is powerful."

Reyna shook her head violently. "I have been listening to them talk. Even they are not so certain." At that, she began wailing again.

The door to the sitting room flew open and surprise

registered on Solomon's face at seeing her there. "Dear sister," he whispered, "you'd best take Reyna upstairs. No use in having you and Yakob in the same room when tempers are already so high."

Beatríz thought to argue, but Solomon was right. He winked at her as she dragged Reyna to her feet.

"Tell Yakob I send my love," she said in a low acid voice.

Solomon fought a smile. "But of course, *doña-doña*," he said as he gave an exaggerated bow.

Beatríz listened to Reyna complain and carry on as the bell rang five, then six. Their small dark room plunged into greater darkness. Unlike the carved silver oil lamps in the house's common areas, the girls' room had ones made of simple pottery. Beatríz lit the linen wick and waited, watching the shadows of a pacing Reyna dance on their whitewashed walls. Faintly she heard the front door open and close on two separate occasions, and assumed that her brothers had left and she and Reyna would be summoned. Therefore, Beatríz was especially surprised when Solomon knocked and entered her bedchamber.

Running his hand down his face, he pulled his cheeks toward his chin. "Father has gone to see Rabbi Ibn Yahya. Yakob is staying for supper, so I am having a tray put together for you two."

"I heard someone being received. Did Astruga come at last?"

"No," he said. "Yusef."

Beatríz stood and checked that the leather cords were tight around her braid and started for the door.

Solomon stopped her. "We sent him away."

"What?" asked Beatríz, her cheeks suddenly hot. "Why

would you –"

"We are having a family discussion."

"Of which I am being completely left out."

"You are taking care of Reyna."

"You robbed me of an entire day with him. It is because you blame me for Reyna?"

"No. We blame Reyna for Reyna. But it was not a good night. Tomorrow. We told him to come back tomorrow."

Beatríz knew it was childish to kick a chair and refuse to speak to Reyna, who apologized again and again, but with so few days left before Yusef's departure, she felt cheated and hurt, and knew of no other way to show her displeasure.

CHAPTER 3

The next day, Beatríz was invited to sit with Yusef's mother, Miriam, in the afternoon and to stay through the evening meal. Beatríz took out her embroidery, yet jumped at each close of a door and footstep on the cobblestones, thinking it might be Yusef. She put the wrong color in several places and had to cut threads that had tangled due to the constant throwing aside of her frame.

At last, Miriam suggested they talk. "You will be part of this family soon," she began. "Is there anything about us you would like to know?"

Beatríz thought for a moment, then her mind was yanked out of the room by a male voice in the alley. But the voice was of an old man, so Beatríz turned her attention back to Miriam.

"Can you think of nothing but my son?" Miriam asked, not quite impatient.

Beatríz reached for her glass of port, conscious of the high color in her cheeks. "The time is short. Each moment apart feels . . . wasted."

Miriam picked up her own glass and rolled it between her palms. "It would seem he feels the same. He has shared his desire to have you stay with us if your family leaves, or if we are all forced out of Portugal. He has said you have agreed to this."

"I have," Beatríz said, her voice strong. "I have yet to tell anyone else, but it is what I want."

"Good," Miriam said. "If there is time, Yusef should speak to your —"

The door swung open and Yusef strode into the room. He stretched out his arms for Beatríz. "I have been missing you all day."

Beatríz ran to him, but stopped midway across the room, feeling Miriam's gaze.

"Go. Go," Miriam said. As Yusef enveloped Beatríz in an embrace that made her legs weak, Miriam added, "*Dois e bom, tres e demais.*"

Yes, three suddenly *did* feel like too many in the room.

Smiling, Miriam left, but not without a kiss on her son's cheek and announcing, "We will eat soon. Do not linger too long or the food will be cold." She left the door open.

Even so, Yusef brought Beatríz to sit beside him. He lifted her wrist to his lips and kissed it so softly that Beatríz's skin tingled all over. He let the tip of his tongue trace the blue veins that hid under the pale surface of her forearm, and her breath quickened. A clatter in the hall made them jump. A servant muttered curses and slammed around to clean up. The mood was broken, and Beatríz decided that caution was best and folded her hands in her lap demurely. Yusef leaned back and exhaled loudly.

"How are things at the port?" Beatríz asked, her voice unnatural in her own ears.

Yusef tilted his head, studying her, and nodded as if to say that they were, indeed, wise to talk for a while. "All is fine. We have procured enough wool to make the journey to Messina profitable."

"Good," she said, not meaning it at all. The thought of his leaving hurt inside her bones.

They sat quietly for a moment before Yusef said, "So my mother and father think they will go to the Maghreb if an edict of expulsion is passed."

"Oh," said Beatríz. "South? I had expected them to go to Italy or . . ." Her voice trailed off, as she had not thought beyond that.

"If Italy is no good, they would have to cross the sea to the Maghreb anyhow, which is to be avoided when possible, or they would have to continue east to the Ottoman Empire. There are Jews living comfortably in Constantinople. The Maghreb makes more sense since my father's strongest contacts are in Safi and Fez."

"Safi? Where is that?"

"Near Fez, though Safi is on the water."

She picked at a loose thread on her sleeve. Fez was said to be dry and devoid of hills, rivers and trees, which were the very things that made her love Lisbon. If Safi was similar to Fez, she did not believe she would like it. "It will be hotter, I should think, being farther south. And it is far from here."

"Not so far. A few days' sailing. And what does it matter how far it is from Lisbon, if we will not to return?" Beatríz stiffened, but he pressed. "Béa, what did you think you were going to do? It cannot be just a walk over the mountains this time. There are few places left for us to go."

"I know. Of course you are right." She paused then added, "Though I wish we could go to England or France or – or the German lands. I remember snow from the mountains of Toledo. It was magnificent."

Yusef pressed his lips together. "You know Christendom is closed to us. The English expelled the Jews two centuries ago, and that one by one all of the other countries of the north followed suit. There are no other options."

"Except for some cities in Italy. Where my family might go." She ignored the tightness in Yusef's jaw. "I heard my brothers speaking of it with my father. We could all –"

"No, Béa. We cannot all travel together. There are too many of us. It is better business to separate. And safer."

She frowned and took his hand in hers. "You make it sound so easy to leave a place and one's family," she said, tightening her grip, "yet, having been born in Portugal, you have never been forced to leave your home."

"Yes, but I have traveled farther than you have ever gone, and I can tell you that there are wonders to behold."

"In Safi and Fez?"

He hesitated. "I think you will find the change most interesting. The people speak Arabic, and the Muslims rule, and so the sights and sounds and way of life will be quite different."

"Different could be exciting," she said, but felt restless. Trying to wrap her mind around beginning anew once again, she rose. She leaned against the window, looking out at men and women rushing by, carrying bundles and greeting each other. People she knew. People she considered friends. "Will we be safe to live as Jews?"

"Yes. The Muslims are too busy trying to keep out the Christian invaders to bother with us." He came to stand beside her. "I am not saying it will be easy, but I am asking you to be strong."

She looked into his grey eyes. "A new life. As long as we are together, it will be wonderful."

Putting his arm around her waist, he kissed the top of her head. "Come. My mother is waiting for us."

The night before his departure, Beatríz could not sleep and so snuck out of her house and went down to the water. She knew it bordered on dangerous and it was definitely unseemly for her to walk alone at dawn, but her desire to see Yusef silenced her caution. The sun rose, turning the gleaming white buildings that dotted the hills of Lisbon pink, then orange, and the water, stretching endlessly before her, seemed to catch fire. So as not to disturb Yusef, she stood at a fair distance, but he spotted her standing along the sea wall and came toward her.

As he moved in for a kiss, she drew back. "You have been drinking," she scolded.

"I cannot stand the thought of going. I was drowning my sorrows."

"What a shame for you. I will not kiss you until you do not smell of drink. Go do your work and I will wait."

He twisted his lips. "You tease me." But when he moved forward again, she put up her hands.

"Work," she said. She knew the quicker he was finished, the more time they would have together. And knowing she was there would cause him to work faster. She watched with great pleasure as he confidently leapt on the gangplank and hurried about the ship.

By the time the sun was a full fist above the horizon, all cargo was stowed and the captain was calling final instructions to the crew. Yusef held his hand high above his head and she raised hers back to him. They met a few paces from where his ship was moored, and she laced her arm through his.

She led him into an area where crates were stored in busier times, backing far enough into the salt-scented cavern so that none could see them without coming entirely in. They had found this secluded spot a few years earlier, but had only stolen a quick kiss before he had left. They were shyer then, and more certain that their time of waiting was soon to end. Now, desperate for somewhere to be out of the watchful eye of parents and siblings, as well as sailors, she continued deeper into the shadows and leaned against the damp wall. He pressed his body to hers and she felt heat in places she was supposed to ignore. His breath was quick. She laced her fingers on the small of his back and moved her hips so he pressed harder against her.

"Béa," he groaned, "you are making me lose myself."

She stood on her toes and pulled his head down. Her lips parted and his tongue slid into her mouth. She sighed. Suddenly, he took her by the waist and hoisted her to sit on a stack of crates, then leaned in and kissed her again. He reached down and took the hem of her dress between his fingers and lifted it to her knees. They were very still. It was a moment of decision. It would be so easy to do what they both wanted to do, to have it done and stop holding back.

"I could take you right here. Right now," he said.

She lifted her chin, daring him. "But you won't."

"But I could," he repeated.

"But," she said, a teasing smirk on her lips, her chin raised even higher, "you won't."

Each stood, enticing the other, wishing the other would forget propriety, forget laws. Their gazes locked. Their eyes sparkled. Their sharp breaths echoed off the vaulted watermarked ceiling. Beatríz looked away first, and tried to focus on the puddled floor rather than the heat radiating from his hands.

She started at the feel of his fingertips on the bodice of her dress. It was cut modestly, but his skin tracing its edge, working its way along the rise and fall of her chest was maddening. She clasped her fingers around his hand to stop the temptation, and he leaned his forehead against hers.

"I hate this waiting," he said. "Surely there is a rabbi somewhere who can marry us."

She leapt off of the crate and tugged him toward the light. "Let us find one."

"Béa, I have to leave in less than an hour."

"Then walk quickly." She was yanked to a halt, and turned to see Yusef's lips tucked between his teeth to stop his smile.

"Béa, you are too impulsive. Even if we found a rabbi, we would not have time to consummate the marriage."

"If walking is too slow, then let us run."

At this, Yusef chuckled, and Beatríz joined him. She knew it would not happen, though part of her wished it could.

"Your love is that pressing?" he asked.

"Something is that pressing," Beatríz said and winked.

After a moment's silence, though, Beatríz sobered. She leaned against the town wall, the gates of her virtual prison. "But there are other women out there, Yusef," she said, gesturing at the sea. "You are a man. If you chose, you could have a girl on any shore. I understand the way of the world. But for me . . . I must wait for you.

Yusef softly touched her cheek. "I do not want anyone but you. And as for taking a girl on the shore, it sounds very sandy, so I would rather not, thank you very much."

Beatríz paused a moment, then shoved him, trying not to

smile. He put an arm around her and led her back to the bustling dock.

"Yusef!" called the captain. "We are ready to hoist sail."

Yusef nodded and turned back to Beatríz. He furrowed his brow and suddenly looked pale. "I cannot bring myself to leave you, and yet I cannot bring you along."

"Soon, love," she said. Standing on her toes so she could kiss his neck, she lingered a moment to inhale his sweet musk. "Come to me soon."

Yusef held her so tight she lost her breath. Then he turned quickly and jogged the gangplank. He ducked into the hold and Beatríz moved toward the gates, and neither of them looked back.

CHAPTER 4

Dearest Béa,

I will not be home in time for Pesah.
Goods are sparse due to land wars, so we must wait
until the roads are passable once more. I will return
to you soon, my love.

– Yusef

Beatríz had read these words daily for weeks, and each time it brought on a wave of fury and disappointment. If she did not treasure each letter from Yusef so, Beatríz would have ripped it in frustration. Passover was once Beatríz's favorite holiday, but after receiving Yusef's news, she felt no joy in it. Where once making matzoh and readying the good silver had broken the drudgery of her daily lessons, now each chore reminded her that she would spend it without Yusef.

In the week before Passover, Beatríz and Reyna were sent daily to the marketplace. If it was not more onions they needed, it was a shank bone. Or cloth. Or candles. The servants were too busy to do such time consuming tasks as going to the market. Typically, Beatríz welcomed any chance to go out, but the newly overcrowded streets were suddenly disquieting. She had no idea why thousands of Jews were flooding into an already bustling city. When her father would not answer her question, she asked a man she knew in the marketplace. "King's orders," the fish seller explained curtly, though he could not or would not say what the purpose was. She held Reyna as they stepped over families lining the streets and elbowed their way to the vendors' carts, feeling sorry for the newcomers struggling to find shelter.

But the day before Passover the streets were absolutely empty. Beatríz was in such a rush to retrieve a much-needed herb that she did not register the change at first. It was not until she and Reyna were halfway to the market that foreboding crept into her and she slowed her pace. Beatríz noticed shuttered windows, a mewing cat, an odd din in the distance.

Then from around the bend came a man dragging a boy of seven or eight by the collar and carrying a girl of about four as if she were a sack of linen. The little girl was kicking and shrieking, and the boy fought to release himself from the man's grip. Beatríz recoiled and wondered if it was merely a father disciplining his children.

Moments later, a woman screamed, "Give my children back!" as she ran into view.

Another man caught up and seized her arm. "Follow or return home, but the children remain with us."

Weeping, the woman submitted and trailed the group

down the narrow street.

A door opened and a lanky man from whom Beatríz often bought olives at the marketplace forced a group of children out. She knew they were not his. Their mother came from behind and pushed the man. He, in turn, punched her so hard she fell to the ground. Reyna yelped, and Beatríz grabbed Reyna's arm to keep her from getting any closer. Staggering to her feet, the mother continued after the man, but as she neared, he stopped and punched her again. This time she remained dazed on the cobblestones. Reyna moved to help her, but Beatríz protectively pulled her sister in the opposite direction.

A man Beatríz did not know was approaching them quickly.

"Look away and do not speak," Beatríz whispered. Arm in arm and holding their breath, the sisters continued walking.

"You there," he called. Beatríz tugged against a hesitating Reyna and kept going until the voice insisted, "Stop. Immediately."

Beatríz considered running but was not certain Reyna could keep pace or if running would bring more trouble.

"How old is she?" the man asked, pointing at Reyna.

The sight of his frayed clothing, oily hair and sunken cheeks made Beatríz even more wary. "*Perdóneme?*" she asked, using her thickest Castilian accent in an attempt to slow down the conversation enough to let her think.

"Hoooww ooold?" he asked again slowly in loud and deliberate Portuguese.

She wasn't sure what was happening, but Beatríz had only seen small children dragged away. Was fourteen old enough? A dull shout came from a crowd in the distance, and all of them turned their heads to listen. When only silence followed, the man brought his attention back to Beatríz and to silent, shaking Reyna.

Beatríz took a deep breath and said, *"Diez y ocho."*

The man was whispering to himself and counting on his fingers, so Beatríz, still holding Reyna, eased a step back. He put his hand up and, narrowing his eyes, said, "That's eighteen." He took a step forward and put his dirt-smudged face close to Reyna's.

Beatríz tried to look confused by his words as she pulled Reyna behind her, putting herself between the man and her sister. *"No entiendo."*

He leaned closer and Beatríz recoiled at the sour smell of his hair. He said, "She don't look eighteen."

"She looks young, but –" Beatríz caught herself speaking clear Portuguese.

Very quickly he said, "You was tricking me. You speak perfect Port'gese."

"Better than you," thought Beatríz.

"If you know what I'm saying, you tricky Jew, I bet she's younger than you say. None of you can be trusted. No wonder they's rounding you all up."

Beatríz sucked in her breath and felt Reyna move close against her back.

Another group of children passed by. Two older boys were scratched up and their clothes were mussed. Their escort's face was gouged. Each boy held the hand of a whimpering toddler and kept trying to shake off the grasp of their guards.

"Help me with them," the cut man hollered in their direction.

"She is eighteen," Beatríz insisted as the filthy man looked away. She took Reyna's hand and began running. Reyna looked over her shoulder, causing them to slow down. Beatríz hissed, "Home. Now. Do not stop or look back." The girls ran tripping on their skirts and dainty shoes, their breath ragged. They passed no one else and entered their house panting.

"Mamá!" shouted Beatríz, her chest heaving. "Mamá!" When no one answered, Beatríz continued into the kitchen with Reyna, speechless and pale, still in tow. The servants looked up and Beatríz commanded, "Do not answer the door. If anyone enters by force, do not reveal that Reyna is here." Beatríz pulled a sack of rice away from the front of an unused storage cupboard. "Reyna, if they come, hide in there. And not a word."

Reyna and the servants nodded, all wide-eyed. When Beatríz turned to leave, Reyna sputtered, "Where are you going?"

"I have to know what is happening." When Reyna moved forward, Beatríz stopped her. "You must stay. It seems they only want children today. I will come home soon. Tell Mamá . . ." She hesitated, imagining her mother's hysteria and realized why her father kept matters quiet. Beatríz had shaped herself to be different, but hated to contribute to her mother's ignorance. And yet. "Tell her nothing . . . unless you must." She smiled as confidently as she could and walked out.

The streets were deserted. Beatríz hurried toward the cobblestoned square. She stepped carefully over a tiny shoe at the entrance and became part of the jostling crowd. The grand square was too small for the number of people inside – so many that she was driven up against one of the perfectly kept white houses that faced the cathedral. Someone was speaking up front, but Beatríz could not hear. She tried to push her way closer, but frantic parents would not let her pass. She turned and left the square, hurrying along a parallel alley until she reached the street closer to the cathedral, stunning for its height of five stories and dual stone towers. She had always wanted to see the stained glass windows that reminded her of flowers, but had never dared to go inside.

The crowd was dense, but even from the shadowy edges Beatríz could hear what was being said.

"I say again, the children will be converted," called out a priest. "Any parent who agrees to become a Christian can keep his child. If not, the child will be sent to live with a good Christian family in the countryside. Any of you who refuse to convert will not see your children again."

A cry went up, and parents held their children closer. A man – not a Jew since he lacked the red fabric circle sewn on his cape that so clearly marked the others – looked at his feet and then slunk out of the square, bumping Beatríz as he left.

Children were shoved and squished, elbowed and clung to. Men at the perimeter forced parents attempting to leave back into the square.

"I will throw him in the well and follow him in myself!" shouted a man to the priest, holding his own child in the air. The toddler grasped at the air as if to steady himself, his eyes wide.

"And so you will both go to hell heathens and unredeemed," answered the priest, his even voice echoing. "But I will not stop you."

A murmur rippled throughout, but no one went into a well as far a Beatríz could see.

"Beatríz!"

Beatríz turned and was surprised to see her sister. Strands of Astruga's hair had escaped from the tight bun and her wild eyes darted.

"Help me. They have taken my children."

"Where are they?"

"I do not know, you fool."

Beatríz stood on her toes, barely able to glimpse anything past the sea of dark hair and glittering hats. Then she saw a familiar face. "Look. With the priests by the font."

Beatríz and Astruga snaked through the crowd together. As they neared, Beatríz asked, "What do you plan to do?"

Astruga stopped short and her nose nearly touched Beatríz's. "Be baptized."

Beatríz sucked in her breath.

Astruga's pursed her lips and huffed. "People change religions like they change shirts. What does it matter as long as I get my children back?"

Was it as easy as all of that? Astruga began pushing through the crowd again, and, in her shock, Beatríz forgot to follow. Astruga's arm reached back between the shoulders of the people who had closed in around them, and pulled Beatríz through.

Near the fountain, Astruga was so focused that she did not realize they were separated again. Astruga drove forward, pushing and shoving, until she was at the feet of a sallow priest. Beatríz could not hear their words, but the priest gestured a cross over Astruga and sprinkled her with water, then did the same to her puffy eyed children. She enveloped them. Astruga glanced into the crowd, but did not acknowledge Beatríz in particular. Her gaze dared her neighbors to argue with the logic of what she had done.

Beatríz stood unsure of whether to return home or not. Then a shrill cry burst from a woman near to her. "Not my babies!" she screamed.

The priest lifted a golden rod and flicked it at the

scratched up children Beatríz had spotted on the street. "Will you accept Jesus Christ as your personal savior?" he called to the mother. When she shook her head, a sturdier looking priest grabbed hold of both boys and used their helpless bodies to part the seas before him, removing them from the area. The mother fainted but the denseness of the crowd prevented her from hitting the cobblestones.

A wide-eyed girl and her shivering little sister were presented next. Beatríz turned away to leave the square, but could not. She was forced to witness as child after child was baptized, as parents decided whether to do likewise or chance losing them forever.

Not until after the dueling bells in their sturdy stone towers had rung out for vespers was the crowd thin enough for her to make her way home. When she arrived, she went straight for the receiving room. Her brothers were there, as were her parents. All looked stricken and her first fear was that Reyna had been taken.

Solomon rushed up to Beatríz and threw his arms around her. "They are gone. My dear darlings gone."

She held up her sobbing brother and stroked his hair as their mother had once done to comfort them.

Their father said, "We will go into the country and pay to get them back."

Beatríz wondered what money he had for this. Perhaps Astruga and Yakob, who surely had enough to pay her dowry but never would, could help Solomon.

Yakob scoffed. "Do you truly think that they would pick guardians who could be so easily bribed?"

"Name me one thing money cannot buy."

"Forgiveness," cried Solomon, and all fell silent.

"Where is Reyna?" Beatríz asked.

"Hiding in your room," her father said. "Though it seems the danger has passed."

Solomon buried his face further in her neck.

"And yours?" Beatríz asked Yakob, hoping all was well with the children who had mastered their father's imperiousness.

"They were not discovered. My wife is with them."

Beatríz did not want to know how they had managed it, for it might only make Solomon feel more like a failure.

Silence filled the room again and Solomon broke from Beatríz's embrace. He straightened his velvet hat and poured a glass of port. Beatríz came to his side, so he gave her the glass, poured himself a new one, tipped his head back and swallowed all at once. Then he poured and drank another. And another. Beatríz set down the glass, laid her cheek on his back, and noticed the dampness of the cloth. The fact that he had sweated through in his anguish made her wish he had made the same choice as Astruga.

Yakob spoke. "The king has done this to force our hands. You know as well as I that King Ferdinand and Queen Isabella have been begging for him to do something for years. They think the Jews living here are a bad influence on the *conversos* who stayed behind in *Sepharad*, and need to feel confident that the converted are truly converted."

Beatríz added, "Yusef said they need King Manuel to keep those of us living in Portugal from flaunting our freedom and enticing others to cross."

Yakob scowled at having been interrupted. "Yes. King Ferdinand and Queen Isabella want the *conversos'* money as much as anything, and every time one of us leaves their realms, their Catholic Majesties have fewer rich people to tax."

"But this plan of King Manuel's – to get us to convert – did not work today," Beatríz argued.

"No, it did not," he said with exasperation, his eyes fixed on a corner of the ceiling rather than her. "All did not willingly hand their children and themselves to the church."

At this, Solomon slumped to the floor and Beatríz knelt to continue holding him.

Yakob continued undeterred. "So I am certain that he will force us to leave, and soon."

"Do not be ridiculous," their mother began. "King Manuel needs us Jews too much – our skills, our money. We are physicians and artisans and merchants who pay him a great deal in taxes. He would never kick us out."

Solomon added in an angry growl, "He wants our money, yes, but if he can make us all practicing Christians – subjects whose Judaism he can stamp out – then it is the best of both worlds for him."

"And," added Yakob, "with Jews here remaining in contact with the *conversos* of Castile, King Manuel is under pressure to convert us or send us far away. Soon we will not be any more welcome here than we were there . . . if we do not convert."

"I do not believe that," said their mother.

Yakob looked down his nose at her. "Mamá, you have trusted what Papá has said too much. He has been reassuring you with those words, but he has known all along that change is coming." His mother shook her head, so Yakob turned to his father. "Papá, tell her." When his father said nothing, Yakob pulled at his beard, almost smiling.

Beatríz wondered what had turned him and Astruga so sour, so cruel. What had befallen them before Solomon and she and Reyna were born? Or had they been that way naturally?

Yakob explained with sick pleasure, "Letters between kings have been exchanged, plans have been made, loyalties are being questioned, investigations have begun. They are torturing and imprisoning people all over Castile and Aragon, former Jews suspected of being false Christians, like Papá's cousin, Noam. The religious leaders want to know that the converts are truly faithful, while King Ferdinand and Queen Isabella want the former Jews' faith and their coins. They must have both to satisfy themselves and their people. King Manuel will be no different, I assure you. The trouble will follow us here, Mamá. It already has." He let his words hang for a few seconds before sitting down and appearing to clean his fingernails.

Beatríz wanted to yank his beard, thinking that, since he obviously had no heart, it might be the only way to cause him the kind of pain he was inflicting on their mother.

Beatríz's mother looked at her husband, her eyes pleading. His guilty face gave her the answer she had been dreading and she began to weep. "You did not tell me," she keened.

Beatríz exchanged knowing glances with Solomon. It would not be the first time her mother had heard only what she wanted to hear or that her father had covered the truth. She heard her father whispering in his most conciliatory tone, and suddenly, her mother stormed out of the room yelling, "No. No!"

Solomon interrupted the uncomfortable silence that followed. "We cannot stay in Portugal. That much is certain. After I find my children," he gulped, "I will leave."

Yakob nodded. "The eight months' permission we were originally granted to live here has long since passed. This can come as a surprise to no one."

Their father shook his head sadly. "But for five years all has been well."

Yakob argued, "Until now. Time is up and we must convert or leave. No message could be clearer."

"Yes. Yes. If they come for the children again," said their father, "Reyna might not be so lucky. Yitzhak has not seen his babies in years. Not since they were taken to São Tomé. I cannot imagine such a fate."

Solomon began to shake and said, "São Tomé is worse than death. That uncivilized jungle island they call a plantation."

Beatríz shivered at recalling the story. How, after the terrible journey to São Tomé, many children were left exposed to the elements. Rumor had it that some were even devoured by dragons. The absolute truth, though, was that those who survived became slaves.

"Those children," Solomon continued, "will never see their par —" His voice broke off and he buried his face in his hands.

Their father pulled at his beard. "I could not bear that, losing my Reyna. And if we move, we can find a new court to break her betrothal to Moises."

Yakob rose and put his hand on his father's shoulder. "Then we go." His words hung in the silence. "Where?"

Their father said quietly, "I think it best that we all travel in different directions."

Solomon asked, "If our business is a joint venture, why go in separate —"

"So at least one of us might live." Everyone stopped and looked at Beatríz. "That is why, is it not, Papá?"

Beatríz's father straightened his belt. "Must you always be so direct?"

Beatríz knew he would not be so irritated if it were one of her brothers who had guessed at the truth. She pressed, "So I am correct?"

He nodded perfunctorily. "Astruga will stay." He frowned, not repeating why. "My best connections are in Venice, so Mamá, the girls and I will go there. Solomon, you –"

"No," interrupted Beatríz. When her father turned, his face, already red, grew darker, but she would not allow this to stop her from continuing. "I am staying, as well."

"To become a Christian?" scoffed Yakob.

"No." Beatríz fought back a snarl. "I will stay with Yusef's family until he returns. We will wait here in Lisbon. But if we must leave before his return, I will follow his parents and wait elsewhere for him."

"You will come with us, Beatríz," snapped her father before turning back to his sons.

Her temper rose. Nothing could make her go with them. Of that she felt certain. Not propriety, not their wishes.

She balled her fists. "I will not leave. Yusef is expecting this."

The men stopped speaking and looked at her.

"Who knows if he will make it back in time? Or ever?" Yakob said.

His words felt like a slap but she was determined not to allow the conversation to turn again. She would not be like her mother, weeping elsewhere while important decisions were being made.

"I have to hope he comes."

"Will hope feed you?" pressed Yakob. "Will hope keep you from being attacked in the street? This is no game you are playing."

"He will come back to me."

"Yakob speaks the truth, my darling," said her father. "These times are uncertain. If we leave you unaccompanied, unprotected, what will become of you?"

"His family will protect me. And what if he comes home and I have left? How will he find me?"

Her father's face softened. "We will send word."

"Not good enough."

Yakob clucked his tongue, so Beatríz turned away from her brother. "Papá, you betrothed me to Yusef when I was a girl, and I have spent my life preparing to marry him. Now you want me to forget –"

"Not forget. We have a contract that we will try to honor. Eventually."

Beatríz gasped. "Try? No, Papá. I will not leave and I will not marry anyone else. I love him. Yusef is the man I want."

"Love will not shield you."

Solomon put an arm around her, but even his warm touch could not soothe her. He murmured, "Neither God nor man can protect you from those monsters out there if they decide that they have had enough of the Jews. There are rumblings in the streets every day when I walk to the port. We are not safe here."

Beatríz pulled out of his embrace. "I will take my chances."

"You are a fool," sniffed Yakob.

"And where do you plan on living if I agree?" asked her father.

"With Yusef's family. They have already said I may. And we will marry upon his return."

"The impudence!" interjected Yakob.

"You spoke to them without your mother's and my permission?"

"Disgraceful," said Yakob as he crossed the room to sit and glare at her.

Beatríz turned her back completely to him. "Papá, his mother offered when I spent an afternoon with her. Yusef's father is your closest friend and —"

Yakob called out, "I do not understand why Yusef would want a girl such as you. At least my wife knows her place."

Beatríz whirled around. "Yakob, I am not interested in your simpering, simple little wife. Would she even know how to find the front door of your house if you did not show her where it was?"

Yakob rose and came at her. Their father rushed between them, his arms creating a shield around his daughter. "Leave us!" he shouted at his sons. Solomon pulled Yakob out the door, and Beatríz and her father were left to catch their breath.

"Why must you make things so difficult?" he asked.

Beatríz stared at him, unsure if he meant her desire to remain or how she refused to be docile.

He went to the side table and, with shaking hands, poured himself a glass of wine. "I cannot pay your *nedunya* to Yusef's family, Beatríz. If I cannot collect on my debts from Castile, and I cannot collect on my debts here once we leave, I will have nothing. Hardly enough to survive. Like our early days in Portugal. You remember? No money to live on our own. Accepting charity for clothes and food. And once we had our home, we had no money to furnish it and no servants to help with anything. This time it could be worse. At least if you come, we might be able to find you a man who will expect less than Yusef's family."

"Yusef does not care. He is not interested in money."

"But, *Amor*, his parents are. They have blocked his pleas,

as well as ours, to let you marry and for me to pay off the debt over time. I do not know what shall be done if I leave you and cannot gather the money."

"I do not believe you. They asked me to join them."

"I do not pretend to understand the motives of others. Abrão is one of my oldest friends, but . . . "

Beatríz did not want this to be true, and was not sure whom to believe. She knew money had been the delay, but she also knew her father would do or say anything to protect her. And protecting her, as far as he knew, meant keeping her close. She only knew one thing that she could state without hesitation: "I will not marry another. And I will not leave without him."

Her father sighed and emptied his glass. Then he turned and looked deep into his daughter's determined eyes. "If you are sure this is what you want, I will speak to his parents myself."

CHAPTER 5

Dearest Béa,

This letter to you is from he who kisses both your hands and both your feet.

I cannot guess when I will be able to return. Nothing is going according to plan. Goods are scarce and we have traveled to a new port in hopes of better trade. Be strong for me, Amor. I will come to you.

— Yusef

Beatríz had not told her family what the letter, which arrived as the last bits of the household were being crated up, had said, lest they changed their minds.

She had been amazed by the speed with which her parents had their house packed. Before six weeks were up, they were saying their goodbyes. The boat for Venice was set to depart, and Yakob's family would leave for Constantinople within days. Beatríz's belongings had been brought to Yusef's family home already. Solomon was still scouring the countryside in search of his children.

The morning of her family's departure, Beatríz and Reyna rose early. Through her tears, Reyna tied on Beatríz's sleeves. Beatríz fixed Reyna's braid, and she thought with deep sadness that she would miss this routine, as well as her noisy, thrashing bedfellow. She could not keep herself from thinking of everything as a "last" – the last time reminding Reyna to fold her nightdress, the last time letting Reyna borrow her hair oil, their last laughs together.

She kissed the back of Reyna's head and clasped her arms around Reyna's jaggedly heaving chest. "Reyna," she gently teased, "if you use all of your tears now, you will not have any left for when the boat unmoors." Reyna tried to laugh, but only snuffled harder causing fat tears to splash on Beatríz's knuckles. Beatríz released her sister and turned her around so they could face each other. "Yusef told me Venice is magical. And Venetian men are rumored to be quite romantic." Reyna wiped her eyes and Beatríz continued, "You are lucky that Moises' family has not chosen to go there, as well. In all of this madness, it seems they have dropped the matter of your betrothal. But promise me that you will not accept gifts from any new men you meet," she admonished, smiling.

"Papá says he wants to marry me off as soon as we arrive since he does not have you there to protect me."

Beatríz shook her head. "I believe he is making a joke." Beatríz touched her sister's cheek. "But listen to what they say and be careful. Mamá will be in no condition to mind you for many months, if history repeats itself. Befriend another unmarried Jewish girl, one who has been living there for at least a year, and let her guide you. The unspoken rules will be different, not just the laws."

Reyna nodded and looked as if she were about to cry again.

Beatríz led her out of the room and down the dark wooden stairs. Their father was standing in the entry where he had stood with Yusef three months before. Three months. Beatríz's heart sank.

Her mother stood facing the wall, as she was wont to do when she fought and lost an argument with her husband. Beatríz ignored it and walked to her father. He put out an elbow and they began for the port along with Reyna, her mother, and a few servants who carried the last of their belongings.

Wordlessly they walked past white house after white house, through square after square until they could see the water. There were more boats than Beatríz could ever remember seeing. The normally fresh salt air was tinged with the sweat of people and the urine of animals. "Are all of these people leaving?" she asked, holding a gloved hand to her nose.

"King Manuel is trying to make it difficult for us to leave by making this the only viable port. He wants us to convert and remain, but the threat of expulsion is finally being taken seriously. I think the city will only become more crowded." He pulled her arm closer to his side. "Do not go out alone after dark and do not come near the waterfront at all. I beg you."

Beatríz nodded and kissed his cheek. "I think I will leave you here," she said stopping at an archway before the last incline to the water. "There will be no room in that chaos for proper goodbyes."

He held her and she tried to lock into her memory how he

smelled inexplicably of cinnamon and joy. She turned to embrace her mother, though her mother's arms were limp around her. Beatríz gave her puffy-eyed sister one last quick hug and stepped back to regard her family. Swallowing a lump in her throat, she lifted a hand to wave, afraid that if she tried to speak, tears might betray her. She turned away before they could say anything, and she hurried back under the archway of the city gates toward the Jewish quarter.

At Yusef's house, she was welcomed warmly. His mother showed Beatríz to her room instead of a servant. She opened the door to a small white room with no decoration but for a small bouquet of wildflowers, which had been placed in a lovely, colorfully painted clay vase by the narrow bed. "The room is not fancy," Miriam apologized. "And not as spacious as Yusef's. But it seemed improper to put you there even with him gone. I hope you understand."

Beatríz nodded and noticed her trunk had already been unpacked and her dresses hung. "Might I go in his room to sit, or would that upset you?"

Miriam hesitated. "It would be . . ."

Beatríz had not been in the house for five minutes and already she had offended Miriam. She wanted to kick herself or take the question back, but Miriam nodded and gestured down the hall.

"I did not mean now," Beatríz said, her cheeks burning. "I . . ." She clutched her hands together. "Thank you."

"This will be good," said Miriam, and Beatríz wondered if she truly meant 'good' or actually meant 'educational' as in, it would give her information while there was still time to break the *Erusin*. "We will get to know one another before we must part ways."

"Part ways?"

"Once Yusef comes, we will surely end on different shores. Much like your family, we might be safer apart. So though you have been dear to us all of these years, I will be pleased to create memories of you to hold until we meet again."

Beatríz sat quietly long after Miriam left and pondered this strange day.

That evening, Dom Abão held out a letter to her. "From my son."

Beatríz did her best not to snatch it.

> *In the name of God.*
>
> *My lord and master and crown of my head, my father, my honored Rabbi Ibin Yahya, may he be protected by his creator and savior.*
>
> *Do not plan to come east. Other merchants say to go south if you can.*
>
> *Has Beatríz's father agreed to let her travel with you? She did not say so in her letter. Ask Dom Vidal yourself if you must, but do not let her leave with them. I beg you.*
>
> *Your son,*
Yusef

"Have you not written to him of the arrangement?" he asked.

"I did. He must not have received the letter yet." She hesitated. "Though that was weeks ago. He should have –" Her face felt numb, but then she told herself not to worry. "He moved ports. I am sure he will receive it soon."

"Even so," said Dom Abrão, "Write again to be certain.

And give me the letter this time. I will hand it to a sailor I know. Letters are more likely to get there if you know the man delivering it."

She knew that. She had learned in her early days that most men would throw a letter into the sea if they did not have any connection to you. One sailor had even done it in front of her. She had shouted at the man, but the paper was coming apart and her carefully chosen words were washed away before he finished laughing at her fury.

"Do not worry, my dear. He will find out. How was your first day at our home?"

She told him as they went to sit with Yusef's mother and await the evening meal.

The first week passed as pleasantly as might be expected with her heart yearning for all across the sea. She seemed to be getting on well with Yusef's parents, and had not embarrassed herself since the first day. Each afternoon, Miriam received visitors and then the ladies embroidered, which Beatríz hated, but it was expected.

"May I ask you a rather personal question?" Beatríz inquired after a friend of Miriam's came to bid them goodbye before leaving for Naples. When Miriam laid down her needlework, Beatríz continued. "How could you bear it when your husband was away?"

Miriam raised her eyebrows and smiled slightly. Then she leaned forward and picked up her wine, but did not drink it. Instead, she leaned back again, rolled the dainty glass between her palms and appeared to be counting the beams on the ceiling. "I cannot say it felt like anything that needed to be borne."

Beatríz frowned and opened her mouth to speak, but

checked herself, as the question she wanted to ask would be impertinent.

"I was more accustomed to being alone than with him, given how infrequently he was home. When he returned," she lowered her voice before saying, "it sometimes felt like an imposition."

"But in the early years?" Beatríz could not imagine finding Yusef to be anything but a welcome presence. Yet she realized that the older women she knew all seemed to find their husbands disagreeable.

Miriam, put down her glass and softened her voice. "In truth, I did not know my husband before we married, and was not sure I liked him even after the wedding. It took some time, but the caring grew. And now our lives are tied together, so what happens to him affects me. When he was away, I always wondered about his wellbeing, but I never dwelled on his absences. I accepted them as a necessity of his business."

"Do you worry about your sons when they are traveling?"

Her voice deepened. "That has been harder, I admit."

Beatríz could not imagine hurting more than when Yusef was gone, and wondered how she would take her own children sailing away. Fleetingly she thought she could not stand it, and would, therefore, attempt to keep from having any. But she wanted children with Yusef. Many of them.

"You truly love my son."

Beatríz nodded, and, overwhelmed by feeling, bent her head down toward her needlework to hide it.

"Do your parents know of your intimacy?"

Her eyes darted up. "Intim – " Beatríz felt dizzy and flushed. "We never –"

Looking suddenly surprised herself, Miriam said hastily, "I

do not mean to suggest anything improper, but it is clear that the strength of your feelings is uncommon."

Beatríz hesitated. What could she say? She knew that her feelings were powerful, but were they rare?

A welcome interruption came when a servant entered holding two letters, one for Miriam and one for Beatríz. The women looked at one another as each took the paper, rose, curtsied, and retreated to her own room. Beatríz scrambled up the stairs and shut the door behind her, breaking the wax seal and sighing at the sight of Yusef's writing. Her joy did not last long.

> *Dearest Béa,*
>
> *It is with great sadness that I tell you I will not be leaving Tripoli as quickly as planned. The ship has been loaded, but the captain says he fears leaving port. Pirates are marauding so freely that he does not wish to put us at risk. He is a good man. I trust him and would make the same choice were I not so desperate to come home to you.*
>
> *We are waiting to see if enough boats are willing to depart at the same time and perhaps protect each other with sheer numbers. At least if our ship were overrun, there would be others nearby to fish us out of the water should we survive an attack.*
>
> *I am sorry. I look up at the stars each night and hope you are looking at them, too. It makes me feel we are not so very far apart after all.*
>
> *Besos y abrasos.*
>
> *- Yusef*

It charmed Beatríz that Yusef would switch into Castilian, her most comfortable language, when he wanted her to feel most loved or comforted. She had taught him phrases of affection in their early days, whispered in sitting rooms or as they walked chaperoned along the shore. But the last words did not make up for the rest and so Beatríz lay on her bed weeping into her pillow until she was called for the evening meal.

A few weeks later, a knock at her door startled Beatríz awake. In a quiet voice, Miriam said, "Beatríz, come quickly."

Beatríz rose and pulled on a dressing gown. She tried to think if Miriam's voice had been cheerful behind the urgency. Could Yusef be waiting just downstairs and in moments she would find herself in his arms, kissing his perfect, soft lips?

She opened the door and half expected him to be right in front of her. Miriam gestured down the stairs with one arm, inviting Beatríz to go first. Beatríz noticed a frown on Miriam's brow, but was still lost in the fantasy of Yusef's return. And so it came as doubly surprising when it was, in fact, Solomon standing in the entryway.

"Solomon!" exclaimed Beatríz, skipping steps in her bare feet in her rush to reach her brother.

"Ssshh," whispered everyone, bringing Beatríz up short. She looked around confused as Miriam and Abrão bowed their heads and closed themselves into the formal sitting room.

Only after the door had closed behind them did Solomon say a word, and even then, he kept his voice low. "I have very little time," he said.

"For what?"

"Before I must go. My wife told me not to come, but I could not leave without saying goodbye."

"Did you find your children?"

Solomon removed his hat and crushed it between his hands, making Beatríz assume he had not. Her chest ached for his loss. But to her surprise, he nodded. "They were living with a farmer and his wife." Even by the light of a single candle, Beatríz could see his face was drawn. She reached out and touched his arm and he pulled her into an embrace. "I stole them, Beatríz." He shivered.

She pulled back. "Stole who?"

"The farmer did not want to let them go. Said that money would not sway him. Said I had no claim on my children anymore and that he would raise them correctly under the protection of the church. We argued and I . . . my babies were being held back by the farmer's wife, crying for me . . . and I –I took a chair and I hit him. He just lay there not moving." Solomon's eyes were wide and the corners of his mouth twitched as he added, "I am fairly certain that he is alive. The blow was not all that hard."

"And his wife?" she whispered.

Solomon looked down again. "She started screaming, and my children did too, and I was afraid she would run for the neighbors, so –" His voice broke off and he yanked at the edges of his emerald green hat. "I struck her and tied her up. I imagine a neighbor found her or she freed herself, but . . . there was so much blood."

Involuntarily, Beatríz took a step back.

He watched her reaction and shame blanketed his face, but then his jaw set and he straightened. "You would know if you had children."

Her breath was knocked out of her. It was not her fault

that she had none. And yet that fact divided her from him, from a world she could see like sweets through the window.

"Solomon," she finally said, "I do not condone violence, but at least you have your children back." She stepped closer to him now, resting a hand on his arm. "They had no claim to your babies, and they were complicit in something so very wrong." For good measure, she added, "They got what they deserved." She tried to sound sure.

Tension left Solomon's body.

"Now what?" she asked, her voice crawling out of her throat.

"We run. My family is already hidden on a boat that leaves at dawn."

"Where are you going?"

He shook his head. "It is too dangerous to tell you, I think." He closed his eyes as if chasing away the memory of what he had done. "Someone investigating might come here, and you cannot tell them if you do not know. It will keep us all safer, I hope." He paused. "We will be changing our names, as well."

Beatríz gasped. "But how will we write? How will I find you?"

He touched her cheek. "You will not. This is truly goodbye."

And for the first time in as long as she could remember, she was overwhelmed with sadness and loss over something other than Yusef's absence. She threw her arms around her favorite brother, and cried, "No! That cannot be!"

"Perhaps one day . . ." He would not promise the impossible. "I must go. I love you." He squeezed her hard.

She wanted to keep him with her, to make him take her along, to scream that he was lying about everything. Instead she took a breath and said, *"Elohim she'tishmor aleinu."*

"God protect you, too," he said before kissing her forehead and slipping out into the darkness.

Months passed without good news or bad. Beatríz grew accustomed to the sadness that sat on her chest and lived behind her eyes, and though she burned to take action, there was no action to be taken. There was always talk about moving, but even Miriam and Abrão seemed unwilling to go before Yusef made it back. Abrão kept abreast of the news through his contacts at the court, but any word of a definitive plan or a final date of departure was always tempered with a shrug and, "We shall see. There is time yet."

But one day in early autumn, Abrão rushed into the sitting room and said, "We must make our way to the waterfront. The king has commanded it."

"Is he expelling us?" Beatríz asked, leaping up.

"No one is certain. If this is it, we might need to leave immediately."

"Let me gather some essentials."

Abrão nodded curtly. "Yes. Always thinking, Beatríz. I will tell Miriam to do the same."

She threw a dress, a comb, and some undergarments into a pile. Then she reached for her travel bag and paused when she saw its button. Beatríz recalled how she had come to possess that particular button on her journey over the mountains from Castile.

A more decorative button had fallen off and she had traded for this. A boy named Davíd, one of Solomon's dearest friends, had been traveling with them and had demanded a kiss on the cheek in exchange for a button from his coat. She had hesitated, but the practical side of her knew she could not accept it for free lest it be considered a sign of betrothal, but she had no money to offer. She had snatched the button from Davíd's palm first to be sure he would not take it back once he had what he wanted, and he had held her sleeve lest she try to run off. The kiss had been quick, but her lips seemed to burn for hours. Confused pleasure and shame had mixed equally, for she did not like being coerced, but she did like Davíd.

Beatríz had hidden the button – chipped and made of plain wood, nothing like the bronze floral one that had tumbled away – for a few days, afraid her parents would question from where she had gotten it. Her cheeks burned each time she thought of the kiss and she considered tossing it aside more than once.

Sitting on her narrow bed in Yusef's house, Beatríz picked up all of Yusef's letters and considered just bringing a few. The stack was so large and she had practically memorized them anyhow. But then, just seeing his familiar scrawl bathed her in peace, and she could not bring herself to leave even one behind. She shoved them in her bag and struggled to button it. Then she touched her earlobes to be sure the ruby earrings Yusef had given her were in place.

She waited at the bottom of the stairs for Miriam and Abrão determined not to show any fear. Yusef's mother and father could not know she was scared, that she dreaded the changes she knew would come once they walked out into the streets to follow the king's edict. If she showed fear, they might try to hide things from her, and she needed information.

Eventually Yusef's parents walked down together, looked around their house as if memorizing it, and the three of them exited. Beatríz squared her shoulders. She had moved before. She could move again. A house was just a house. Who was in it made the difference.

The streets were busy, as they had been for weeks, and the sunlight made the white buildings gleam. The day seemed too perfect for anything to be wrong. Nothing alarmed them at first except for the eerie quiet. Even the children seemed to know this was no time for joking.

They were nearly out of breath by the time they crested the hill on which perched the most magnificent structure in the city. The castle seemed to stretch the length of Lisbon and was surrounded by a formidable stone wall upon which soldiers stood watching the commotion below. Two pointed towers stood above all else flying the banner of Portugal. The white of the country's newly adopted flag stood out against the brilliant blue sky, while its coat of arms, bearing five blue shields in the shape of a cross, vanished and reappeared as the wind blew.

Trudging up the hill, Beatríz had seen people moving with relative calm, but as they got closer to the palace, people were racing in different directions. Some were talking, some shouting. Some were alone, some were escorted by men in black robes or ruffians like those who had dragged children away from their parents months before.

Beatríz tried to hear what was being said but only caught snippets.

"All are to be converted."

"Judaism is outlawed."

"Drown anyone who does not comply."

"Turned to slaves."

"Closing the ports."

She knew the king planned to get rid of the Jews, but

would he really accomplish it through forced conversions and locking them in?

Abrão led them to an official in a plumed hat. "Rodrigo!"

"Abrão," the man said, extending a hand. "My friend, you must hurry home. I think if you stay in your house you will be safe."

"But the decree?" Beatríz asked, ignoring the man's surprise, probably that a young lady would intrude upon a conversation. Miriam and Abrão did not react, having grown used to, and even grown to appreciate, her boldness.

Rodrigo said, "I believe the king will concede when he sees the mayhem this is bringing. They anticipate great problems in the countryside if the messages are not clear. Accidental drownings. Attacks. No one knows for sure."

Miriam's face twisted as if she had just bitten into something bitter as she said, "Queen Isabel will not care if there is mayhem as long as the Jews are converted or leave. This was the condition of their Catholic Majesties' marriage contract with King Manuel, if you recall."

Then let us go home," said Abrão. "Perhaps we can avoid conversion."

Someone slammed into Beatríz sending her sprawling. The skin of her palms ripped as she skidded along the cobblestones and landed on her stomach. Her bag kept her from hitting her head as hard as she might have. She scrambled onto her feet only to be spun around by whomever chased the person. "We should hurry," she said. "People are growing frantic."

A child's cry caught Beatríz's attention. A little girl in a traveling cloak was standing on tiptoes searching the crowd. Her wailing grew louder by the moment.

"Come, Beatríz," insisted Abrão, tugging at her elbow, but

Beatríz pulled away, rushing for the child.

"Are you lost?" Beatríz asked, kneeling so their faces were level. The little girl nodded vigorously, unable to speak past the tears, her wide brown eyes reminding Beatríz of Reyna. Beatríz hoisted the girl onto her hip. The girl clutched at Beatríz, small fingers digging into her neck. Beatríz cooed and soothed her. "We will find your family. Shush now."

"Beatríz!" shouted Abrão, "We must go. She will find her way."

"No! I will meet you at the house."

Miriam began, "What if —"

"I am not leaving her," Beatríz argued, feeling that compassion even the midst of chaos was a must. She had been abandoned and disappointed too much herself to act blithely about a child's fear. "I will come as soon as I can."

Just then a woman barreled through the square, her face pale and frantic, her eyes searching.

"Mamá!" cried the girl, wriggling from Beatríz's grip and sprinting toward her mother.

"Dolce!" shouted the woman, and then she slapped the child across the face. The girl reeled and Beatríz started forward, but the mother clutched her daughter and stammered, "I — I thought I lost you. Come. We must get back to your father." Dolce buried her face in her mother's shoulder, and was carried away as the mother smothered the girl in kisses.

Beatríz turned on her heels, considering how love and fear intertwined at times, and joined Yusef's parents who were waiting for her by the statue.

"You cannot help everyone," reprimanded Miriam. "You must put yourself first."

Beatríz did not remind her that Miriam and Abrão might

have gone ahead without *her* if self-preservation trumped all. Instead, she tucked in her lips to hide a smile and agreed.

The three walked back down the hill through the maddeningly meandering streets, but just as they neared their house, a tall priest in a robe too short for his frame stepped in front of Dom Abrão.

"Abrão," he said, which surprised Beatríz. How did they know each other? The priest's tone lacked malice as he said, "It is a fact. You will become a Christian today. Do not resist. I can protect you. The church can protect you."

Dom Abrão looked at Miriam and she looked back at her husband. A decision was being reached in a way Beatríz could not see. What would she do if they did plan to resist? It might compromise her future with Yusef. She did not want to be converted, but it seemed the safest choice.

When the couple began to follow the priest, Beatríz stopped holding her breath. They had not asked what she wanted, but as an unmarried girl, much to her irritation, no one ever did.

They arrived at the door to a tiny chapel just as a small group was pushed through the door. The other priest was shorter and stronger than the one that accompanied them, and he did not use words to convince. He smoothed stray hairs over his shiny, balding scalp, took the head of the family by the collar, dragged him to a shallow pool and shoved his face in it. The man came up sputtering but had the wherewithal to dive for his wife. He held her out of reach of the short priest and said, "Gently, sir." The priest did not heed the plea, but grabbed the woman and dunked her as well. The children were next, and all sat shivering and wailing in the dim, low ceilinged chapel, which seemed filled with smoke from the multitude of offering candles.

The tall priest looked at Abrão and Miriam. A stained glass lamb in a peaceful pasture towered over him and threw a green light across his reddish cheeks. "That man," he said, gesturing at the balding priest, "disagrees with the order. He thinks the king is merely creating hundreds of heretics, and he plans to expose them as frauds and punish them. I, however, believe this to be a blessing. God will reward you for what is done here today."

Beatríz stepped forward. Miriam reached out a hand to her, but Beatríz said, "I will go first." It was to be done whether she understood or liked it or not, so she saw no reason to delay.

Their beatific priest did not immerse them in the pool as Beatríz feared, but crossed their foreheads with damp fingers and smiled. Beatríz did not react because it did not seem real. Was that all? Was she a Christian? It made no sense.

After finishing with Miriam and Abrão, the priest pointed at the red circles of cloth on their garments and suggested they remove them. Then he drifted away and into the street, presumably looking for his next converts. Beatríz was wary to remove hers, which confused her. She had begrudgingly worn a similar badge in Castile, and this one in Portugal, but if she stripped off the dreaded marking, she felt something of her would be taken away.

Abrão took a knife out of the scabbard Beatríz had not noticed hanging from his belt, and sliced at the threads of his own star and then Miriam's before handing the knife to Beatríz. Deciding it was the safest choice, she worked the star loose, and Miriam and Abrão threw theirs to the stone floor.

Beatríz rolled hers between her fingers a moment more then let the cloth flutter away.

Staring at it, she considered her religion. It was part of her.

The ritual. The predictability. The songs. The chanting. The familiarity of it all comforted her, especially during times of change. And yet she had always hated being crammed into small synagogues for prayers, admiring instead the larger churches of the city. She had hated being separate from the men during services, while Christian boys and girls stood side by side. She did not care for being left out of society and pushed out of countries because of being a Jew. Always suspected. Always at risk. Perhaps this conversion was what she had wanted without even realizing it.

Her stomach twisted as she considered this thought and her future. Had she angered God by not fighting against this? Would she be forsaken? Punished? Or had she just been set free?

CHAPTER 6

Beatríz was aware of the pandemonium as they walked, but forced herself not to let it sink in. Instead, she asked Yusef's parents where they were going.

"The port," Abrão said, guiding his wife through the crowded streets.

"Why?" Beatríz asked. "We have been converted. Now we can stay and wait for Yus–"

Abrão stopped short and pulled her to the side, allowing another group guided by a priest to pass. He leaned close and said in a low voice, "We are still Jews. Do not let a sprinkle of water make you forget it. We are safer in another land."

Beatríz's legs went weak. "B-but Yusef –"

Miriam stepped closer. "There are ports he will check first, and if we are not in one of those, he will continue to look."

Beatríz's stomach sank knowing that could take months more, but she was willing to leaving. The plan had been set.

She followed Yusef's parents listening for distant sounds like seagulls rather than the immediate shouts and begging that surrounded her, and thought of the last letter she received from her sister.

> Beatríz,
>
> In the name of God.
>
> Venice is lovely. And you were quite right – Venetian men are handsome. Not that I am allowed out to see much of them.
>
> Our living conditions are hardly as comfortable as they were, for Papá's friend had only had one room to spare and we are all sharing it! It would be hard enough, but Mamá spends her days crying and her evenings yelling at Papá. It would be nice to have someone to talk to.
>
> I wish you would come to us and let Yusef find you here. Would you at least consider it?
>
> May God have mercy on you and grant you the best and health.
>
> > Your loving sister,
> > Reyna

She would not consider it, but thinking of her sister among the canals and safe from this bedlam gave Beatríz a moment of relief.

The docks were filled with people trying to convince captains to take them aboard, but each one was offering the same answer: King Manuel had declared that no ship could leave the harbor with New Christians for fear that the former Jews would revert to their wicked ways as soon as they were off his shores. No matter what argument was offered – money, a long history of being Christian, assurances that the authorities had no way of finding out and therefore would not punish a captain – no one seemed to be convincing enough.

Beatríz had to jog to keep up with Abrão as he moved undaunted through the crowd. She spotted familiar faces now and then, but did not stop to question her friends or even acknowledge them. When they reached the end of the walkway and had still not found a boat to take them, Abrão said, "There are always ships that moor farther out. Captains with, um, shadier reputations. I think we should continue on."

She did not like the sound of it, but felt they had no choice. They climbed boulders and a hill, and when they reached the crest, Beatríz saw a ship anchored a short way off the shore and a group surrounding dinghies.

Miriam struggled with her skirts and her heft as they climbed the rocks, and insisted the others go ahead. Beatríz and Abrão split up to approach captains, and at the first ship, Beatríz was told that they were full. She did not mind, as it was headed for Candia, which was incredibly far and not one of the places Yusef's family had contacts, meaning he would not think to find them there first.

She met Abrão on his way back. "Good news," he said. "The captain I just spoke with is Genoese and does not care who his passengers are. He was here to unload cargo, and with the conversions and chaos at the port, there is nothing to transport out. The passengers' bribes will make the short crossing to north part of Africa worth his effort. There is room for us and the boat leaves immediately."

"That is wonderful," Beatríz exclaimed, trying to believe it.

His eyes drifted to where Miriam stood out of breath, and said gravely, "I could only get the two of you aboard. He is asking for more money than I brought. More money than I could have imagined this would cost. But you two go ahead and I will follow soon. I will send word to Yusef about where you have gone." Beatríz opened her mouth to argue, but he said, "Not a word. Miriam will refuse to get on if she realizes what is happening. I do not care what you do or say to her, but make sure she stays on that rowboat."

Beatríz feared what this meant, knowing perfectly well it might take him some time to find another captain willing to break the king's decree, and that harm could come to him in the meantime. She could offer to stay in his place, but he knew the options and was asking her to go instead. Abrão had been like a second father to her. When her family had first come to Portugal, he had provided comfort and a home for them all without ever complaining, and had eased her way at every turn. She recalled the first time Yusef sailed away, when Abrão had stood with her on shore, holding her around the shoulder while she cried silently, assuring her that Yusef would return. After all Abrão had done for her, she would do what she could for him. She would help get Miriam to safety.

Beatríz's mind sharpened. A lie. She would need a lie.

Abrão gathered Miriam, and together the three walked toward the water. He raised his arm in a high wave and the captain pointed at him. Miriam was pulled onto the nearly loaded dinghy, and then Beatríz. The sailors' hands lingered even after she was steady on her feet. Beatríz pretended not to notice and scooted toward Miriam along the weathered bench.

"That is all we can take," shouted the captain in heavily accented Portuguese. "No room," he said in Castilian. He switched to Italian to say something to his crew, and Beatríz thought he told them to hurry.

It took Miriam until that moment to notice Abrão was not aboard. She rose and Beatríz yanked her arm, hoping she would go without a fight. It was not to be.

"Abrão!"

Abrão slipped into the middle of the crowd that was still calling to the captain.

Miriam shouted for Abrão again and then tried to climb over Beatríz. Miriam was twice the width of Beatríz, but Beatríz had made a promise. She blocked Miriam's way first with her leg, then with her body.

"Sit!" said the captain.

"My husband!" she shouted.

"Miriam," Beatríz said, hoping to feign confidence well enough to cover the quaver in her voice, "he is going to his mistress."

Miriam's head snapped toward Beatríz and she froze. "What?"

"His mistress. He cannot leave her here unattended, so he is making arrangements for her care before he joins us. He did not want me to tell you, but you should know why he is staying."

Miriam blinked several times, peering over her shoulder to see who might have heard this insult. By the averted gazes, she knew everyone had. "Is this true?" she asked Beatríz.

Beatríz tried to look convincing. "Yes."

Miriam thudded onto the bench and turned her back to the shore.

The crew leapt over the side and began to heave. They kicked up small rocks at first, but the rowboat jolted toward the waterline and soon the men were splashing as they shouldered their burden. Beatríz noticed Miriam's shoulders shaking. The crew jumped back into the boat rocking it so hard water lapped over the sides. Some women screamed. The sailors picked up oars and they slipped toward the ship.

The rowboat pulled along side the ship and the passengers were helped up the ladder. Miriam struggled to climb while holding her bag, but would not accept help or even acknowledge Beatríz's offer to take her things. When it was Beatríz's turn, she decided to once again ignore the lingering hands on her bottom meant to 'help' her aboard and the fingers that slid across her breast as she was lifted over the rail. She did, however, move quickly toward the mast where the other passengers huddled.

The captain leapt confidently onto the wheelhouse and addressed them. "We will arrive in Safi in three days. This is not a passenger ship, so I hope you understand you will be expected to sleep on deck. I apologize for the inconvenience." He then turned and called orders to the crew who snapped into action, leaving Beatríz to wonder why he was so indifferent to the decree of King Manuel.

Beatríz noticed the crew spoke many languages but found ways to communicate with each other. Castilian, to her surprise, was the linking language. She watched them begin to hoist the sail, pull on a rope she assumed held the anchor, and do each job with ease and excitement. Or perhaps it was her own nervous excitement that colored her perception. Although the men in her life were on boats so often that they probably knew the name of every task and job aboard, Beatríz had never traveled by sailboat. And so, despite the bewildering turn of events that day, she felt a thrill as she watched the gleaming sails flutter and billow.

It was not until a breeze blew dark curls in her face and the passengers had clumped at the stern to watch Lisbon fade into the distance that the discomfort of Beatríz's lie wrapped its fingers back around her throat. Now that there was no way off, she figured it was safe to tell Miriam the truth.

"Miriam," Beatríz said stepping to her side. Miriam kept her eyes fixed on the city they had called home. "Miriam, I lied. There is no mistress."

Miriam looked quickly at Beatríz, her mouth opening and closing.

"Dom Abrão knew he could only get the two of us on board. He told me to make sure you stayed with me."

Miriam's eyes narrowed, and before she walked away, she said to Beatríz, "That was very cruel. And very wrong."

Beatríz nodded to no one in particular, feeling like a thorn had lodged in her stomach. Beatríz had repaid Miriam's endless kindess with a lie that cut too deep.

A woman had been watching the exchange and waved Beatríz over. "These times sometimes call for extreme measures. Come sit with us for now. You will sort this out later. I'm Jamila."

Beatríz did not even know that she was walking, but suddenly found herself a few paces away and lowered herself onto a coil of ropes next to Jamila. A group of women sat nearby speaking in hushed tones about whom and what they had left behind.

Jamila was younger than Miriam, but older than Beatríz. She had piercing eyes and a liveliness in her face, even when she was not speaking. Some of the women had babies in their arms or young children hanging on them, but Jamila sat alone. She angled slightly to include Beatríz in their group.

"Who are you traveling with?" Beatríz asked.

"I am alone."

Beatríz cocked her head. What woman would travel by herself? "What about your husband?"

Jamila smiled. "I never married. To be honest, I never wanted to, and someone needed to care for my ailing father, so it was a matter of convenience. After he passed, I helped my sister with her children. But my sister left months ago and I stubbornly stayed, assuming all the running would be for naught. Foolishness. But I will join them in Fez, if a crossing through the desert can be made from Safi. I am relieved this ship was staying on the Atlantic side of the Maghreb. I feared I would end up on the Mediterranean and have to find my way back past Gibraltar."

"Are there other Jews in Safi?" Beatríz asked.

Jamila nodded. "There are Jewish quarters in most cities of any size throughout the Maghreb, just like there were across Europe before all the Jews were expelled." She pinned a loose curl behind her ear. "The coastal cities have been trade centers for us for so long that you will find many established Jewish families there. My worry is whether there will be space for us, given these past months of Portuguese unrest so closely following the edict of expulsion from *Sepharad*."

Miriam passed by, and Beatríz tensed. Jamila reached out a hand and patted Beatríz's arm. "We are all being asked to do things we would not normally do. She will forgive you."

Laughter from the crew stabbed Beatríz's ears. The land where she had met and loved Yusef fell out of view, and the horizon beyond which she hoped to meet him again remained empty. The boat rocked and swayed, and time passed. They were given bread, which Beatríz choked down without tasting. Before she knew it, the moon glistened on the black water, a sight too beautiful for such a night, yet that is what she felt as she watched Miriam sit with her back turned just a few feet away.

The next morning, Beatríz kept her distance from Miriam, but knew where Miriam sat at every moment, and shifted every time she shifted. Sometimes she watched from the corner of her eye, sometimes she stared outright hoping her intense gaze would magically turn Miriam's head toward her own. But as the sun rose and began to sear her skin, Beatríz could wait no longer.

She walked slowly in Miriam's direction, trying to ignore the others who were looking at her. When she was standing very near, she paused, hoping Miriam would look up at her. She did not. Beatríz cleared her throat. The silence between them was filled with the flapping sails and the creaking hull.

"Miriam, I —"

"Can you get me some water, dear?" Miriam interrupted quickly.

"Anything," Beatríz answered, swallowing the lump in her throat hard, then again, and again as she walked.

With shaking hands she pulled the ladle from the water barrel and poured it into a tin cup. When she turned, a drunken sailor (perhaps more hung over than drunk judging by his squint) was leaning against the wheelhouse. He made a lewd gesture at her, causing Beatríz to fling the water in the air. He and his friends laughed as she swallowed her fury and turned back to the barrel. Water seeped into the leather of her boots, and this time she had to concentrate even harder to get any water in the cup. She walked deliberately past the man, forcing herself not to react to the feel of his hands on her lower back as she continued squishing across the deck toward Miriam, thinking of Yusef's warnings of the dangers at sea.

When she handed over the cup, Miriam thanked her without looking. The other women watched as Beatríz backed over to the rail and slumped into its broken shadow to pass the day, trying not to notice the men staring at her.

She observed that the ship hugged the coast all day, but then as evening approached, they left sight of land. Her last glimpse of Portugal had been the day before, and now they were crossing the small waterway between Gibraltar and the Maghreb. She wondered if she would see the land of her birth, or the land where she had fallen in love, ever again. The ship would continue southwest to a city where she had never been and where she knew no one, and the thought gave her a pang of melancholy.

When the moon was high above their heads and all were fighting off sleep, two drunken sailors came to where she was standing. The one who had gestured lewdly and grabbed at Beatríz earlier in the day trailed the other. The one in the lead, whose hair was pulled back into a ponytail, pointed at Beatríz.

"Here's the one I want," he said in Castilian. He struggled to keep his balance as he took Beatríz's chin in his hand.

"Do not touch me," Beatríz said, jerking her face out of his grip.

He stumbled back then came at her again. "I will do what I want." Then he threw his arms around her. Beatríz struggled, knocking them both to the ground. Beatríz rolled away and scrambled to her feet. The sailor staggered up, furious, his hand going for his knife. Licking his lips, he said, "I'm gonna kill you or fuck you. Either one will do."

Out of nowhere, Miriam stepped in front of Beatríz. "Why do you want her? She's inexperienced."

"Because breaking a virgin is what we bet on around here. I won tonight, so I get to pick my virgin."

"Well," began Miriam, "that's a shame for you. She is not a virgin."

Beatríz fought to hide her own surprise at this.

"She was engaged to my son, a merchant who sailed off some months ago. He had her before he left. I was furious and thought to leave her behind, but we promised her dead parents that we would care for her. I will do that, but she is ruined, so I will find my son another wife. A pure wife."

Beatríz could not believe the string of lies coming from her future mother-in-law. She wondered if Miriam was fabricating as they stood in the moonlight or if she had been planning the story in case of such a confrontation.

Miriam continued, "But as for being with her, I cannot imagine what you would gain. She is neither a virgin nor experienced enough to bring you much pleasure. She would not know what to do."

The pony tailed sailor swayed as he turned his head to look at his friend. His friend raised his shoulders slightly and the men nodded at each other. "We will have someone tonight. That is a fact." His eyes roamed the deck.

"Have me," Miriam answered.

Beatríz grabbed onto Miriam's arm, but Miriam stepped forward shaking off Beatríz's hand.

"You? You're old."

"Not as old as you might think. But I have been married long enough to need some tricks to keep my husband interested. I am willing, but you must forget the girl."

"No," hissed Beatríz.

Miriam took another step closer to Beatríz's would-be assailant and kissed him hard, her mouth open, her arms wrapping around his back. Beatríz felt nauseous at the sight. Miriam whispered seductively, "Take me and leave her be."

Beatríz covered her mouth with her hands to hold in a scream.

Laughter burst from the men when they began leading Miriam away. Beatríz turned to Jamila and said, "We must stop them."

"No. This is what she chose."

Beatríz began to move forward, but Jamila clutched her, saying, "Do not look. Do not think. Do not hear. It is not happening."

Beatríz heard a strangling noise coming from her own throat.

As the men turned, the man with the ponytail said, "She is mine first tonight. I won the bet, and I do not want to poke around in your filth."

"She's not a virgin and I beat you at cards last night when there weren't any women. I should go first."

They began shoving one another, and the shoving turned to punching. Ponytail knocked the other man down and grabbed Miriam. They began using her like a rope in tug of war.

Another figure moved toward them. "I warned you on the last leg of the trip," shouted the barrel chested man whose hat had fallen off in his rush to cross the ship, "that fighting would not be tolerated."

"But captain —" began the shorter man.

"Shall I make myself clearer that I will not allow discord among my crew?" Moonlight glinted off his raised sword, and the men stepped back, leaving Miriam to stare wide-eyed at the captain. Beatríz thought the captain was warning the men or would hurt them but he pointed the sword at Miriam, then raised it above her head. In those moments, Beatríz felt sure it was for show, a warning. As the sword sliced through the air, it created a silver rainbow, which Beatríz found eerily beautiful, still certain there would be no contact. But then a crack — Miriam's head was split open. Blood and ooze began pouring down her gown before her body even hit the deck. Beatríz's scream could not be singled out among the cries of the women around her.

"Now neither of you can have her," shouted the captain.

Hands held up Beatríz as her knees buckled. "No. No. No!" she thought. Other words would not come as she stared at the body of Yusef's mother splayed on the deck, vacant eyes fixed on the heavens. She stood numb as the captain regarded his blood-spattered shirt with irritation.

"For causing a disruption to my peace," scolded the captain, "you will get rid of her then swab the entire deck. That should take the fight out of you."

Beatríz did not blink as she watched the men cursing each other under their breath. Then they took Miriam's body and threw it overboard as carelessly as an empty sack. At the sound of the splash, Beatríz vomited.

"Aw, I'm not cleaning that up," said the sailor who had touched Beatríz by the water barrel.

"We will do it," said Jamila. "We will also clean the blood."

The man with the ponytail hesitated. "The captain said we do it. If I let you, we could get punished ourselves. And I don't like the captain's justice much." Walking away, he said under his breath, "I knew taking these Jews would be bad luck."

Beatríz did not blink. Or speak. Or breathe. Gentle hands touched her. Moved her away. Voices soothed.

What would she tell Yusef? It was her fault.

CHAPTER 7

Beatríz did not speak for the rest of the journey. She moved around only when necessary and another woman always followed her, though Beatríz had not asked for an escort. When sitting against the rail, she covered her face with her hands, blocking out the sight of the cruel sailors, the too-bright sun, the sympathetic faces the passengers, and the world she suddenly hated.

She could not get the sight of Miriam's sliced head out of her mind. Never before had Beatríz seen a murdered body. Dead bodies, certainly, but from disease or accident. This woman – who had been like a second mother to her – had been protecting Beatríz. And now she was dead.

Was this what the world beyond Lisbon had to offer?

She sat still, so still, hoping to make herself invisible, and hoping the rest of the journey would pass without incident. She had begun to pray, but wondered which God to pray to, and if God was interested in a convert's prayers. Worse, might this not be a punishment for her conversion?

Eventually land appeared on the horizon and everyone

else cheered. Beatríz turned her head, but could not feel anything. The swath of water grew narrower, and dusty land dotted with glimmering white and tan buildings nudged away more of the sky. The crew and passengers readied themselves to disembark.

Beatríz had been staring at Miriam's bag for two days. She crossed the deck and opened it tentatively. The commonplace items Miriam had hastily gathered a thousand regrets ago greeted her. A dress. The long shirt she wore under her dresses – her *camisa*. Letters. They had packed nearly the same things. There was little of use to Beatríz, but she could not bear to leave the bag behind.

Making her way safely onto the gangplank and the down the incline with her own bag slung across her chest and Miriam's bag in hand was challenging, but she flinched away from help at the top. She lurched out of the grasp of the sailor waiting to help her at the other end then tumbled into him when the ship rolled on a wave. When he reached to lift her up, she kicked at him and he cursed her.

Once on solid ground, Beatríz did not follow her shipmates nor did she wish anyone farewell. Keeping her eyes down, she waited for everyone else to pass through the gate and then studied the city.

It was smaller than Lisbon and completely surrounded by a tall, brown wall the thickness of a man with his arms outstretched. The opening to the gate was not a mere round arch, as she had been accustomed to in Lisbon. There were three curves at the top that reminded her of flower petals. Instead of seven hills, there was only one, but it was steep. The buildings clutching to the incline were tan and white, stone and mud brick, wood roofed and tiled. There was no uniformity, no common aesthetic. Some seemed newly built while others were crumbling or partially constructed. She spotted two towers right off, and realized that, as they had no bells, they must be minarets, from which Muslims were called to prayer. One was on the side of the city where she stood, and the other far up the hill.

A fisherman dropped a basket of silver fish with protruding teeth onto the sand not three strides away from Beatríz, sending her scuttling back. Then a woman picked up one fish from the pile, threw it onto a cutting stone, hacked its heads off, tossed it into a new basket and reached for another fish. She did this with such speed that Beatríz marveled at her skill. But the pooling blood reminded Beatríz of Miriam, and, queasy, she moved away, up the slight incline toward the gate.

A Portuguese flag flew overhead, and the armored soldiers gave Beatríz pause. She had been told that Safi was under Muslim control, making it ideal for Jews wishing to escape. Beatríz also remembered, however, Yusef telling her that the Portuguese were attempting to conquer port cities across the Maghreb. Would she be forced to live as a Christian here, too? Or could it be that the soldiers had more pressing problems, namely protecting the city from the Muslims, who surely would want their city back?

And then a question startled her: Did she care?

She pushed it aside.

The soldiers did not seem too concerned with those coming or going, so she followed the example of the pedestrians ahead of her, looked down at the ground and moved into the shadows of the city.

With each step, she became more and more determined to push bad memories away, to use each new sight, sound, and scent to try to help her forget. But it did not work. Every woman's face became Miriam's. Every man's became the captain's. Everything reminded her that she was alone in a new city. Alone. Her hand drifted to Miriam's bag where she knew Yusef's letters rested, dreading his reaction to his mother's death. Could he ever forgive her? Pressing her eyelids together, Beatríz breathed in deeply and tried again to forget.

Beatríz was not sure which way to go, so she followed a young boy with a hoop in his hands. The child scampered quickly out of sight, but she continued in the same direction. There seemed to be little order to how the buildings and walks were constructed. The first street she traveled twisted and turned more tightly than any she had ever seen. When a woman came toward her, Beatríz had to turn sideways to let the woman pass.

As she made her way further up the hill, the streets widened and took on some order. The houses were more newly stuccoed and freshly painted. Beatríz was mesmerized by the variety of doors, both their shape and color – blue like a calm summer sky, green like an angry river, red like blood when it first hits the air. There were round and pointed top doors, small and chipped ones, some studded with metal circles, and others criss crossed like baskets. She wended her way further to the outskirts of the town and found that in some places there were stairs of stone, while in other places, the earth itself was carved into steps.

Beatríz came to an archway that curved inexplicably across the street. With nothing lovely about it, one could not even declare it decorative. While she was considering this oddity, it occurred to her that she might be in the wrong quarter. In fact, she did not even know if Safi was divided into quarters at all. The first person she approached spoke no Portuguese or Castilian, so she decided to make her way to the center of town where she might have more luck finding information about Safi and the family Yusef's parents had known.

For weeks, Dom Abrão had worked with Miriam and Beatríz to memorize the names and locations of people he knew in various cities. Had Yusef's father known that they might be separated or that she might end up alone?

She found herself on a street that acted as a marketplace, though it was not large enough to be the main market for the town. Wares hung from hooks and across the narrow alley. Each small booth was full from floor to arched ceiling with all manner of glitter, beast, and fabrics. A stall with stacks of pink and silver fish, along with flat, winged sea creatures was wedged between a man selling rope-soled shoes on one side and a family hocking pots on the other. The smells were punget – hot animals, cooked food, spices, rot, and feces all mixed, making Beatríz want to simultaneously take in everything and hold her breath.

She pulled a coin from her bag and bought a flatbread whose local name she did not know. As she savored the seeds and spices hidden in the dough, she wondered how, in a small city, she could be having so much difficulty finding what she was looking for.

The two sacks of belongings Beatríz carried grew heavier as she walked, and the rope that tied Miriam's began to cut into her hands. Even in the shadows, it was so hot that Beatríz felt as if she were inside a brick oven. At last, with aching legs and dwindling patience, Beatríz found someone who spoke her language and, thankfully, knew whom she was looking for.

Even before reaching the Jewish Quarter, the crowd thickened. The lucky few that had recently found passage out of Portugal joined those wise enough to leave before the forced conversions, and all of them had arrived years after the exiles from Spain. Many had moved on to other cities in the Maghreb, but enough Jews remained that Safi was overrun.

Beatríz pushed through thick, dirty crowds that sat and stood in the streets and filled the squares. Bundles and trunks littered the way, tripping more than one passer-by. Beatríz kept her head down and did not react to her behind being pinched and her body being groped. The strangers' roughness was so unlike Yusef's welcome caresses – his skin on her skin, exploring, whispering, stroking – which had nearly driven her mad from wanting more. These men touching her without permission was unseemly, but she said nothing, too afraid to speak up in case the answer came, once again, via sword or worse. Whatever she did would be to keep herself safe until she found Yusef.

At last she found the house she had been looking for. Beatríz knocked and a servant opened the door. The servant did not return Beatríz's smile nor did she seem to understand what Beatríz asked in Portuguese. Beatríz tried next in Castilian, then pointed at the name painted next on the door and read out aloud. Beatríz suspected the servant was being intentionally difficult and fought to keep her temper in check. With a barely concealed smirk, the servant disappeared into the house, closing the door firmly in Beatríz's face.

Moments later, Beatríz heard the tap-tap of a woman's shoes on tile and the door swung open. A fat woman with full lips was suddenly facing her, her head wrapped in dark material. The blonde hair peeking from under the purple veil took Beatríz aback until she remembered Miriam saying that the lady of the house had been Italian by birth. Yusef had told her of the blondes of Italy and points north. She had not realized any of them might be Jews.

The blond woman offered nothing but pursed lips and raised eyebrows, so Beatríz spoke first. "My name is Beatríz," she began. When no answer was given, Beatríz searched for something more to say. "Uh, you see I am expected. My betrothed is Yusef, son of Dom Abrão."

The woman narrowed her eyes. "Where is Miriam?"

Beatríz felt the energy rush out of her legs. "She . . . she was killed on the passage."

"And Dom Abrão?"

"He stayed behind. Are you Anna, wife of Simeon?" When the woman merely twisted her mouth, Beatríz added, "Miriam and Dom Abrão said you were aware that I would be joining them."

Tucking blond strands under her veil, she backed into the shadows. "Well, you cannot stay here," she said, beginning to close the door.

Beatríz took a step in to wedge herself between the doorjamb and the frighteningly heavy door. "But –"

"How do I know if you are who you say you are? You could have heard information on the boat. No." She tried to shove Beatríz out, but Beatríz bent her knees and held firm.

"I have nowhere to go. I could work for you. Sleep among the servants."

"I have ample help. Besides, my husband has a wandering eye. I do not need a pretty girl under my roof. Goodbye." With great force, she pushed Beatríz who stumbled.

Beatríz slapped the slammed door, but the woman did not open it. Beatríz pounded with both fists. Then she hit it harder. Nothing. Hands stinging and panic rising, Beatríz slumped against the wall to collect herself.

The light turned orange at the tops of the houses and then

eased to a cooling blue, and still she sat. A man approached the house, eyeing her suspiciously. Simeon, she was almost sure.

"May I help you?" he asked, his gaze wandering from her dark, wavy hair, to the neckline of her dress, and settling on her lips.

Beatríz shook her head and scuttled away. If his wife knew he had come home with Beatríz still out front, her troubles might double. All she needed was a jealous wife and a lusty husband making a scene over her presence. And seeing the way he looked at her, she was not sure she wanted to sleep under his roof or to be beholden to him.

She roamed a bit among those left on the streets, those like her with nowhere to go. She weighed her options and considered the fact that technically, she was a Christian. Perhaps she could travel to another quarter and find a church where charity might be offered. But maybe they would see through her and turn her away. Many before her must have tried the same trick. But *was* it a trick? She had been baptized.

She thought about her religion. What it meant to her. For her whole life, she had gone through the motions of prayers and holidays without thinking. It was what she was.

She recalled standing in the women's gallery of the synagogue, wishing she could go downstairs to Yusef and be with him during prayers. Wishing she could knock down the screen that stood between them and tell him how she appreciated him, loved him. She would kiss him and –

Then it occurred to her why men and women were separated during prayers. To keep one's thoughts on God and eyes on the prayer book. Or, in the case of women, most of who did not read, to keep them caged while the men served God. Caged. Did she mean that? Yes. She did. She was in a cage when she was not allowed to be with Yusef. And she felt trapped by a religion that made her the target of hate and suspicion.

The weather was turning unexpectedly chilly, especially compared to the heat of the day. Beatríz guiltily reached into Miriam's sack and pulled out a shawl. Wrapping it tightly around herself, trying to ignore Miriam's lingering scent in its folds, she continued to walk, hoping to find a solution. As she neared the end of town, the crowd only grew thicker. At the same time, she noticed a more potent smell. To her deep surprise, Beatríz found herself at the edge of the trash heap, an expanse alive with movement. Dizzy from hunger, Beatríz thought for certain she must be imagining it. But upon closer inspection, she noticed that people were crawling among the refuse. Mouth agape, she watched as one person after another seemed to be settling down upon the piles.

"Nowhere else to go," a half-buried man called out in Castilian-tinged Portuguese. "Once you get past the smell you will find it is the perfect solution." He picked up an empty sack and shook off rotting peels of some sort. "This will keep you warm, dear. And the treasures you can find in this place will surprise you: bones still encrusted with meat, shoes with few holes. God provides. Join us."

A few days ago, Beatríz had been sitting on comfortable furniture with nothing more pressing to do than pick the color of thread to use in her needlework or to reread Yusef's letters. Now she was faced with sleeping in a heap of rot. The shift was dizzying.

Beatríz forced the corners of her mouth into a polite smile and backed away from the man, bumping into new arrivals as she did. Turning and walking, Beatríz again fought the sinking feeling and told herself she would solve this problem without sleeping on the molding rubbish of the city. She had, unfortunately, been too optimistic. She staggered with fatigue until she found a doorway in which to lean her body and promptly fell asleep.

She was awakened by a splash of water in her face. Dirty water. A servant shouted at her. Though Beatríz did not understand, she got the gist and hurried away. Out of sight of the still shouting shriveled woman, Beatríz sank onto her haunches and dried her face and hair with the shawl. For some reason, drying off fishy water with sweaty wool struck her as funny and she began to chuckle grimly. Certainly some passersby must have thought her mad, but Beatríz was too tired to be embarrassed.

Yet she sobered to think of how quickly her situation had grown desperate. When her family had been forced to leave Toledo, they had arrived in Lisbon to the comfort of Dom Abrão's. And Miriam's. Beatríz swallowed hard, trying not to think of her split skull. Instead she thought of her family's journey to Lisbon. Crossing the mountains had been a struggle, but her family was together and somehow it had made things seem less frightening. It was ironic how Beatríz, who had longed for the adventure of traveling again, had sunk low so quickly. Yet she had never thought she would undertake her travels alone.

Had she done the right thing in leaving her parents?

She considered walking to the waterfront and trying to find a boat bound for Venice. Not only did she not have enough money for such a long passage, the thought of facing sailors without any protection seemed foolhardy. And had she not wanted adventure? To be independent and to get away from her mother's moroseness? Mostly, leaving Safi now would mean that Miriam's sacrifice had been for nothing. She could not allow one setback – enormous as it was – to undo it all. Besides, what if Dom Abrão did arrive in Safi? Or Yusef? No, she would stay. She could manage this.

Beatríz spent the day inquiring about rooms but to no avail. As evening approached once again, she found herself standing at an abandoned construction site – or a destroyed house. She could not tell. There was a roof and walls, but no shutters or doors. Beatríz looked down the street one way, then the other, and stepped inside. She moved through the entry way and into the courtyard, and, to her disappointment, she saw a fire pit with coals still glowing. While she was not the first one to think of living there, she did not plan on being thwarted and so let her sack fall to the dust.

"Out. Out," someone hollered.

Beatríz turned. The voice came from an opening on the second floor. A withered old woman was waving her arms wildly as if the motion could sweep Beatríz away.

Beatríz put her hands on her hips. "Is this your house?"

The woman turned and Beatríz could hear her rushing down the stairs. The woman hobbled quickly over and came very close to Beatríz, pointing in her face. "I live here with my family. You go."

"Do you own this building?" Beatríz asked. "Do you pay rent for this house?"

The woman lowered her finger but remained close enough that Beatríz could count the wrinkles on her forehead. "No."

"Then you have no claim," Beatríz said, knowing perfectly well that if a man lived there, that was all the claim that would be needed. When the woman did not respond, Beatríz knew she had won. "I will go upstairs."

"No. That is where we sleep. My daughter and her baby. She is a widow."

"There must be more than one room."

"No. There are other people, too."

"Down here, then."

The old woman shook her head as she pursed her lips. "Dangerous. Many come in and out in the night."

Beatríz thought of the possible dangers, of who might poke around while she was sleeping. But what choice did she have? She announced, "There is nowhere else but the garbage heap, so I will sleep here." The woman crossed her arms, so Beatríz asked, "Have you any authority here or are you simply too selfish to share this crumbling spot with someone in need?"

The old woman did not answer, but stomped to the pit and began to stoke the fire. Beatríz walked to a covered corner of the courtyard, threw her bags down, and laid her head upon them, falling asleep without removing her shoes.

Beatríz awoke to someone tugging her hair. She opened one eye and saw a toddler standing over her. Drool ran down the child's chin and snot encrusted her nose. Beatríz sat up and took in the girl's plump cheeks and wide clear eyes. "What is your name?" Beatríz asked.

"Lola," the child squeaked.

"I am Beatríz."

"Bay-a-zees," Lola nodded, her curls bouncing.

Beatríz smiled.

Lola's mother pushed Lola out of the way and addressed Beatríz. "You get your own food and do not speak with my daughter. I do not want her to grow attached to anyone else who might disappear." With that, the woman called to Lola and vanished upstairs.

Beatríz felt sorry for the young woman, widowed and alone, living in this abandoned house. It was hard enough for

Beatríz to think of herself. She could not imagine the
challenge of having a child to care for in the midst of this
madness, though her womb panged at the thought of a child
of her own. She decided to be friendly if the woman would
allow it. Making an effort toward another person might help
Beatríz stop thinking so much about Miriam.

The sun sank and the courtyard grew dark. Beatríz
wrapped herself in her still-damp shawl and watched yet
another woman trudge up the stairs without giving her so
much as a second look.

The old woman had been correct: others did come and go
throughout the night. Beatríz considered what she might do if
anyone tried to steal her belongings or molest her. She
thought she would scream. But who would hear? Who would
care? Beatríz scooted into the farthest corner, and luckily no
one bothered her.

The next day, still exhausted since the night's sleep had
been fitful from nightmares of Miriam's murder, Beatríz
decided to help the women of the house whose names she
still did not know by buying food. She had found some coins
in Miriam's bag, and reached into her own for fresh clothes
then hesitated. Who knew when she would get a chance to do
wash? And who would help her tie on her sleeves or do up
her bodice?

As she set out in the soiled dress she had worn since the
day of her conversion, she thought about clothing, and the
endless arguments she and her mother had had over her style
and modesty. Such frivolous discussions. Would she rather be
with her mother arguing over stiff skirts versus flowing ones
now? No.

Beatríz wended her way through the streets, remembering
the feel of Yusef's fingertips along the scalloped fabric at her

chest, and hardly realized she had found the main square that held the large marketplace. In the center, there was an open space for selling animals, for carts moving goods, for semi-permanent stalls draped with fabric for shade. All around were buildings full of ground level shops. One stall came after another, much like on the street she had walked the day before, only this market had row after row, building after building devoted to selling goods.

Leather bags, beads, pots, pans, hats, baskets, sacks of spices, piles of dates, even musical instruments filled every free space. Around the next corner, men hammered metal, painted wooden frames, wove patterned rugs and richly colored blankets. Women baked flatbreads and rolled out fabrics. Beatríz forgot her troubles, moving quickly to see it all, thrilled by the new sights and sounds and the freedom to go where she pleased when she pleased. Until she reached the counter of animal heads with their cloudy eyes staring at nothing. She walked past with a shudder trying not to think about Miriam and seeking a place to catch her breath.

She leaned on the counter of a stall to quiet the quaking of her legs. Her fingers brushed a bowl of green olives stacked tall and glistening in light made softer by a length of blue fabric strung overhead. Plump purple olives were in the next bowl. Then tiny ones so dark they looked nearly black. Beatríz's stomach rumbled, and this, of all things, triggered a powerful homesickness.

The vendor's soft eyes and ready smile made her look twice. In just a few days, she had forgotten about kindness. Her shoulders relaxed and her stomach was released of its gripping sorrow. She handed him coins and thanked him as he handed her a small sack.

She tried to listen to conversations as she wended her way

through the crowd, hoping to gain information about how to survive in this new place. Two men stood huddled under the fishmonger's canopy. "A caravan is being set for Fez," said one.

"Will you join?" asked the other.

"What have I got to lose? The worst that happens is I die in the desert."

"You would rather die of thirst as a Jew than live as a Christian?"

Beatríz considered this. She thought she did not especially care how she lived, as long as she was free to live as she pleased. Restrictions were plentiful as a Jew, so being a Christian for a while, if not forever, had to have some appeal. Why did the man not see that?

The first man said to the other, "Would you call this living?"

The two men laughed grimly, and Beatríz thought to move on until the second man said, "Lucky we did not go to Venice. The Plague has hit them hard."

She froze. Her family had not mentioned a plague in the letters she had received in Lisbon. Had they remained unscathed and chosen not to worry her? Had they written to tell her, but she had missed the letter? She decided to write to them as quickly as possible.

She needed paper. Surely someone in the many stalls was selling it. And perhaps a quill and ink. Unless she could borrow that. The city had proven somewhat unfriendly, but there might be someone kind enough to loan both to her. She walked back and forth along the rows looking for the proper stall, suddenly unable to hear or see anything except for what each lacked.

At long last, she found the right shop. As she dug into her

purse for her coins, she hesitated. There was certainly enough money just then, but would her coins last? And how would she walk around with ink and keep from spilling?

"Just the paper, I suppose," Beatríz said, biting her lip as she looked longingly at the bottle.

The woman, whose eyes shone brightly, said, "We have a table for rent along with the ink. You must buy the quill."

Beatríz nodded.

The woman gestured to the stool, and Beatríz sat. Then she paused to think. She ought to write to Dom Abrão and Yusef. Though her heart squeezed at the thought, keeping Miriam's death from them would be cruel. So she had three letters to write and very little time unless she wanted to hand over a great deal of money for the rental. But how to write such delicate things?

The first was easy. She briefly told her parents that she had arrived safely in Safi and hoped they were well. She left out the rest.

And at that moment she understood that she could not trust the letters she received. She knew that, unless absolutely necessary, her family, and maybe even Yusef, would likely hide the sordid details and challenges they faced. Her spirit shrank within her skin and she felt lonelier than she ever had in her life.

Setting out a new piece of paper, she wrote, "My dearest Yusef," and stopped. She wanted to tell him all. She wanted to unburden her guilt. She wanted to have him put his arms around her shoulders as she wept and told him that it had been his mother's choice but that if she could have, she would have – what? Would she have given her life for Miriam's? No. Would she have offered up her body to stop the fight? No. So what?

Forgetting the time, she put the quill in the bottle and covered her face with her hands.

She felt a hand on her shoulder. "*Senhorita,* what is the trouble?" the owner of the stall asked.

Beatríz listened to her jagged breath echoing off her palms and answered, "I have bad news to tell."

"In my experience, it is best to make it quick and simple." The woman patted Beatríz again and turned to sell a customer a length of twine with which to tie a bundle.

Beatríz looked at the page with Yusef's name and set it aside, picking up a blank sheet instead.

> *Dom Abrão,*
> *In the name of God.*
> *It is with difficulty I write to tell you that Miriam perished during the passage. I will remain here.*

Beatríz considered telling him the details but thought better of it. What else then? She thought a moment and then added:

> *I am overwhelmed by a sense of loss, and can only imagine what you must be feeling. I am filled with regret and sorrow for the loss of such an estimable woman.*

She signed her name. Quick and simple. The woman had been right. Beatríz felt lighter for having written the words.

Yusef's was not so easy. As far as she knew, he had always told her of his fears and of the dangers he faced. He had never wanted secrets between them, and she did not want to be deceitful. And so she put the paper in front of her, the quill trembling, poised past the greeting.

All that we feared has come to pass and more. I cannot think of what to write but the truth. We were forcibly converted in Lisbon, and your mother and I left your father at his insistence. And the worst – your mother was killed trying to protect me on the ship. I

Unable to write more, she touched her fingers to her lips and squeezed her eyes shut. Just a few more words and it would be done. She dipped the feather into ink once more.

am sorry. She was good to me.
I love you and think of you with every breath. Hurry to Safi. I will wait for you.
With all the love in my heart,
Béa

She set the quill down and folded the letters, writing the men's names on the outside, wondering if Yusef was still in Messina or if he had moved on by now. When she attempted to pay the proprietor for the time and ink, the woman waved away the offer. Beatríz could not think how a profit could be turned with such charity, but she thanked the woman and said she would be back again soon.

The letters weighed heavily in Beatríz's hands, so she hurried through the crowd. She needed to get to the waterfront, but the labyrinth of the city thwarted her. Each time a street bent and sent her back uphill, she cursed. She became blind to all other things in her attempt to get to the boats, not caring who she bumped as she began to run.

By the time she reached the city wall and passed through the gates, she was dripping with sweat. She wiped a palm on her skirt and switched the letters to the dry one as she headed for the docks. Peering at the various ships' flags, she tried to think what her better bet was: a language she knew or where she thought the ship might be heading. She knew perfectly well that she ran a risk sending letters with a stranger, but she had no other choice.

A Portuguese flag flew on the closest mast, so she called out, "Are you going to Lisbon?"

A sailor shook his head.

The next flag seemed familiar. "Venice?" she asked.

The man nodded and spoke with grand gestures of something flowing (Beatríz guessed he meant the canals) and of something tall (she thought he might be referring to a famous building of some sort). She held up a letter and he waved his hands in front of him and said something else she did not understand. Beatríz feared it was about the plague, but did not wish to dwell on the possibility.

A Spanish flag came next, but the ship was going to Genoa. And the next was off to Barcelona. She thought to give the letter to them and hope someone who knew her father in that port city might send it on to Venice, and then her father might send Yusef's letter on to Messina, but she decided to be patient and kept walking.

A Portuguese flag flew over the last ship and Beatríz found it was going to Lisbon. When she held up her letter, two sailors waved her onto the gangplank to deliver it. Nearly jumping with excitement, she started up the narrow piece of wood. But halfway there, a third man came to the rail. Something in his expression caught Beatríz's attention, and she found herself unable to move forward. The man narrowed his eyes in a deep smile. Or was it a grimace? A menacing leer? He was missing his front teeth, which she noticed when he licked his lips.

Suddenly, she thought he might be the sailor who had blown her a kiss on the boat to Safi – the one who had later come for her. But then she noticed that this man had reddish hair and was thinner. Not the same man, but it did not matter.

With a galloping heart, Beatríz backed down the gangplank unable to turn away from that face. A body pressed against her back and she screamed, nearly losing her balance as well as the letters.

"Excuse me," said a deep voice.

When hands gripped her shoulders she pulled away and spun around, this time tipping so far to her left that when she jerked to the right to keep from falling, she did lose her balance. The man grabbed her around the waist and held her until she was stable again.

"You're going to make us both go for a swim," the husky man said. He was a full head and a half taller than she, and Beatríz's neck hurt just trying to keep eye contact.

"Do not touch me!" she shouted, and he lifted his hands to the sky. "Let me off."

"It would be easier if you went up since you're nearly there."

"No! You back down. Now!" Beatríz ignored the laughter behind her. A group was gathering to watch how this would end.

Amusement in his eyes, the man scooted down the narrow plank without needing to look at his feet, his hands in the air, and fingers wiggling the entire time. When he leapt onto solid ground, doffed his cap to her and bowed, his friends erupted in cheers. Beatríz's eyes filled from relief and frustration. Had she misread the situation so badly? But when she turned her head to the toothless howling man, she saw the sword slicing

Miriam's head open. Holding her bag and letters to her chest, she looked down.

"*Senhorita*," the man said gently, but when he touched her arm, she jumped. "Did you need some assistance?"

Beatríz nodded, but, unable to rectify his kindness with the vision of blood that lingered in her head, she could not look up. Beatríz held out the letters, also unable to speak.

He looked at each and said, "We do not typically carry letters for those we do not know. But since I gave you such a scare, I would be wiling to help. We are more likely to find boats going to Venice and Crete when we get to Lisbon, and at least it would be on its way."

Beatríz forced her eyes up to meet his, said, "Thank you," and hastened away. She had to trust that he would do as he promised and not throw her letters into the ocean. She would have to trust many people now that she was on her own, but knowing which ones was proving to be harder than she had suspected.

CHAPTER 8

Beatríz found her way back to the abandoned house before dark. Only after arriving did she remember that she had wanted to bring food to Lola and her family.

Her desire for peace evaporated the moment she stepped into the courtyard and saw what the old woman was wearing: Miriam's dress. Beatríz had tucked Miriam's bag into her sleeping corner assuming no one would know it was there. But the crone had.

"What do you think you are doing?" Beatríz asked.

"What?" asked the wrinkled olive of a woman.

"That dress is mine."

"Looks t'big for you. You's skinnier than this," she said holding out the green material, a cruel smile revealing where her teeth had once been. Since the elderly lady was neither as tall nor as fat as Miriam, the dress dragged in the dirt.

"It does not fit you either," Beatríz argued, her voice wild. "And even if it was the right size, it was not yours to take." Beatríz felt heat rushing up her neck.

"Consider it rent." The woman turned back to her

cauldron.

Fury splintered through Beatríz's, and she moved forward with a raised fist.

"You touch my mother," called out Lola's mother from behind her, "and you had best sleep with one eye open."

Beatríz spun around. The younger woman had a knife, presumably for cooking, but Beatríz was not convinced Lola's mother would hesitate to put it to other uses.

Anger still crashed inside Beatríz, but with no way of getting back what was rightfully hers, she stormed into the corner to see what else was missing. Only the letters remained in the bag. Gone were the comb, the mirror, the *camisa* and the shoes. She threw the sack, growling as it hit the ground.

"We'll give you bread for a few weeks," the old lady called out without looking up from her work. "Consider it a trade."

Beatríz did not answer. Even if she had put her guilt and grief aside and tried to sell Miriam's belongings, she might not have done much better at the market, which was already flooded with unwanted items. Beatríz nodded, unable to look at the thieves.

When Lola's grandmother brought the flatbread, Beatríz's heart nearly cracked at the sight of dust already ground into the dress that Miriam had worn on the night of Beatríz and Yusef's betrothal.

Two years earlier, just after Beatríz's seventeenth birthday, a grand party had been thrown to celebrate the marriage agreement. Having nine witnesses in addition to the rabbi would have been enough, but it was not in any of their parents' nature to let an important moment pass without making an event of it.

The house had hummed in preparation. Before the guests had arrived, Beatríz put on her best dress and let Reyna fuss with her hair, wrapping her plaits with leather and adorning them with bejeweled pins. Beatríz's mother had strutted like a peacock, ordering the servants to place platters here and glasses all around the courtyard. Her father had relaxed in his sitting room with her brothers, drinking port and laughing easily. Her sister, Astruga, and her husband had stood uncomfortably in the entryway.

Beatríz had been called down when Yusef arrived. He had received her formally as if they did not spend free afternoons hiding in corners kissing. They had walked together into the courtyard and Beatríz had gasped at the loveliness of her mother's work. Flowers festooned tables and blooms were even tied onto the pillars. Candles flickered from silver candelabras, which, she realized, must have been borrowed from neighbors, for her parents had never owned so many. Everything had glowed, especially Yusef. He had pressed his lips to her palm and she had thought she just might faint on the spot.

Family friends had trickled in, taking up glasses and mingling. Beatríz and Yusef had held hands despite the scandalized looks of some of the older guests. But their parents, happy for the blossoming affection that had helped solidify the business relationship between the families, had not warned against the public display.

Once all were gathered, the fathers had stood with the rabbi and called for attention. The rabbi had held a paper and asked Beatríz and Yusef to step forward. "Yusef and Beatríz, do you wish to be married?"

Yusef had squeezed her hand and said, "Yes."

Beatríz was more overcome than she had expected to be, and could barely force out the word, "Yes." The crowd had chuckled, but Beatríz only noticed Yusef's smiling eyes, eyes whose unique color had stopped her short for their beauty the moment they had met.

"Do you have the gift?" asked the rabbi.

Yusef had held up a gold coin for all to see, and like a sunrise, it filled Beatríz with warmth. Beatríz's hand quivered as she opened her palm to receive it. His heat lingered in the metal as she had clasped it to her chest.

"Good," said the rabbi. Then, turning to the fathers, he had held out a contract that the men had had drawn up before the ceremony. The agreement had dictated the legalities of what each would be owed in case the betrothal was broken and a marriage did not take place. Even if Beatríz had been close enough to see it, she would not have looked at the details. What had it matter since nothing would stop her from marrying Yusef?

The rabbi had handed a quill to her father. "Write your name here."

Yusef had kissed one of Beatríz's cheeks after her father had signed and the other cheek after his father had signed. The fathers had shaken hands and applause had echoed off the courtyard walls. Beatríz buried her face in Yusef's chest and let him squeeze her. She had breathed in his musky scent and dreamt of the day they would share a life and share a bed.

Beatríz and Yusef had stood together all evening. Even when having separate conversations with their backs to one another, they had kept their fingers laced, creating a perfect V with their bodies.

The only solemnity of the evening was when Beatríz's friend, Sól, had approached. "I am so happy for you," Sól had said. She had seemed to be smiling, and so it had been especially surprising when Sól's face then crumpled.

Beatríz had tightened her grip on Yusef as she leaned

closer to Sól.

"My husband is so unkind. I wish –" Sól's voice had broken off as she threw her arms around Beatríz's neck.

Beatríz had put her free arm around Sól and waited for her childhood friend to stop weeping. "I have not seen you since your wedding. What was that, almost a year ago?" Beatríz had asked.

"My husband will not let me out of the house. He fears I will run off with a younger man." Sól's head had snapped over her shoulder to be sure her hunched, grey haired husband could not hear. "The only advantage to his being so old is that he has no will to touch me. I suppose for that I should be grateful."

Yusef had turned to join their conversation. A longing had spilled out of Sól's gaze, and Beatríz inched back against Yusef so his heat radiated against her shoulders.

Sól had looked away, her forehead wrinkling. "Congratulations," she had whispered before disappearing into the house, her husband limping in her wake.

"Why is your friend troubled?" Yusef had asked, stroking Beatríz's hair.

Beatríz had shaken her head. Then she had leaned into him further and sighed. "We are lucky."

Miriam had come over to them in an emerald dress that offset her jade eyes perfectly. She took Beatríz and Yusef in her arms and whispered, "*A união faz a força.*"

"Yes, strength comes from union, but not only in business," Yusef said, holding Beatríz tighter around the waist. "I will be stronger with Beatríz at my side."

"We will all be better for having Beatríz in our lives," said Miriam, kissing them both again before easing back among the guests.

Years later and a world away, Beatríz stared at the woman in Miriam's green gown with consuming hate. She wanted to knock that old bag of bones down and strip it right off of her. But she did not. She sat powerless and dumbstruck, and her anger turned inward. She had nothing left of Miriam except memories, and all of it was her own fault.

Beatríz rose in disgust and decided that she would have to move away from the wrecked house and the ruined women as soon as possible. First she had to gather information. She wanted to know how people improved their lives in Safi. Beatríz spent the following weeks avoiding Lola's family and eavesdropping on pairs of women whispering in corners, and men sitting under canvas awnings in larger groups, drinking tea or port, joking and arguing passionately about the best way to manage and escape.

In the marketplace, Beatríz only heard bad news. Warlords were fighting to take over Fez. Or was it another city? There seemed to be an ongoing land war out in the desert, so even if one survived a crossing, one might walk into a war. More alarming was the rumor that Muslims were coming to attack Safi. No one knew for certain when or how, but the theory was that they wanted their city back. Beatríz, and the people she overheard discussing the possibility, did not think that the skeleton army the Portuguese had left to hold Safi would scarce protect anyone.

One day in the market, Beatríz heard men talking about a caravan they had formed. They were well supplied, and planned to gather for departure the next day. Should she join them? But she had no way to leave word so that Yusef could find her. She would not go. Not yet. But she would observe what they brought and how they were organized. If things did not improve in Safi, she thought she might join the next group of trekkers across the desert.

CHAPTER 9

Beatríz slowed as she approached the arched gates on the side of the city that led away from the ocean and into the sandy dunes. A group was gathered at the soldiers' checkpoint. She inched closer to the guards, staying at the edge of the crowd.

"But we are Christian," one man was explaining.

"Of course," replied a soldier, his voice thick. "But what were you at Easter?" When no answer came, he said, "No one goes to Fez. No one."

"Except the Muslims," grumbled the man.

"If we let you leave Safi, who's to say you won't turn back into Jews? Our orders are to keep you all here." He turned to his companion. "You would think since we stand here day after day saying the same thing the word would spread. Why do they keep coming here?"

Beatríz leaned against the rampart wishing for some shade. So no one was allowed out. Now what? She decided to return to the abandoned house. Perhaps she could rest, for another sleepless night and not enough food had conspired to give her a throbbing headache.

Lola's screams could be heard from a fair way off. Beatríz hesitated. Did she really want to hear the little girl have another tantrum? It was bad enough to be woken at all hours by the poor thing's nightmares, but the daytime crying was sometimes too much to bear. She could leave quickly, but she wanted to take some bread at the very least if she was going to disappear for the day.

She stopped to let her eyes adjust to the darkness of the entryway and was surprised to find soldiers inside. Lola was trying to get to her mother, who was being held by one of the men. Beatríz's stomach clenched.

"We will not leave," said Lola's mother.

"But you must," answered the soldier. Beatríz noticed a scratch on his face, likely put there during a struggle before she had arrived. "You do not pay rent for this spot. The owner has returned and he wants his home."

The old woman, who was gripping her granddaughter, spat over Lola's head onto the floor. Her wrinkled, sour face looked like the toe of an inside-out stocking.

Lola's mother said, "There is nowhere to live and you will not let us leave this wretched city."

The other soldier, whose back was to Beatríz, said, "You can leave by boat."

Lola's mother pulled against the soldier holding her. "Who has the money for another voyage?"

The soldier with his back to Beatríz took off his helmet and lowered his head. "I know it is difficult –"

"You know nothing," snapped Lola's mother.

He straightened up and put his helmet back on.

Beatríz thought his voice sounded familiar. Something in his tone or cadence. But she was distracted by his next words.

"Be that as it may, you must leave this house immediately. You should collect your belongings."

The soldier holding Lola's mother let go and she, Lola, and the old woman rushed to each other before gathering pots and blankets. The soldiers were waiting for the women to finish, and Beatríz knew she ought to leave. But she stood rooted, unable to think of where to go next and wondering why the man sounded so familiar. Then the soldier who had removed his helmet turned around.

Beatríz gasped. "Davíd?" she asked, straining the eyes she was sure deceived her. The pointed chin, high forehead, and jutting cheekbones all seemed to be those of her brother Solomon's childhood friend, the one who had demanded a kiss for a button on their journey out of Castile.

The soldier cocked his head. "Do I...Beatríz?"

Beatríz smiled broadly. "I cannot believe it is you." A laugh worked its way out of her, taking with it some of the anxiety that had lived on her chest for weeks. "How good to see a familiar face."

"How good to see *you*. Many times I wished we had also gone to Lisbon. Coimbra was far less exciting. But what are you –" He stopped himself and his forehead creased. "Escaped from Portugal?"

Beatríz nodded.

"And your family?"

"Scattered."

"Where is Solomon?"

She shrugged and willed away the lump that formed in her throat. Solomon had been right the last time they spoke – it was best not to be aware of his location.

The other soldier left them to talk and decided to hurry up the process of clearing the house. He reached for Miriam's bag. "Stop!" Beatríz shouted across the courtyard. "That is mine."

The man frowned, but let the empty satchel drop to the ground again. Beatríz ran over and snatched it to her chest.

"You are not living here, are you?" Davíd asked with unmasked distaste.

She straightened herself up, not wishing to show how much she hated this place. "I am. Or rather *was* living here."

"Why?"

"There is nowhere else to go. I have been waiting for my betrothed."

Davíd looked at the water stains on the walls. "Waiting with whom?"

Beatríz held the bag tighter. "I came with his mo – family."

"Were you all living here?" he asked.

"There is no 'all' anymore," Beatríz said, swallowing a lump in her throat. "Just me. I am alone now."

"Being alone here seems like a poor idea."

"I know," she said firmly. "But it is a fact."

Lola toddled down the stairs with her mother and grandmother. The women did not stop to look at the soldiers or at Beatríz. As they passed, however, the old woman spat again, and this time, the glob landed on Davíd's tunic. To Beatríz's surprise, he did not move.

The other soldier pushed the women out through the doorway and then turned back. "To the next house?"

Davíd shook his head, wiping away the spit with a grimace. "Later. Go to the tavern and we can finish before supper."

The man bowed slightly and disappeared.

Davíd walked with Beatríz onto the street, but made no

move to leave her. He looked back at the wreck in which she had been staying and asked, "How have you been surviving?"

"I have a little money but it's been . . ." She stopped herself and looked at her soiled dress and dirt encrusted fingernails. "It has not been what I expected. When I moved with my family to Portugal, it was strange and crowded, but we had a family take us in. My Yusef's family, in fact."

Beatríz thought of her early days with Yusef. She recalled how shyly they had looked at one another across the dining table on the first night she was in Lisbon. When she thought no one was watching, she had studied his handsome face and thick hair gleaming in the candlelight, thinking him the loveliest boy she had ever seen.

Living together had been complicated. She was taught to stand primly aside if he passed her in the halls even though she wanted nothing more than to touch him. She had never felt so strongly about a boy and did not understand why she could not stop thinking about him. Because she wanted to be with him at all times, she tried to keep her distance. And yet he seemed indifferent, averting his own gaze, keeping quiet. His indifference maddened her. It never occurred to her that he might be avoiding her for the same reasons.

Her parents did not observe the added difficulties and tensions, like the night he had accidentally seen her in her nightdress. Beatríz thought she would die from shame. And desire. As much as she loved every chance to be near him, she could not wait until her family moved out so she could breathe and sleep again.

On the third day, Yusef stopped right in front of her in the hall and smiled. He had asked a question. She was not exactly sure what he had said, for she did not yet speak Portuguese, so he had pointed at the door and made his fingers look like legs walking along an invisible floating street. Without thinking about what her mother would say, she had agreed.

Before her Portuguese and his Castilian had improved, she and Yusef had each spoken in their own language with gestures and attempts to find common words, of which there were many, though the sounds were slightly different. They laughed raucously at the misunderstandings and the lengths to which each would go to tell a story. He took her around Lisbon and showed her the sights, and they ducked into shadowy corners of the courtyard of his home to talk and sit close, their affection growing as quietly as blades of grass.

David snapped her out of her reverie. "And is Yusef…eh…'gone' as well?"

"No," she said with a chill at the thought. "He is elsewhere. For now." To dwell on his absence made her chest ache, so she asked, "You are a soldier for Portugal now?"

David sighed. "Yes. I left my wife and child to fight battles I do not care about."

"Is she a Christian?"

"Like me. *Anusim.* Just after we married, my wife and I decided that being Christian would be easier. It was better for my business and I did not have to worry for her safety, or that of our family. And after I was pressed into service, I knew I had made the right choice. She could remain in Portugal, the land of her birth, while I left to do my duty here. Unlike you and I, she never had to leave her home, and the thought of it scared her terribly. It matters not what God everyone *thinks* we pray to as long as they let us live our lives in peace, no?"

"And coming here is living in peace?"

Darkness flashed across his face before it settled into a sad longing. "It is one thing to fashion a cannon, but another to invade a city and do the killing. I did not want to go, but in that matter I was not given a choice. Weapons makers such as myself are in demand. They say we will return home within the year. I hope it is true." His fingers traced the handle of his sword as he stared into nothingness.

"Well . . . it was good to see you again." She looked down the street considering a direction to begin anew.

"Where will you go now?"

She shrugged, feeling no desperation. Just a vague irritation that she would, undoubtedly, have to fight for whatever spot she found.

After a moment's thought he said, "Come live with me."

She raised her eyebrows, unsure of what he was suggesting.

"Live at the garrison. Nothing untoward," he said, his laughter coming easily as it always had. "We have needed help for some time. The last bout of plague killed a number of our servants. It will not be glamorous. I hesitate to even tell you that the work will be washing and cleaning. Assisting the cook." When Beatríz did not object, he continued, "You will be safe. The soldiers are gentlemen, on the whole."

Her answer was ready as soon as he had said "nothing untoward." It would not be so bad. She had never been as pampered as some girls she knew, for there was a stretch of time after their arrival in Lisbon when her family did not have enough money for servants. Secretly cooking, cleaning, and washing clothes were essential tasks undertaken by Beatríz, her mother, and her sisters to keep their house looking posh for visitors even when their larders had been nearly bare.

She nodded and Davíd smiled.

"Excellent," he said as they began walking again. "*La compañía en la miseria hace a ésta más llevadera.*"

"I am happy for your company, too," she said, "but you do not seem miserable."

He raised his eyebrows. "Hundreds of miles from my wife and child? Pretending to be what I am not? I would not call this the dream of my life."

As they began walking again, she caught sight of little Lola and her mother and grandmother sitting in the shade, with nowhere to go. "Davíd," she began, torn by her hatred of the grandmother for stealing Miriam's belongings and her sympathy for their situation. "Is there room for more at the barracks? Those women from the house –"

"The ones who spat at me?" He laughed but checked himself when he saw she was serious. "It is not a place for children, and we have no need for so many."

She glanced at them once more, her stomach squeezing, then followed Davíd.

Davíd walked along, somewhat unaware of the crowds parting fearfully in front of him or the fact that Beatríz had to jog a bit to keep up. She did not mind, actually, and found it fun to be treated with less care than her father and even Yusef did. He gestured broadly and, as a hint of a smile was always in his eyes and on his lips he spoke about the doings of his life in the years since moving from Toledo to Portugal's other large city, Coimbra.

She wondered what had left him confident when so many others had been broken of late? She supposed the protection of his position afforded him this luxury. He knew he would be fed. He knew he would have a place to sleep. He could walk and someone would move out of his way. And his religion could not be ignored. Would she no longer feel the need to look over her shoulder if she embraced Christianity? Or at least pretended to?

David slowed his step to match hers and guided her down a more crowded street. Many homes had deep brown pottery vases as tall as her waist flanking their doorways, and passersby had to wend around them. Beatríz could not figure out their purpose beyond being decorative, but she found them intriguing despite their inconvenience. It seemed so perilous to leave breakables where they could topple at any moment. But then, maybe the people of this town had grown accustomed to tenuousness and had decided that keeping something of beauty, however passing, was worth the risk.

"Can I help you carry your things?" David offered.

"It is not so very much," she answered, easily holding up her light bag.

He stopped, his eyes wide, and reached out. "Is that –" he began, his fingers touching the wooden button keeping her satchel together.

She nodded and blushed at remembering trading the button for a kiss.

Pulling at his chin, he said, "I was impudent for having done that. You were my friend's sister, and young. I had no right to demand anything, especially that. I could have just given it to you."

She turned the bag so they could no longer see the button. "It was a long time ago. We were both foolish then. You should no more have asked than I should have done it, but as long as you do not try such tricks again, I shall forgive you." She smiled and he nodded in agreement.

David pressed his palm to her back as they moved among strangers, and the gesture seemed too familiar, but it allowed them to stay together as the crowd jostled.

As they neared the water, the streets narrowed and leveled out slightly. The air was fresher here than in the odd wreck of a house on the twisted street where she had been staying. David slowed in front of a sturdy, sand-colored building – a gatehouse. Next to the gatehouse was a wider building, a mosque. From the soldier standing guard, she realized that the Portuguese army had confiscated the mosque to use as their barrack. The other barrack, she knew from her morning excursion, was on the opposite side of the city, at the top of the hill facing where a land-based army might attack.

David gestured in front of the larger structure and said, "Your new home."

Beatríz was happy for somewhere to live, but also felt uncomfortable that it had been someone else's sanctified space. How would she have felt if a synagogue were made into barracks or a barn? For all she knew, that was precisely what was happening in Lisbon, and thinking of it, she felt a twinge of remorse.

A sentry opened the door and David explained that Beatríz would be the new servant.

David told her, "After the men see you at supper, they will remember. Then you can come and go at will."

They walked though the archway and into the enormous open courtyard with a fountain in the center. All around, from the ground up, tiles of earth tones and white created fantastic designs that reminded Beatríz of flower blossoms opening and rays of sunshine reaching out exuberantly. Above her head, the walls were of stucco, and every inch had been carved in swirls and patterns like leaves and teardrops. There were no depictions of real things, like in the synagogues back home where graven images were forbidden.

This was now a place of war and business, not worship.

An empty shed stood next to a fire pit over which large cauldrons hung from hooks. Only chickens and a rogue goat populated the dusty space in the middle. A pen at the back contained a pig and a sheep as well. Horses neighed in their corral. A groom walked across the courtyard and waved to the blacksmith who was working in a shaded corner.

Beatríz had an odd feeling in her stomach. "Will there be any women?"

Davíd nodded. "Our cook. We call her 'Blanca'."

"'Call her?' What is her real name?"

"We do not know. She had her tongue cut out and she cannot write."

Beatríz stepped away from him. "You did *what* to her?"

"Not us." He laughed, though Beatríz did not find anything funny about it. "We took her in. She had her tongue cut out at some point. Likely for heresy. Odd business. Anyhow," he continued casually, "she can gesture and will show you what to do. But you will find her conversation rather dull."

Beatríz tried not to show her distaste for his lack of concern.

They walked up two stone steps and ducked into a narrow hallway. Davíd stopped. "You will assist Blanca when you are not needed elsewhere. I should imagine that between washing clothes and helping her you will not have much free time."

Beatríz sighed, relieved by the idea of keeping busy. "Thinking is my greatest enemy. I will be glad for the work. And glad to know you are here." She sucked in her breath, wondering if these last words appeared too forward, and if she was unwittingly putting out signals to men. Men like the ones on the boat.

She swallowed hard and watched Davíd for signs that he

took this as something more, but he merely appeared to agree. "I will be happy for the company, as well. When possible, I will take you around the city. A woman should not travel alone."

He opened the dark wood door to the kitchen. There were glass windows (a small thing that Beatríz had come to miss greatly), a long table and a few rickety chairs. A straw mattress was rolled up in the corner and Beatríz felt a rush of excitement at imagining being able to sleep comfortably for the first night in many weeks.

"How quickly my fortunes have changed," she said with awe, and then laughed at herself. "Changed and changed again. I thank you for this good turn."

Davíd nodded and said, "Blanca, this is Beatríz."

Beatríz had not noticed the woman kneeling in front of a cabinet. Blanca stood slowly. Keeping her chin low, she studied Beatríz. All Beatríz could think about was the missing tongue. Then she took in Blanca's deep-set eyes, her porcelain skin, and her tremoring hands. Beatríz wondered how Blanca managed to chop food with hands that shook so noticeably.

"Beatríz will work for you," Davíd said. "I will leave you to get settled." He bowed and went to meet the other soldier who was probably drunk at the tavern by then.

Blanca gestured to Beatríz to put her bags in the corner. Blanca then pointed at Beatríz to push up her sleeves and motioned to the plucked chickens on the table. Beatríz stepped forward ready to work.

Blanca placed chickens in pots followed by spoonfuls of oil, cilantro juice, and onion juice. As the women peeled garlic and pounded almonds, Beatríz was amazed that Blanca's hands did not shake while she worked. Blanca put the garlic, almonds, and salt into the pot and Beatríz realized Blanca had to be Andalucían, given the ingredients she was using, or at least she had learned to cook from one.

Safya, an Granadan servant Beatríz's mother employed in Lisbon had made this very dish . . . when her mother did not object to the exotic ingredients and style. Beatríz had dreamed of visiting her beloved Safya's native home in the south as she watched her cook, and had always loved the change in menu – not just the strong vinegar, basil, green rue, and citron leaves, but also the *murri* and bee balm. Beatríz would sit in their kitchen in Lisbon watching their cook work, and would take the foreign herbs and flowers in her own hands to smell them. The sour green rue always made Beatríz's nose sting, and bee balm was her favorite, whether the petals were dried or freshly cut.

Standing next to Blanca, the minty, fruity aroma filled her with peace and nostalgia.

Blanca added some sort of wine Beatríz would later learn was called *nabidh,* and the women moved to clean and set the tables. Beatríz followed Blanca away from the front gate and into an open walk. They strode under curved archway after curved archway, and Beatríz noted more lovely mosaics on the walls and on the scalloped columns.

There would be, it seemed, twenty men in the large dining room down the hall, and five servants eating in the kitchen. Beatríz had not eaten with servants since she was a child, but she did not care. The cooking smells were making her dizzy, for she had not eaten since early morning when she had walked to the gate to see about the caravan's departure. It occurred to her that Lola and her family might not be so lucky as to have a meal coming at all, let alone one as delicious as what she was helping prepare.

When they got back to the kitchen, Blanca pulverized a few *dirham* each of Chinese cinnamon, pepper, cinnamon, cloves, and lavender, while Beatríz cracked eggs into a bowl. Then Blanca beat the spices into the eggs and covered the contents of each pot with the egg mixture. Next, she dotted the whole thing with egg yolks. Finally, Blanca pointed to the pots then lifted her fingers to the sky as if to say, "God willing," which was what the cooks she knew always said. Beatríz noticed that the tremor was back in Blanca's hands now that the work was done.

Blanca stretched and Beatríz took this as a sign that they would rest a moment. Her arms and back ached, unaccustomed as she was to hard work, but she was determined not to show Blanca. She looked out the window and saw the sky darkening a bit. Noises from the street were muffled but growing louder. Evening prayers for the pious were done, and all seemed to be headed home for a meal. Within the building, Beatríz heard new noises. Footsteps on the other side of the closed door. Low vibrating voices of men. Laughter. The clanking of a metal latch, which she supposed was from the front gate. Her heart sped up as she thought of being one of only two women locked in the barracks, but she told herself she had to trust Davíd that no harm would come to her.

The footsteps grew steadier and a young man not wearing a uniform opened the door. Blanca reached for two of the pots. Beatríz took two others and followed Blanca back to the large dining room where the soldiers were getting settled. The men met the pots with hoots and claps, and one cheered, "*Blanca, quieres casar-te comigo?*"

His friend said, "You want to marry her over some measly chickens? What if she had served stuffed lamb with cheese?"

"Then I would drag the priest in here right now and not even ask!"

The men laughed as they reached to serve themselves. Blanca, who had blushed throughout the exchange, backed out of the room, and Beatríz made to follow.

"Wait," called Davíd and she stopped, folding her hands demurely in front of her. He tapped his knife on his cup. He spoke in Portuguese, as he did any time he was with the men and not alone with her. "This is Beatríz, our new servant. She is an old friend of mine and is not to be touched."

The men nodded and, though Beatríz expected more questions or ceremony, they dove back into talking and eating. Davíd winked and she stepped quietly out of the room, relieved.

"Stuffed lamb with cheese?" she thought with disgust. Milk and meat together? Not kosher. What was she to do? Eat what she was given, she supposed. She had spotted the pig in the courtyard. There would be *jamon* at some point soon. Pork. She sighed. There was a first time for everything. Eating what she was served would keep her from starving, and also from being identified as a secret Jew among men who might care about such things.

Was she a secret Jew? She had not prayed lately. In fact, she had had no more than a passing religious thought in weeks. What *was* she?

After the meal, the men left and Beatríz and Blanca cleaned. Beatríz's hands stung from the hot water and harsh soap, and her back throbbed from the new kind of work. Bitterness momentarily surfaced as she thought about her sister Astruga in her Lisbon home surrounded by servants, but Beatríz resolved not to think of it again.

When at last they were finished cleaning, Blanca pointed

to the mattress in the corner. Beatríz was not sure if they were to share or if Beatríz would lie on the floor, but at least they could finally sleep. Then the door opened and the soldier from the dinner table who had asked Blanca to marry him held his hand out. Blanca lowered her head and nodded to Beatríz, then followed him out.

Had they gone for a walk? But Blanca did not indicate that she was coming back. Perhaps they slept together. A sin. But Beatríz could understand it. She wished Yusef would walk in just then and stretch out his hand for her.

Beatríz began unrolling the mattress and jumped at a knock on the door. She prayed it was not some soldier looking for Blanca. Or worse, her. When it was merely Davíd, she exhaled audibly.

"Ah, you found the mattress. Good. Blanca spends most nights with Miguel, so you should be set then." Beatríz was stunned into silence, so he continued. "I will see you after mass in the morning, unless you have any questions."

"Am I expected to go to church?" she asked, unsure if she wanted to or not.

Davíd leaned against the rounded doorway. "No. Blanca works to set out breakfast and prepare dinner. We should talk about religion soon, but you get settled for now." He bowed and left.

She sank onto her mattress, and before she could even think over how her life had changed in one day, sleep consumed her.

CHAPTER 10

The next morning, Blanca and Beatríz rose before the sun and made pots of soup, then set the tables with old bread that the men and servants dipped in the broth. Beatríz was busy, but with Blanca not speaking, Beatríz had more time to think than she had hoped. Time to think of where Yusef might be, whether her parents and Reyna had been affected by Venice's latest plague, of her brother, of Miriam, of Abrão. Her stomach clenched as she cleared the tables and washed the pots, and by the time they took a break to let dough rise, Beatríz could hardly breathe.

Blanca sensed Beatríz's agitation and gestured to the door, so Beatríz walked out to the courtyard.

Once again, Beatríz was impressed by its beauty and immensity. There was room for an entire stable of horses, which housed five at the moment. Work areas occupied two of the corners and seemed to be large enough for two men to work in each. And Beatríz thought that the twenty soldiers living here all could march ceremonially in the middle and not feel cramped.

Water whispered down three levels of a fountain in the middle of the courtyard. Around and within the fountain's base were intricately painted brown, green, and white tiles, and there were swirls Beatríz recognized as writing. As a child in Toledo, remnants of the Moors' architecture and art had been everywhere, even inside their synagogue. Beatríz never understood why there was Arabic writing on the walls of a Jewish house of worship, but there was.

Beatríz walked to the fountain and cupped her hands, pulling cool water to her mouth. How lucky to live in a place with its own source of water, and not have to continually walk into the nearest square for it.

She heard hammering from the work area and moved toward it. To her surprise, Davíd was standing behind an anvil. He stopped when he saw her and doffed his cap.

She gave a perfunctory curtsey and said, "I expected you to be out...soldiering."

He laughed. "I am not on patrol most of the time. I go when needed, but usually I spend my time making and fixing cannons, muskets, and swords. He usually does the more mundane tasks," Davíd said, gesturing to an aproned man to his side.

The man shook his head good naturedly as he picked up a horseshoe and began brushing at it. "He does not respect the beautiful simplicity of what I make. Where would our horses be without me?"

Davíd turned to the fire and moments later withdrew a glowing red stick.

"Did you learn this from your father?" Beatríz asked Davíd.

"Yes. And *he* learned from his father." The other man took the horseshoe toward the stable, so Davíd quietly said,

"I do not know how our family became the weapon-making Jews rather than jewelers or moneylenders, but it has been a good business for us." Davíd banged and shaped the stick until it was flat. "How are you getting on with Blanca?"

"Well," replied Beatríz trying to sound confident, but her hesitation caused Davíd to look up.

"But?"

"But I am restless. The work is honest and she is patient, but I am terribly distracted. All I can think is that I sent letters weeks ago and have had no reply. Or maybe I have." Beatríz laughed at herself. "For all of my eavesdropping around town, I have not learned where letters are brought for those of us without a known address."

Davíd threw his hammer aside. "Come," he declared.

Beatríz was taken aback by his sudden move and outstretched hand. "Do you not have to work?"

He smiled. "Fashioning killing tools can wait an hour. Let us go to the rabbi's house. Letters for displaced Jews are sent there."

"Rabbi?" she asked askance. "If there are supposed to be no Jews, then how —"

"The army knows perfectly well that there are Jews who wish to remain Jews and that rabbis live and work within city walls. As long as no one is especially obvious, the soldiers have more important matters to attend to. For now."

Beatríz's anticipation had her walking faster than Davíd. He caught her by the elbow as they huffed up the hill. "Patience, my friend. The letters will be there or they will not. Let me savor this break from work."

She slowed her pace grudgingly.

He stopped in front of a house Beatríz had passed many times before. Considering the large number of people that often gathered outside, she wondered why she had never thought to ask about it. Then again, given that it was supposedly a secret, she might not have been told the truth.

Davíd led Beatríz to the end of a line. A few people slunk away as the two approached, and she and Davíd were left a wider space when others joined the line. Beatríz found it curious that people would be so intimidated by the uniform. If only they knew he was a Jew like them who, as a boy, had dreaded stamping on a spider, and who ran promptly home when his mother called. The strangers only saw the helmet and sword, and whispered and stared.

At first, standing with Davíd made her feel important, but then she began to worry. Most news spread not by letter but by word of mouth. She had made herself conspicuous by being with Davíd, and surely someone might talk. It was unlikely that anyone even knew who she was, but her unease deepened. While it might help her family know she was safe, it might also be spread that she was in the company of another man. Yusef might hear.

Her color was high and Davíd, noticing the flush, offered to wait for her while she sat in the shade.

"No," she answered, suddenly quite self-conscious. "I know what to do…so, sir," she said, raising her voice to be overheard, "I thank you for you assistance."

His face was full of questions. "See you tonight, then."

She nearly fainted at this. "At the garrison. To serve supper to the soldiers. Indeed."

He furrowed his brow and bowed. "Yes of course."

As he walked away, Beatríz felt her stomach flip for how she had treated him, but she knew it had to be done. She could explain later. The line closed tighter around her, though no one engaged her in conversation. She had been with a soldier and that was enough to breed mistrust.

The line moved slowly, but at last she entered the rabbi's home. Inside a large group of people bustled around. Two women stood before a man at a small desk. Trays of drinks were brought out. Paper was stacked in corners and a few older children pulled letters from a sailcloth bag and were sorting them.

The rabbi, much younger than Beatríz had expected, waved her forward. He looked her up and down quickly and then asked her name.

"Beatríz of Lisbon. Daughter of Dom Vidal. I am hoping there are letters for me."

The rabbi turned to the teenage boy who stood at his side, and the boy moved to a corner filled with small piles. It looked incredibly disorganized to Beatríz, with stacks leaning precariously to one side and others looking as if they had already toppled. The boy stood with his hands on his hips, and Beatríz, finding the suspense unbearable, decided that if he took much longer, she would volunteer to help him look.

The rabbi distracted her with a few questions. Was she married? When had she arrived? How was she finding Safi? Where was she staying?

She tried her best to mask her impatience and to reply politely. She was uncertain about the reason for his questions, but she could not take time to consider it while she kept half an eye on the boy. Beatríz was unable to speak once she saw him take hold of a small bundle. He returned and held it out to her.

With shaking hands, Beatríz reached out for the letters tied together with twine. Once they were between her fingers, she froze, arms still outstretched.

"They are yours, I assure you. The boy can read them to

you," offered the rabbi.

Beatríz shook her head. "I can read," she said, ignoring his unmasked shock.

She brought the stack slowly closer, praying under her breath that one would actually be from Yusef. When she saw his firm script, she let out a gasping cry. Covering her mouth with one hand and clutching the letters with the other, she offered a quick *"obrigado,"* in thanks and pushed her way out onto the street.

Leaning against the wall of the rabbi's house, she did not care who saw her pulling the letter open as tears streamed down her cheeks. Upon seeing the page filled with his glorious writing, she was overcome and closed her eyes again. Her heart thrashed within her chest. She held the paper up to her nose hoping a little of his scent might still be on it, but it smelled like ink and mildew.

With ragged breaths, she began to read.

Dearest Beatríz,

I have been writing to you in Lisbon for weeks, but as I have not had a reply, I can only guess that you have left. I am hoping you have followed my parents' plan and are in The Maghreb. I know my father's hope was to reach Safi in particular. I pray that this letter finds its way to you.

I am not certain if you have heard the news. I am in prison, but I am well.

When our ship attempted to land in Malaga, the captain asked for our papers. Since we were entering without permission, all of the Jews were arrested.

We have been told that we will be put to death unless ransom is paid. Please do not fret. I assure you this is customary, my love. If not for the threat of death, many would not pay, preferring to remain locked away for a set time and then going on with their business some months later.

I had hoped (as is often the case), that someone from the Jewish community of Oran would pay as they had so often in the past. However, with the large influx of Jews to The Maghreb, and the number of us in need of assistance all around the Mediterranean, they are less willing to do so, especially for people they do not already know.

By the time this letter arrives, I imagine I will already have been released. I have sent word to my uncle, my father, and my brother. One of them will send the money. I have no doubt.

My parents' preparations should have made life comfortable for you in Safi. I will come to you when I can.

My heart is ever yours,
Yusef

Prison. Put to death. Ransom. Beatríz read the letter once more, her eyes fixed on certain words that would not release her. He could say it was common all he liked, but he was locked up far away and she was powerless to help. A teardrop fell, smudging his signature, making her cry all the more.

Beatríz floated to the soldiers' compound, unable to read any of the others letters. Another might be in the pile announcing his release. But if it was not, if there was only bad news, she did not want to be on the street when she learned of it.

Davíd looked up when he saw her emerge from the shadows of the entryway, and when he noticed her unsteady gait he rushed to her. "What is it? What news?"

Beatríz could not force the words out. She held the paper toward him.

When he tried to take the letter from her, she could not loosen her grasp. He gently pried her fingers off, keeping his eyes locked on hers all the while. "Beatríz, whatever it is, I will help you. Let me see," he soothed. His eyes skimmed the letter and she noticed his forehead crease. He looked up, his voice bright but his expression grim. "He said not to fret."

"He is in prison, Davíd. How can I be calm?"

"Because being in prison means he is still alive. You must not worry. He has more experience with these matters, and if he is confident, you should be, too." He held the letter out for her to take back, and asked if she had opened the rest. When she shook her head, he asked if she wanted him to read the rest to her.

"I can do it, but I am afraid of more bad news."

"You read? How?"

Fidgeting with the twine that lay loose around the stack, she explained, "Solomon taught me."

The corner of one side of Davíd's mouth turned up. "Your brother was always a troublemaker."

The mere mention of Solomon made the chasm in her chest bottomless. "My parents were quite angry with him." She sighed at the recollection of how her parents had beaten and punished both her and her brother. "But one cannot unlearn such a thing." She looked at the letters again and bit her lip, dreading the news they might contain.

He squeezed her shoulder and said, "Read them out here so I can be with you if you need me."

She nodded, grateful for Davíd's understanding. He walked back to the fire and she leaned against a pillar near his work area. She tucked Yusef's letter onto the bottom and opened the top one. It was from her sister.

Beatriz,

In the name of God.

A letter was delivered to me that you had written to Dom Abrão. The servant said Dom Abrão left Lisbon some time ago - the day after the conversions began, in fact - and so the man did not know where else to bring it. Did Dom Abrão never reach you? To say I am worried would overstate my feelings, but it gave me pause. Should you be in a strange city without a man, take care to return to Mamá and Papá immediately.

I would offer to have you come to me, yet I cannot imagine your being legally allowed back in to Lisbon. A man was captured while attempting to sail into port under cover of darkness, and not only was he arrested, but his family's business has been confiscated, as well. I will not risk my security to help you if you get caught, so do not attempt to return.

God have mercy on you in Safi, and may He grant us both health.

Astruga

So her sister would not help her. This was no great surprise. And Dom Abrão was missing. She could take her sister's advice and find her parents, but Yusef might already have been released and on his way at that moment. And what if the men she had overheard were right and Plague had closed the port of Venice? What then? If her ship was turned away, no one would know where to find her and she might end up even farther away and in a worse place than the garrison of Safi with an old family friend. No. She would wait.

Beatríz smiled as she opened the last letter. She assumed her father's missive would describe the sights and sounds of Italy, details that had fed her wanderlust as a child. Upon seeing so few lines, her heart froze.

> Beatríz,
>
> God has taken your sister and your mother. Do not come to Venice. I am leaving, but do not know my destination. I will write when I am settled.
>
> Your lord and master,
> Your loving father

Beatríz felt herself losing her balance and grabbed on to the stone pillar. Both gone? It could not be. The women of her life. They were supposed to help her dress for her wedding. They were supposed to attend the birth of her children. They were supposed to spend afternoons together and fight over who was hosting holiday meals. But all of those dreams vanished with the stroke of a pen. With the bad fortune of her father choosing Venice over another place to run. She sank down and wept for them.

She could feel Davíd hovering nearby, but did not have the strength or will to even look up at him. It was too much loss at once. Too much to bear. What bad news would come next? She did not want to know. Instead, she wished she could simply vanish from the earth.

She jumped when a hand touched her arm.

Davíd did not ask, but took the letters from her hand and read them quickly. "Dear God," he said.

Beatríz stared into his eyes and said nothing.

"You are with us now, and we will keep you safe until Yusef arrives."

Beatríz's face squished up and she gripped the pillar harder. "Blanca must need me," she said, her chin quivering.

"Take a moment."

"No," she replied, folding the letters and pulling the twine around them. "Work will help." She walked a few unsteady steps and turned back, ignoring Davíd's worried face. "We can talk this evening. But not about this." She nodded determinedly, praying that acting confident would make her feel confident, and disappeared into the kitchen.

Blanca looked up momentarily and gestured to a pile of herbs. Beatríz tucked the letters into her bag and grabbed a knife. She put a handful of greens on the wooden block and hacked away, hoping her fingers were not among the shapes that swirled in front of her eyes. For once, she was thankful that Blanca had no tongue to ask her any questions.

CHAPTER 11

After hours of chopping, stirring, serving and cleaning, Beatríz was too tired to mourn or worry with force. Davíd knocked on the kitchen door just as she and Blanca were wiping the last plates. Blanca swept her hand to the door, so Beatríz felt free to walk out into the night air with Davíd.

As they sat on the edge of the fountain, Beatríz said, "Tell me how to be a Christian."

Davíd lifted his eyebrows. "Let us begin with how not to be a Jew."

Beatríz nodded and relaxed. He would respect her desire to forget, if only for a moment. Or perhaps they were not ignoring it for this was, in truth, the best way he could help her now.

"You must never put on fresh clothes on a Friday or Saturday. Never be seen separating milk from meat. Do not rest on Saturday unless all around you are doing so."

"And church?"

He paused and dipped his hand into the water, which suddenly reminded Beatríz of standing at the baptismal font with Miriam and Abrão. Had it been less than two months since she had been converted?

"You will come with me tomorrow. Do not worry that you do not know what to do. Many do not."

She thought about this. As a female, Beatríz had never been expected to know much of Judaism either. She had never been asked what she believed or what she understood of the words and rituals. Her only responsibility was to help keep a kosher home. What she had known about being a Jew was that she was one. It was her community. Her identity.

Davíd continued, "And those that *do* know are often so careless about the rituals that they hardly move or even speak the prayers aloud. Some even sleep. You will find it is not as alarming as you might have believed, and you will find the church's air a relief from the heat."

"When do we go?"

"After you clean up from breakfast. If you have another dress, you should change into it. Sunday is the day for such things."

Beatríz and Davíd were joined on their walk to Mass by a handful of men from the barracks. When Beatríz inquired about the rest, she was told the others did not go regularly or were sleeping off a hangover. Beatríz found this most surprising at first, but then considered the fact that many of the Jews she knew did not worship regularly, either.

The men joked loudly as they walked and were given as wide a birth as the streets would allow. Davíd held her elbow loosely, sometimes including her in their conversation, sometimes steering her around filth in the streets. His movements were protective without being territorial. She wondered how his wife fared without him to offer such services and hoped she had a family in Coimbra that could fill the void while he was abroad. At the thought of family, Beatríz's pace slowed.

Davíd misunderstood and leaned in, whispering, "No one will know you are a Jew. And if they do, they will not say anything."

The men walked toward the door of the great mosque at the center of the city that had been converted to a church. Beatríz pulled against Davíd but he pressed his hand on her back and led her inside. She deeply disliked the idea of worshiping in a stolen place. Then again, she disliked having a religion forced upon her. It seemed oddly fitting to be a Jew turned into a Christian entering a mosque turned into a church. It was all as jumbled as she felt..

Davíd had told her that prayer rooms of mosques were typically empty except for carpets covering the floor. Filling the place were rows of pews, paintings and an altar with a towering cross behind it. Many of these items must have been shipped from a great distance. So much effort to transform the place. The Portuguese were making it clear that there was no room for Islam in their world.

The mass began. Beatríz sat next to Davíd and watched every move the priests made and listened carefully. Each word spoken in Latin or Portuguese promised to unlock some mystery – the mystery of why she had been kept separate from others, of why she had been forced to move and move again, to lose her family, to lose her love. One priest held a chalice in the air and spoke again, but she understood nothing.

All present were invited to receive communion, but Davíd told her to stay where she was. "If anyone asks, say you have not gone to confession," he whispered. "Do not go up until you are confident with the words and motions." He slipped into the aisle and joined the line of men and women having circles placed in their mouths.

Beatríz could not help but look around to see who else remained in their seats. Two women and one man sat in place. "Could they also be Jews?" she wondered. She felt incredibly conspicuous and fought the urge to slide down in her seat.

She was studying a painting of a man with a dozen arrows penetrating his flesh when Davíd joined her once again. He knelt and motioned for her to do the same. She got on her knees, and tried to match his laced fingers and bowed head.

At first she moved her lips in an empty mirror of the others prayers, but then in the quiet, she began to think of Yusef. *"Please, God,"* she begged, allowing the pulsing murmur of the congregation to push her thoughts forward, *"let him be safe in your hands. Guide and protect all that I love. Let us find one another again. Forgive me for being in this church. Or help me to see that this is right."*

At a bang at the back of the room and a flood of light, Beatríz's head snapped over her shoulder. A knight on horseback darkened the doorway and then rode right into the church. Beatríz actually blinked a few times to be sure her eyes were not deceiving her. She moved onto the bench, unable to close her mouth or look away. Davíd got off his knees and sat so close that his hip touched hers, his eyes fixed on the horseman making his way toward the altar.

In a voice that boomed from the curved ceiling, the knight called from inside his helmet, "Father, give me absolution before I go to kill the infidel."

"I cannot," the wiry priest said as he backed away from the horse that threatened to trample him. "There is no crusade. There is no papal directive."

The knight unsheathed his sword and held it high. "I am going to kill Muslims. I do not need the Pope to tell me what must be done."

"I am sorry, but if you go on your own, it is murder."

Turning his horse, the knight seemed to be addressing the congregation as much as the priest. "You priests are always complaining that there are no true believers. That most people believe in nothing, not even an afterlife. Well, unlike many – some present here, I imagine – I believe in Jesus as our Lord and savior. I believe in God's wrath and in God's love. I believe in heaven and hell. I need you to absolve me of this sin."

"My son," said the priest, raising and curving his arms as if to embrace the horse-backed knight, "while what you say fills me with joy, what you are suggesting goes against one of the Commandments. I cannot wipe away murder."

The knight lowered his sword to the priest's shoulder, making Beatríz cringe, but then lifted it again. "I will be absolved. Are you the man to do it?" When the priest shook his head, the knight warned him. "I will use this blade to get what I want. I ask you again!"

"No, sir!" cried the gray haired priest.

The knight pressed its sharp tip into the holy man's collar, releasing a trickle of blood. Beatríz wanted to look away but found she could not, and when the knight lifted the blade high in the air, a strangling noise filled her throat. Images of Miriam and the ship from Lisbon flashed through her head, and she grabbed onto Davíd.

The knight swept the sword down stopping just short of cutting the priest's head off. With a chuckle, he turned to the young priest and turned the sword on him. Keeping the blade's edge just under his ear, he said, "I am sorry your friend would not comply. You will. Absolve me or I will end you both."

The younger priest, face white, raised a shaking hand and painted a cross in the air. Satisfied, the knight kicked his horse and galloped out. The young priest sank to the floor staring into the blinding light, not noticing that the older priest was yelling at him about God's will. A few men rushed forward, though most scurried down the aisle and out the door.

Gripping the pew, she said to Davíd, "I thought he was going to kill him."

He grimaced. "As did I."

"We have to stop him."

"Who?"

"The knight."

"Stop him? Are you mad?"

"We must keep him from killing the Muslims."

"Why? It is none of our concern. And it is his job. Or his personal crusade. What does it matter? There is no stopping one who wants to kill. Let us go, Beatríz."

Beatríz turned to look over her shoulder once more.

Still in shock, she found she could not move, so he dragged her into the square where he sat her in a shady spot. He was pale and shaking himself. Other soldiers asked if he would walk home with them, but he waved them off under the guise of helping Beatríz.

"I might have made that sword," he grumbled. "I fashion death. It is nothing until I see it firsthand."

"Have you been in battle?" she asked, reaching out to touch his quaking hands.

He nodded.

"Have you killed anyone?"

He looked away and nodded.

She sank heavier against the wall. Even Davíd, gentle Davíd, had taken a life. She could not understand this world.

They sat for a time watching men and women heading in and out of the marketplace. They carried baskets in their arms, carpets over their shoulders, led animals on ropes.

"I need a drink," Davíd said rising.

"On a Sunday?" she asked, half joking since, for Jews, nothing was sacred about that day.

"Any day is a good day for a drink," he answered grimly. "I will bring you home first."

After the events in church, all Beatríz could think of was leaving. She wanted to get away from this city that terrified her with its thieves, its murderers and its stolen mosques. But without Yusef, she would go nowhere.

Any day that she could, she went to the rabbi's to check for letters, but no new ones had arrived. She tried not to worry, knowing full well that even if Yusef had received a letter and written back straight away, a ship might or might not have been coming to Safi directly. It was also possible that his jailors might not be willing to give him paper or pen, or would rip up anything he wrote rather than bother to send it. In grimmer moments, she allowed herself to consider that he might already have been hanged.

And so she was in shock when the rabbi's assistant, Yoshuah, pulled a letter from a stack and handed it to her with a smile.

> *Béa,*
>
> *I was in ecstasy when I received your letter. Though the news was not all good, knowing you are safe made my heart swell.*
>
> *Thank you for informing me about my mother. She*

was always brave and one to put others before herself. She died protecting what I treasure, and that makes me love her all the more.

My father wrote to tell me he was leaving for Safi. I know you can offer each other comfort in these trying times.

As I have only one piece of paper today, please ask him to write and tell me if he has been able to arrange for the money to be sent. I am sure he has, but with the hours stretching endlessly in this prison, I cannot help but be haunted by doubt.

If I could put my arms around you, I would ask nothing more of life. Take care, my sweet love.

- Yusef

He did not blame her for his mother's death. Beatríz turned her face to the too-bright sky and closed her eyes, letting the sun bathe her in forgiveness. She had not wanted to believe Yusef would hate her for causing his mother's death, but there had been a small part of her that feared he might.

Her mind set on "love," "put my arms around you," and "ecstasy." She imagined him kissing her cheeks, then her neck, which always made her toes curl, especially when he ran his tongue along her skin, up and under her ear. She looked around, wondering who could see the color that had risen in her cheeks. Tucking the letter into her bodice, she went home to help Blanca.

Later, as she worked in silence, she considered the letter again. In her own selfishness, she had forgotten one important part. Yusef did not know his father had gone missing. She would have to tell him, but not yet. Too much bad news all at once might be too much for him to bear.

Yusef had written to his uncle and brother. One of them must have pieced together the funds for Yusef's release by now. She hoped it was true. Her stomach squeezed again at the thought of him sitting in prison. All she could do was wait.

Beatríz listened intently to conversations as she served their meals. Surrounded by the men who controlled the city, she learned a lot. Her question of escaping Safi for Fez was answered by the soldiers' complaints of being undermanned. Jews were slipping out of the gates at night because the few men on guard often were too drunk or too sleepy to notice. She also learned that some people escaped by day. Beatríz overheard a seasoned soldier quietly berating a new recruit. "Do not ever again let me find you turning down a sizeable bribe from a Jew or a Christian. What is it to us if those people want to fry in the desert? If they offer us enough money, we say yes. Take as much as you can and go for a drink."

Going alone, however, was foolhardy. That week some Bedouin had rescued a couple that had nearly died of thirst and starvation. A sand storm had pinned them down and they had barely managed to crawl to where they were found.

Conversation after conversation led her to understand that the average soldier did not care who came in or out as long as he lived long enough to make it home. And most men could be made to forget about their wives with a smile. Beatríz made a point of tying her hair back and of not making eye contact with the men when possible, for she did not wish to encourage a familiarity that might get her into trouble.

Davíd was the only exception. They spent much time together free from social constraints and rules that would typically dictate their behavior. It did not go so far as meeting in private, but they had an ease one could only have with an old friend.

One evening, Beatríz sat out with him in the courtyard enjoying the night air. She had had a rare opportunity to bathe, and she marveled at having gooseflesh from the breeze that rustled her loose, damp hair. Davíd offered his cape, but Beatríz was not cold enough to want to put anything dirty next to her newly clean skin.

"So your brother stayed in Toledo, no?" she asked, suddenly nostalgic for its lush hills and its cliffs that drop off to the river. "How has life been for him?"

"Frightening at times. He and his wife and were questioned once by the inquisitors, but they have nothing to hide and, luckily, were not falsely convicted."

"Have others you know been found guilty?"

"Yes. They have had to wear the *San Benito* sign through the square for not eating pork and for putting on fresh clothes on a Friday night. These habits are hard to break, but they should be more careful. I choke down pork and remain covered in soot. And my brother was lucky. Having to wear a sign that announces deceit for all to see is nothing compared to the tortures that await those found guilty of worse."

"But does the deceit not trouble you?"

"What is in my heart is my business. Every man is false in his own way. If not with religion, then it is in his relationships or in his business. I will not feel shame for pretending or for changing. I received the gift of life from God, and the best gift I can give in return is to continue living. God understands sacrifice and compromise."

Beatríz thought for a while. Astruga had not cared about giving up her religion, and Davíd was not troubled. So why was she hesitating? First, she did not believe in Jesus. Could that piece be put aside? Or could she ignore that one part? She thought not, as it seemed crucial to being a Christian. How could she say words she did not believe and did not understand? Then again, she had not understood most of what was said at the synagogue, for, as a female, she had not been taught much Hebrew, so the words were as empty as the Latin she heard in church. It was being forced that upset her so much. If she did not believe in Jesus, how could she go to church? And after what she had seen at Mass, she had not been able to go back. Davíd warned that she would have to join him, but he was not pushing too hard.

When she turned to discuss her concerns with him, she found him staring at her. "What?" she asked somewhat startled by the softness in his face.

"Nothing," he replied. He stood and said, "It is late. I should return you to your quarters."

"Yes." Beatríz did not want to leave the salt air, but something in his look made her know it was time to part ways.

As they walked, Beatríz was somewhat embarrassed by what she wanted Davíd to explain. "This is an odd question, perhaps, but I keep waiting for Blanca to claim her mattress, and have been surprised to . . . find myself alone each night."

"Yes. Miguel is a lucky bastard." He chuckled at her scandalized expression, and added, "They are getting married tomorrow, so it will finally be legitimate. Why he would want to ruin the perfect arrangement is beyond me. Perhaps she is with child," he said casually.

Beatríz's eyes widened, though she felt foolish reacting in such a fashion in front of Davíd who was, once again, inexplicably unconcerned with sin or scandal.

But Beatríz had spent her life being bombarded with the importance of purity. Her mother would rail against her father for allowing Beatríz to run about town with Yusef, which neighbors had seen and reported with disapproval. Melancholy washed over Beatríz as she realized she would never be around her mother's tantrums and lectures again.

"You know," David explained, pulling her back to her new, strange existence, "Blanca once had a husband, but the man was hanged. Back when she lost the tongue. Nasty business." He flipped the ends of his cape over his shoulders. "Anyhow, she and Miguel seem to get on well, so she can start fresh. Maybe find some happiness in this Godforsaken world."

"David, I cannot understand you. How can you tell such stories so . . . so . . . matter-of-factly?"

He pressed a hand on the wall behind her and leaned in so close she could feel his breath. In a whisper, he said, "Beatríz, all I have seen in my relatively short life has been beyond my comprehension. The only way I have been able to avoid going mad has been not to think and not to feel. I suggest you do the same."

And with that, he pinched her cheek and began to walk away. "Rest up," he said, calling back. "There will be a feast and dancing tomorrow after the wedding. And you will have to join us at church."

Beatríz lay awake that night. She knew David offered sound advice but was finding it hard to follow. When at last it became clear that she would not sleep, she rose and began preparing the morning soup to spare Blanca some work on her wedding day.

Beatríz wanted to be happy for Blanca, but all she could feel was jealousy. Envy coursed through her with such strength that she had little room for any other emotion as she served the meal and even as she entered the church. Beatríz would have given anything to be standing before the priest at that moment with Yusef, and she would have happily ignored standing in front of a cross rather than under a chuppah. She would have been able to forget that no one in her family was there to celebrate with her. If only Yusef were there. If only. If only.

Before she realized it, the ceremony was over and everyone was rushing forward and clapping their hands on Miguel's back and shouting, *"Parabéns."* Blanca beamed at the good wishes and blushed when Miguel lifted and carried her out of the church to the great whoops of his fellow soldiers.

Davíd had been right. There was dancing late into the night. Bleary from lack of rest the night before, Beatríz stumbled a bit more than she would have otherwise, but it was a night of mirth.

She recalled the thrill of dancing with Yusef, especially in their early days together when they were not accustomed to touching or being alone. She loved being escorted by him onto the dance floor, standing breathless in the moments before the music began, his hands resting on her back or elbow. When the dance forced her away from him and into the arms of another partner, she thrilled each time she circled back to him or caught his eye as they all swirled and leapt. He always found a way of sneaking in a few words of love or a kiss just as they rounded away from their watchful mothers. His mother thought he ought to ask other young ladies to dance, but he refused.

Beatríz danced with most of the soldiers at Blanca's wedding, laughing and chatting about everything that did not matter in life. Happy and carefree for once, she fell onto her mattress at dawn. But within the hour, the newly wedded Blanca roused her to begin work again.

CHAPTER 12

Beatríz and Blanca continued to work together as they had before the wedding. Beatríz did not notice any coming baby, and she did not feel close enough to Blanca to ask. In fact, Beatríz never knew what to say to the mute woman, and so Beatríz spent her days in near silence musing about her own life.

As weeks turned to months, Beatríz got to know the rabbi a bit from her regular visits to his home. She wished she had the strength to resist running there every time a new ship landed, but she could not. For weeks she had been turned away with a gentle shake of the head and good wishes, but one afternoon, so late Beatríz feared she would miss serving the evening meal with Blanca, he reached behind him and pulled out a letter.

Beatríz ripped it open as she stood in front of the rabbi's desk and immediately wished she had not.

My love,
I had hoped that someone in my family would reply
to my letters, but I have received nothing. The date for

my execution has been set and, in truth, I fear for my life. I hesitate to ask this of you, but perhaps you could write to one of your relatives for assistance.

Behind the bars that trap me, I dream of you. It is not the dampness of this cell that freezes my soul, but thinking I will never see your lovely face again. It is not death I fear most, but the thought of never touching you again. I dream of holding you, my Béa, and pray that God brings us together once more.

Yours forever,
Yusef

Execution.

Execution.

Beatríz sank to her knees and held the letter to her chest. The rabbi and the boy rushed to her side and tried to help her up, but she felt as if her bones had evaporated. Someone brought her a cup, but she could not reach out for it nor sip when it was pressed to her lips.

"What do I do?" she implored of the rabbi.

He remained still, not knowing the cause of her sorrow but accustomed to the unraveling of lives. Kneeling down beside her, he laid his hands on hers. "Whatever you must," he soothed. "Can we help?"

All grew very narrow and dark around Beatríz as if she had created a spyglass in front of her eye with cupped hands. "Paper. I need paper."

"You write, too?" the rabbi asked.

She nodded and was brought to a chair where she dashed off letters to Astruga and her father. Someone in Venice might know where her father had gone and forward it to him and, if not, that person might read the message and be willing to help. She thought and thought of whom else might assist, but her mind was muddled. Yusef's parents were gone. She did not know where his brother was. Solomon was at large. Friends had scattered after she left. There was Yakob. They might hate each other, but could he deny his sister this most important help? She hoped not.

With the three letters newly sealed with wax and a hasty *"Obrigada,"* she ran down to the docks. She knew a merchant friend of Davíd's was loading a ship headed for Lisbon. She hoped she could find him in time; if not, she did not know who would willingly bear her letter.

This time, driven by panic, she did not care who might leer as she ran up the gangplank of the ship. The merchant, Ricardo, was standing near the opening to the hold. When she called out to him, he approached, his eyes warm with welcome.

"Can you take this for me?" she asked, holding out one letter.

He studied the writing and nodded. "Anything for a friend of Davíd's. Especially a pretty one."

She ignored the compliment, the weight of each passing moment pressing down on her. "When do you leave?" she asked.

Ricardo's brow furrowed as he glanced over her shoulder. "As quick as we can. That ship came with the Plague."

Beatríz turned and looked at the ship flying a flag she recognized. The golden lion on a red background was Venetian.

"When did it arrive?"

"Only this morning, but once they explained that many people on board had died or were dying, no one was allowed to disembark. The soldiers are guarding them now."

Beatríz stared at the neighboring ship. There were people lining the edges and shouting. Some spoke Italian. Some Catalán. Some Portuguese. She looked among the faces for her father.

"Shall I take just the one or all three?" Ricardo asked looking at the papers Beatríz was absently crinkling.

She held the letters that were the key to Yusef's release. Who knew when and if the other ship would be returning to Italy? And if the Great Pestilence had truly arrived in Safi, it could be some time before anyone else would land. Decisively, she handed the other two over. "Please, *senhor*, if you meet any ships bound for Venice or Malaga or upriver to Seville, pass the others on."

"None dare enter Venice these days, but perhaps Seville." He took the letters and winked. "You got a husband in each of those ports?"

She swallowed hard and tried to play along with his joke, hoping that he might be more likely to remember the letters if she did. "Of course. Never can have too many husbands. Especially husbands that are far away."

Ricardo guffawed and hit the letters on the rail. "Good luck to you," he said, wiping his eyes. "Lucky husbands to have a woman like you."

She lowered her eyes and walked back down the gangplank. She hurried over to the Venetian ship and spotted Miguel as she neared. He was busy talking to the captain and the conversation did not seem to be going well. Miguel held his unsheathed sword and kept shouting "No!" to whatever was being said.

Beatríz decided to use his distraction to her advantage. She walked as close to the other side of the ship as she could, and leaned on the rope to keep her balance. A young blond woman on board spotted her and waved.

"Do you have any food?" the woman shouted.

"No," Beatríz answered. Ignoring the woman's look of desolation, Beatríz asked, "I am looking for my father. Dom Vidal of Lisbon, formerly of Toledo. A merchant." She hesitated before adding, "A Jew."

The woman looked over her shoulder, leaving Beatríz to wonder if she would have been more attentive if Beatríz had had food. "Wait," the woman said and left the rail. Moments later she pulled someone to where she had stood.

"Sól?" Beatríz shouted, unable to believe that her childhood friend was standing before her.

Sól smiled brightly. "Beatríz!"

"Is my father aboard?"

"No. No one else we know. My husband died on the passage," she said as mildly as if she had lost a shoe or a handkerchief.

"Oh," answered Beatríz, keeping her shock in check. "And are you well?"

"So far. But we would all feel better if we were allowed on land. Supplies are short and the journey has been distressing."

Hands on Beatríz's shoulders shocked her. She whirled around to find Miguel's face very close to her own.

"What are you doing here?" he inquired.

"Looking for my father."

Miguel's face looked ashen. "He is not on board, is he?"

Beatríz shook her head.

"Good. Then be on your way."

"My —" Beatríz began to argue but was startled by a something brushing past her leg. She screamed and jumped back as three rats the size of cats scurried down the rope from the Venetian ship. Beatríz shuddered and shook out her skirt. "Filthy creatures. I hate nothing more than rats."

"Impossible to keep them off the boats. Or on them. Go home, Beatríz. Blanca will need your help."

She took a moment to wave at Sól. "Good luck. If you make it off the boat –"

"Home, Beatríz," insisted Miguel.

Beatríz waved once more to her forlorn friend and went back to the barracks. On her way, she kept itching, so when she arrived, she changed dresses and violently shook out the one she had worn at the docks. When she looked at her leg, she noticed a few red bites.

"Do you need any washing done?" she asked Blanca. "I think I ought to boil my skirt and *camisa*. There were rats at the dock and I'm afraid one of them might have set fleas on me."

Blanca shook her head and pointed at a goat carcass, cleaned and ready to be butchered for the evening meal.

"That's going to take some time," Beatríz said with a sigh. "I just think if I do this now…" But when Blanca put her hands on her hips, Beatríz threw her aside her dirty dress, rolled her sleeves up and grabbed a knife to help Blanca hack apart the beast. She would wash the clothes when she found the time.

Within days, Beatríz's world was unraveling.

The men around the table stopped speaking when the women entered to serve, but Beatríz could hear the word 'plague' floating on whispers. Fewer men arrived on time for meals and they all ate faster. Beatríz knew terrible things were happening on the other side of the barrack walls, but she chose to ignore it, hoping that the troubles would drift past them like paper boats on a river. But it was not to be.

Blanca was the first one Beatríz saw take sick. When the women were cleaning up after supper, Beatríz noticed Blanca having difficulty staying on her feet, blotting her forehead and clutching her stomach. At first, Beatríz smiled, thinking Blanca might be with child. But then Blanca collapsed.

When Beatríz grabbed hold of Blanca, she felt the fever. Beatríz loosened the laces of Blanca's dress and spotted a swollen area on her neck circled with blackish red splotches. Beatríz snatched her hands back. Blanca's eyes rolled back in her head and she moaned.

Shaking all over, Beatríz ran for the door. Like in a nightmare, she found herself unable to make any noise at first. When her voice came, it was ragged and strangled, but no one answered the call. She stumbled into the courtyard hoping to find Davíd working. The space was empty and silent. Beatríz spun around and around to find someone or to hear something, but there were only the horses scraping their hooves in the dust and a rooster pecking.

Beatríz went to the gate and found a soldier arguing with a crowd.

"We cannot help you," he was shouting. "No other soldiers are here. And if they were, what could they do? Get back! You cannot come in. No, I cannot take your child. Back, I say!"

He nearly beheaded Beatríz when she tapped him on the shoulder. His look was wild but changed to sheer concern as soon as he saw it was she. "Beatríz, hide yourself within."

"Where is Miguel?"

"Out with everyone else. They are scattered around the city dealing with corpses. It is all happening so fast."

Beatríz hesitated, unsure of why she could not comprehend the magnitude of what he was saying. She had heard of outbreaks, but she never thought she would find herself trapped in a city filled with the pestilence. "What do I do?" she asked.

"Stay away from the infected."

She blinked a few times. "Blanca."

His eyes widened, and then he began shoving townspeople and locked the gate with a definitive clang. He rushed into the kitchen and froze at the sight of Blanca writhing on the floor.

"I did not know what to do," Beatríz said, her voice weak and apologetic.

"We have got to get her out of here," he said.

"And put her where?"

The man looked around as if the answer would present itself in one of the corners. "I do not know. We should find Miguel," he said.

"Well we cannot leave her like that." Beatríz considered putting Blanca on her own mattress, but thought better of it. "Can we get her to their bed?"

They struggled to get the thrashing young woman out the door.

"Just put her inside. I suppose you will have to guard the gate while I find Miguel."

The soldier scuttled off after dropping Blanca on the mattress.

Blanca was shouting incoherently and vomited. She was clutching her head and the shouts turned to screams, sending chills from Beatríz's shoulders down her legs. She took the cloth and wiped Blanca's face, then continued loosening Blanca's dress.

Beatríz wondered if Reyna and her own mother had suffered so. They must have. Beatríz wanted to know how long it had lasted. And then she did not. Best not to know.

She was not there to help her family, but she would be for Blanca.

Once Blanca was in nothing but her *camisa*, she quieted down, and Beatríz went to wash. Before she could think what she was doing, she had dipped her hands into the fountain. When she saw the mess begin to float off, she yanked her hands back up. *"Oh no,"* she thought. *"I polluted the water."* She grabbed the overturned bucket and dipped it in, trying to scoop up any traces of vomit. After a few minutes, she felt fairly confident that she had been successful. Nothing but leaves floated within the basin, and she sighed with relief.

Beatríz hurried to the gate and asked the soldier if he knew where Miguel might be found. He said pointing to the nearest square. "The men are searching houses. So far, those taking sick have lived by the water. That boat, the one from Venice, was sent away, but maybe someone snuck off and is hiding in one of these houses."

Beatríz shrugged, wondering what happened to Sól. She hoped food and fresh water were put onboard before it set sail, and wondered where – and if – her friend would land.

The soldier opened the gate a crack and Beatríz squeezed out into the middle of the crowd that tried to maneuver past her and sneak into the compound. They pushed against her and she had to jab her elbows against the ribs of more that one person to reach the other side of the crush. She was suddenly put in mind of the day she and Astruga made their way to the center of the square, the day her sister had chosen to be converted rather than let her children be taken.

Once clear of the pressing, panicked group, Beatríz was able to see the transformation of the city. Everyone she passed looked tense. Everyone rushed. Shutters were closed. A corpse rotted in the street and a lone dog was ripping the person's flesh, but no one ran it off or even seemed to notice. Beatríz hunched her shoulders and moved away, crossing her arms in front of her as if that would protect her from the sickness.

She spotted a helmet across the square, but it was not Miguel, so she continued on. Around the next bend, she found him standing next to a cart. When she looked closer, she realized the cart was piled with bodies. She covered her mouth with her hands and the lingering smell of Blanca's vomit kicked her stomach into her chest.

With a grim look on his face, Miguel turned back to the house.

"Miguel!" Beatríz called out. She could not bring herself to move closer to the house or the cart.

With some irritation, Miguel came to her. "Why are you out here?"

"Blanca . . . is sick."

Miguel grabbed her arm. "No."

Beatríz did not want to tell him the rest, but she knew Blanca needed him. "Her fever is high."

"Is she coughing?"

Beatríz thought a moment. "Not that I know of."

"Then there is hope," he said before running off.

The soldier left by the cart called after Miguel, and when Miguel did not turn back around, the man threw his hands up.

"Blanca has it," Beatríz said softly.

The man's irritation turned to sorrow, and he struck the wheel of the cart. Then he turned away and offered a young man money to help him take the bodies away.

"What will you do with them?" Beatríz asked as each man took hold of a handle.

"Burn them, of course. It's what we always do. There always seems to be Plague here in The Maghreb," he said with disgust.

Beatríz was so disturbed that she turned the wrong way and wandered uphill instead of back to the barracks.

At the same time she realized her error, she saw Davíd with a soldier she did not know. He must have been from the other barracks. Davíd was hammering boards against the front door of a house. Beatríz assumed the family had died and the men were trying to prevent anyone from going inside. But as she moved closer, she heard pounding that was not a hammer.

A small voice from within pled, "Please, *senhors*, do not leave us with our father. His body stinks."

The men continued with their work as if they did not hear.

"We will starve," called out another voice. "We have little food and water. You cannot do this."

Davíd took another nail from between his lips and held it in place.

Beatríz moved forward. "Davíd."

He turned and the nail fell to the ground.

"There are people inside," she said.

"I know."

"Are they sick?"

"No. But they might be."

"And if they are not?"

Davíd turned back to his work and punched the nail through the board. Then he and the other soldier stepped away from the door behind which the shouting continued.

"Davíd, you are killing them!" Beatríz shouted.

"This is my job," he said, he face full of hate and regret. "Let me do it in peace."

"That is wrong."

"Is it better if they come out and sicken others?"

Beatríz did not answer. Inside the boarded up house someone wailed.

"Davíd, let them out!" she begged, walking to the door and trying to pull the boards off.

Davíd wrenched her arms away and threw her against the wall. "Leave it." Then he called to the small crowd that had stopped to watch. "Anyone caught prying off boards will be put to death." He turned back to Beatríz and pointed very close to her face. "Anyone."

Beatríz heard a muffled weeping from the other side of the door. "Are you sealing all of the homes of the sick?" she asked.

"As many as we can." Then he and the other man began to walk away.

Beatríz suddenly felt full of spite, so she called out loudly, "So will you seal off the barracks?"

"Why would we do that?"

"Because Blanca is sick."

Davíd swooped at her, pinning her against the brick wall with his forearm. "Quiet," he hissed. "Do not let such news be known. Go home."

Her gaze was so fiery she would have set him ablaze were he made of paper. Davíd backed away and she straightened up, still feeling the press of his arm on her chest. "You are a hypocrite," she said just loudly enough for him to hear.

"Go, Beatríz," he said, his voice softening. "Take care of Blanca. And yourself."

Beatríz would not answer. She knew there was a logic to all he said and did, but she could not calm herself so quickly.

Back at the barracks, Blanca was worse – delusional and

shivering violently. Miguel mopped at her brow but she was not soothed in any way. Miguel looked hollow and lost. When Beatríz asked how she could help, Miguel waved her away without looking up from Blanca's ravaged body.

Beatríz went to prepare flatbread with cheese for any soldiers arriving just then, and an *adafina* for anyone coming in later. Beatríz had learned to cook *adafina* from their Jewish servants. By Jewish law one could not cook on the Sabbath and this dish could sit on the fire for a day and a half, the flavors growing richer over time. She would tell the guard about it so the men would feel free to come into the kitchen all through the night.

She had hoped the rhythm of the cutting and stirring would help clear her mind, and it did at first. But when she added onion to the pot, the sizzling oil set her thoughts popping. How could Davíd push her? Who would grow sick next? Was Blanca still alive? Would Beatríz herself live to see Yusef again.

No. She could not allow herself to think. Cook. Stir the onions. Add chickpeas. Add garlic. Add potatoes. Beatríz scooped dry beans into the soaking bowl for the next meal and went to get more water. Standing at the fountain, she paused and prayed for the health of those she loved. Then she filled bucket and went back to the kitchen.

Beatríz looked at the dead lamb on the counter. She did not have the heart to cut into it. To make up for the lack of meat in the evening meal, Beatríz decided to add both honey and chopped dates plus extra potatoes and eggs to the *adafina*.

Suddenly, Beatríz thought of Reyna as a small child clapping her hands while leaning over the *adafina* pot. Reyna had loved to see how the eggshells were dyed reddish brown by the onionskins. The thought made Beatríz both happy and sad at the same time with the sadness winning out. She reminded herself not to think.

Beatríz stirred in spices and water, and threw in chicken from the last evening's meal for good measure. Then she remembered the *kouclas*. These dumplings had always been her favorite part of the *adafina*. Beatríz mixed onion, egg, flour, parsley and salt, and tied the little lumps into cheesecloth. After dropping the bundles into the stew, she stood back satisfied with the first meal she had ever cooked alone. Some women buried their *adafina* underground to cook over embers, but Beatríz would use the bread oven so the men could serve themselves at will.

Beatríz went to check on Blanca, but nothing had changed. Blanca was still in anguish, and Miguel was still helpless. He told her not to waste her time with them, that he would call her if necessary.

Beatríz set the table and decided to wash her dress after all. She scratched absently at the fleabites on her ankle while she waited for the water to boil. She would have washed something of David's if he were around to ask, but did not offer to wash Blanca's linen. She ought to have, she knew, but she just could not face the filth just then.

After hanging her dress and thin white *camisa* to dry, she spread out her mattress and hoped to rest a little. Men came in to the barracks, but only one asked for food. He was satisfied with the cheese Beatríz had set out in the dining room and so the *adafina* continued to cook undisturbed.

David came late in the evening. He knocked and murmured her name, and she invited him to enter. He took his cap into his hands and asked if she might step out with him into the courtyard.

She rose and her cheeks blazed recalling their last

conversation. "We can speak here in the kitchen, if you wish," she said with as measured a voice as she could muster.

He nodded and leaned on the table. "How is Blanca?"

"She is doing poorly."

Davíd looked at steam coming from the large covered pot. "Did you do that by yourself?"

"I am not as helpless as you think."

He lowered his eyes. "I know. Béa, I –"

The word shocked her. "Beatríz," she insisted. "Only Yusef calls me Béa."

"I am sorry." His face reddened. "Beatríz, I want to apologize for laying my hands on you. It is simply that…well…all of those bodies and the begging…. Everyone is afraid but I do not know what to –" His voice broke off and he looked to be biting the inside of his cheeks.

"I understand," she said gently. "These are trying times."

"Yes. We begin it all again at dawn." With drooping shoulders he left the kitchen.

She thought she ought to say something more, but no words came to her.

In the morning, she was not hungry and few men came in for food, so she remained on her mattress until Davíd came to see her.

"Blanca has begun coughing up blood. Do not go to her," he said. "She will not last the day."

Beatríz's head began to throb and she pressed her temples with her fingers. "How much worse can this get?" she asked.

"Much worse, I fear. I have not seen an outbreak like this in my time here. Stay in the barracks if you can. People are frightened, Beatríz, and who knows how they will behave?"

They both had been raised with tales of angry, frightened

mobs attacking innocents in the street. Jews were a favorite target. They were blamed for bringing the disease and sometimes blamed for poisoning the wells. Jews had been rounded up and burned by the thousands from England to Bohemia, homes were looted, and adults and children alike were beaten when they were not murdered. Even non-Jews suffered accusation of sin and were told that secret pacts with the devil had brought on the suffering. Beatríz wondered if such things would happen in Safi.

Beatríz wished Davíd a safe return before lowering her aching head onto the mattress. It was not until she felt the tenderness in her armpit that she began to worry. Within minutes, her upset stomach turned to full nausea. She tried to stand, but found her legs were weak. She crawled to the door and opened it before passing out.

CHAPTER 13

In the haze that followed, Beatríz felt herself being lifted and she heard muffled voices. Her skin prickled and everything spun around. She threw up and tried to clean herself and the area around her, but hands grabbed her arms to hold them still.

Her mother, Reyna, and Miriam sat vigil that day. They cooled her forehead and took turns singing to her. And when it grew dark, they lit candles, which made their faces glow in the soft light just like at her betrothal party. Beatríz smiled to see them all and thanked them for coming.

"I have been so lonely without you," she tried to say, but Miriam wiped her brow and shushed her. "Where is my father?" Beatríz asked. "Mamá, where is he?"

Her mother leaned forward, her face more relaxed than Beatríz could ever remember it, and pushed hair out of Beatríz's face.

"Can you tell Yusef I am sick?" Beatríz asked. "Reyna, tell Yusef I need him."

Reyna put her hand on her heart and mouthed the word

she always used when describing Yusef and Beatríz, *"Suerte."*

"No," Beatríz insisted. "We are not lucky. You say that again and again, but we are apart and he is in prison, and I am dying – and you are dead. You are dead!" Suddenly full of panic. And as she tried to sit up, blood ran from Miriam's scalp and into her eyes. Reyna's hands and neck were covered with sores. Beatríz began to scream.

"Ssshhhh," the women all said as they reached for Beatríz.

"Get away! Do not touch me!" The wall next to her mattress trapped Beatríz. Hands pulled at her and she screamed again. The pain seared through her head and her skin felt pierced by a thousand pins.

"Let go," a voice soothed. "Stop fighting."

And Beatríz did. She lay still whispering, "Yusef."

Beatríz woke to find Miguel propped against the cutting table. Her eyes stung and she closed them again quickly. Every inch of her screamed. She coughed, but it was a rasping cough, not wet and bloody as Blanca's had been.

Blanca. Was Miguel in the kitchen waiting for Blanca? Beatríz's head hurt more from the thinking and a moan escaped her lips. She heard Miguel scuttle toward her.

"Beatríz? Are you awake?"

She thought she moved her head, but was not sure.

"Oh, thank God," he said.

She opened her eyes a slit.

"Where is . . . " She could not find the energy to finish her thought.

"Davíd will be back soon," Miguel offered, though that was not for whom Beatríz had begun to inquire.

"Blanca?" she whispered.

Miguel looked away. Understanding what was happening

was like wading through waist-deep water. Eventually, she realized that Miguel was sitting with Beatríz because he no longer had Blanca to care for. Blanca had not survived, but by some miracle, Beatríz had. It was as simple as that.

"Water," she whispered. Her temples pounded.

He rose quickly as if glad to have something to do. He handed her a cup and said, "Davíd hardly left your side for these three days. He would not hear of anyone else caring for you, but at last, he surrendered to sleep this morning. With Blanca...I said I could."

She tried to reach out to him, but could only lift her arm part way before it fell to the stone floor. Miguel took her hand in his before lowering his head and weeping softly to his chest.

Davíd found them like that.

"Davíd," Miguel said, wiping his cheeks, "you are supposed to be resting."

"Is she –" Davíd rushed over.

"Her fever broke. She is awake," said Miguel.

Davíd exhaled audibly as Beatríz blinked a few times. A deep crease folded into his brow as he knelt down.

"She will recover. Sleep, my friend," said Miguel. "Davíd, you can do her no good if you are asleep on your feet."

She heard Davíd walk to the door, hesitate, and then continue out.

She heard footsteps again, but instead of Davíd returning, it was a young soldier. A stench brought with him made Beatríz gag. She had no strength to cover her face, so she breathed through her mouth instead.

"Good God, man," said Miguel. "What have you done to yourself?"

"I heard that bathing in human urine will protect me.

Better that than take sick, no?"

"Why not dip a handkerchief in aromatic oil or burn incense?" Miguel asked from behind the crook of his elbow.

"I do not believe in those. But I put a 'stink' under my bed."

"Dead animals in the barrack? You had best take that out immediately. No need to attract more vermin. And I suggest that you wash, as well."

The young man stormed out.

Miguel sat next to Beatríz again. "The city has gone mad with ways to keep the Great Pestilence at bay. Church bells are rung constantly. People line up all hours at the doctor's to be bled. Some soldiers have been firing cannons, which upset Davíd, who claims they are making more work for him." He shook his head, and then his face grew dark. "There is no cure as far as I can tell. And even if there were one, what good —" He sighed leaving his sorrow unspoken.

The light caught a gold disk hanging around Miguel's neck. Beatríz had never known Miguel to wear jewelry and wondered if it had been Blanca's. With some effort, she pointed to the dangling metal.

Miguel touched it and blushed before tucking it in his shirt. "A talisman for health. It cannot hurt, I suppose."

Why had Beatríz lived when so many perished? As Yusef's mother would have said, "*A morte não escolhe idades.*" It was true: death did not take sides.

"I had a wife before Blanca," Miguel said, leaning against the cutting board once again. "My father arranged it. I had never met her, but in the sketch I was shown, she looked beautiful so I agreed. But while she was fine of face, she was also cruel. And worse, she never stopped talking. Never. She talked in her sleep. She talked as she cooked. 'Now for the salt. In with the lard. That is a fine chicken. Stir. Stir.' And those were tame comments. She criticized me constantly, even to my own mother who grew to hate my wife – my first wife – with an unstoppable passion. Being sent abroad was a relief, I swear to you."

"Where is she now?" asked Beatríz, whose neck and head felt as if someone were stabbing her.

"Dead." He shrugged. "I had hoped that Blanca would give me a son, but…" They sat in silence for a while. "I will come check on you later, Beatríz," Miguel said at last.

Beatríz nodded, and when next she pried her eyes open, the room was dark and Davíd was curled up on the floor next to her. She reached out and touched his hair, but when he stirred, she snatched her hand back and pretended to still be asleep.

The sickness did run it course, but not before killing a quarter of the population of Safi. Many considered themselves lucky for two reasons: one, it could have been worse; two, there was more available housing. Within weeks, the screams were only of playing children and of fighting spouses. There were more prayers for the dead to be said, and everyone left alive to say them murmured an extra prayer of thanks at having been spared. This time.

Beatríz began to find comfort in the church visits she made with the soldiers, marking time and using the break in her routine to reflect. She ignored the painting and statues of suffering, focusing instead on the beatific Jesus and the peaceful Virgin Mary, hoping to hold a child of her own some day. Though that hope was beginning to dwindle.

Eventually, boats began docking again, bringing with them

fresh supplies of slaves, goods from far off lands, and the possibility of news. Beatríz resumed her visits to the rabbi's house, though she was turned away with nothing time after time. Even so, she did not lose hope. She enjoyed the air, regaining her strength, and the chance to see how the city had changed. Some houses were abandoned. New slaves worked in certain households. Fewer children played in the squares. But on the whole, everything seemed remarkably like before. She thought more should be different to mark the tragedy, that the very colors of the stone ought to be different, but they, like so much else, remained the same. Everyone breezily said the pestilence was common in the Maghreb and since it would surely be back, one had to simply live life. But Beatríz could not dismiss it so easily. She often dwelt on having seen Miriam's dress in a pile of refuse. What had become of little Lola's family? What would become of her if she stayed in this city?

With Blanca gone, all of the cooking fell to Beatríz. She did not mind, though she found the lifting and scrubbing tired her as never before.

The days ran into one another punctuated only with fruitless visits to the rabbi and deciding what dishes to prepare.

Until the day it rained. It did not simply rain, it poured. It was as if God realized he had done enough to make everyone miserable and wanted to bless Safi with clean streets and fresh water in their buckets. Beatríz loved the sound of the downpour slapping the stone walls and wooden shutters, and tried to match the rhythm of her chopping to the beat.

When at last she was free to go into the courtyard, she wandered over to Davíd.

"Lovely day," he said with great sarcasm, setting aside his

tools.

Beatríz shrugged and said, "I think it is. When was the last time you saw rain?"

She leaned out and let the drops tickle her face and hands. Giggling, she flicked her wet fingers at him and he shoved her out from under the awning. She pulled him into the open courtyard and then she ran back beneath the taut canvas. Looking to the sky and stretching out his arms, Davíd let the downpour soak his hair and shirt. Beatríz noted his fine figure emerging from under the saturated fabric and closed her eyes quickly, concentrating on the now thunderous deluge.

"Come out here," he called.

"No." She laughed, her eyes still shut tight. The sound reminded her of lying in bed with Reyna listening to October storms pound the tile roof of her parents' house.

Davíd ran to her and threw his arms around her to get her wet.

She wiggled out of his grasp and teasingly protested the mess he made of her dress, so soiled and limp from constant wear these past months that it reminded her of a beggar's. Squeezing his cheeks, she asked, "Is that any way to treat a lady?"

She let go to shake out her dress again, and when she looked up, she noticed his face had gone slack. His eyes locked onto hers and he did not take heed of the water dripping down his brow. Her stomach flipped as she recognized the hungry sadness in his eyes. Turning her head away quickly, she stared at the rain.

She waited for Davíd to say something, and when he did not, she steadied her breath before murmuring, "Davíd, you have a wife."

"Who is not here."

Beatríz frowned. The cascading water filled the silence between them.

If not for Yusef, she would have reached out to touch Davíd's wet skin. If not for Yusef, she would have pressed her lips to Davíd's. If not for Yusef, she would have let Davíd dampen her clothes as he pressed his body against her.

She studied the watermarks on her shoes.

She still wanted Yusef. She still had to believe.

His voice curled around her. "I loved you when we were children. Why do you think I made you kiss me over a button?" he said. "I feel this is my second chance."

"No, Davíd."

He slipped his hand into hers, and she pulled her hand free, more slowly than she should have. Her heart pounded as she turned to face him. He blinked a few times, his longing gaze pulling her soul closer. She backed her body away.

"I hope you will not put me out because of this, but I cannot betray your wife or Yusef. I am sorry."

She walked out of the gate toward the rabbi's house, concentrating on her footsteps rather than the burning she felt on her back as he watched her go.

As if by divine message, or divine reprimand, Beatríz received a letter from Yusef that day.

> *My sweet Béa,*
>
> *Wonderful news. Your sister, Astruga, sent the money for my release. I am free and working to save enough for passage to Safi. If need be, I will join a crew and sail with them until I can reach you. With God's help, we will be joined soon.*
>
> *- Yusef*

The rabbi's wife, Rebecca, who asked the glowing Beatríz of her news, congratulated Beatríz. They speculated that it might take Yusef a month to reach her, but certainly no more than two. Rebecca said they could arrange a ceremony on the docks if that was what would make Beatríz and Yusef happy. Beatríz hardly noticed the rain, or anything else, as she made her way back to the compound.

Davíd crossed the courtyard as she entered.

She thought of walking away but decided it would be rude. "I have had a letter from Yusef. He is safe and on his way." Her feelings were jumbled – regret, joy, anticipation, concern.

Gone was his bravado, his confident stance. In its place were loneliness and yearning in a man who knew he would never get what he wanted. "If you have decided that our friendship should end, I understand."

She shook her head. "We can talk of Safi. Of our work."

He ran his fingers through his hair and nodded.

She began to walk away and turned back to ask, "Davíd, I remember when I was ill… making a mess of myself. Yet, when I woke, I was clean and in a new dress."

Davíd's cheeks pinked. "I – it needed to be done. You were very sick."

"You changed me?"

"And washed your dress and *camisa*," he interjected. "Miguel helped and –" He second-guessed the explanation he had meant to be reassuring. "Nothing was – We did not – Circumstances –"

Beatríz bit back her embarrassment. "Thank you for your help." She paused and added, "That is not why you suddenly…feel differently, is it?"

"No! My feelings were from before I saw you – I mean to say, you are lovely – I – no, that is not what I – but you *are* and –"

"Never mind." She blushed and walked away, adding, "I will see you at supper."

She carried on with her work, but could not stop thinking of his seeing her naked. He had had his hands on her body, had washed her, had dressed her. These were intimacies only mothers or nursemaids were to have, not a friend, perhaps not even a husband, and certainly not a man she hardly knew. That Davíd had seen what Yusef had not pained and shamed her. It did not matter that he had done it to help her. She could never tell Yusef. Not ever.

As she served that evening, she was careful not to look at Davíd, though she knew he kept his gaze fixed on her. Instead, she listened to the men and, before she had dished out to everyone, she was already frightened by their talk.

"The timing could not be worse. A siege now will be devastating."

"We haven't the manpower to protect Safi."

"Then write to the commanders and –"

"And what? We are already surrounded and the commanders have been unwilling to reinforce us for months."

"But all has been peaceful."

"They knew the threats were real."

"With so many of our men gone and the city decimated, how are we supposed to keep the warlord from conquering?"

A silence fell and Beatríz set a pot on the side table hoping to hear the rest by pretending to stir.

"More wine, Beatríz?" requested Davíd, and she had to leave.

When she returned, their conversation had changed to topics less appropriate but also less alarming. Not especially interested in which prostitutes had survived and were open again for business, she left the room wondering when she would learn more of an attack. Unfortunately, she did not have long to wait.

CHAPTER 14

Explosions woke Beatríz the next morning. At first she thought there had been another outbreak and canons were being set off to ward against the pestilence. But the next canon fire was followed by shouts and the distinct sound of crumbling. When she ran out, she discovered she was alone in the compound but for the sentry at the gate.

His voice was tinged with panic as he told her, "We are surrounded. The attackers number in the hundreds and we are not thirty men. All is lost."

"What will happen?"

"Hope they do not kill everyone, I suppose."

Beatríz held the gate to steady herself. She noticed anew the scalloped archway, the striped pillars, and the mosaics. "They will want their mosque back, I should think."

"At the very least."

Beatríz was not sure where to go.

As if reading her thoughts, the soldier said, "It is difficult to breech the city walls, even when they are so poorly guarded. They will likely attack one spot at a time until they realize our numbers are few. Go inside. You should be safe for today."

Not the least bit reassured, Beatríz went back to the kitchen.

Two soldiers came into the compound that afternoon covered in soot. Beatríz followed them and hid in the shadows outside the storeroom as they gathered weapons.

"It is the safest choice," one was explaining.

"Surrender is safe?" asked the other.

"Saf*est*, not safe."

"They might kill us."

"They promised not to."

"Promised? The infidel cannot be trusted."

"It is our best hope. If we try to fight, we are dead men. At least this way we have a chance."

The clatter of swords on the ground momentarily masked their conversation. They emerged from the storeroom with arms full.

"We could be captured. Enslaved. *Killed.*"

"Or we might be set free."

Beatríz stepped out from the shadows. "Will they come for everyone or just the soldiers?"

The men spun around.

"Beatríz!" said the taller soldier. "How much did you hear?" When her silence answered, he exchanged glances with the other man and then said to her, "You need not worry."

"I am worried," she said. "Will *I* be captured or enslaved or killed?"

The man's face twitched. "It is possible."

Beatríz's legs went weak. "Even if you surrender?"

She jumped at the sound of a canon being shot.

"We should go," he said, and the two men left without

another word.

Beatríz had the rest of that day and most of the next alone to worry. She did not hear any significant changes.

Late in the afternoon the second day, David came rushing into the kitchen. "Beatríz. You are still here?"

"I was told to that this was the safest place."

"Not anymore. We are surrendering, but God knows what that means for us. Run and hide, Beatríz. Do not let them find you in here. Do not let them find you at all."

"But David, where will I go?"

"I don't know. I cannot help – Beatríz, the men are expecting –" He stopped and his forehead wrinkled. "Grab your bag. Follow me."

She hastily shoved her letters and extra dress – the one she had wanted to wash just before Blanca took sick – into her satchel and buttoned it. David reached out a hand and she took it after just a moment's hesitation. He pulled her out of the compound and through the panicked crowds and winding streets. They huffed up the hill, stopping at a sealed up house. David unsheathed his scabbard and began prying away a board barring the door.

Beatríz suddenly realized what he was doing. "I cannot go in there."

"You can and will," he said. When he tossed aside the board, he glanced at her face and froze. Softening his tone, he added, "There are no corpses in there. The house was empty before we did this."

"No." Just thinking about the illness made her shudder.

"Beatríz, be reasonable. You can hide here and –"

"No!" She put her hands on her hips.

"This is foolish. If those men rampage and you are found on the street –"

Beatríz shook her head violently, unable to bring herself to walk into the sick rooms.

"Then I take no responsibility for what happens to you," he said.

"I am not asking you to do any such thing. You are not my husband, Davíd, nor my brother. You are not anything!"

Davíd stormed away before she could apologize. She would always wish she had.

Beatríz stood in the doorway for a while unsure of what to do or where to go. Suddenly a surge of low calls came from the direction of the south gate where Beatríz had seen caravans assembling. The invaders had entered the gates. The sound of breaking glass held her frozen in the doorway. Angry shouts and terrified screaming came from just around the bend. She knew she had to run but could not decide on a direction. If she were spotted in this quarter, she would be known to be a Portuguese Jew or a Christian, and was not sure which might be more dangerous. She had to get out.

She ran west toward the near-empty section of the city, the quarter where the few Muslims who had remained after the Portuguese take-over resided. As she passed under an archway that separated their quarter from hers, she spotted a group of veiled women gathered on a balcony watching the siege. Beatríz's lungs stung and she paused to catch her breath, slinking into the shade. Suddenly, a veil fluttered to the street in front of Beatríz. She waited for someone to come out for it. Monstrous smoke began billowing into the sky from somewhere across the city. Beatríz stared at the veil again.

"Para tí, señorita," Beatríz heard someone say in Arabic-accented Castilian. *"Sácala."* The woman pantomimed picking something up and pulling it close her chest. All but one

woman had retreated inside. Round brown eyes looked out from a veil, and Beatríz could tell the woman was smiling. More glass broke, close this time, and the woman gestured at Beatríz to cover her hair and pin the veil under her eyes. Beatríz complied, securing the material as quickly as she could with trembling hands.

"*Gracias!*" Beatríz shouted. "I will bring it back if I can."

The woman clasped her hands and looked to the sapphire sky. "*Inshallah.*"

If Beatríz's father could see her in a veil, he would be furious. But he wasn't here. She ran.

Beatríz skidded to a halt. Men with swords were crowded into a square. Beatríz turned and looked around. She made out a door left slightly ajar on the side of a house. She crept over to it and peered inside. The small area had been abandoned for some time and was filled with rotting boards and random refuse. Beatríz slid inside, trying to pull the door shut but found it jammed a hand's length open. She scuttled in and wedged herself in the farthest corner behind some forgotten material. Her rapid breath made the veil flutter. She thought of removing it, but was afraid to be found so exposed.

Someone pulled at the door. Beatríz braced herself.

A girl around Reyna's age entered and pulled the door shut. Beatríz whispered. "Come here."

The girl jumped.

"Come here," Beatríz repeated, but the girl did not seem to understand what Beatríz said, so Beatríz waved her over.

The two knelt in the corner for hours. People passed by their shelter, some running, some shouting, some alone, some in large groups. The sun sank and the streets turned from orange to blue. Then someone yanked the door, pulling extra hard as it caught on one of the cobblestones. The girl tightened her arms around Beatríz. A man entered, calling something in Arabic. The girl tucked her lips between her teeth and pinched her eyes shut. The man poked his sword into some cloth that dangled from the roof, then looked into one corner before walking out. The girl trembled against Beatríz.

They stayed where they were until morning, Beatríz fighting off sleep in the hopes of seeing any danger coming. When all had grown quiet and Beatríz felt somewhat confident that they could try leaving their haven, they struggled to stand on their cramped legs. To Beatríz's surprise, the girl hugged Beatríz tightly before waving goodbye. Beatríz thought to go with her, but the girl belonged in the Muslim quarter and she belonged across the city.

Beatríz wanted to return the veil, but could not remember which house it had come from. She walked to her own quarter, and, unsure of what might await her, she decided to keep on the veil after all.

There had clearly been struggles while Beatríz was hiding, as evidenced by collapsed walls, broken pottery strewn everywhere, and odd bits of clothing left in the street. But on the whole, Beatríz did not find as much destruction as she had thought there might be. Perhaps the soldiers had been right to surrender. Maybe the siege had been easier because of it.

She crept toward the mosque that had been the barracks and saw a pile of the soldiers' possessions lying in the street being picked through by neighbors. Beatríz thought to join them, to salvage what she could and return it to them, but she did not want to draw attention to herself nor did she know where the soldiers might be. Blanca's spare dress was snatched out of the pile by a hunched over woman and, uncharitably, Beatríz hoped the disease was still lurking in the seams.

As she rounded the corner, Beatríz nearly fell over a man crouched against the wall, stolen goods laid out before him.

"You will profit from the misfortune of others?" she asked, not attempting to mask her fury.

The man shrugged, not the least disturbed by her accusation.

Beatríz looked more closely. She saw Miguel's talisman. Ricardo's doublet. David's scabbard. "What happened to these men?" she whispered, unpinning the veil that covered her crumbling face.

"You were David's friend, no?" he asked.

Beatríz nodded, then looked more closely at the man. "You – you sold milk to us."

"Yes. My goats were taken during the invasion, so I will scavenge for now."

More gently, she said, "I'm sorry to ask again, but why do you have their things? Where are the soldiers? I thought they surrendered."

"Seems they did not like the idea of a surrender after all and chose to attack at the last moment when they were supposed to be handing over their weapons. Took a few of the infidel with them to the other world, but a waste of lives, if you ask me."

Beatríz had many questions swirling in her head, but her mouth could form none of them.

"Not all of the men attacked, though," continued the man. "Some were at the barracks preparing to leave. Like David."

"He is alive?" Beatríz asked, grabbing the man's sleeve.

"Was when they dragged him out."

Beatríz's momentary relief was swept away. "Dragged? Where did they take him?"

The man shrugged with one shoulder. "Somewhere to be held for ransom."

Beatríz covered her mouth and sat back on her haunches. "Ransom?"

The man reached out and patted her with his dirt-encrusted fingers. "Do not fret, *senhorita*. He is lucky. Lesser men are turned to slaves or killed on the spot. As a weapons maker, your friend is valuable to both the invaders and the Portuguese army, plus he comes from a wealthy family. Someone will certainly pay to bring him home."

Beatríz touched Davíd's scabbard lightly as if it were his hand rather than a sun-warmed piece of metal, wondering if she would ever see him or Miguel again. Anything was possible.

She rose, unsure of what to do next. She had nowhere to live and little money. Commotion in the barracks where the invaders – or rather, former citizens of the city – were reclaiming the mosque sent Beatríz in the other direction. Where to go? The only other people she knew were the rabbi and his wife, so she wandered up the hill to their house.

When she reached the rabbi's street, she noticed it was especially crowded. People were milling around with bundles and talking excitedly. Beatríz made her way to the rabbi's house, but could not make it through the door. She was just turning away, when she heard, "Beatríz? Are you joining us?"

Beatríz turned and found it was Rebecca, the rabbi's wife. Beatríz asked, "For what?"

"We are leaving. My husband has decided to be Moses and lead our people to a new land."

"Will it take forty years?"

Rebecca laughed a tinkling laugh. "I hope not. I should like to give birth on solid ground," she said, laying her hands on her mildly protruding stomach. "We will not go far. Perhaps to a town where we are the only Jews. Perhaps not. But somewhere we are welcome. Will you join?"

Beatríz knew she ought to, but was terrified. What might await her on a new ship? This time there was the rabbi and other men he knew, but could they protect her from sailors causing mischief? Beatríz doubted it. She twisted the button on her satchel nervously, weighing her options.

"What will you do if you stay?" Rebecca asked.

Beatríz shrugged, unable to voice her fears.

"Then come. We will find you a home and employment. And we have safety in numbers."

Beatríz thought. She had nowhere to live if she stayed, and the only people she still knew in Safi were about to leave. "Rebecca, how will Yusef find me?"

Rebecca hesitated. "I cannot say for certain he will know where we are, but we should be able to send word back once we are settled."

Beatríz's heart sank. "Should?"

Rebecca, who was a head shorter than Beatríz, reached up to the younger woman's face and held Beatríz's cheeks in her hands. "Beatríz, there are no certainties in life. But I am confident that those left behind will help Yusef find you."

Beatríz mind prickled with unanswerable questions. "How many will go?"

"About a hundred," Rebecca said, gesturing to the crowd in the street. "The rest did not want to take their chances."

"Perhaps we could leave a list with someone? Of those of us who chose to leave. In case anyone comes looking."

"There is not much time, I fear."

"I can do it quickly, but I need paper."

"Oh yes. You write. How unusual," Rebecca said. "We are leaving in a moment for the ship, but you can try."

Rabbi Aharon greeted Beatríz warmly and his young assistant was sent to find her paper. She set herself up on the street with the boy holding the bottle of ink, calling for anyone who wanted to be included to come forward. Only half of the travelers' names ended up on the paper before they were set to go, but the rabbi placed it in the hands of his most trusted friend. And so with a slightly less heavy heart, Beatríz watched the city she had nearly come to think of as home disappear from sight.

CHAPTER 15

This journey was far less traumatic than the one that brought her to Safi, though it took her the first afternoon and a sleepless night of cowering in a corner to learn that the crew would not harass her.

The ship traveled north, passing through the narrow strait near Gibraltar, the ship hugged the coast for a few more days and made its way east. Small towns and seaside villages cropped up now and then, but the travelers were headed for the large city of Oran. The Mediterranean Sea was dotted with boats of many sizes, and Beatríz could not help but wonder if Yusef might be on one of them or just beyond the horizon.

During the journey Rebecca and Beatríz were scarcely apart. They came to know one another well. Both women were inquisitive and opinionated. But while Rebecca quietly observed and whispered advice to her husband, Beatríz questioned him and then questioned his responses. More often than not he indulged her with answers, but Beatríz knew she had pushed too far on one occasion.

The men had been debating what to do about a group of Jewish women who were singing on the ship. Some of the men thought this ought to be forbidden, as, according to their beliefs, a woman's voice was never to be heard in song. Other men disagreed, saying that hearing a woman's voice was only forbidden during prayer.

"But does it not say in the 'Song of Songs'," interrupted Beatríz, *"Let me hear your voice, for your voice is sweet and your face is beautiful"?"*

A few men looked at her with wide eyes while others turned their heads completely away. As a woman, she was not to question, and certainly not to interrupt.

One man mumbled, "She quotes such filth?"

"The Torah is filth?" Beatríz asked, particularly upset that what she viewed to be the loveliest of poems, biblical or otherwise, was being disparaged.

Rabbi Aharon rose and quieted everyone. "Let us be careful with our words, my friends." Then he faced her, and said, "According to the Talmud, a woman's singing is akin to nakedness."

Beatríz nearly laughed. "I assure you they are hardly the same."

The grumbles of women behind her and the red faces of some of the men told her she had overstepped.

"I mean to say," Beatríz stammered, "I – I mean to ask, how is a spoken voice so very different from a singing voice?"

Rabbi Aharon looked around at the expectant faces of his new congregation. "I think we can agree that they are different."

"If a woman has a lovely speaking voice – musical, even – should she never be allowed to speak?"

"A woman is not to speak or interrupt all!" shouted one

man, whose wife lowered her head and walked away.

When Beatríz opened her mouth to argue, Rabbi Aharon put up a hand to stop her. "Please go back with the other women," he said, his eyes fixed on Rebecca's, and Rebecca pulled Beatríz by the elbow.

"You should not speak to him like that," Rebecca admonished.

Beatríz was taken aback. "What have I done that others have not?"

"Other *men* have pressed. But you should not think you are equal to a man."

Beatríz watched the rabbi's set face, his hands clasped behind his back as he walked. "I have not challenged him. I did not say he was wrong. But if I do not understand, I must ask why. It makes no sense that I should believe him just because he says something."

"You believe him because he is a rabbi."

Beatríz pressed her lips together.

Rebecca continued, "He knows more than any of us."

"Yet he is human. Can he make no mistakes?"

Rebecca paused and watched him study the horizon. "As a husband, yes. But I cannot question his beliefs, his knowledge, or his leadership."

Beatríz shook her head. "Does God not encourage learning?"

"God commanded *men* to study. Do not insert yourself into their world. Your job is to help men, not to question them, not to give your opinion, especially when others can hear." When Beatríz's only response was to clench her teeth, not wanting to offend her friend but unwilling to agree, Rebecca added, "You and I respect one another despite our differences. But when you express yourself openly, it feels like disrespect. Respecting me means respecting my husband and his authority."

Beatríz fought the urge to laugh and the urge to cry.

The rabbi resolved the issue an hour later when he walked over to the women. "I am not ready to rule that women should never be heard – though sometimes it might make life easier," he said with a twinkle in his eye. "I believe that if the women of this ship would like to sing as a group, they can do so quietly, for not all of our people share the same beliefs about women's voices. The men who object may plug their ears. For my wife has a lovely singing voice, and I am sure can control my desires while we are all stuck on the deck of this ship for the next day or so." He tapped his fingers on the rail. "Anything else you absolutely must know, Señorita Beatríz?"

Beatríz smiled. "I think I shall give questioning a rest. At least for today."

The rabbi laughed first, followed by everyone sitting nearby. Rebecca relaxed and nodded to her friend.

At last, the city appeared. What surprised her most was that it was flat. This would be the first time she lived in a place where she did not spend her days walking up and down hills, having to watch her footing and her skirts on an incline. As the ship got closer, Beatríz thought the city of Oran looked much like Safi: a high surrounding wall, boats at the dock, low buildings, save for the relatively towering minarets. But hearing the call to prayer, she knew living in a Muslim city would be different, though how different, she was not sure.

She did not see any crosses or church spires, and had heard that the Christians had not yet successfully taken Oran.

At least here, if Rabbi Aharon gained permission to enter with his followers, she could live as a Jew. But what did that mean now? Living without her own religion had not seemed to matter much during the past six months. Would she welcome the return to Judaism or would she feel stifled by it?

Stifled. The word spun in her mind like bats around torchlight. How odd that that word came to mind. Since leaving Lisbon, she had felt freer. Adrift and scared, but free of expectation. Was that the loss of her religion or being away from her parents? She did not know. Now, living among Jews again, she was unsure how her existence would change. Already there had been arguments among the men on the ship about women's behavior, and Beatríz feared more restrictions.

If there had been no siege on Safi, would she have continued going quasi-contentedly to Mass? Could she have developed a sense of community with those people? Or had she been content because she viewed her situation as temporary?

Rebecca's touch startled Beatríz. "My husband would like you to accompany us to the house of the *sharif*. You will be presented as my cousin."

The *sharif* was the man who ruled the city. Beatríz, in her worn out dress and with her rumpled hair, felt self-conscious at the thought of being presented as anything at all to a man of such import. "What purpose will my presence serve?" Beatríz asked.

"The *sharif*, it is said, appreciates beautiful women and putting you in front of him might sway him."

Beatríz blanched and whispered, "What will I be expected to do?" She imagined dancing or showing an ankle or, heaven forbid, becoming one of the *sharif's* wives. Beatríz felt trapped. Was this why she had been invited to travel from Safi? Was she to be the sacrifice her community made at the altar of security?

Rebecca took Beatríz's hands in her own. "You will stand with me. It is mere show, according to my husband. Perhaps the *sharif* will assume there are women from our group who would willingly join him at his palace, but we would never suggest that nor allow it. Knowing such loveliness could pass him on the streets might be enough."

"Might."

"No harm will come to you. I promise."

And so with great consternation, Beatríz followed Rabbi Aharon and Rebecca to the palace. She noticed the city was in better repair than Safi had been. Fewer buildings were crumbling, more doors were painted, and less whitewash was chipping. The city felt more relaxed and prosperous. The streets were wider and even straight in places.

The clothing on the people they passed was brighter – more white tunics on men, more brightly dyed and thinner fabrics on the women. Feeling as if she were being baked by the strong midday sun, Beatríz wished she could be wearing such light cloth. Even if she were wrapped, as some of the women, from head to toe in what looked like giant translucent winding sheets, it still looked cooler than her thick gown which felt leaden and which kept all cool ocean breezes from reaching her skin.

They approached the palace, the most formidable looking building in the city. It was not especially decorative on the outside – a plain sand colored building with high walls – yet the entrance spoke of the grandeur they would find inside. The rounded door was gold and the height of three men, and around its frame was carved dark wood. Guards flanked the entrance, and she found their elaborate uniforms of high turbans with feathers, colorful tunics, and swords glinting in their shining belts stunning.

The rabbi approached one guard, and as the men conferred, Beatríz noticed the other guards staring. Beatríz wished a large number of their men had accompanied them from the boat, for truly, what would prevent any one of the *sharif's* men, if not the *sharif* himself, from spiriting her away? Or from taking Rebecca for that matter. Then again, what match would unarmed Jewish men be to the sentries of the great house?

Within moments, Rabbi Aharon was waving them forward, and Beatríz's stomach began to twist. As they walked through the high arched doorway, Beatríz said a prayer and kept her eyes low, fighting both the desire to run and the desire to appreciate the beauty of the place and its people.

When they were led through a cavernous entry and out to a courtyard cooled by the shade, Beatríz could not help but peek. The design reminded her of the barracks in Safi, which had once been a mosque, with colorful *zilij* tiles used to create lovely designs like flowers. Above the tiles, creating a second story was carved white stucco nearly blinding in the sunshine. The columns here were not covered in tile, but looked like ribbons wrapped around them, for they were carved in swirls. Gold colored lamps with delicate cutouts in the metal hung every few feet along the edges of the courtyard, and Beatríz could not help but think how lovely it must have been when they were all lit. The surrounding overhang was made of dark geometrically carved wood topped by tile roofs. The trickle from a small green and white tiled fountain echoed soothingly.

A man approached who towered over Rabbi Aharon, his

long limbs swimming within loose fabric cinched around his narrow waist. His carefully folded turban elongated his thin face. The man gestured at jewel toned cushions set in a square – a place Beatríz assumed was meant for conversation, and the men sat. Beatríz and Rebecca stood a few paces behind the rabbi. Rebecca suddenly looped her arm through Beatríz's, and Beatríz, could feel her tremble.

"Are you the *sharif?*" asked Rabbi Aharon.

"You will speak with me."

Beatríz wondered if he was a son or brother of the *sharif* or an assistant.

Rabbi Aharon cleared his throat. "We are seeking refuge. As you likely know, Safi was seized, and though the disagreement was between the Muslims and the Christian conquerors, we felt it prudent to move on."

The tall man pursed his lips, which made him look as if he had smelled something unfortunate. "Our city is already crowded. To accept another hundred people might stretch us to our limits."

Rabbi Aharon kept his voice steady. "I understand. But you should know that we are artisans and traders, lucrative professions."

The man looked bored. "I will tell you a story of another boatload of Jews that arrived some time back. Only the rabbi came ashore. While he was speaking with us, the captain of the ship stole his goods and allowed his crew to rape the women. The rabbi, as you can imagine, was quite disturbed by this. We had not planned on letting him stay, but once he demanded our assistance and asked that we mete out punishment for a man that was not even under our control, well, his fate was sealed. We sent him away."

"But he was wronged," Beatríz said aloud without

thinking, and Rebecca pinched her hard.

The man's face twisted as he turned sharply to face her. "You let a woman speak?" he asked, looking back at Rabbi Aharon. He opened his mouth as if to continue his story, but turned his angry gaze upon Beatríz once more. "What should we care of a man we do not know? He did not pay taxes to us. There was no agreement of protection. Why should we intervene in a matter that, besides being incredibly commonplace, did not concern us?"

"Because there is a thing called human decency!" Beatríz replied, her cheeks on fire.

"Beatríz, silence!" growled Rabbi Aharon.

She knew she ought to heed him, but she could not. "The man asked for shelter, a man who would have paid taxes, yet you refused him. Then he was attacked and you turned your back on him."

The man rose and stepped forward, his height compounding his air of menace. "The impudence —"

"Beatríz, you put us all at risk," Rebecca hissed.

Rabbi Aharon moved to shield the women and bowed his head in reverence. "This young woman lived a life quite different in Portugal. Some, though not most, of our people allow their daughters, wives and sisters to speak their minds. That would, of course, change if it pleases you." He glared over his shoulder at Beatríz. "We will not make a nuisance of ourselves if you grant us safe harbor, and will show our gratitude with timely payments and a promise to stay out of your court system. We are self-sufficient. We are skilled and brave men, all."

A new voice joined, and the tall man jumped to the side and bowed. A plump man with a beard as white as broken waves, stepped around an ornately carved white partition

Beatríz had not noticed at the far end of the courtyard. After he spoke, the tall man translated into Castilian. "The *sharif* said, 'You are mistaken.'"

The *sharif* strode across the room and came very near to Beatríz. When he spoke, the tall man translated again. "You have brought more than brave *men*, it would seem." The *sharif's* eyes sparkled as he hitched his fabric belt higher over his paunch.

Beatríz lowered her eyes and tried to put her arm back through Rebecca's but Rebecca shrugged her off.

"The man we refused was weak and unlucky. He returned with his people to Barcelona and convinced them all to convert to Christianity. What if I had found a place for him and his people, and at the first sign of distress, they had run off leaving me without my taxes? Then where would I be?" He was looking directly into Beatríz's eyes, or rather, looked up into them.

She straightened her back, trying to look far more courageous than she felt, and to think of an answer that might please him. "If you had punished the captain and his crew, you could have confiscated the captain's goods, as well. Then the Jews would have been settled by now and making money, thereby lining your pockets with their labors. Instead, you have been missing that amount for these many months, and so I should think it is time that you welcome some hard working, skilled Jews into your city."

No one breathed, and more than just Beatríz prayed. If she were allowed to survive, if she were allowed to roam free, she promised not to be so bold and foolish as to open her mouth when she knew she ought to be quiet.

The *sharif* ran a finger along her cheek and she held her breath. As his touch drifted down her neck and onto her bosom, she closed her eyes and wished once again that she had not allowed herself to be brought as bait and been wise enough to stay silent. "Your women are immodest in many ways," he said, "but I like to see exotic foreign faces in my city, and I like spirited women. Would you give any of them to me as payment for your stay?"

"No," Rabbi Aharon said quickly, probably, Beatríz thought, more to protect his wife than her. "We have money, but I promised everyone safe passage and a free life. I keep my promises."

The *sharif* took one last liberty with Beatríz's flesh before turning his attention back to Rabbi Aharon. "The difficulty is this," explained the *sharif* in a thunderous voice, and the assistant continued to translate, "the Jews that are already established in this city pay their taxes to the king."

Aharon's voice was both placating and strong, a quality Beatríz admired. "We have no treaty such as the Jews who came here before us. Our taxes could be all yours."

"But when the king finds out, he will try to make you *his* Jews."

Rabbi Aharon's voice fairly purred. "I am sure a man of your stature could convince the king otherwise once you and I have a treaty between us."

In the silence that followed, Beatríz peered from below her brow. The *sharif* had put his hands on his waist and was pacing. He stopped and said firmly, "If your money comes regularly, you can stay." He added, "As for your living arrangements, you will have to squeeze into the Jewish quarter. Should you need more room, you may go beyond the outside wall of that quarter."

The translator drew up a document reflecting the agreement. Rabbi Aharon took the signed scroll and they left the palace to share the good news with their shipmates. Beatríz was able to relax a little as they walked away from the palace, but she would never be completely at ease while living in the city with the *sharif*, whose reputation for marrying girls against their will she learned of quickly. Having her face known and admired would not allow her to let down her guard as she had at times in Safi. And she knew she had to make amends with Rebecca once again.

The next round of negotiations was to be with the established rabbi of Oran, Rabbi Simuel. He was older than Rabbi Aharon, adopted the local custom of wearing a turban rather than a traditional hat and hooded cape, and appeared to have no family, judging by the lack of women or children's belongings in his poorly lit home. Books and documents littered every flat space, and the table was hastily cleared for this discussion.

Rabbi Simuel's reception was brusque, and he was not the least bit swayed by the presence of Beatríz or Rebecca or the news of skilled workers. "This quarter is crowded. Our community has its ways."

"I am not seeking to change your community. I am simply asking you to allow me to bring mine in."

The men went back and forth sometimes in Arabic, sometimes in Portuguese, sometimes in Castilian or Hebrew. Beatríz was amazed at Rabbi Simuel's speech, which was peppered with Arabic and spoken in an unfamiliar accent. She eventually learned that his family had lived in Oran since before his birth. They had been Valencians who left during the great conversions of the fourteenth century, and, being isolated, maintained the Castilian native to Valencia at that time. Rabbi Simuel's sentences included words that seemed very old-fashioned to Beatríz's ears, which, she thought, must have further muddied the men's conversation.

Without warning the men were on their feet and Rabbi Aharon was shouting, "I have a signed agreement with the *sharif*. There is nothing you can do to stop us from living here."

"*Sharifs* come and *sharifs* go. That paper is only as good as his life. You had best pray for the long life of this *sharif*."

Rabbi Aharon lowered himself slowly, the final thump as he sat echoing resignation. "We will stay, and so you and I must agree on duties. I am willing to make concessions. I will do the weddings and brisses of my people, but the fees can go to you."

Rabbi Simuel narrowed his eyes and added, "You will also contribute to my school. We are in need of a new roof and you will pay for it even if your students remain with you."

Rabbi Aharon gripped the bench. Beatríz could not see his face, but imagined it was as red as his neck. "The roof, yes. Once that is paid for, no more fees to the school. And my students *will* stay with me, you can be sure."

Beatríz was not aware of Rabbi Aharon having any students, unless the boys who assisted the rabbi were students. If they had not been, they *would* be after this conversation, no doubt.

As negotiations continued, talk halted occasionally as each man stopped to find a word in Arabic, Castilian, or Portuguese. Beatríz wondered if each man entirely understood the other. There were times when she could not follow the jumble of accents and words.

The next part, however, was clear and caught her attention as it concerned her.

Rabbi Simuel flicked his fingers in Beatríz's direction as if she were a passing dog. "Your women do not have their hair covered completely."

"No."

Beatríz touched the scarf she had been given by the Muslim woman during the siege. She no longer tied it as a veil, but it was still modest compared to the caplet and elaborate plaits of her days in Lisbon.

"They will follow our custom. It is too tempting, too distracting to see strands hanging loose." Rabbi Simuel's face wrinkled in distaste. The possibility that he did not like women at all, not simply their hair, crossed Beatríz's mind.

Rabbi Aharon, who Beatríz noticed loved to touch the bottom of his wife's braid when they passed on the ship, hammered the table. "No. You know that custom, unlike the Jewish laws of *halahah*, is up to each group. In this regard, we shall do as we wish."

"It is a dangerous thing to differ on such important matters. Let me give you an example of where the mixing of customs has been leading my people. I have noticed of late Jewish women leaning out of windows like the Muslims where they can be seen by passersby."

Rabbi Aharon leaned forward slightly. "Muslim women are not supposed to be seen either, true?"

Rabbi Simuel nodded, his face neutral.

"It is very hot here. If their men allow it, I should imagine it is because they are making exceptions based on reality, bending to accommodate life as it is lived rather than trying for an unattainable ideal."

Rabbi Simuel rose so quickly his bench fell over. "If this is how you view God's law, then I cannot see this arrangement working."

"Leaning or not leaning out of windows is not God's law. Custom and *halahah* are not the same!" Rabbi Aharon answered sharply. "You will have our money. What more is there to discuss?" He rose and stepped lithely over the bench. When he reached his wife, he turned back. "Except living arrangements. How shall we find rooms in this quarter?"

"Without my help." Rabbi Simuel walked out of the room and closed the door with a bang.

The Jews of Oran were more accommodating than their rabbi, and arrangements were made individually. Rabbi Aharon was honored with the privacy of an empty flat. Rebecca took Beatríz aside and murmured, "I cannot have you live with my family. There is little space in the rooms we have been given. I hope you understand." Beatríz did. A young unmarried woman in the home of a married man who was not her kin would be scandalous. And yet, she was without a home.

She was introduced to a tanner and his family. A shed at the back of his property was converted into sleeping quarters and two other single women who would live there, too. While it was a relief to have a place to live, the tanners and dyers used urine, dog feces, and bird droppings for their work, and Beatríz nearly gagged each time she entered their section of the Jewish quarter. And she could never help but worry that she carried the smell with her even when she left, though Rebecca never mentioned it. Rebecca did, however, ask Beatríz to leave her shoes outside during her visits.

The stink aside, Beatríz considered herself lucky. The other options were to live in tents on the outside of the city wall where the threat of marauding tribesmen was constant, or to bake on the rooftops under tarps that hardly protected newcomers from the elements. And though she did not live with the rabbi and Rebecca, she ate at their table for most meals and assisted Rebecca, who was slowing down as her pregnancy progressed.

Rebecca preferred to stay close to home and asked Beatríz to purchase goods from the market, giving Beatríz the opportunity to explore the city. Feeling protected by her association with the rabbi and more accustomed to being alone than in her early days in Safi, she finally felt able to enjoy the more adventurous aspects of her displacement.

At a first glimpse, Beatríz had thought Oran was just like Safi, but because Oran was under Muslim control, the goods and customs were more authentically of the Maghreb. The bags of spices held ground powders whose scent she did not recognize. Signs were written in Arabic swirls that she could not read. Baskets were woven in geometric patterns she had never seen. Shoes were made of cork and some had pointed toes. There was even a food – a fruit, she was told – that was oblong and bright yellow. These fruits grew in clusters and had thick inedible peels. She had heard Yusef speak of bananas, but never thought she would taste one. It took some time to work up the courage, but once she did, she fell in love with its solid texture and sweet taste. Whenever she could, she would buy one, though Rebecca asked her to keep both the fruit and the peel out of her home, for the syrupy smell made her sick to her stomach.

On one of her first forays, Beatríz's ears perked up at the sound of music, and she moved to an area not covered by vaulted roof or cloth awning. A small group of men in white turbans were chanting and pounding on small flat drums held in their hands while the women trilled. It sounded to Beatríz like birds in distress or in love, and after the initial shock of the sound, she found herself unable to keep from tapping her feet to the rhythm. Each woman was covered in elaborate jewelry made of what looked like silver coins and large pieces of amber. Coins even dangled from their head coverings. The robes of each varied dramatically in color. Beatríz marveled at one woman whose azure dress had large-plumed yellow birds woven directly into it.

"Berbers," a man said as he sidled next to her. "Mountain people. They mostly stay out of cities, but if they have business, they pass through. And armies hire them for their fierceness in battle. Terrifying horsemen."

"'Course, they're hard to control," said his friend.

Beatríz could not help but be surprised by the sight of the men addressing her. They were in turbans and robes, but they were speaking Castilian. They had likely left in 1492 and been in Oran as long as she had been in Lisbon. The clothes made sense. Why hold on to anything from your homeland when you were clearly not going back? And the flowing robe certainly seemed more comfortable in this heat than the cloaks and thick leggings the men she knew wore. But when she tried to imagine Yusef dressed in the loose fitting cotton robes that reminded her of nightshirts, she could not keep herself from chuckling.

Beatríz did not answer either man lest they take a reply as an invitation to familiarity. She continued to move through the bazaar sorry to leave the music behind.

During mealtimes, Rabbi Aharon told the women about the town and his work, and of the other Jews he was meeting. He told them that five years prior, after the expulsion from Spain, one large group of Jews had arrived with their own rabbi but he had died during a plague some time back. For the past few months, Portuguese Jews had been streaming in, though no group as large as theirs. Rabbi Simuel was charging them extra taxes, telling them it was the only way to keep peace with the *sharif*.

The largest challenge already presenting itself to Rabbi Aharon was the number of established residents seeking his advice and assistance. Rabbi Simuel seemed disinterested in helping anyone that did not bring him money, yet Rabbi Simuel hated anyone coming to Rabbi Aharon.

To Beatríz, the most pressing concern became the state of widows, or rather the women who could not prove they were widows – the *agunah*. Once Beatríz knew of their suffering, she could not stop thinking about it. A woman was not allowed to work, and without a husband to bring her money, she could not eat. Many of these women had no proof of the deaths of their husbands, and therefore could not remarry. As times grew harder and the city more crowded, the charity of the citizens shrank, and the women were growing more desperate. They begged daily, but more and more were starving to death. In fact, Rabbi Aharon had presided over two funerals within weeks of their arrival. Since there was no fee, Rabbi Simuel did not object to his performing the funeral rite, and Rabbi Aharon returned from each silent and disheartened.

One morning, Beatríz stared at her bread and broth. Hearing women's cries from outside, she did not have the heart to eat.

Rebecca closed the shutters, which did little to muffle the sound and much to cut out the breeze. "Beatríz, if you were to walk out there at this moment carrying that bowl, each woman would get a mere bite. What good would it do? You must eat and keep yourself strong."

"But how can I forget them?"

"Do not forget. But there are limits to what can be done."

Beatríz lifted the slice to her teeth and tore off a small piece. The bread felt like sand in her mouth. She listened again to the cries. "Do the rabbis not see what their stubbornness is doing?"

"It is not a matter of stubborn. It is the law," Rebecca insisted, standing very straight. "My husband does what he can, but he is one man in a large city."

"I know, but if he would agree to grant *halitza* to those women, he could save them."

"*Halitza?* It is serious to break a marriage contract, Beatríz. Without proof of death, he cannot release an *agunah* from the obligations of Levirite marriage."

Beatríz pushed her bowl away, the broth lapping over the brim and onto the table. "Ignoring the reality of their situation makes him complicit in their deaths."

Rebecca's gasp told Beatríz she had overstepped. Beatríz sat frozen in the uncomfortable silence, watching the spilled soup seep into the wood grain. She excused herself with an apology, uncertain of when she would be welcome again at Rebecca's table.

CHAPTER 16

Lacking occupation or company, Beatríz sat that afternoon in the courtyard of the tanner's house watching him work. He stood at a vat of urine, dipping the hide up to his elbows, working the material between his hands, and hanging it to dry. Then he took another hide, scraped it clean of hairs and flesh, and began again.

After a time, he stretched his arms above his head and wiped his hands on his stained pants. Even dry and washed, the tanner's forearms remained yellow and Beatríz imagined the stench that must have lingered on him. What could his wife have thought as he touched her with those hands? Even coming home from a long journey, Yusef had been able to quickly wash off the scent of his hard work, hardly pausing to do so before coming and greeting her with sweet kisses. She tried to imagine Yusef smelling foul. But it was honest work that allowed the tanner to support his wife and seven children. So what if it caused them to wrinkle their noses? Or perhaps his wife and children had come to associate that smell with comfort and care. There were, Beatríz was coming to understand, so many ways to live.

"Nothing to do at the rabbi's house?" the tanner asked, shading his eyes from the sun.

Beatríz shifted and smoothed her tattered skirt. "A disagreement."

"Ah. May I?" he asked, pointing to the ledge upon which Beatríz was perched. She nodded so he sat at a respectful distance. "Personal or religious?"

Beatríz thought a moment. It was, in fact, both. "Religious, I suppose."

The tanner shook his head and studied his cracked hands. "Rabbis complicate things. Or religion does. With a little time made for thinking, I imagine we average men could figure things out for ourselves."

Beatríz shrugged.

The tanner mused, "Rabbis have the luxury of time and learning. I suppose we pay them for their time so they can do the thinking for us. Since they produce nothing a man can hold, maybe they make rules to show us that they are doing something."

Beatríz said nothing, but wondered if he might be right.

"Five or six years ago, before the expulsion brought all of the Jews of Castile to our land, scholars here were irrelevant. They sat alone, discussing mysticism and philosophical ideas that interested no one but themselves. I tell you, they had brawls – actual fist fights – over issues that most Jews could not comprehend, let alone care about. With the expulsion, to the surprise of us all, these bookish, legal minded scholars," he said, spiting at the last word, "were suddenly rendered relevant!"

He rose and scooped a handful of water from a barrel into his mouth. Beatríz recoiled, wondering what the water could have tasted like. Then she realized it must have tasted like the rest of his day.

"When their communities fell apart," he continued as he covered the barrel, "these Jews from Toledo, Barcelona, Valencia, and so on, lost their true leaders – merchants. Great merchants who had helped shape society fled every which way, leaving common people grasping for guidance. Leadership and solace are now sought from rabbis."

The tanner spit again. He wiped his chin with the back of his hand and Beatríz stared with rapt attention, wondering how this ordinary man had come by such a vocabulary and the ability to formulate such thoughts.

"Then people began asking questions. Religious questions. Personal questions. Questions that until recently had only been academic suddenly needed answering – problems brought on by forced conversions, by voluntary conversions, by separations, by deaths, by dislocation. These problems had to be solved, and people turned to rabbis to solve them."

He grabbed a new hide and dipped it into the murky liquid. "In my family, the boys were raised to be learned, but as soon as I was able to earn money, I was forced to cease my studies. But my brother, the pride of our mother, became a scholar. From the time he was a boy, we only saw him on feast days and had to listen to him pontificate about things none of us cared about. I scoffed at him, dreaded him. Now I live under his rule."

"Who is your brother?"

"Rabbi Simuel," he said, as he slapped a skin into the pool of urine.

Beatríz spent the evening thinking about Rabbi Simuel, about brothers, loyalties, and changes. Her thoughts swirled until she felt sick. Where were her brothers? How many more changes and losses could she endure?

In the morning, despite her weariness from a poor night's sleep, she rose and left the tanner's compound. She could not hide forever, and she had to get out of the cloud of rot and waste that hung about the place. But with Rebecca angry with her, she had nowhere to go.

The stench was only slightly less pungent on the street, for behind each door on that street, another tanner or dyer did similar work. Beatríz took care not to let her skirt drag in the liquid that ran down the middle of the walkway and found a place to sit. She had been loitering for the better part of the day when a stranger stopped in front of her.

"I hear you write," said an old woman, her gnarled hands shaking as she pointed directly at Beatríz's face.

"I do," said Beatríz, sitting up taller, unsure of how the woman knew such a thing.

"Can you help me write a letter?"

"Of course. Do you have paper and ink?" Beatríz asked.

The woman rested her hands on her hips and jutted out her chin. "No. Do you?"

"I can get them and come back here. But it will cost you."

"I have money if you can write."

As she hurried to get the needed supplies, Beatríz recalled when her family lived in Dom Abrão's house, when they had first moved to Lisbon. Thinking all were out, she had settled in the courtyard with a quill and paper. A noise made her look up.

Yusef was standing in the doorway staring. "Are you . . . writing?" he had asked.

She had gripped the quill tightly. "Yes," she said reluctantly.

He chewed words he did not ask. Stepping forward, he asked, "How did you learn?"

"Solomon."

She worried he disapproved until he walked to her side. "You make your letters beautifully," he said. He traced the last one she'd written, and her face flushed as she imagined it was her skin he touched. He asked, "When I travel, will you write to me?"

"Of course," she said too quickly.

He opened his mouth to say something, then smiled and turned to go. But not before his fingers had brushed her knuckles and drifted all the way to her wrist. An accident? She thought not. Her skin tingled and she could not breathe. He liked her.

Writing had brought them together.

Beatríz's step hitched, thinking about how long it had been since she had received a letter from Yusef or anyone else she knew. She had to push such thoughts away, even the hope that she would be found here in Oran, and considered how she might turn writing into a business.

She thought about the woman in Safi who rented out her stall when Beatríz needed to write letters for Yusef. Beatríz had been more comfortable making arrangements with and emoting in front of a woman rather than a man, who might take her unaccompanied state or her fragility as an opportunity of his own. She realized that this might be a way for her to support herself for a while. She would charge little money at first and might gradually increase the fee if word spread that she was fair and competent.

Beatríz let it be known that she would set up in the square of the Jewish quarter. Before long, Beatríz had a small business that helped repay the tanner and his family for the food they had been giving her without complaint since Rebecca no longer fed her three times a day. The other women with whom Beatríz shared the spare room helped clean the house and minded the younger children; Beatríz was relieved to have her own way to contribute to the household.

One afternoon, a girl came to her and said she had no money, but wondered if Beatríz would help her anyway. Something in the child's expression stopped Beatríz from refusing. There was maturity in the young face, the kind etched by hardship. The girl did not want Beatríz's charity and asking for it seemed to be physically painful for her. Then she removed a ring and held it out for Beatríz to take, saying it had been her wedding ring and she would part with it if Beatríz demanded payment, but it was the last object of any value she had. Her cheeks were sunken and a scar grooved the length of her neck, disappearing under her bodice. She also had scars around her wrists.

Beatríz refused the ring and took out a sheaf of paper from her bag, forcing her gaze away from the white scars. "Do you know the words you would like me to write?" asked Beatríz, setting the paper on the rough plank she had co-opted for a desk.

"Yes. It is to Don Yonaton."

Señor,
In the name of God.
Healths and blessings to you.
I am writing once again to ask if you have news of your eldest son. If he is dead, please inform me of the details. If he is alive, please explain to him that I am in need of his

formal declaration that he will not have me as his wife. My last letter went unanswered. If you did not receive it, let me say again how sorry I am to bear the ill news of the death of your younger son, my husband. If you did receive my last letter but did not answer because you find the matter distasteful or disturbing, I am sorry. Yet I must remind you of the desperation of my state. Please send a reply with haste.

She paused. "And sign it Clara."

Beatríz closed the inkbottle and rubbed her hand, weary from writing so quickly to keep up with the torrent of words Clara offered. Clara's voice during the dictation was steady, business-like.

Beatríz had no blotter so she held the paper still to ensure the writing did not smear. "I am sorry to hear of your husband's – of your loss," Beatríz said. She could not help but consider that if she were already married to Yusef and something had happened to him, legally one of Yusef's brothers would have to marry her. If they did not want to, they would have to formally declare a break of their obligation and bond.

Clara leaned against the stones of the city wall and looked up at the gulls flying overhead. "I have nearly grown accustomed to my husband's absence," she said, her voice heavy. "I saw him drown during our escape and was finally able to make Rabbi Simuel accept the fact of it, but he insists that I get documentation from my husband's brother before granting me *halitza*."

"Yes, most rabbis are reluctant to release a woman from Levirite marriage," Beatríz said, thinking of her argument with Rabbi Aharon and Rebecca about this very issue.

"I have never met his brother and hardly knew of his

existence. I ought to have lied when Rabbi Simuel asked about him."

"Escape from where?"

"São Tomé."

Beatríz gasped. "The island of Jewish slave children? So you were taken from your parents the first time the Portuguese tried to force conversions?"

Clara pressed her lips together, keeping her eyes on the soaring birds.

"I heard dragons ate the babies," whispered Beatríz.

A cluck escaped Clara's lips, as if she had answered the question often and found it distasteful each time. "There are no dragons except in stories." After a time during which Beatríz was too embarrassed to speak, Clara added, "Large lizards."

Beatríz shivered, unsure if the lizards had, in fact, eaten babies. She could not bring herself to ask more about it, so she tried, "I thought no one escaped."

Clara leveled her gaze at Beatríz. "Few did."

"What did you do? As a slave."

Clara's face darkened and she touched her scarred wrists. "I will not talk of life there. My husband and I escaped and he drowned before we reached land."

"You seem so young. How old were you when you married?"

"Thirteen."

Beatríz expected more of story, but Clara offered nothing. Instead, she sank onto her haunches and huffed. "After all I lived through, it would seem my undoing will be a stubborn rabbi. A man here in Oran wants to marry me but I am still considered bound. For now, I have nowhere to live except the streets and he refuses to have me in his home without a legal marriage. Other women find men who are willing to bend and live together without the proper papers, but I found a moral man, God help me."

"Send your letter," Beatríz said, "but I will go to Rabbi Aharon and speak to him about this."

"He is the new one?"

"Yes. He is kind and thoughtful." Beatríz tucked the ink and quill into her satchel and buttoned it. "Now that I think of it, you ought to come with me. When he sees your scars and hears your story, I cannot imagine he will deny you."

The women stood and color rose in Clara's cheeks. "Would it help if my Davíd came with us?"

Beatríz started at the name. Could it be? No, of course not. She wondered if her Davíd was well. – Hers? She pushed away the thought of his captivity and the guilt that came with the memory of him.

"What a thing to find another Davíd," she began to think, and then realized how many "Davíds" she had known growing up. But back home it had been "Davíd the miller" or "Davíd the dyer" or "Davíd, the son of Avraham the tailor." There had been no need for further clarification. Growing up in Toledo, the population of Jews all seemed to know one another, and then in Lisbon, after a few months, she felt she knew everyone in her community.

But this Davíd Clara spoke of was just "Davíd." Davíd from where? Davíd who did what? It occurred to her that like this Davíd, she was not known and she did not know others. The region was littered with people cast out from their homes, moving frequently to find a better place in the world – a place that would have them, a place that might give them joy or at least some peace. With desolation, she grasped that it might be a very long time before she found such a place or knew her neighbors so well once again.

Forcing the quaver out of her voice, she said to Clara, "Perhaps you ought to bring Davíd to Rabbi Aharon. Meet me within the hour."

Beatríz waited down the street from the rabbi's house feeling apprehensive about facing Rebecca once again.

Clara strode around the bend confidently, pulling Davíd behind her. Since being offered a glimmer of hope, Clara had transformed. She turned and said something to Davíd, who put his arm through hers. He was older than she, but not shockingly so, and was bent a bit at the waist as if he had been carrying heavy loads for years and had grown accustomed to that position. Enthusiastically, Clara introduced them and Davíd responded with a sheepish nod. Together they went to Rabbi Aharon's door, and to Beatríz's relief, his assistant Yoshuah, not Rebecca, answered and escorted them in.

Rabbi Aharon greeted them warily from behind a stack of papers. Once Clara had told her story, he eyed Beatríz and glanced over his shoulder – to see if Rebecca was within hearing or not, she felt sure. He rose and suggested they go for a walk. As they made their way toward the docks, Rabbi Aharon's eyes only met Beatríz's once, at which point he sighed and shook his head almost imperceptibly.

"Clara, Davíd, I understand your situation," he began once they were outside the city walls. "But Rabbi Simuel has told you what needs to be done."

"You believe," Beatríz interrupted, "that some unknown man has more claim to her than Davíd?"

"Well, yes."

"What if the brother is already married? Is having multiple wives legal?" Beatríz scoffed.

"In these cases, the second wife would be of a different sort. Not someone to share the man's bed, but more of a ward." He added, "It is the law."

"And what was the need for such a law?" Beatríz pressed.

Rabbi Aharon absently tugged at whiskers on his cheek. "To ensure that a woman would be taken care of in the event of her husband's death."

"But Davíd is willing to care for Clara. How can what you propose make more sense?"

Rabbi Aharon opened his mouth and closed it. "Might I suggest a compromise?" he asked, looking at Beatríz rather than the couple at the heart of the argument. "The letter should be sent. If there is no reply within one month, I will perform the ceremony myself. I will bypass Rabbi Simuel's directive. One month."

Everyone standing there knew that it would be highly unlikely that a letter would return within that time, and that this compromise was in fact a victory for the couple. And for Beatríz.

Clara threw her arms around Davíd, who stumbled back at first, then held her tightly and whispered something in Clara's ear that made her laugh. He kissed her cheek and thanked Rabbi Aharon. Clara thanked Beatríz and said she would come visit her in the square soon.

Beatríz and Rabbi Aharon were left standing alone.

Rabbi Aharon cleared his throat. "Rebecca will not like hearing about this."

"Rebecca is lucky that you are alive and healthy," Beatríz said, her eyebrows raised. "Lucky. Many are not, and these laws of men —"

"Laws of God."

Beatríz clenched her hands and continued, "These laws are

causing great suffering. If you died tomorrow, would Rebecca be able to find your brother and force him to care for her and the coming child?"

Rabbi Aharon lowered his head. "He was going to Naples. I hear there has been complete chaos with half a dozen armies attempting to seize control of the city. I have not heard from him at all."

They stood in silence for a moment then he added, "Beatríz, it seems you have skills I could use. Would you be interested in continuing your letter writing at my home and bringing my attention to matters that might be seen... differently?"

With little hesitation and much amazement, Beatríz agreed.

He began leading Beatríz back within the city walls. "Rebecca misses you. She knew I did not agree with you and she was willing to lose you rather than to question me. She has been so fragile since we were forced out of *Sepharad* and away from everyone she loved. I have been the only constant in her life. And she knows that the nature of my job is to make unpopular decisions at times, so she is determined to shield me from criticism and to support me when others do not."

Beatríz nodded. She would have defended Yusef the same way.

As they approached the square that would send them in separate directions, he said, "I will explain to her what has transpired today, and perhaps she will have you back as a guest in our home. If not, she will have to grow accustomed to having you as a worker."

Rebecca was cold to Beatríz at first, but softened when she heard the women's stories and saw how her husband was able to help them with little trouble. Rabbi Simuel objected vociferously and threatened to go to the *sharif*, but never did. He also denounced Rabbi Aharon to his congregation, which only served to swell the numbers of Rabbi Aharon's followers. It was one of the few happy conclusions Beatríz experienced since leaving Lisbon.

Rabbi Aharon also decided that given the times, finding dead husbands' brothers was too difficult and made exceptions whenever fitting. He still wanted evidence of the husband's death, however, and that proved nearly impossible for some widows and abandoned women. Beatríz made extra money by forging letters from supposed witnesses, and she never knew if Rabbi Aharon realized the handwriting was actually her own.

CHAPTER 17

Beatríz's ambivalence about her community and her religion deepened. She felt lost and disconnected, not wanting to tie herself emotionally to people who might soon vanish anyway from disease or siege or another expulsion, and was frustrated by Jewish customs and laws that she had never bothered to question in the past. She found reasons to avoid services, occasionally wandered into a church, and often stopped to listen to the call to prayer emanating from the minarets.

In defending her choice to accept conversion, her sister, Astruga had snapped, "People change religions like they change shirts." Beatríz mulled over that statement often. She felt naked with no ritual, no family, and no man. And yet, she could not change her circumstances and could not decide where she belonged.

Beatríz was both relieved and dismayed to be in the rabbi's house when Rebecca's labor pains began. Beatríz excused herself from her letter writing. The midwife was sent for, but was otherwise occupied and explained that with a first birth, there was no rush, leaving Beatríz to tend to Rebecca alone.

As the night and Rebecca's suffering dragged on, Rebecca grew frantic. "Do not let me die, Beatríz."

"Rebecca, you are not going to die."

"How can anything with this much pain and blood end in anything but my death?"

Beatríz smiled. "I might not have done this myself, but I have witnessed a few births, including that of my sister, Reyna. I am fairly certain that pain and blood are the natural course of things. You know this to be true."

Rebecca nodded, her pale face drenched with sweat. "I need to walk. Will you help me?"

Beatríz obliged and circled the room with Rebecca, stopping when Rebecca needed rest or when she doubled over. When she could, Rebecca would speak. "I always thought I would have my mother and my sisters aid me when my time came. But I did not conceive when we were still in Valencia, and it has taken nearly six years for me to be able to carry a child this long. Loss after loss has been agonizing for us both, and I came to think I was being punished for some sin."

"Rebecca, far more sinful women have had children. In fact, it seems that sinful women have more of them, no?"

Rebecca raised her eyebrows and then began to laugh. But her mirth did not last long for new, more intense pains brought back her panic.

At long last, the midwife entered. Her assistant soon followed, holding a steaming mug. With soothing words of encouragement, the midwife held it to Rebecca's lips. Whatever the brew, it calmed Rebecca. The midwife checked under Rebecca's gown and patted her knees, saying all was well. Beatríz stepped into the shadows of the room and watched as Rebecca grunted and squatted, shifted and howled until the sky began to pink.

When the midwife finally pulled the baby out, Beatríz was overcome by wonder, followed hard by aching jealousy. To see Rebecca holding the child and kissing it, then presenting it to Aharon who wept with joy and kissed his wife, stung Beatríz. She was aware that to feel anything but delight was petty, yet she could not help but wish that the baby had been her own and that the kisses were from Yusef. She felt nearly sick with wishing and regret. Could a year already have passed since they were together?

Around the time the baby began to sit up, Rabbi Aharon leapt up from a pile of letters just unloaded from an incoming ship. He raced across to Beatríz, holding a paper out to her. When she saw the writing, her hands shook.

> *My love,*
>
> *I have been writing to you for some time, but not having received a response these many months, I am losing heart. Feeling sure of your constancy I do not fear that you have found another, and cannot allow my mind to think the worst. And so I assume you have left Safi and pray that some kind-hearted soul knows for which shores you were bound and will send this onward.*
>
> *Luck is not on our side. I have been detained by wars throughout the region. Every attempt to cross the Mediterranean has been thwarted. At each port and on the open sea, the captain has repeatedly been told to turn back. This madness cannot last forever, but I do not know how long you must wait.*
>
> *There are no safe harbors. I spend hour upon hour pondering our future. I have begun to wonder – should*

we find one another – *if we would not be better returning to Portugal and living as Christians. A compromised life might be better than no life at all. I hope you do not think ill of me for suggesting such a thing. We will likely be denied reentry, but it might be possible.*

As always, the hours away from you torment me. My love remains undiminished by time and distance. Above, I crossed out my words of doubt. I <u>will</u> find you and we will be together.

Ever yours,
Yusef

Beatríz tried to see through her tears to read it again, but failed. She heard Rabbi Aharon ask the woman with whom Beatríz was working to come back another time, and Beatríz felt hands on her shoulders.

"Is the news bad?" Rebecca whispered.

Beatríz had been crying from relief at knowing that Yusef was still alive, but then considered the question. He was unable to reach her. And yet the letter had. How was it possible? If the letter had come mostly by land, why could he not? If it came by sea, how could the captain not have found the same route? It was maddening and Beatríz was not sure how much more she could take.

Unable to speak, she held out the letter to Rebecca who passed it to her husband to read.

Rabbi Aharon exclaimed, "Wonderful that the letter arrived at all. You will see. Yusef will come through that door any day and you can go back to Lisbon if you like. Or begin anew."

A young woman's voice came from near the door. "Yusef from Lisbon?"

Beatríz's heart flipped. She swallowed the lump in her throat and scratched out, "Yes. He is a merchant. Son of Dom Abrão."

"He is dead."

All of the air was pushed out of her. She neither blinked nor moved. Everything was loud and silent at once. Someone was holding her, but the touch felt distant.

"No. I have a letter," she heard a voice say and realized it was her own.

"Letter or not, he – he is dead."

She blinked, silent for a moment, taking in the woman's words, then exploded. "Liar!"

The shorter woman bowed her head and said, "*Senhorita*, I have no reason to say anything but the truth."

"Then you are mistaken," Beatríz insisted, her voice firm, but her legs turning to liquid. "It could not be the same Yusef."

"But I assure you –"

"No!" screamed Beatríz. "You are sure of nothing. Nothing!"

Rabbi Aharon put a hand on her arm to calm her. She pulled away from his grasp, but when she saw sympathy painted across his face, her outrage drained away, along with her ability to stay on her feet. When she slumped, his hands and Rebecca's were there to catch her.

She could hardly get enough air in her lungs to say, "It cannot be true."

"Beatríz," Rabbi Aharon said gently, "let them speak."

"It cannot be true," she said again, to herself as much as anyone else.

Someone pressed a cup of wine into her hands, and after a few sips, she rose. Standing tall, jaw set, she said, "I need to know."

"Explain how you came to know Yusef," he said to the women.

"We met him on the ship," answered the shorter one whose tangled dark hair and sunken eyes Beatríz suddenly hated.

"What ship?" Rabbi Aharon asked.

"One attempting to get to Algiers. We were all together for nearly two months, sent from port to port."

"You are Beatríz, then?" asked the other woman.

Beatríz sucked in breath at the sound of her own name and nodded tightly.

"He spoke of you often," she explained. "He shouted at the captain that he was not doing enough, that you were waiting, and that a way had to be found to reach you." The woman smiled at the memory and Beatríz hated that smile, for it was of a moment Beatríz had not been there to share.

Rabbi Aharon cleared his throat and asked, "How did he, uh, die?"

Tears sprang into Beatríz's eyes and she stood rigid.

The women looked at each other and the first one answered. "Our ship was boarded at sea. The men were dragged off to the galleys." She said nothing more and silence seeped into every corner.

Eventually, Rabbi Aharon stabbed the air with, "And?"

"No one survives the galley, sir. No one escapes. He is gone."

Beatríz felt herself surfacing. No tale of stabbing or hanging. No beheading or fever. Suddenly clear, she said, "So he could be alive."

Rabbi Aharon put his hand on her arm. "The galleys are as good as dead. You know that."

The woman with the sunken eyes said, "Our men were being beaten as the chains were put on them. The sailors said anyone who struggled would not survive for long and that there were always men to be found in other ports to take the place a fool who resisted."

The other woman added, "Beatríz, he was fighting fiercely, shouting that you were waiting. The lash came upon him many times and his back was ripped –"

"Enough," shouted Rabbi Aharon, throwing his arms around a swooning Beatríz. "Is there anything else you must add – sparing any unnecessary details?"

The blond one wrung her hands and said softly, "A storm of surprising strength came without warning within the week that sank and capsized many ships."

The pause that followed was unbearable. Beatríz slipped to the ground when the other one added, "Including Yusef's."

On her hands and knees, Beatríz screamed, "She did not see him die! She does not know!"

"Yes, Beatríz. Yes," Rabbi Aharon said, stroking her back. "Yoshuah, take these women into the kitchen and find them something to eat," he instructed someone. "Rebecca, help me bring her to our room."

"She does not know!" shouted Beatríz, fighting against their clutches.

Beatríz screamed and cried and gasped and paced the small room Rebecca shared with her husband and baby. Rebecca had what Beatríz wanted and could never have with Yusef. Not ever. But Yusef was not dead. He could not be. If he was gone, what was left for her?

Each time Rebecca tried to reach out for Beatríz, Beatríz pushed her away. But Rebecca was not daunted and tried again. And again.

The sun set on her grief and Beatríz continued to cry. She thought she had no more tears left and then more would come. Beatríz refused food or drink and sat alone keening when Rabbi Aharon finally insisted that Rebecca step away and eat with him. When Rebecca returned, Beatríz was rocking on the edge of the chair staring at the cracks in the wall, whimpers rising and falling from her lips.

"Beatríz," Rebecca said, resting her hand on Beatríz's knee, "it is nearly time for sleep. You will stay with us, I hope."

Beatríz merely rocked.

"What will we do with her?" Rabbi Aharon asked.

Rebecca answered, "She can sleep on the kitchen floor if you can get blankets. Have Yoshuah ask the neighbors if they have some, or even an extra mattress."

Eventually Beatríz was led to the kitchen, but she did not lie down. She continued to sit and rock, lost in the loop of agony, imagining Yusef's split back, the lash coming down upon him as he was chained to a bench where he would row until he died, the waves crashed over the boat, breaking it apart, sweeping him under, dragging him down. She clutched at herself, beginning again with the lash on his back.

"Grab hold of him!" she cried.

She woke to Rebecca stroking her back, shushing her. "Wake up, Beatríz. A dream, Beatríz. There is no one here."

Forcing open her eyelids, Beatríz realized Rebecca was right. There was no one. She was no one. Without Yusef, what was she? Her entire purpose had been to wait and then to be his wife. Without that, what was she? What was she to do?

Looking around the kitchen, Beatríz saw the room with new eyes. It was small and dull and domestic. A compromise.

Not her home. She did not want to be there. She rose and took hold of her bag, starting for the door.

"Where are you going?" asked Rebecca.

"To the docks. Someone must be leaving for somewhere near Crete. Perhaps those women are mistaken and he washed ashore."

"Washed ashore where? Who knows where he was or where the ship was?"

Beatríz had to steady her legs. "I have to try and find him. I cannot stay here and wonder."

"Beatríz, you cannot go."

Beatríz spun around. "I can and I will. There is no reason for me to stay."

"At least have Aharon write you a letter of introduction."

"What would it say? Who I am? Who am I, Rebecca? Betrothed of Yusef? Daughter of Don Vidal? No. They are gone. I am not even Beatríz of Lisbon or Toledo. I belong to no one. I am nothing."

"You are the guardian of their memories. You are a letter writer. You are my friend."

"I will have to be all of those things from somewhere else, Rebecca. I cannot stay." Beatríz began walking away, but stopped. How could she leave Rebecca so coldly? Putting her arms around Rebecca, she whispered, "Thank you for everything. I…" Too many words flooded at her, and she was overcome by emotion. She could not allow herself to feel anymore, so she kissed Rebecca's cheek and headed to the waterfront, every inch of her aching.

At the docks, she hesitated. The sea held dangers known and unknown. But leaving by land was impossible. She had to take her chances.

She found a small sailboat in the final stages of preparation and forced herself not to think. She approached and a man stepped forward who spoke accented Portuguese.

"I am Onur," said the short man with kind eyes. "Do you need help?"

"Yes," she began. "I want to go."

"Where?"

Beatríz shrugged.

Onur grimaced and turned to the man standing with him, a stern looking fellow who shook his head as Onur spoke. The man muttered something elaborate and Onur explained, "My brother, Yavuz, says he does not trust a woman who does not know where she is going, and that women aboard are bad luck."

"What about her?" Beatríz asked, pointing at a veiled woman near the hold.

"Nesrin is my wife. Yavuz thinks we should not bring her on our trade journeys, but ever since our village was attacked, I refuse to leave her behind."

Beatríz's heart clanged with the wish that Yusef had held the same conviction. Of course, she might have ended up at the bottom of the sea with him if she had, but would that have been worse?

Yavuz looked her over, grumbled, and gestured dismissively before turning his back to her, yet he did not walk away. Beatríz might have been offended another day but had no energy left to feel anger with anyone; she merely had the will to lurch away from the city of Oran.

"I can pay," she said, reaching with uncooperative fingers to remove the ruby earrings that Yusef had brought her as a gift. "I must leave here."

Yavuz, his back still to her so she could see fine hairs

sticking out from under his turban, said to the wind in perfect Castilian, "How do you know you can trust us?"

"I know nothing." She added quietly, "Please bring me to another land."

Onur spoke to his brother insistently in words Beatríz did not know. Yavuz crossed his arms and said something sharp in reply. Onur turned and spoke to Nesrin, who lowered her head as she answered his question.

"My wife thinks we should oblige, and adds that she would welcome the company. Yavuz agrees, but says it is against his will. His name means 'stern' and you will find our parents named him well. You may, then, ride with us."

Beatríz let the earrings fall into Onur's palm before he helped her aboard. Watching him tuck Yusef's gift into his purse was so painful that Beatríz nearly snatched them back and ran to Rebecca. But she could not give in to that weakness.

She allowed Onur to lead her to Nesrin. Nesrin's smiling eyes, the only part of her face showing from behind her *niqab*, were a shade of green Beatríz recalled from late summer trees in Toledo. Nesrin pointed to Beatríz's bag and then to a corner near the steps that led below deck. The area below was small, Beatríz would sleep and sit on the spot where she threw her bag.

As they moved out to sea, relief and regret battled equally within her. Beginning anew might help her forget all that she had been. At the very least, she thought, her life could not get any worse.

CHAPTER 18

Day after day, Beatríz helped Nesrin as she best could, but, as there was little to do, she mostly sat and thought of all that was lost. Watching the sun rise and set, she pushed away as much despair as she could, turning herself numb. They seemed to sail endlessly on a sea of emptiness.

But one afternoon, Yavuz cried out and pointed. When Beatríz looked, she saw a large ship headed directly toward them. Onur and Yavuz yelled and scurried, and soon Beatríz understood why. A solid black banner whipped atop the towering mast. Pirates.

The men huddled together then scattered about shouting orders to one another. Beatríz moved to sit by Nesrin who shrank into a shadow not daring to look over the side at the approaching enemy as Beatríz did. Beatríz felt certain that the pirates would just rob them of anything valuable and leave, but that did not keep her breath from catching in her throat.

The large ship came along side theirs with raised oars and lowered sails. Someone called down to them, but Beatríz could not understand what was said. The men on her boat looked at one another and Onur shook his head. The pirate pointed his sword and repeated himself. Onur shook his head again. The pirate motioned to his shipmates, a handful of whom leapt onto the rail, took hold of ropes, and began to lower themselves over the side.

Onur walked quickly, knife in hand, to where Beatríz sat. Beatríz shrank back, but he was coming for Nesrin. In one swift move, Onur had kissed his wife and slit her throat. Beatríz screamed as blood spilled over his fingers and soaked the front of Nesrin's dress, then watched with fascinated horror as Onur laid his wife's head gently on the deck. He looked at Beatríz and held out the knife, questioning rather than threatening. Beatríz stuck her hands in front of her, hoping to shield herself from a blow.

"They said they will take our women. You do not want that," he said stepping closer, the sun glinting off the blade.

"Don't," she said, bracing herself for the cut.

Instead Onur threw the knife to Yavuz who stood in front of the goods they had planned to sell in Constantinople. Before Onur had time to help his brother, a pirate sliced Yavuz with a sword. He fell to his knees cursing and clutching his side, calling to his brother. When Onur moved forward to help him, the pirate rested the sharp blade against Yavuz's throat, daring Onur to take another step.

Beatríz was so busy watching the men that she did not realize anyone had come up behind her. Suddenly, she was jerked to her feet.

"N – nu – no!" she stammered.

She was handed to another man who pulled her up along the rope with him as if she weighed no more than a pillow. Beatríz looked at the small sailboat disappearing beneath her,

Yavuz still writhing in pain, and Onur staring helplessly at the mayhem. She was dropped onto the deck and scuttled to her feet. Bundles were thrown up and over the rail including her own. She knew Yusef's letters were in there but made no move to retrieve them.

"What will you do with me?" she stammered. "I cannot row."

The sailor who held her laughed. "We will use you as we please. As long as you please us. You look pleasing enough." He ran his hand along her bottom and she jumped away.

Another pirate grabbed her and stuck his hand down her bodice. Beatríz screamed and tried to move, but he held her tight and kissed her.

"No!" shouted someone, and Beatríz exhaled with relief assuming whomever it was planned to protect her honor and her body. A stocky man, sunburned where hair should have been, came closer. "No free tastes. You know how this works. Are you a virgin?" he asked her.

She nodded, her bottom lip trembling.

He smiled broadly. "Not for long. Gentlemen, get your purses and your cocks ready. As always, the highest bidder breaks her."

The men shouted out sums while she struggled and begged. Finally, a hairy man with an open shirt was named the victor. He stepped forward and called for them to bring her below and then to hold her down. She kicked and wriggled until their grips were so hard she knew bruises would linger as a reminder of this horrible moment. The man unfastened his thick leather belt with a clink that Beatríz swore she heard above all over sounds, and he dropped his thick wool pants. She screamed as he threw her skirt over her chest. He yanked her hips so her knees bent and the men still holding her ankles stepped around to the side of the table. Her arms were stretched over her head and when she tipped her chin to see who was holding them, she felt a searing between her legs.

Her eyes felt pushed out of their sockets and ringing filled her ears. As he pushed further into her, stretching her inside with cruel power, she imagined Yusef standing in the room trying to stop them. Her flesh ripped more and tears swirled her love away. She screamed again. Or he did. Or both. He collapsed onto her and the crowd cheered.

And like that, she was ruined.

If there were a crumb of kindness in these men, they would have left her to her pain and dismay. But they lined up and paid the first mate for the pleasure of being next inside the newly deflowered girl. When at last every man had finished, she thought she would be released. Instead she was thrown in a cell with nothing but old straw scattered on the floor and a pot. Broken in every way, she leaned against the hold and wept.

However memorable, the first time was not the worst. Beatríz wished she could disappear each time they came for her, wished she could make her mind linger elsewhere. But Beatríz saw every filthy hand, every fat stomach, every nose hair. She felt every thrust and scratch of stubble, every scrape at her back, every hand forcing her arms to be still. They came for her and came for her and came and came, and there seemed to be no end to it.

Alone, hour after hour, day after day of dreading the next time she would be dragged from her cell, she thought of her pain, thought of her fear, and sometimes thought of her past.

A memory that returned again and again was a time she and Yusef had taken a walk with her brother as a chaperone. Solomon had skulked off, leaving the couple under a

Jacaranda tree to plan their futures.

Beatríz, who did not want to be left behind again when Yusef went to trade, had announced, "I will become a merchant. Travel the seas with you. Gather spices and wool and bring them from port to port in a ship we own together."

Yusef's eyes had danced. "But who would trade with a woman?"

"Other women merchants. There must be some. We will band together and make more money than anyone would expect of mere females."

He leaned back on his elbows in a pile of petals. "And where would these women be found?"

"Hmm. The Venetians are immoral and the Ottomans have new ideas. I dare say I would find a partner or two in those lands."

He nodded sagely. "The beginnings of a fine plan. There are female traders in some ports, but the seas are dangerous."

"You say that, but I do not believe you," she said airily.

His mouth twisted. "What would you do if pirates boarded our ship?"

She picked up a twig and held it out, then swished it from side to side. "Fight them off and take the treasures from their hold."

He tugged the twig out of her hand, snapping it to prove how weak she was. "They are dangerous men, Béa. They would take you from me and keep you for themselves."

"Keep me for what?"

He pressed his lips together and his gaze slid to the ground.

"Oh," she said, her stomach flipping in discomfort. Not ready to be serious, she asked suggestively, "And if you were a pirate, what would you do to me?"

His eyes met hers and he raised himself up on his knees. "If I were a pirate? Well . . ." He looked her over. "I would choose you above any other girl we captured." He ran his fingers through her loose hair. "I would make you my own." He let his hands settle on her hips, making her body burn as he inched forward, their chests touching. "I would never let you go." He kissed her hard, and she lost all thought. All care.

"A-hem."

She pried her eyes open, and saw her brother standing above them. Yusef leapt away, a rush of air coming between them. Modesty ought to have made her leap, as well, but all she could think was that she wanted Yusef pressing against her again.

"I think it best that we all go back home," Solomon said.

How could they have joked about this?

A few days into her imprisonment, the captain came to the gate and pointed at Beatríz. "My cabin boy is getting you a basin. I want you to wash before you come to me."

Beatríz's stomach turned and she nodded. He was the one man on the ship who had not touched her, and she nearly wept to think of what he, as the most powerful, might do.

"Do you have lice?" he asked.

She knew she did. She had been itching like mad since her first night in the cell. But she shrugged, not sure why he wanted to know.

"Have the boy comb out your hair. It will take a while. Do not let him rush."

The door was unlocked and Beatríz shuffled to the galley, for she ached inside and out. She had not walked freely for so many paces in a while and the movement jarred her. The captain left her with a boy, eight or nine years of age, who was pouring a pan of steaming water into a tub. Beatríz wondered who he was, where his mother might be.

The boy handed her a grayish cloth and stepped back. He made no move to leave and she realized she was to wash in front of him. She held the strap of her *camisa* between her fingers, poised to remove the cloth, and bit her cheek. While she knew every man on the boat had seen her naked, had touched places meant for only Yusef, she still wished that this boy was not seeing her like unclothed. She slipped the strap over her shoulder and he turned away, attending to some potatoes that needed peeling.

She stepped into the tub that was too small to sit in, and bent to wet the cloth which grew brown almost immediately as she wiped at her legs. Bruises emerged – purple, green, pink, and red– some healing, some fresh, on her ankles, her calves, her thighs. She squatted and felt sure that a coarse brush could not scrub the filth all away. If she had lye, she would have shoved it inside herself to burn away what had been left. Burn away what was left of her.

The water was so murky she could no longer see her feet. She asked the boy if there was more clean water and, without looking up, told her he was heating it for her hair. She tried to clean her fingernails, caked with dirt, blood, and skin. She scrubbed her neck, wincing when she touched the bite marks an especially excited younger sailor had made on her the night before. More bruises emerged on her arms and wrists. Her skin reminded her of a full moon, cratered and shadowed in spots. Without being asked, the boy came to wash her back and took the cloth and scrubbed. It was odd to Beatríz to be touched without malice, without lust. She closed her eyes and imagined Reyna running warm rivulets of water the length of her spine.

He stepped away and handed her a cloth that she used to dry and wrap her body. "You don't want to get back in that shift," he said balling up her *camisa* and tossing it into the fire. The boy walked back with a basin and a comb and a clean cloth for her to wrap herself in. "Best sit on that chair and lean your head back, Miss," he said.

He lathered her hair with a sharp smelling something, nothing like the flowery soap her mother had the servants make. Her mother said perfumes would attract a man and encouraged Beatríz to use them often. Beatríz never wanted to attract a man again. If only the pungent soap was strong enough to make her invisible.

The boy stood on a box behind her chair and yanked the comb through her hair. She heard snaps as strands broke off. At first she thought it hurt, but she realized it was not real pain and let her mind quietly shut down. She was safe for a while and though he tugged and picked, she actually fell asleep sitting upright.

When the boy was done, he told her to stay where she was and offered her soup. "Can't have you dirty yourself by going back in there," he said, gesturing with a ladle at the cell. Beatríz did not turn to look at her residence, but nodded and lifted the spoon in agreement.

Bluish light streamed through a porthole. The cook entered and clanged about. The men were coming to eat soon and Beatríz tried to fold in on herself as if that would make her undetectable to them. The captain thumped down the stairs before the other men and held out a hand to help her up. Reluctantly she took it and rose, still wrapped in the cloth from her bath.

"Where are your clothes?" he asked.

"Burned," she said.

"Something clean," he called impatiently to the boy, who ran off into the captain's quarters. The captain walked, still holding Beatríz's hand. It was a familiar gesture that stung Beatríz as she thought of strolling with Yusef along the docks.

The boy held out a nightshirt and the captain screwed up his face. "Something for a woman, idiot," he said. Then he snapped, "Never mind. Go." The captain closed the door behind the scampering child, and handed the nightshirt to Beatríz. She lowered her eyes and readied herself to be naked in front of another man, but then the captain walked to the window and looked out, giving her an unexpected moment of privacy.

When her turned back, he smiled at the nightshirt that nearly touched the ground. "Perhaps something more suitable tomorrow," he said.

So was she to stay with him until morning?

She winced as he walked toward her.

"No need to fear," he said. "I do not need to attack women to get them into bed." His soothing voice frightened and calmed her at once. It would not be unlike a man to feign kindness only to hurt her more than the others, she felt certain. And yet, perhaps he was true. "I will not touch you if you do not want me to. But stay here tonight," he said. "I grow lonely without a bedfellow."

He patted the mattress but she did not move.

He nodded. "They have abused you. I can understand your reluctance, but if I had wanted to simply have you, it would have been done by now." He waved her over and she perched on the edge of the bed, ready to run, though she knew it would do no good if she did. "You look tired. Would you like to sleep?"

Beatríz could not make sense of the sudden change in her circumstances. Violence had become so common that she no longer trusted gentility. Or was he the proverbial wolf in sheep's clothing? Either way, she was exhausted and a bed with actual sheets was too inviting. If she were molested, at least it would be on something less splintery than the mess table of prior nights.

She slid onto the bed and nearly sighed at the cool softness. To her surprise, the captain said, "Good. I have some charts to check. I will lock the door behind me, so enjoy the quiet."

Before allowing herself to plummet into sleep, she watched him leave. She noted the crispness of his collar, the precise cut of his blond hair, and that he had not stunk when he came near, in either breath or in body. He did as he promised, locking the door, the jangle of the keys fading into the chorus of voices and clattering flatware.

Beatríz awoke with a start. She was not alone. The captain was . . . at his table. Reading. Her heart thumped against the mattress and she lay still hoping not to attract his attention.

"Good sleep?" he asked without lifting his head. She did not answer and he continued to read.

Beatríz stared at him unable to rest, ready to flee or fight, though he did not turn his gaze from the leather bound tome. The light outside the window disappeared and they floated once again in anonymous darkness.

At last he turned out the lantern and approached. Beatríz's heart sped up. The captain sat with his feet on the ground, but set his hand on her leg. "Would you mind if I touched you?" he asked.

Unsure of what game he was playing but unable to lie, she answered with a quaking voice, "Yes. I mind."

He took his hand back. "I told you, I will not force myself on you." He kicked off his boots and wriggled under the sheets. "I would ask, however, that you stay in the bed with me. I come to miss my wife at night and would appreciate a warm body next to mine."

"Wife?" she whispered, unable to reconcile this brutal life with a domestic one.

"Of course," he said, raising himself onto one elbow. "Many of my men have wives in some port or other. Men take liberties on the sea that might not otherwise be acceptable. And life is more . . . disposable out here, as well. We fight. We fuck. We die." He shrugged. "Our wives like the money they get from our journeys and we like the freedom. I think they like being left alone while we're gone, truth be told."

Had Yusef taken such liberties? She could not imagine her sweet love holding down some girl and having his way with her. But were the wives of these men thinking the same? What of the men on the ship she had ridden with Miriam? Pirate or sailor, she had not been able to see much of a difference. She prayed Yusef had never done unto another's as he would not have had done unto his.

The captain rolled over and went to sleep. Despite her best efforts to remain alert, the soft bed pulled her below the surface of consciousness.

In the morning, the captain rose, pissed in a pot, and dressed. Through slit eyelids, Beatríz watched him rummage through a trunk and pull out a white slip, shake it, hold it in front of him, and lay it on the mattress. When Beatríz was a child, servants would flutter her *camisa* onto the bed and leave her to her rest as the captain did for Beatríz now.

The captain locked her in, and she knew it was to protect

his freshly cleaned property from others more than to keep her from running, for where was she to go? She sat up and touched the slip. Where did it come from? Another girl, no doubt. One who shared his bed. One who had been stolen, she imagined. Where was the girl now? Beatríz examined it for signs of struggle or bloodshed but found none. She shuddered and set it aside, content in his nightshirt for the time being.

Beatríz worked up the courage to stand and look around the room, though every time she touched something, her hand sprang back as if stung. By the time the sun was strong, she had risked taking a book off the shelf and had brought it to the bed. It was a dull account of an explorer, but it was the first book she had laid hands on for months, and she drifted into the world of the adventure nevertheless.

When the keys entered in the lock, Beatríz jumped and hid the book behind her. The captain seemed not to notice the high color on her cheeks. He nodded as he entered, kicked off his boots and flopped onto the bed. "Storm coming," he said. "Better rest while I can."

Beatríz sat very still, her knees tucked under her chin, waiting. But he slept. When he rose, he put on rain gear and wished her well, adding that the cabin boy would comb her hair out again before the seas grew heavier. Beatríz was mystified. Why his civility? Could it have been that knowing she was his alone that took away the urgency?

The boat rocked and creaked, though Beatríz could not say she feared its breaking apart. She almost wished it would, even if it meant she herself perished. Actually, considering her own death was the thought that calmed her most.

By morning, the seas quieted and the captain stumbled into his cabin hardly acknowledging her and slept again.

Having spent most of the night awake herself, she decided to rest.

She awoke with his arm across her and his body close. His snoring came as a relief and she tried to move out from under his grasp, but he stirred and pulled her close again. "María," he whispered, "*sálvame*." Was his dream of his wife or of the Virgin? And from what was he being saved? Hell? A snake? Falling into a well? Beatríz smiled – the first smile that had broken across her face in weeks – to think of the possibilities. Her smile turned to a laugh and his eyes opened.

"I was dreaming," he said.

She giggled accidentally. "I know."

"Did I say something?"

She took a moment, wondering whether to tell the truth. "You were calling for María."

He flushed. "A nursemaid," he said. "Did you have one growing up?"

She opened her mouth to answer then closed it again.

"Not going to tell me? How about your name?"

She shook her head.

"Why? We spend night after night in this bed and I have been a gentleman. Do you not owe me at least some information about yourself?"

"No," she said sitting up, very serious again. "Because then it will be yours. I would rather die with my memories than give them to you. You have enough of me already."

He nodded, and she thought he looked a little wounded. "Would you like to know about me?"

She did, in fact, but shrugged and looked away.

"I imagine you notice to how I speak. See how I act. A bit different from the men I lead, no? I am an educated man of good birth. I was to be a pilot on a proper ship."

Beatríz looked back, eyes wide. "What happened?"

"The money's better in this."

"But the girls? The robberies?" she asked, pulled into conversation despite herself.

He smiled. "How is it so different from your average merchant ship? At least we are honest about our thieving."

She felt her brow furrow as she thought of Yusef's panic after his last return to Lisbon. He had been at the mercy of the men who owned the ships, and their deeds had frightened him. At least now he was free from fear – fear for himself, fear for her. She clapped her eyes shut tight, keeping the tears inside her lids.

"I have spoken of something close to you. Your husband is a sailor?"

She shook her head and exhaled slowly. "Touch me if you like, but do not ask about my past."

He hesitated. "May I?"

She nodded, realizing that even if Yusef had been alive and they found each other, he would no longer want her. What did it matter if one more man touched her after all the others that had? At least this one let her wash and gave her clean clothes and asked permission to put his hands upon her. She lay back and stared at a crack in the painted beam as the captain slipped inside of her.

The strangest thing was how easily they fell into a routine. Each morning, he rose and went on deck, came back for meals, and studied charts before inviting her to join him in bed. Most nights he wanted her, but sometimes he was content to stroke her arms and breasts and hips and talk about his life. He spent the most time telling her about his childhood in Mijas, staring down at the Mediterranean wishing he could sail away from his Andalucían home then wishing he could return once he had.

Beatríz wept often to think of what had become of her. However, she hid her sadness whenever she could lest he tire of her moods and turn her out to the mercy of the others. She knew this time of relative peace could not go on indefinitely and wondered how it could end.

Her answer came one afternoon . . . she could not say how long it had been. She thought she could recall at least twenty sunrises, but with nowhere to mark them, she was not entirely certain her count was accurate. Just outside the captain's locked door, she heard an argument beginning.

"You can't keep that girl all to yourself." Beatríz recognized the voice as that of the first mate.

"It is not good for morale to have a woman in that cell screaming and crying."

"It is not good for morale," the first mate said, his tone mocking the fancy word, "for you to be the only one with a woman. The men need to put their dicks in somethin', and the cabin boy's got other work to do. No one cares 'bout the girls screamin' but you."

"I have no stomach for it," said the captain.

"For what? *You're* keepin' her prisoner."

"I do not force her."

The first mate laughed. "If we were in port and you gave her a choice, do you think she would stay? You know that girl'd run off quicker than a lynx."

Silence prickled Beatríz's skin.

"I like her."

"Then let us get another –"

"No. Because the new one will cry and I will hear it while I am trying to work or sleep."

"Captain, if you don't want such things on your ship, then

you oughta change professions. Or find a crew of decent men. If there is such a thing. But sir, I swear you'll have a mutiny on your hands if you don't turn that one over or let us grab a new girl."

Another painful pause.

"We were planning to land in a week –"

"Another week's too long. The men're restless."

Keys jangled and Beatríz leapt to her feet, trying to think of an argument to defend herself. No words came.

The captain walked in running his fingers through his blond hair. His bright green eyes met hers and he looked away quickly. She knew he had decided, and her whole body tingled with fear.

"Captain –" she started to say, but her mouth was so dry the rest would not come out.

"Have the men keep the noise to a minimum," the captain said tightly.

Beatríz watched him walk to the window and look out. That was it? He was just going to hand her over like that? After all they – What? There was no reason for her to believe this would end any other way. She felt herself disappearing into the blackness of fear, but snapped out of it when the first mate grabbed her arm. She screamed and lunged for the captain.

"Please! Please do not send me back to them!"

The captain did not turn to face her, and the first mate began to chuckle. He grabbed her around the waist and started to pull her out of the captain's quarters.

"Beatríz!" she shouted. The captain turned his head a little, and the first mate paused. She felt encouraged, hoping that a bit of personal information might make him feel connected enough to her to continue keeping her for himself. "My name is Beatríz. I grew up in Toledo."

The captain turned his head. Back to the window.

The first mate pulled at her again. "So Beatríz from Toledo, what'll we do with you?"

And with that, the brutality began anew.

She lay on the straw, sore and cold, wondering how many nights had passed, when a pair of feet came into view. She did not move. He could drag her if he wanted, but she would not make it easier for him. Whoever he was.

The figure squatted, and a straggly-haired boy came into view. No, not a boy. Youthful, but almost a man. Cleaner than the others. Softer around the eyes. His fair skin pinked at the ears and at the neck. She noticed that freckles dotted his nose and cheeks as he titled his head so their eyes could meet.

"Why do you scream? It only encourages them," he said.

Beatríz did not answer. She could not force herself not to cry out, though she knew perfectly well it goaded them on. She wondered what kind of men took extra pleasure in the pain they inflicted. They said her screams made it like having her maidenhead again and again.

"You're Castilian? We rarely get those."

Beatríz would like to rip Castile off the planet, sink it beneath the sea, and consume it with fire, taking all its men with it.

"I wish I could help," he said softly.

Beatríz studied him. He seemed sincere. He had been with her, sure, but he did not seem to be doing more than satisfying a need. His acts did not humiliate her, punish her.

She lifted her head slightly. "Then kill me," she said.

His mouth fell open. "Miss, that's not what –" He gulped. "You cannot want that."

"Why not? What is left? Are they going to let me go?"

He shook his head slowly and she closed her eyes. Her heart pounded within her chest as if to remind her that it beat steady and strong and wished to go on beating. She hated her heart.

"They have taken everything from me. All hope. All dignity. Kill me or go away."

He rose and locked the cell behind him.

Beatríz rocked along with the boat and listened to the waves lapping at the hull the way the men would lap at her breasts. Every movement, every sound, made her think of them. Every time they called out to one another above deck, she shuddered. Eventually the sun began to set and Beatríz's soul cried out. They would come for her soon. She covered her eyes with her stinking hands and prayed that the ship might hit a rock and sink.

The lock clanked again and Beatríz whimpered.

"Do you swim?" whispered the freckled man-boy.

Beatríz uncovered her eyes and nodded, completely bewildered by the question.

"I have an idea," he said, his voice filled with excitement. "It will hurt, but if you can swim, you might live."

She thought. Did she want to live? And what could hurt more than what had already been done to her. She sat up.

"I've seen them kill the girls when we come to a new port. I think that it's what they are going to do to you."

Beatríz sucked in her breath, shocked that she was shocked. She wanted to die and they were going to kill her. She should have been relieved. But she wanted to die in a way that was her choice at the very least.

"They'll cut you and throw you overboard. I can do it," he said. "But I can try to cut you so you won't bleed to death."

"Why? Why would you do this?" she asked, trembling.

He shrugged. "I like the captain. He likes you. And I'm not like them," he said, his voice soft like the captain's.

The thought of the captain, who passed her cell several times a day without looking, made her stomach turn.

"I hope to run off one day," the young sailor continued. "Become a doctor. The doctor on the boat's been training me, so maybe…" His voice trailed off as he looked over his shoulder. "I have to slice your neck, but I think I can do it lightly enough to draw blood and nothing more." He produced a blade and Beatríz drew back. "Hide this cloth," he said, putting the cotton in her hand. "Hold it to the wound once you're safely out of sight. If I can, I'll pretend to knock a barrel over once I've thrown you overboard. You can use it to stay afloat."

It all sounded quite possible, but Beatríz's head spun at the thought of it. If she drowned, so be it. But what if it did not work? What if they caught him and punished him? Then her?

He looked over his shoulder again. No one but the cabin boy was around and that child was trained to never speak of what he saw. "It should look like we struggled, so scratch my face."

"What?"

"Scratch me."

Beatríz had so much anger within her that if any man but this one had stood in front of her, she would have gladly clawed his eyes and ripped at his throat. But with this one before her, she could only feel relief.

He took her wrists in his and yanked them roughly at his face. She pulled back. "Do it!" he shouted. When her arms remained soft, he leaned in and kissed her. With blinding fury, she sank her nails into his face and drew down. He leaped away holding his cheeks and cursing.

"I'm sorry," she said.

He waved her apologies away and took a moment to collect himself. "Well done," he forced out. Then he straightened his doublet and lifted the knife. Beatríz clutched the cloth. Her chest clenched because, if this was her moment to die, she knew she would go with a soiled soul. She did not know how to make amends for sins not entirely of her making, and with no one to pray for her.

The sharp edge slipped across her neck like Yusef's lips. Immediately she felt warm liquid soaking her *camisa* and trickling down her stomach. Her eyes flew open to the boy's worried face.

"Still alive?" he asked.

She nodded before swooning. She felt him carry her on deck.

"What in hell…" a sailor called.

"Jesus, boy, what have you done?" The voice was the captain's.

"She attacked me when I went for her," she heard the boy say. Beatríz tried to remain very still. "We'll be in port tomorrow, so we can get someone new."

"But she was a fine one. All that fighting and screaming," said someone in the crowd that seemed to have gathered.

The men laughed.

"Eh," said the freckled boy, "a virgin's a virgin. Must be one or two still left. Maybe someone younger this time."

Beatríz's stomach flipped at the thought of a little girl being bought or captured and abused by them. It would not be the first time or the last, she imagined. Even so, Beatríz was so horrified that she considered sitting up and accepting her fate if she could protect another girl. But she did not. She could not allow them to touch her again.

"Time to go," the freckled boy said, and the crowd jeered as she plummeted into the waves.

The cool water enveloped Beatríz and after the initial shock, she opened her eyes to see which way the bubbles floated. She let herself drift and only gave the smallest of kicks so they would not realize she was still alive. Being sure to reach the surface face up took some doing. She played dead in the half-moon night and only looked for the barrel after the ship had floated away.

CHAPTER 19

Beatríz woke with a start. She was laid out on a table like the one she had been thrown against again and again on the ship. She sat up quickly swinging her arms, smacking into a woman who jumped back in shock.

"Don't touch me," Beatríz shrieked, tucking her knees under her chin and wrapping her arms around her legs.

The woman held up her hands and said something in Arabic. The tone was reassuring, but Beatríz had no trust left. When the woman called loudly over her shoulder to summon someone unseen, Beatríz dropped her forehead to her knees and cringed, wondering what punishment would walk through the door.

Beatríz heard a man's voice. "You must speak one of the Frankish languages?" he said in Castilian. She did not answer so he asked, *"Castellano? Catalán? Portuguese?"* Beatríz remained silent, and he said something to the woman.

"You were mumbling in both Castilian and Portuguese when I found you," he continued. "My Castilian is better than my Portuguese, so I will speak that unless you tell me otherwise."

The lilting rise and fall of his voice colored the tree-spotted hills of her language with fine desert wind. Despite her fear, Beatríz had to know who addressed her so beautifully in her native tongue. She lifted her head slightly. The young man had wavy black hair that reached just below his ears. He was clean-shaven, though a dark shadow of stubble outlined his strong jaw, and thick eyebrows topped almond shaped eyes that were the color of straw. Beatríz wondered where such light eyes had come from since most men she had met, especially those native to the Maghreb, had dark eyes. And then it occurred to her that she did not even know if she was in the Maghreb anymore.

"My name is Ibrahim. What is yours?"

Beatríz pressed her lips together. For so long she had sequestered everything true about herself. A benevolent tone would not trick her into releasing any of it so easily. The captain had been kind, too, but he had still misused and betrayed her.

"There is time for names, I suppose. I should tell you that I found you at the water's edge and brought you here. This house belongs to my grandmother, as well as myself, and you are welcome to stay with us until you have recovered."

Beatríz gave no answer.

"You have clearly endured something terrible. My grandmother means to help. The women of our town turn to her for care, and, though you have no reason to believe me, I swear she will be good to you."

Beatríz rested her chin on her knees and looked at the woman. She had the same almond eyes as her grandson, and though her head was covered, Beatríz knew from the eyebrows that her hair was gray. Unlike her tall, slim grandson, the woman was short and round and moved with a noticeable limp.

The woman held up a cloth tucked in her palm, and deep lines fanned across the woman's prominent cheekbones as she blinked and smiled encouragingly. The cloth dripped water onto her wrinkled bare feet, but the woman did not seem to notice or mind. She waited, her partially toothless smile never wavering, as Beatríz decided whether to allow herself to be helped.

"She was going to bathe you," Ibrahim continued, "but you woke. Would you like her to continue?"

"No!" shouted Beatríz, pulling her feet even closer to her body. When Beatríz shook her head, she felt a tightness around her neck and reached to touch the source. A cloth had been wound around her throat, and when she pressed on it, pain leapt from the place where the young sailor had sliced through her skin. She gasped at the memory as much as the gash. Ibrahim and his grandmother stepped forward, eyes wide, but Beatríz buried her face in her knees again. She heard whispering.

"My grandmother has cleaned the cut and is worried she has bound it too tightly. She wants to loosen the bandage."

Beatríz shook her head, ignoring the pain the movement caused. She did not want to be touched ever again. The man spoke to his grandmother and it sounded as if she were arguing with him.

"*Señorita*, my grandmother is worried about the other wounds on your body, as well. They must be tended to or they will fester." His voice was calm but had a pleading undertone. Was he afraid for her health or afraid of his grandmother?

Beatríz did not move.

He said something else to his grandmother. When she argued, he answered her more forcefully then said to Beatríz, "Excuse us. We will leave the washing cloth and basin here. There is salve in the clay pot by your feet that you can apply yourself, but there are sores that she insists you will not be able to reach, and she has offered to assist you with those. When you are ready."

Beatríz nodded to her knees, half hearing his words.

"Ah. Em, my grandmother's name is Samira. She will wait in the other room until you call for her."

The door closed and Beatríz lifted her head again. She was alone on the kitchen table. A fire had been lit under a pot, though in the absence of any scent of food, Beatríz assumed Samira was heating water for cleansing. A bar of rough soap sat in a small bowl and next to that was larger ceramic bowl filled with murky water. Beatríz leaned over and saw bits of sand floating at the top of the clouded liquid. She took the cloth Samira had left and dipped it into the water. Beatríz's hand sprang back at the warmth. When was the last time she had touched anything warm that was not flesh? When she wiped her arm with the slippery linen, it reminded her of sailors sliding their bodies across her. She dropped it and buried her face in her hands.

The sound of her crying must have brought Samira, for, within moments, the woman's hand was on Beatríz's shoulder and her voice was cooing in Beatríz's ear. At first, Beatríz cringed. But then her breath slowed. The woman's voice soothed her like her nursemaid's once had, and feeling like a child again, she allowed Samira to wash her arms, her hands, her shoulders. She did not flinch when the material passed over the welts and cuts on her back, for the pain was so slight compared to what she had endured, and her mind traveled far from the table and the kitchen and the night.

She thought of purple jacaranda blossoms and Yusef's full lips, Davíd dripping with raindrops, her pride at cooking the *adafina* alone, hiding in the corner of the darkened shed when the man with the sword poked at fabric near to where she crouched.

But then Samira began to wash Beatríz's legs, and Samira exclaimed. Beatríz followed Samira's gaze to a puss-oozing mark on her inner thigh that had clearly been made by a full set of teeth. Beatríz's hand sprang to cover it and her face flushed. They would know what had happened, what she was. Samira gently lifted Beatríz's hand aside and held the cloth up, her eyes asking permission to proceed. Beatríz nodded, and Samira washed it, shaking her head with pity. She reached out and squeezed Beatríz's hand, cracking Beatríz's heart. Samira applied salve, muttering as she worked. Beatríz listened to the flow of incomprehensible sounds, never uncovering her face.

After a while, Beatríz noticed the touching had stopped and looked up without thinking. Samira was at the pot. When she returned, she had new linen and a fresh bowl of steaming water. Samira pointed at Beatríz's face and then pantomimed washing her own face. Beatríz suddenly thought of Blanca, sweet, tongue-less Blanca, who helped Beatríz learn of a new world without ever speaking. Beatríz realized she wanted to stay in this place where words did not matter and actions were kind.

Beatríz wiped at her face, though only a few grains of sand were on it. She wondered how long she had spent in the sea. It was dark outside, but she could not think that she had reached land on the same night that she had been tossed into the water. But she could not remember having floated in the daylight. She would never know how long or far she had traveled, only that she was lucky to have landed where she did.

Absently, Beatríz scratched her head then froze. The lice which had tortured her since she was thrown back into the cage were still nestled against her scalp, hiding between the strands. Nauseated and suddenly frantic, Beatríz sprang from the table and ran for a large knife she had seen near a stack of onions. When she snatched the carver and held it to her own neck, Samira screamed.

Ibrahim barged through the door to find Beatríz sawing at her hair.

"Stop!" he shouted.

"I want it gone," Beatríz said without pause.

They all gasped when the blade sliced free and Beatríz was left clutching a handful of dark curls.

"Your hair is beautiful. Why have you done such a thing?" Ibrahim asked.

Beatríz thought of the men dragging her by it to get her onto the table, calling out the names of their gods and their mothers as they fell on her, breathing heavily into her hair. Her hair. Hair that had once filled her with pride. Hair that she had combed and scented. Hair that she had adorned for Yusef. Now soiled. Now hated.

She took the knife against her neck again and began to saw outward. If only she could do it faster. Cut it all off. Or turn the knife the other way.

"Wait. Please."

Something in Ibrahim's voice made her pause, though she kept the knife pressed against the strands, waiting to begin again.

"I can see your hair offends you, but your feelings might change. If you continue, you will be left without this loveliness."

Beatríz shook her head. He did not know there was no loveliness left, neither inside nor out. She was as befouled as her hair. She began to push the blade again. "I will cut it as short as I can," she began, the bandaged cut on her neck stinging with each word. "And then I want your grandmother to shave my head."

Ibrahim sucked in his breath. Samira pulled at his sleeve to understand what was being said, but he did not take his eyes off of Beatríz. "Muslim women do not do such things."

"I am not Muslim," she said, readying another handful of hair.

"Even so, I know she will not. Let her tend it. She is skilled at combing thoroughly and has ways to kill the —"

"No. I will do it myself, if I must, but I want it off." Beatríz was frantic to continue, but an itch came so strong that she set aside the knife to scratch her scalp. If she had touched an actual bug at that moment, she would have run and leapt out of a window just to end her own agony. But when she stopped scratching, her head spun and all of her energy suddenly left her. Beatríz sank to the floor shaking.

Samira and Ibrahim conferred in hushed Arabic.

"My grandmother will help you cut it, but she will not shave your head. That is something . . . that she will not do. And you cannot do it yourself. Please do not try. You will hurt yourself and upset my grandmother."

Beatríz shook her head slowly, her resolve weakening.

"You can veil yourself."

Her lips trembled. "Men might not see, but they will know what lies underneath."

"Men show respect to women who are modest and covered."

Beatríz knew the pirates would have taken a head covering off as quickly as they had removed her dress and the result would have been the same. And yet, on the skiff that was overtaken, she had had her hair free while Nesrin had not. Could that have made the difference? No. Nesrin's husband, Onur, had killed her to preserve her dignity, to protect her from soul-killing shame. Then again, on the ship from Lisbon, the sailors had been able to take hold of her free-flowing curls, beginning a chain of events that ended in Miriam's death – or ended in her kneeling in this room with clumps of hair littering the brushed stone floor.

Beatríz pled feebly, "Ask her again to shave it."

"No. I will not ask again what has been answered. Her generous spirit will wrestle with it, wanting to please both you and Allah. A woman of her years should not be exposed to such inner turmoil."

The man seemed more concerned with his grandmother's happiness than with the battered, half-dressed woman who sat before him covered in welts and lice. And this made Beatríz suddenly like him very much.

Beatríz nodded and Samira disappeared to find a comb and a more appropriate blade. Ibrahim offered his hand to help Beatríz off the floor and onto a bench. When Samira returned, Ibrahim took his leave of them and Samira began to work. As strands and clumps of curls fell into Beatríz's lap, Beatríz cried with relief and despair. Her hair was all that remained of her former life other than her memories. But there were no blades sharp enough or hands skilled enough to excise her recollections. Even the lovely memories of before shredded Beatríz's heart and threatened her sanity.

After the remnants of her hair were combed with strong smelling liquid, Samira hung an amulet around Beatríz's neck.

The swirls of blue and white looked less like the eye Beatríz imagined they were meant to be and more like the Berber fabric she had seen in her first days in Oran, which suited Beatríz fine. Wild horsewomen could protect her, or clay eyes, or wizened grandmothers. She did not care. She only hoped to be safe for a little while.

Beatríz was dressed in loose flowing fabric, her head was covered and the material tied at the back to avoid rubbing against the wound on her neck, and she was led to a bed where she fell into sleep before the lamp next to her was blown out.

She woke in the morning to playful shouts on the street and thought she was in her bed in Lisbon. As her eyes fluttered open, the spare walls and bright light streaming through the unshuttered window took her by surprise. Turning her head to look around, her neck twinged and the truth of where she was startled her out of her stupor.

Beatríz forced her body to stand and she looked outside. Another town baked by sunshine that never lit the narrow streets all at once. The sand colored houses were crumbling in spots. Dirt covered the walkways, not cobblestones, and a dip ran the length of the street, hard and cracked. Beatríz presumed that these were for runoff of waste and rain, though it looked like there had been no precipitation in a good long time here. The air smelled of the sea, a scent she once loved and which now turned her stomach. She held her breath and pinched her eyes shut to forget.

Giggling forced them back open. Veiled women walked among children who darted one way then the other, playing a joyful game of tag among the folds of their mothers' robes, much as her sister, Reyna, used to hide in the brocade curtains of their home. Beatríz turned from the window.

She was not in Sicily or Barcelona or Lisbon, of that she was sure. Where was she? But as quickly as curiosity came upon her, it vanished. It did not matter where she was. Only that she be left alone.

The man – Ibrahim was his name – had said she could stay until she had recovered. How long would that be? She wanted to stay right where she was. In truth, she never wanted to walk outside again.

Samira entered with a bowl and held it out toward Beatríz. Beatríz was not sure if she was meant to wash again or if it was food. Then she saw the spoon and shook her head. Samira nodded encouragingly and said something, then pointed to her heart. Beatríz did not know how her heart and soup were connected, and merely considering food sickened her. She shook her head again and lay down on the mattress, turning her back to Samira. Beatríz heard Samira leave the bowl on the floor next to her and walk out. Feeling guilty for dismissing generosity, Beatríz closed her eyes and fell back asleep.

The light was waning when Beatríz awoke. The bowl remained where Samira had left it. The evening call to prayer floated in through the window on a light breeze, carrying with it the scent of salt water. Yusef often smelled of the sea. So did sadness and violence. Beatríz turned to the mattress and cried, trying to muffle the sound.

When at last she was quiet, there was a knock on her door. In a scratchy, weak voice, Beatríz asked the person in.

Ibrahim entered. "Ah, you are awake."

Beatríz shrank back, thinking he might have put on the show of propriety the night before but was coming now to harm her. As he smiled genuinely and remained in the doorway, she felt her anguish lift a little.

"My grandmother says you have not eaten today. We are sitting for our evening meal. My cousin, Anisa, is here with her husband. Will you join us?"

Beatríz thought. She wanted to. She did. But she was so afraid. It had been a lifetime ago that she sat around a table eating in a civilized fashion with people who only wanted conversation and company. The memories of Rebecca, of Miriam, of her mother, of the captain, of the cage, were too strong. She could not force herself to stand and so shook her head.

"My grandmother would like to bring you food then. And after you eat, she should treat your wounds and comb your hair again."

Beatríz touched the scarf still tied securely around her short hair. She could not meet Ibrahim's gaze, but nodded. She knew that the jagged way she was seeing everything was caused by not having eaten in . . . she did not remember when.

The soup was spiced with something Beatríz did not recognize, but she loved it immediately. It reminded her of the offloading ships on the docks of Lisbon, ships full of carpets, exotic animals, and mysterious baskets trailing unfamiliar scents. Yusef would walk with her and tell her of his journeys, pointing to goods and describing the lands from which they came.

Beatríz put down the spoon and looked out the window again.

Ibrahim came to collect her bowl and frowned when he saw it was mostly full. "You must eat to heal."

Beatríz did not answer.

"My grandmother will be offended."

"I am sorry, but I cannot." She sat on the edge of the bed and put her head in her hands. A thump made her look up and she saw that Ibrahim had brought a stool to her doorway.

"May I?" he asked, and, though the question suddenly reminded her of the captain, she nodded. Ibrahim sat on the stool and studied her until she had to look away. "We are very much alike, you and I."

"How?"

"We both know sadness."

Beatríz winced.

"Different sadnesses, yes, but we must fight for our joy now."

"I have no fight left. I wish –"

"What?"

"I wish I had drowned."

She had expected Ibrahim to say something, to argue. That he did not speak comforted her. When she looked in his direction, he was staring out the window.

After a time, he spoke in hushed tones, still looking into the beyond. "Many times I have thought, 'What can I do to end my pain? What can I do to cut out this heaviness, this scorching reminder of all I have lost?' But I have never had the courage to do harm to myself. And now that I have met you, Beatríz, I truly believe that I could not do it because Allah wanted me to find you."

Beatríz shook her head. She did not believe that was true. Did not want to believe in anything. She shook her head again.

"It is what I believe. You do not have to. But why else would I have been walking at the water's edge, a place I never go at night? Why would I have stopped at the moment, at that place, to look out at the dark water, something I never allow myself the painful luxury of doing? No, I do not believe in coincidences. I was brought there to find you."

Beatríz's cheeks burned. "I am not worth anyone's time or attention, let alone your God's."

"Who are we to question? Maybe I was to find you so that more bad men did not."

Beatríz shuddered, and did not want to go on discussing fate or other ways she might have been found. "What is this place?"

"Djerba, an island near Tunis."

"Near Sicily?" she asked, trying to locate the spot on her mental map.

"Far, far closer to the Maghreb, but yes, if you went north and slightly east across the water you would reach Sic–"

A knock at the front door interrupted them, and Ibrahim left the room. Beatríz heard women's voices, and the door closed.

Ibrahim reappeared and said, "Having reached this uncommon age, many turn to my grandmother for guidance and she never refuses anyone at any hour. I told my cousin, Anisa, to take over, for she has observed our grandmother in the healing arts, but Anisa claims her knowledge is not nearly good enough. It would not matter anyhow, for our grandmother will not slow down. She loves her work. But it takes its toll on her."

"How old is Samira?"

"She stopped counting in her late forties, and anyone living past that is, of course, quite special." He took hold of the stool. "As we are alone now, I will leave you. Call out if you are in need of anything. Good night."

CHAPTER 20

When the door closed, Beatríz lay down and tried to fall asleep rather than think. But every noise set her heart pounding, every voice echoing in the streets reminded her of someone she would never see again or someone she hoped she never would. She pressed her palms to her ears and pinched her eyes shut. "Please," she thought, "please release me." But it was not to be.

She tossed and turned in a nightmarish half-sleep until she could no longer take the frustration, then flung herself onto her feet and into the big room. Beatríz wandered around breathing deeply, hoping that if she filled her lungs enough, it would help calm her. But there did not seem to be enough air.

Her eye caught a line of jars next to the cutting block and she suddenly forgot her effort to breathe. She wanted to open each lid to smell the spices, to see which ones she recognized and to study the ones she did not. But when she reached for the first, she hesitated, unsure if a clank of pottery would bring Ibrahim into the room or if Samira would be angry to have her possessions disturbed. Her hand froze in mid-air and she thought of standing in the captain's cabin, reaching for his book, wondering what punishment might come from touching what was not hers.

Her hand snapped back to her side and she was suddenly overwhelmed by memory and fatigue. But she could not go back into her room. The street noises were duller in the kitchen. She moved to the table, climbed onto the bench, and rested her head on her arms, her nose nearly touching the wood. The dull scent of ashes, soap, and animal fat reminded her of hiding in the kitchen with her mother's cooks when her mother did not want her underfoot or was having one of her sad days, of which there were many.

Beatríz leapt at a touch on her shoulder. Samira's face came quickly into focus and Beatríz remembered she was safe. Samira stroked Beatríz's head and smiled with closed lips. Then she gestured spooning food into her mouth. Beatríz shook her head and Samira's smile faded. Samira lowered herself stiffly onto the bench beside Beatríz and explained something, which Beatríz was sure involved eating to stay healthy. Beatríz lowered her head again, breathing in the reassuring scents of the table.

A door opened and Ibrahim began to welcome his grandmother. His voice broke off when he saw Beatríz. "Are you in need of something?" he asked her, his voice laced with worry.

"*Everything*," she thought, but merely shook her head.

He hesitated then moved to stoke the fire. Samira stopped him and used the table to rise, then hobbled into her room.

Ibrahim covered the pot and made to leave.

"Ibrahim," Beatríz asked, wincing at the pain when she turned to face him. Touching the bandage, she tried to remember what she wanted to know. "Whose room have I taken?"

"Mine. But do not worry."

Beatríz's forehead wrinkled. The thought of being in a man's bed startled her, and then she nearly laughed at the resurfacing of her old sense of modesty.

"Where are you sleeping?" she asked over the bitterness in her throat.

"The floor."

"That cannot be comfortable."

Ibrahim shrugged. "I will not have a lady sleep on my floor like a dog."

The blood drained from Beatríz's head. A lady? Where? She had become a dog or worse. She deserved no more. Why was he insisting on kindness when he knew what she was?

"I cannot sleep," she managed. "At least one of us should."

Ibrahim shook his head. "That is your room. It is yours until you choose to go."

The soft roll of his R's soothed her. He bade her goodnight and she blew out the lamp before returning to her room.

She finally slept, but the nightmares came and would not release her. Reaching hands, dogs tearing her to pieces, giant lice biting her neck and beasts pinning her down. Whether she screamed out loud or in her dreams she did not know, but she woke in the half-light of dawn bathed in sweat and short of breath. She would not allow herself to sleep again and pinched herself every so often to make sure she did not slip into slumber.

Beatríz heard Samira rise and begin to cook. She heard Ibrahim murmuring to Samira over the clank of cutlery. Beatríz wanted to rise, to see them, to take comfort in their company, but she could not make her legs move. Instead, she remained in anxious silence, her still-vivid dreams coiling around her.

Eventually, Samira entered with a bowl and bread. Beatríz's stomach clenched from hunger, but still she could not make herself eat. She lowered her head and Samira left the bowl again, stopping a moment. Beatríz hoped she would not speak. Even though she could not understand Samira, even a kind tone or an unintelligible plea would force the tears out, would make Beatríz confess the nightmares that haunted her. But Samira closed the door, and Beatríz lay on her side as still as she could trying not to think.

The light intensified and punctured the space between the shutters, changing the shadows as the day wore on, warming the room beyond bearability. But Beatríz did not rise to let the air in.

She stared at the bowl across the room. Despite all of her efforts not to, as the shadows blurred with dusk, she finally slid onto the floor. With shaking hands, she waved away the flies, lifted the coarse ceramic, and then brought the wooden spoon to her lips. The coagulated soup exploded with flavor and tasted of love. It made her weep and she kept eating. She did not deserve this food. She did not deserve this care. She pressed her fingers hard against her cut forcing the pain to smash the goodness. And then she lifted the spoon and did it all again.

Beatríz pulled herself back up onto the mattress and sat with her knees tucked under her chin until the room grew dark and Ibrahim entered, candlelight streaming in behind him.

"Ah, you ate," he said, lifting the empty bowl from the floor.

Beatríz dug her nails into her palms and the pain calmed

her mind. "I would not allow myself to die in the water and I cannot starve myself now. Help me, please. Please end this misery."

"End?"

"Kill me."

Ibrahim leaned back against the wall. "Killing another is against both of our religions. As is killing yourself."

"What do I care of religion?"

He tilted his head. "God does not want you to die."

"God does not care."

"God rescued you from the water."

"I do not believe that God watches me. Chance and a barrel saved me," she said, her teeth dripping fury. "And if what you say is true, then God put me on that boat to be attacked.

"Perhaps it was for a reason."

"Then I hate God."

Ibrahim stood quietly for a moment. "I can understand your anger, but we are all tested. I can help you see –"

"The only thing I want is to be dead. If you cannot help me with that, you cannot help me at all." She slid down on the mattress and turned away from him. Ibrahim walked away without another word and closed the door behind him.

Convinced there was no way out of her life, Beatríz rose the next morning and ate. And the next day. And the next. Each time she swallowed, she fought the desire to cry, for every bite ensured she would live another day. Samira and Ibrahim spoke of the positive – that she was eating and growing stronger. But they did not remark on what was clear – that sadness still threatened to drown her. They ignored it with their words, but she felt them watching her, exchanging glances and whispers, encouraging her to join them in the routines of their lives.

Finally Beatríz, unable to sit another day in silent terror, accepted Samira's invitation to help Samira in the kitchen. Though Beatríz barely said a word and could not muster a smile, Samira brightened each time Beatríz ventured out of her room and began talking immediately. Before long, Beatríz understood words like "cut" and "stir," and when she did not understand, she watched and copied. Most meals were vegetables and bread or grain, but apparently when they had the money, Ibrahim brought home meat or fish and Samira created a feast. Beatríz found something satisfying in accomplishing tasks, of watching something come from her efforts, and of getting to know Samira by deeds and movement if not by words.

First she learned how to preserve lemons, and came to find reassurance in the rhythm and habit of turning the lemon jar every few days – her own sands of time. With each rotation she could mark the fading of the bites and cuts, of the meals she had been able to eat without anger or tears, and of the added bits of sleep.

The cooking surprised Beatríz constantly. The first curiosity had been *Nawasar* – dough rolled flat, cut and boiled, but which retained its shape and size and remained inexplicably soft. It sounded similar to something Yusef had told her he had eaten in Venice, a soft dough topped by sauces. What had he called it? Pasta. Samira and Beatríz cooked the *Nawasar* with a mixture they made of onions, salt, pepper, potatoes, chick peas, and harisa, adding boiled eggs one time and lamb another.

Most surprising was the *Mujabbana* because Samira followed it with the word "Toledo." How did Samira know of the city in which Beatríz had grown up? The rolling of the dumplings brought her back to a time when her eyes barely peeked above the counter and a servant had brought a wooden box for Beatríz to stand on so she could knead the dough under the practiced hands of the cook. Beatríz did not remember what cheese the servants rolled in or if there was cilantro or anise inside of the dumplings at her mother's house, but the dish Samira created was so familiar Beatríz could do nothing but marvel. How had this information traveled to Djerba? By merchant? Another traveler seeking refuge? Or had Samira been the one to move from place to place, picking up recipes along with ways to heal the body and soul? Samira would not understand if she asked and Beatríz found herself unable to question Ibrahim about anything personal.

One morning, Samira picked up a basket and said, "*Al-qaysariyya.*" Beatríz understood that she was going to the covered market, and waved goodbye. But then Samira waved Beatríz toward her and suggested, "*Ta-aal.*"

Beatríz frowned and shook her head. "*La.*" She pointed to herself and said, "*Waggeef,*" not sure if the "stay" she had just said was a command to stay or if she was successfully explaining what she wanted for herself.

Samira pointed again to Beatríz and out the door.

Beatríz shook her head again.

Samira hesitated and then left. Less than an hour later, Samira entered with onions, grain, cheese. And Ibrahim.

"My grandmother says you will not go out with her," he explained. "Why?"

Beatríz swallowed hard. "I do not wish to go out."

"But you have lived here for nearly a month and have not set foot outside. I have not said anything about it, but my grandmother is growing concerned. It is not good for you to lock yourself away. You must put the sun on your face, breathe in the air."

Beatríz felt like a child being reprimanded. "But I...." Her fingers drifted to the cut on her neck, but it no longer stung or felt tender to the touch. "...cannot." She bit her lip so he would not see it tremble.

Ibrahim whispered to Samira and then sat beside Beatríz, asking permission before he did. "Beatríz," he cooed, "you must. We will help you, but you cannot stay inside."

Beatríz inched away. "You are working."

"I said to my boss my workday is done. We will do without meat today. Meat is not as important as your health. Come. We walk outside."

Beatríz looked at them helplessly. "Please do not force me."

Ibrahim knit his brow. "Try."

Something beyond Beatríz pushed her onto her feet and she found herself on the stairs. Samira took the steps ahead of her limping down one by one, which gave Beatríz time to think. She could do this. She could walk outside. Samira and Ibrahim were there to protect her. What was she afraid of? Everything. Everything. Beatríz turned with the intention of going back up, but Ibrahim looked down at her and smiled, a smile that chilled Beatríz for her desire to please him and her certainty that she could not.

"This is good," he said. "You have already come so far."

How could she refuse his kindness, his generous patience? She turned back and dragged her feet down the stairs and onto the cobblestones. But when the light between the buildings shone on her face, she froze. A cold sweat sprang all over and she gripped the doorjamb. Samira placed her hand on Beatríz's arm. Words caught in Beatríz's throat, and her mouth remained in an O.

"Beatríz, come," said Ibrahim.

Beatríz shook her head and felt the air press out of her.

Ibrahim stepped in front of her and bent at the knees so their eyes were level. "You look sick."

Beatríz nodded and began panting with fear. "Upstairs," she squeaked, dizzy and unsure of where she stood at that moment. How would she manage to get up the stairs once she found them with her legs shaking so hard?

"No, Beatríz. You must continue past your fear. Make it leave you."

"Ibrahim I ca –" Beatríz doubled over, trying to get air into her body. "I can't – breathe. I –"

"All right," Ibrahim said. "We will try another day."

Beatríz turned and moved into the secure darkness of the stairwell. Sunblind, she could not see the first step and inched forward. Behind her she heard a woman speak to Ibrahim. The woman spoke quickly and the words sounded sharp, not like the gentle waves of Ibrahim's Arabic. Samira moved next to Beatríz and then began the ascent speaking to Beatríz as if she would understand. And funny thing was, Beatríz did. A little. She knew the woman outside was family and that she would come up.

Only when the door to her room clacked shut did Beatríz begin breathing less jaggedly. She perched at the edge of the mattress, slowly regaining feeling in her face. Her clothes were damp with sweat and she wished she had something to change in to.

When Beatríz emerged, a willowy woman with dark kohl around her bright eyes and a rich purple scarf wrapped around her head stepped forward. Without waiting for

Ibrahim to introduce her, she said in Castilian, "I am Anisa. My cousin says you have a fear of the outside."

Beatríz looked down at the newly swept floor, shamed.

"Many of the people here in Djerba have come from other places with reasons to fear. You must be like the rest and join life, no?"

Beatríz shook her head. She would not. Could not. And she did not need Anisa with her beauty and impatience telling her differently.

"*Keeff*," growled Ibrahim, holding up his hand, which Anisa answered with a toss of her head that made her scarf shimmer.

If gratitude were tangible, Beatríz would have draped it over Ibrahim. Ibrahim and Anisa began arguing as if she were not there. At least they had switched out of Castilian so Beatríz could drift away from their conversation. Eventually Samira turned to her grandchildren and silenced them.

Anisa began to argue again and Samira slammed her hand on the table, shaking her head and shouting, "*La*." Ibrahim and Anisa moved away from one another quickly like Beatríz used to leap from Solomon when their father found them bickering. She missed her dear brother. She rested her forehead on her palms, overwhelmed by memories and the all too familiar longing that had lodged itself between her ribs.

Beatríz turned to Anisa thought of the word for 'how' and began, "*Bahkee…*" and then could not think of how to finish. She wanted to know how Anisa spoke nearly perfect Castilian, so she simply added, "Castilian."

A smile crept into the corner of Anisa's lips. "Yes. And you are learning Arabic, I see."

"Poorly, I think."

"But you are trying." Anisa sat on the bench across from

Beatríz and her gaze cut into Beatríz. "My cousin likes you very much. So much that he has kept you from seeing anyone that might scare you. I scare him, *a laisa ka-dħaalika?*"

"Right," Ibrahim said as he laughed. She realized it was the first laugh Beatríz had ever heard from him. Ibrahim sat on the bench next to Anisa and said, "Anisa, you make me happier and angrier than anyone I know." She playfully pinched him, and Beatríz noticed Samira's shoulders relaxed before she went back to kneading dough.

"Where do you live?" Beatríz asked.

"Across the street with my husband. I thought we might meet the first day you were here, but you would not come out of your room. Since then, I have seen you at the window of Ibrahim's room, but he insisted on keeping company away. But now we have met, so we can be friends, *inshallah.*" Her eyes flicked to the ceiling at her reference to Allah and His will.

Beatríz asked, "And have you always lived here?"

Anisa's eyes danced with confusion. "Has he told you nothing?" She turned to Ibrahim who suddenly looked less amused. "We came from the Maghreb. But, how shall I say, after our own tragedies, we decided to take what was left of our family – just the two of us and our grandmother – and come here. Ibrahim had a friend that had settled on Djerba, and so it was as good a place as any. Better, perhaps, because it is surrounded by water."

"Tragedy?" Beatríz asked, relieved to be drawn in by someone else's drama.

Anisa looked at Ibrahim who nodded and began studying ragged skin around his dirt-caked fingernails. Anisa's gaze lingered a moment on her cousin before she turned it back to Beatríz. "Yes. Our village was attacked by Berbers."

"Or the Tuareg," mumbled Ibrahim.

"I say they are all the same. And what would the Tuareg have been doing by our – It does not matter. Some pack of devils stole our family and our friends, including Ibrahim's wife. They chained everyone and took them across the desert to sell them as slaves."

"Wife?" Beatríz whispered, a chill creeping down her arms.

"She is dead," Ibrahim said as he stood and left the room.

Anisa watched her cousin go then continued. "Ibrahim was trading near the coast and when he came back she was gone. He has never forgiven himself."

"Could he have stopped them?"

"No. He would have been captured or killed, but he says he would have preferred it."

Beatríz thought of her conversations with Ibrahim. He understood her wish to die as few would. But he did not help her end her life. Why not? Because he had forced himself to continue living. Why did she have to face the same fate? Perhaps Ibrahim was more inherently hopeful. Or maybe he had come to think of life as something worth living, though she could not imagine reaching that point again.

"Ibrahim was like a madman," continued Anisa. "He raced into the desert, nearly dying of thirst and hunger. When he crawled back to the village, he swore he would try again. We told him there was no use. The Berber are cruel. They chain the people they capture around the neck, and if one does not keep pace with others, they cut off the head. When the captives reach the slave market, the empty neck rings mark the number that died along the way."

"Did Ibrahim ever find what happened to her?"

"Eventually he reached the market and spoke to the traders that he knew. She never arrived."

Beatríz sucked in her breath. She looked at the door as if she could see him standing behind it, imagining him with his hands covering his eyes as he often did when he thought she was not looking.

"There is an Arabic saying: 'He who sees the calamity of other people finds his own calamity light.' You see, others have their troubles and continue to live. So will you." Anisa rose. "Now that we have met, you must all come to our home to eat. It is three steps across, which I know you can walk without trouble."

Anisa's confidence only partially convinced Beatríz. The steps would be made with sheer will, but she would take them. She could do that much.

Only after the door shut behind Anisa did Ibrahim emerge. "Now you know," he said.

Beatríz rose. "You did not need to keep such a secret from me."

"It was not a secret. It…" He looked away. "I do not like to talk of it."

"May I ask one more question?"

Ibrahim nodded, though his muscles tensed.

"How did Anisa escape capture?"

"Her parents – my aunt and uncle – hid her but were taken themselves. My brothers died fighting and their wives were taken. Many villages continue after such attacks, but ours lost its heart and enough of its people that those of us left behind chose to go." He crossed the room to where Samira stood preparing food, oblivious to the entire conversation, and kissed Samira on the cheek. She patted his hand before continuing her work. "My parents had died some years earlier and I was the only one left to care for Anisa and our grandmother. So the three of us made it to the coast and sailed to Djerba to begin anew."

"How does she know Castilian so well?"

Ibrahim's face twisted cryptically. "She fell in love with a foreign merchant and she made me teach her enough to communicate with him. The man taught her more. He sailed in, stayed for a stretch of time, and sailed away again, only to return as soon as it was possible. They talked and talked and grew to love one another. But he would not marry a Muslim and she refused to become Christian. I assure you the heartbreak was powerful for them both, but some people cannot get past such differences. The man left and she married Fadil. It has been a good marriage for them both. Childless so far, but happy."

They stood in silence. "Fadil refuses to speak Castilian even though many traders do, and Fadil does not like when Anisa does. It will be hard for you at their house, I think."

"No," she said, despite her reticence, "it will be fine. I will learn to speak better Arabic in their company. And she is family." The last word sliced her.

"Shall we practice walking outside until mealtime? My grandmother can stop cooking and accompany us. And though others may disapprove, I can stand at your side and guide you if you think it will help."

The thought of it filled her with dread and she declined. "Perhaps tomorrow," she said and would say again each day of the next week. She would put off going outside until she could not avoid it any longer. The time would come sooner than she hoped.

Anisa began to cook with them regularly and they took turns eating at one another's houses. Fadil openly winced when Beatríz spoke briefly the first night, but he grew used to hearing Castilian at his table. He was a round, quiet man with eyes full of admiration for Anisa. She played at ignoring and dismissing him, but just when Beatríz thought it was too much, that her behavior bordered on cruel, Anisa would tug Fadil's beard or put his turban between her hands and kiss his forehead. Beatríz noticed that Samira clucked quietly each time Anisa kissed her husband publicly, but never said anything more.

It reminded her of Yakob's anger over Beatríz's kissing Yusef. But Beatríz's kisses were hardly as chaste and she had not been married. Not married. Beatríz sighed and concentrated on the conversation that she could hardly follow, her head aching with the effort.

Just as Beatríz could manage the steps to Anisa's without bracing herself, she was pressed to go much farther. One afternoon, Samira called up the stairs as she always did when coming back from the market. Then Beatríz heard a clatter. She ran to find Samira splayed, nose bleeding, struggling but failing to stand.

"Ibrahim –" Samira panted. "*Arjou-kee.*"

Samira needed her help, was begging for it, and yet as Beatríz looked down the stairs, the doorway grew closer and farther at once. Her legs began to shake and she opened her mouth to refuse Samira but could not. Beatríz ran up the stairs and knocked on the neighbor's door. No one was home. Beatríz looked at Samira who had managed to roll on her side to lie awkwardly, blood smeared across her face.

Beatríz crept past Samira and down the stairs, trying not to think of anything but how much she did not want to do what she was doing. She stepped onto the street and crossed to Anisa's. After pounding on the door, she stepped back and looked up. No sign of anyone inside. She stepped forward and pounded again hoping, hoping that Anisa had simply not heard her the first time. No answer. Beatríz heard a shout from Samira and knew she had to hurry.

Where was the waterfront? Ibrahim turned left when he went to work, so Beatríz did the same. A child ran into her before shrieking past followed hard by another boy giggling over the game of chase. It was enough to begin Beatríz's panic in full. The world fell out of focus and tears streamed down her face. She could not see where she was walking and stubbed her toe. She moved toward the dark side of the street reaching out to find the wall. At its cooler touch, she crumbled, putting her hands to her face and sobbing aloud.

Someone touched her and she jumped. A woman she did not know spoke to her rapidly, her face full of concern. Beatríz backed away and into a man with a bright blue Berber turban who grabbed her in surprise to keep her from falling over. Beatríz screamed and slithered out of his grip. Holding her hands up in front of her, she waved away the small crowd gathering to watch. She fumbled along in the direction she thought she wanted to go, trying to set her *niqab* in place to cover her face but with little success.

At the crossroads, she froze. Which way? Down would be right but the streets seemed level. Beatríz gasped and sputtered, holding her sides as if that might force some air in. Beatríz looked down both streets again. She thought she heard Samira shout, but it could have been anything. Beatríz bit her lip and tasted blood.

An older woman limped by and Beatríz took hold of her. The woman spun with wide eyes and leaned away from Beatríz's crazed desperation.

Beatríz managed to remember the words she needed to ask where the water was. "*Ayna…maa*?"

The woman pointed hesitantly and hurried past.

"*Shukran*," Beatríz called after her, knowing the woman would not have wanted her thanks. Only to get away from her.

Having a direction helped Beatríz's panic lighten, but not enough. Her inability to breathe made for awkward progress and she kept stopping to gather herself. She hoped some passer-by had heard Samira's cries for help and at least lifted Samira into the house. Why had she not done so first? Because Samira had begged her to go. Could this have been planned? A way to get her out? No, the blood was real. The moans genuine. The image of Samira's suffering propelled Beatríz onward.

She told herself, "Stop crying. Start breathing." And she did. Then she thought, "Find Ibrahim. No one else cares who you are." With sudden clarity, she hurried down the road until the city wall opened onto the waterfront.

It was lined with boats, mostly small rowboats and sailboats, but a few larger vessels were anchored, as well. Did one of them hold the men who had imprisoned her? She could not make herself take another step and began looking for familiar faces. Then she was more afraid she might see one.

"Excuse me," she asked a man passing by, one she knew she did not know. "Do you know where Ibrahim is?"

"*Laa afham*," he answered and made to walk away.

She broke rules of propriety and held him by the arm. "I know you do not know what I mean....I...*Bint*...not daughter...uh, friend... *Jadda*...of...Ibrahim. Samira?"

"Ah!" The man began to nod. "Samira." Then he launched into an explanation that escaped her but involved his head and a pain. From his enthusiastic retelling, Beatríz assumed it had healed well.

"Ibrahim?" Then she pointed up and down the port.

"*Na'am*," he nodded. "*Ta'aal.*" He waved her along and she followed.

Soon they were standing in front of crates and Beatríz spotted both Fadil and Ibrahim atop the stack. She had never been so happy to see either of them. "Ibrahim!" she shouted.

He turned and leapt down as soon as he saw her. "You left the – What is wrong? You look terrible."

"Your grandmother," she began, but he was racing away before she could say any more.

The men looked at her and she suddenly felt exposed and terrified. She told her breath to be steady and her legs to stay firm, but her body was finished listening to her brain.

Fadil climbed down and spoke to her. She looked at him, exhaustion clouding her mind, making it impossible for her to even try to comprehend what he meant.

"*Namshī*," he said, offering to bring her away, and put out an elbow for her to take.

Beatríz had rarely seen a man walk with a woman in the months since she had left home, and could not think why Fadil would choose to break tradition for a woman he had just met. Either way, she linked her arm through his, wishing it were her brother or her father or Yusef escorting her inside the city walls of Lisbon. How many times she had once longed to stay just another moment at the water's edge, and how quickly she wished to get away from it now.

By the time they reached the house, Samira had been bandaged and settled in her bed. Neighbors crowded the large room and Fadil blanched. Beatríz had been told he was a man who preferred to be alone. And besides, he had work to do – more since Ibrahim would not work that day. He placed his palms together and bowed his head at her before walking back out.

Beatríz wanted to know how Samira fared. People turned their heads but looked at her in confusion or leaned closer to one another to whisper while staring directly at her. She slunk into her room and lowered herself onto her bed.

Anisa walked in and asked sharply, "What took you so long to get help? My grandmother said she lay there long enough for the blood to dry."

A new lump formed in her throat. "I tried. I went but –"

"Are all women of Castile so weak or is it just you?" she pressed.

"Enough!" shouted Ibrahim from the doorway. "She made it all the way to the waterfront. You know that was not easy. After the Tuareg stole your parents you spoke to no one for months, so do not talk of weakness."

Anisa hissed and walked out.

Beatríz rose. "Ibrahim, I am so sorry."

"For what? My cousin's bad behavior or the gossips who stir up trouble?"

Beatríz smiled a little through her guilt. "But I was so slow."

"My grandmother called to stop you, but you were already gone. A neighbor came and helped her up."

"But Anisa said –"

"She is terrified of losing anyone else. She behaves badly when she is frightened."

"So do we all."

Ibrahim tipped his head. "Perhaps. Perhaps. She will not apologize, I think. Instead she will cook you a meal and pretend she never said such terrible things. You must forgive her and not mention it."

Beatríz pursed her lips, wanting to argue the point but

realizing she should not.

"Come. My grandmother wants to see you. She wants to introduce you to the neighbors. And be warned, she wants you to go to the market for her tomorrow." He looked at Beatríz and raised his eyebrows. "You can do it. It is only half as far as the waterfront."

CHAPTER 21

The next day, Beatríz crept out with Samira's basket over her arm. Her veil and *niqab* were reassuringly secure, though the air felt hotter as she breathed through it. The streets, which had been bustling just before she left, were suddenly quiet and Beatríz hesitated, wondering what had caused everyone to run away. Then she heard the call to prayer echoing from atop the minaret. She was unsure if she ought to continue walking since the signs said otherwise. But if she stopped, then what? She would not kneel down, and that would call just as much attention to herself. When Samira and Anisa were busy, they did not always stop. Women here were like women back home – exempt from the ritual of religion when the needs of the home pressed. Men followed the laws much more closely, and their adherence seemed to matter far more than any woman's.

She walked on. Her breath quickened. Her ears perked. Her awareness of every movement and person around her was keen. But as she moved through the peaceful town, she was able to study her surroundings for the first time since reaching Djerba. Around the corner from Ibrahim's, the streets widened enough that four people could walk across with their arms outstretched. The sand colored buildings were low and humble, many did have crumbling facades, but the streets were clean and there was no smell of refuse or rot. It was a smaller town than any she had ever lived in, so it took her little time to make her anxious way to the market.

When she arrived, the final strains of the call to prayer echoed and then went quiet. A few people still milled about, and Beatríz was relieved not to be the only one. The market square was not as large as those in Lisbon or Safi or Oran. Moving toward the stalls, shaded by simple earth-colored cloths rather than the colorful finery like those of the Maghreb, she wondered how different the goods might be. She was surprised to see that much was the same: fish stacked neatly in baskets, spices of umber, amber, and tan domed burlap sacks, metal cookware in bronze, silver, and black hung from hooks and lay piled high. For the first time, Beatríz saw a camel head placed proudly on the counter of the butcher's – a beast she had never known of until coming to the Maghreb. Seeing its long lashes and oblong, peaceful face made her sad, and she hurried toward the fruit seller's with a knot in her stomach. There were no bananas, as she had hoped, but there were olives – larger than any she had seen since Lisbon. She did not purchase the salty treats, however, since Samira had not asked for any and Beatríz had no money of her own.

Buildings emptied of the pious, and the marketplace bustled once again, putting Beatríz on edge. She tried to buy the needed items as quickly as she could to get back to the familiar safety of Ibrahim's home. But even through her anxiety, she could see that the people walking by seemed content and well fed. Friendly. There was less strain on the faces of the locals than there had been in Safi — a place of escape, of disease, and of war. The people of Djerba ambled along in their thin flowing robes, addressing neighbors. They all seemed to know one another. Beatríz thought that she might grow to be comfortable, to even like this new place, but she could not stop her mind from racing to the worst the strangers might do to her, so she bought the items as quickly as she could and hurried home.

She shopped for Samira the next day. And the next. And the next. She never forgot her fear, but she faced off with it each time she reached for the door latch and convinced herself to take the next step. Her pride grew, but she never grew complacent. She remained vigilant while out and said a prayer of thanks upon her return.

It was just after one such trip when Samira knocked on Beatríz's bedroom door.

"*Min fadli-ka*," called Samira.

Beatríz had grown accustomed to Samira's polite entrances. Even in her early days in the house when Beatríz could not bring herself to answer, Samira always had spoken to her as if she could.

"*Ahlayn*," Beatríz replied in greeting. She was pleased to finally be able to offer a few phrases back and loved seeing Samira's smile when she did.

"*Kayf haalik?*"

How was she? Beatríz hesitated. Though it was one of those questions a person asked as naturally as breathing, the answer came hard to Beatríz each time. She thought about it. Today was a good day. She could honestly tell Samira, "*Bi-khayr.*"

Samira smiled her broadest toothless smile as she did any time Beatríz was even the least bit at peace. Then Samira held out a pile of linen. She said something as she patted the cloth and gestured at Beatríz.

"*Shukrân*," Beatríz said, not sure what she was thanking Samira for. She rose and took the bundle into her own hands. Beatríz stared at the fabric, hardly hearing Samira say, "month" and "clean," for she was slapped by recognition. How long had it been since she had needed such cloths? When had she last bled? A tingling came over Beatríz as she sank to the bed. She began to cry even before the word "baby" formed fully in her mind.

Samira gripped her shoulder and was asking Beatríz questions, but Beatríz could not untangle the words or her thoughts. She was on that ship for many weeks, months, and had bled often. But the bleeding could have been from the ways they used her. Often it was. When she was with the captain…. How long had it been? Had she bled then? She did not think so, but what did that mean? Nothing. All of it meant nothing. Except that there was a baby growing in her.

What if it looked like one of the pirates? What if, when it was born, she saw the face of the fat man who broke her, or the freckled boy who released her, or even the captain? If she saw any of their faces, she would kill the child. She knew she would. Better to kill it now before it was fully grown. She could not see any of their faces again. She wanted it out.

What were the words she needed right now to ask Samira to help her? Had she ever known anyone who had done such a thing? Did she need medicine? A tool? How could she get Samira to understand?

"Please" she begged, taking Samira by the hands. "*Arjou-ki,*" she repeated in Arabic. Then Beatríz stopped, unsure of what words to use for what she wanted Samira to do. Cut? Take? Kill? Nothing came to her even though she used these words during her work with Samira in the kitchen. Like one of the beasts she and Samira prepared to eat, she would lay herself out and let Samira butcher her. She could not, would not have this baby.

Samira's eyes held their own sorrow now. She looked from the rags to Beatríz and back, and she began slapping her own face. The gesture upset Beatríz further, and Beatríz backed away. Samira reached out, but Beatríz ran into the kitchen. Just as on the first day she met Samira, Beatríz had every intention of using a knife to solve her problems. She took one from the cutting block and walked to the table, holding the blade out to Samira.

Samira understood perfectly well and began shaking her head immediately and arguing. "*Laa! Laa!*" Samira ran for the window and called across to Anisa, asking her to get Ibrahim.

"No!" Beatríz shouted back. "Not Ibrahim. You, Samira. Please."

Samira shook her head and laid the knife on the mattress. She spoke incessantly to Beatríz, as if speaking would keep Beatríz from any drastic action. The old woman kept muttering and rocking and touching Beatríz's face and muttering more, like an incantation. But to bring what? Peace? Calm? Unless it was the end of this baby, Beatríz could not image needing what Samira had the power to bring.

At long last, Ibrahim rushed in with Anisa close on his heels. He began, as he always did, by addressing his grandmother but kept his eyes fixed on Beatríz. When Samira explained, he fell to his knees in front of them. His face was red and a growl roared from his throat. It was the first time Beatríz had seen him angry, and she shrank back for fear that his anger would be directed at her, the whore he had brought into his home.

"Animals!" he shouted. "How could they – It was not bad enough – Those men –" He rose, his face twisted, and hurried from the room. A clatter of pots falling to the floor made Beatríz jump. Samira took Beatríz's temples in her palms and kissed Beatríz's forehead before walking out.

Beatríz could not understand the kind gesture. This had been her fault. She had insisted on leaving Rebecca and her grief in Oran, had foolishly forced her way onto Onur's boat, had not allowed herself to be killed rather than captured, and had attracted the attention of those men with her immodest hair. She had cried rather than submit and they had come for her all the more. It was because of her own stupidity and stubbornness that she was carrying the bastard child of any one of the disgusting men on that ship. It was her fault. She could not allow Ibrahim or Samira to believe it was any different.

Beatríz noticed Anisa standing across the room with her arms folded. Beatríz braced herself for Anisa's cutting truth. Instead Anisa raised her eyebrows and sighed. "He acts like you are his woman. And even if you were, what good would his anger do? Carrying on can only make you feel worse, *a laisa ka-dhaalika?* Of course I'm right." Anisa leaned out the door and clearly did not like what she saw.

Beatríz was confused. Anisa's disapproval aimed at Ibrahim? Why not at her?

"He knows what men are and what happens when they attack a boat. Or a village." Anisa's face darkened. "He cannot find them and get his – what is the word? – revenge. So the question becomes you. And what to do about you."

Beatríz pressed her lips together, measuring Anisa. "And what is to be done about me?" she asked, trying to keep the sharpness out of her voice.

"Nothing. There is a baby. You have nowhere to go. We care for you until it is born or until you leave. That is that."

"Baby." "Born." The words were like blows and Beatríz felt each one of them deep within. Her face crumbled and she pressed her hands to her stomach. She shook her head and dug her fingers further into her flesh.

"You do not want this baby," Anisa said firmly.

The word "no" caught in Beatríz's throat.

"Of course not. And my grandmother will not help you."

With a quavering voice, Beatríz said, "She will help by letting me live here and taking care –"

"No. I mean help you to get rid of it."

Moments earlier, Beatríz had been so ready to have Samira cut it out. But there was a part of her that was sure Samira would not and so she could act brash and wild, knowing someone would stop her. But Anisa's assuredness hinted at a knowledge Beatríz admitted she was frightened of.

"I can help you," said Anisa tugging at her emerald headscarf. "But you cannot tell anyone. If I were found out, well…."

As her voice drifted off, Beatríz wondered what it might mean for Anisa to be found doing this illegal, blasphemous thing. Imprisonment? Stoning? Having her family reject her? And what might be the consequences for Beatríz? Did she care?

Beatríz swallowed hard and pushed her clenched fists farther into her middle. It was sensitive and hard at the same time. She had been remotely aware of this before but had denied the change in her body. There was no denying it now. The faces of the pirates swam in her head again, making the nausea that she had also denied roll through her.

"I will not tell," Beatríz whispered.

"Act as if all is well. Or not well — but as if we have not had this conversation. Tomorrow come to my house and we will fix it."

Beatríz watched Anisa slip out, then rose herself and walked to the kitchen, stopping when she saw Ibrahim standing at the table, his head bowed so that strands of hair dangled over his forehead, swaying as he shook.

"If I could, I would find —" Ibrahim tightened his grip on the table so his knuckles popped white. "Revenge might be forbidden, but —" He spun away from Beatríz, but for the brief moment that she saw him, she could see his agony.

Why did he care so much? Who was she to him? If she could erase the pain from herself, would it erase the pain for him, as well? Going to Anisa's would mean not having to be reminded of her attack every day for the rest of her life, and that was what mattered most of all.

Beatríz kept to herself that night. She tried not to think about God or sin or her mother or Yusef or Ibrahim or disappointment or danger or the ship or the growing life inside of her. She tried and failed and did not sleep.

In the morning she rose sick and anxious. Samira tried to get her to eat but she refused. Instead she walked to Anisa's and knocked on the door. Anisa answered, her eyes flicking up to the window of her grandmother's house and back to Beatríz again. Beatríz was not even sure if Anisa knew she had looked up.

Beatríz followed Anisa up the steps and into the house. Her husband Fadil was slightly more successful in his business ventures, so their home was decorated with carpets and real chairs rather than flaking paint and benches. There were even cushions here and there covered in thick woven fabrics of reds, blacks, and whites.

Anisa handed Beatríz a small tied sack. Beatríz pulled open the string and fingered the dried leaves and flower heads.

Anisa spoke in a low voice even though they were alone. "Use half of what is in the bag and brew in boiling water. It will be bitter, but drink it all. If by tomorrow you do not bleed, brew the other half. You will feel sick, but that only means it is working. Do you understand?"

Beatríz nodded, mesmerized by the leaves inside. "Have you used this before?"

"No," Anisa answered quickly. "The leaves are not mine. They came from a friend. But I know they helped her and other women, too, though no one dares to speak of such things. Remember, you must not, either. Now go."

Beatríz hid the sachet in her palm and squeezed it tight, feeling relief for the first time since she let herself face the truth about her condition. She began walking to the door but turned back. "Anisa, why are you helping me?"

Anisa put her hands on her hips. "Because what has happened to you is not right. I know."

Beatríz bowed her head and squeezed the bag harder. "Thank you," she murmured.

When she reached her own house, Samira was gone. It was too early to go to the market, so Beatríz assumed someone had needed help, perhaps with a birth. Beatríz shuddered and filled a pot with water.

When at last it was ready, she untied the bag and looked at the leaves again. Half right then. But Anisa said it might not work. Maybe if she put in more, her chances for success would be better. The whole bag might be too much, but maybe not. After only the briefest hesitation, she decided to use it all.

As the water darkened, Beatríz said a prayer. "God, forgive

me for what I am about to do. I know that you are the one
who gives life and you are meant to be the one to take it. But
I cannot have this child. You cannot have intended for me to
suffer like this." Beatríz's thoughts grew dark and angry, but
she pushed them aside since she wanted to speak to God with
the purest of hearts. "If you see fit to punish me, I
understand. I believe I am doing right. Maybe not right, but
what I must. Forgive me."

She lifted the steaming cup to her lips and nearly dropped
the horrid smelling liquid. Anisa had warned her it would be
bad but Beatríz was not prepared for this. She held her breath
and drank as quickly as she could.

Immediately she began to vomit. She tried to hold it in,
sure that if she did not all of the benefits would be lost. Her
efforts proved impossible. She tried to keep her head in a
basin, but soon found her legs weak. When she hit the floor,
pain radiated from her middle. Pain worse than when the fat
sailor broke her maidenhead.

She woke up to shouting. Cold water slammed in her face
and someone shook her.

"Beatríz? Beatríz! What have you done?" Ibrahim's face
came into view before she closed her eyes again. He said
something to someone Beatríz could not see. A woman
answered. Beatríz gasped for breath. All went black.

Samira rocked Beatríz against her ample bosom. The
motion and the smell of cooked onion that lingered in
Samira's clothing sickened Beatríz. Samira murmured a prayer
and held Beatríz closer. Beatríz stopped feeling her grasp. She
stopped feeling anything.

The room was black. Beatríz burned all over and tried to ask for help, but no one heard her. Perhaps she was not speaking. Perhaps she was not moving. A fight raged somewhere nearby. The voices were in Castilian. She was home with her mother and father. No. They were dead. She knew this room was in Djerba. Who was speaking?

"If our neighbors find out, they will kill you."

"They will not find out unless you tell them."

"She could die."

"I told her not to drink the whole thing."

"You blame her?"

"She wanted it. She took it."

"*Oskoot,*" interrupted someone to silence them. Samira, Beatríz realized through her fog. Why had Anisa and Ibrahim been speaking in Castilian? To hide their words from Samira.

During the pause that followed, Beatríz nearly fell asleep.

"Get out!" shouted Ibrahim.

"Grandmother asked us to be quiet."

"I will be quiet when you are gone."

"I will go, but please tell me if she recovers."

Ibrahim offered no reply.

Anisa must have walked to the door because Samira sounded confused and was begging her to stay.

Anisa answered with a melancholy farewell, "*Laa. Ma'ssalaama.*" And with this, the door clicked shut.

Samira entered Beatríz's room followed by Ibrahim. Beatríz struggled to keep her eyes open, and when her gaze met Samira's, Samira shrieked and clasped her hands together. Then she knelt at Beatríz's bedside and stroked Beatríz's face. The comforting touch soothed Beatríz just enough that she lost her fight and let her eyes close.

"*Alhamdulillah.*" She heard Samira's whispered praise of

Allah before everything faded away.

The too-bright sun streamed into her room. Beatríz dragged her hands up to block it but lost control and her palms thumped onto her eyelids. She opened her mouth to gasp, but it felt full of fine sand and no sound escaped.

"How could you do it?" Ibrahim asked from somewhere nearby.

Though he had spoken barely above a whisper, each word thundered inside Beatríz. *Do what?* she wondered. Kill the baby? Nearly kill herself? The answers were so clear and yet she doubted she could ever make Ibrahim, or Samira for that matter, understand. A year earlier in Lisbon, she would have judged a pregnant girl who took a tansy tea as harshly as Ibrahim was judging her. Maybe more so. But Beatríz did not want to apologize. She did not want to explain.

"Are you going to tell your grandmother how I got the herbs?" she croaked.

"No. But I think she knows."

Beatríz tried to lick her lips but it felt like she was running them over with the spice grater. "How long was I...."

"Just last night and part of this morning."

"I am sorry for the mess."

"Yes, my grandmother cleaned your clothes and wiped you of the sickness."

Beatríz noticed she was in a robe of Samira's with its sleeves meant for a shorter woman. She added, "And blood." When Ibrahim merely tilted his head, she said, "She must have wiped me of the blood."

Ibrahim's eyes widened as he realized what she was implying. "No. There was no blood."

"But —" Beatríz sputtered and sat up quick enough to

make the room tip. Steadying herself she touched her stomach, and a lump resisted the pressure. Forgetting modesty, she pulled her gown up to her knees and turned on one hip. No blood. No cloth lay beneath her to protect the sheet. "How?"

Ibrahim pressed his lips together and shrugged, color rising in his cheeks.

"I need Samira in here. Now," Beatríz insisted ignoring the ripping of her dry lips as she spoke.

Ibrahim called for her.

Samira walked in wiping her hands dry. Her expression changed from concern to relief and around again.

Beatríz asked, "The baby is still in there?"

Samira nodded after Ibrahim translated. "*Alhamdulillah.*"

"Thank God? Thank God?" Beatríz's voice rose dangerously. "I wanted it out. How can this be? I nearly died and that – that *thing* is still in there?"

As Ibrahim explained, Samira's face went slack. Then her anger poured out in a torrent of words almost too fast for Ibrahim to translate. "Allah has saved you and you do not thank him? You committed a terrible act, one you should have been punished with by death, but you were allowed to live. You should be on your knees begging for forgiveness, but instead you shout?"

Samira began pacing and crying and Ibrahim took Samira in his arms. Then Samira said something and Ibrahim hesitated. When he refused to translate, she demanded he do so. His gaze did not meet Beatríz's as he said, "She says you might have damaged the baby. She wants to know what will you do if it is born crippled? How will you live with yourself knowing you were responsible?"

Beatríz covered her face. The thought of the baby being

harmed made her ill. Now that she was alive and recovering, knowing that she might have done something worse than kill the child made her want to die all the more. She balled her hands and began pounding her head with them. After a few solid blows, Ibrahim grabbed her. She struggled but was too weak to fight for long.

As Ibrahim held Beatríz, Samira spoke quietly to him.

"She says she should not have frightened you like that. If you had damaged it, it would have died. She does not want you to worry."

Beatríz closed her eyes. "It was not supposed to – Is there a chance I will still – that it will still...."

"Die?" Ibrahim turned and asked Samira.

Samira nodded.

Beatríz held herself very still trying not to feel remorse. She should have been glad at the news. Was this not precisely what she wanted? How could she suddenly feel protective of a baby she had tried to get rid of? Confusions and contradictions bit at her.

Samira excused herself, but not before apologizing again. The apology splintered Beatríz further.

"I wish you had left me to rot on that beach," Beatríz told Ibrahim.

"No, Beatríz. Stop such wicked talk. You are a miracle. You do not see it, but you are. Most would not have survived what you did. There is a reason."

Beatríz said nothing.

"Soon you will learn to see the baby and not what brought it."

Beatríz did not believe him. She knew that every time she looked at the child, nightmares would rise before her eyes. "Maybe it will kill us both when it is being born. I hope it will."

Ibrahim leaned against the wall and sighed. He looked like words were fighting to come out of him. But he said nothing.

CHAPTER 22

Beatríz considered leaving Djerba, but she had nowhere to go. Nowhere. And that fact rooted her in the eye of her personal storm.

Things were different between them after that day. Beatríz was not sure if she was imagining it, but underneath every interaction there seemed to be so much unspoken feeling. Worry. Anger. Confusion. Embarrassment. Relief. She felt watched when she most wanted to be hidden. And when she most wanted to lie still and sleep away her miserable days, she felt compelled to do more work to make up for frightening them. Her compromise was to rise earlier and prepare the morning meal, but to disappear when that was finished. Samira sighed often and watched Beatríz with a pensive face when she thought Beatríz was not looking. Beatríz saw little of Ibrahim, choosing to take her evening meals alone. She could not escape her extraordinary hunger, but she could escape his questioning stares.

She wanted forgiveness as much as she thought she had no right to seek it. And even if she did, even if forgiveness was to be granted by the mortals who had twice brought her back from the brink of death, she did not think she deserved it.

On her way home from the marketplace one afternoon, she saw Ibrahim at a distance moving among the people of Djerba with ease. He was not native, but this had become his home. Ibrahim stopped to join a circle of men trading stories. The worry that seemed to crease his face and the gentle way he moved in his house, melted away as he became a man among men. Suddenly, his head tilted back in a laugh and he patted the shoulder of a man in a black turban. As he excused himself, the men cried out their good wishes before closing their circle again. Ibrahim carried the laugh with him as he walked back to the water's edge.

That evening, Beatríz watched him carefully. He had worked since dawn, hoisted and carried, struggled under the weight of other men's goods, and yet he entered the house without bitterness or complaint. He kissed his grandmother, helped her move a heavy pot from the fire, poured himself a drink and sat smiling as Samira told him about a child whose arm she had set that afternoon.

His gaze met Beatríz's and her stomach flipped. She had not meant to stare at him, and having him catch her sent her from the room with burning cheeks.

What was that? Affection? Interest? Desire? She had thought such feelings had died with Yusef, and there was a part of her, a large part, that wished they had. She did not want to look at men. She did not want men to look at her. She did not want to want.

"Beatríz," Ibrahim called after her, "do not go. Come sit with us tonight." He said it as a question rather than a command.

Beatríz stood on the other side of the door considering the offer while trying to calm herself. Had she done enough to make amends? Had she shown the proper shame for an act she was not entirely ashamed of? Could she sit at the table like she had before? She was tired of being alone.

She opened the door and stopped. "I would like to," she began. Then she tested him with, "Shall we ask Anisa and Fadil to come?"

Ibrahim stiffened and Samira looked up at the name, anger curling her lips. Anisa did not come around anymore, but Beatríz was not sure whose doing it was. Beatríz had seen Anisa at the window once and waved, but Anisa had turned away. Beatríz had not tried again.

"No," Ibrahim said. His voice was sharp, but he softened it when he added, "But come. We have missed you at the table."

Beatríz moved forward self-consciously and sat. Even in the weeks since she had drunk the tea she thought her stomach looked bigger. Her clothes were loose as was the fashion, but she wondered if Ibrahim was watching the growth, noticing how the folds caught differently around her middle. She blinked several times trying to tame her emotions, to ignore the idea of him watching her and the unrelenting pain caused by thinking about the baby.

"Beatríz," Ibrahim asked once she was settled, "my grandmother wanted me to ask if you would like to go to church. Now that you are comfortable going out, perhaps you would like us to show you where it is. There is one, you see. A few Christians have lived here peacefully for some time and —"

"I am not a Christian," Beatríz interrupted. Then she

realized that she actually was.

"Then what are you?"

Was she anything? She felt like nothing. No one. But she said, "I am a Jew."

Ibrahim looked deep into her eyes. "Why?"

"Why?" Beatríz asked almost laughing. "Because that it what I was at my birth."

"And you have chosen to remain so?"

"Why are you a Muslim?"

"Because it is the true path."

Beatríz felt a smile pull at the corners of her mouth. "For you."

"For all."

She sighed. How often had others tried to change her, to stamp out who she was. And yet, she wanted to discuss this. Arguing about such matters felt liberating. Exciting. Certainly better than thinking about poisoning herself.

She asked, "Would you have asked the same question if I said I was a Christian and wanted to go to church?"

He pulled at his collar. "No. But I would have known it was wrong."

This time Beatríz did laugh. His certainty was both offensive and intoxicating. "How can you be so sure? Judaism has been around longer than Islam. And we are, after all, the Chosen People."

Ibrahim leaned in, his eyes sparkling. "Were."

Beatríz reflexively sucked in her breath, but was not truly upset.

Samira asked him to translate, but Ibrahim told her, "Later," without breaking his gaze with Beatríz. "Clearly God has pulled his favor from you. Your people have been suffering for a very long time now, no? Being chased from here to there. Exiled. Murdered. Blamed for everything that goes wrong in the Christian cities."

Beatríz could see a truth in that, but countered, "Perhaps He has not pulled favor, as you say. Perhaps God is using the Christians as an instrument to punish us for our sins. Teaching us a lesson, if you will."

"What sins?"

Beatríz was stunned by the fact that she had never really thought about it. Everyone she knew bandied about the phrase 'punished for our sins' but there never an explanation or a detailing of what precisely needed changing. Jewish law was so intricate, so beyond the understanding of most (and certainly beyond Beatríz) that to question it was absurd. One act she might consider quite wrong was deemed acceptable while another that seemed equally or less important was prohibited.

Beatríz's mind then went to the personal – of the lust she once felt for Yusef, of not having honored her parents enough, of conceiving a child out of wedlock, of not always following the dietary laws of *kashrut*. She was certainly being punished, but her entire community? Were Jews so much more sinful than Christians and Muslims that they deserved special punishment? It did not seem so. Or maybe Ibrahim was right and it was the very fact that they had remained Jews, that they had not accepted Jesus or Muhammad.

"I am not sure," she said at last. "I only know that the rabbis claim we are not good Jews and that we are being punished for it."

"It is self-evident that Islam is the true religion. Allah gave us power over all land, all cities, and all peoples while you Jews are powerless and dispersed and depend on our good will. Allah put us in charge because you have not yet realized what the truth is."

Beatríz thought back to Toledo, then to Lisbon, lingering only momentarily on its lovely trees and hills, its waters, its towers. "You are mistaken, Ibrahim. Where I come from, there are only Christians in charge. How can you say Muslims are all powerful?"

He scoffed like one listening to a child share theories, correcting it without wanting to hurt its feelings. "Beatríz," he said, letting the R in her name roll gently, "everyone knows that the power enjoyed by the Christians is temporal."

Beatríz could not but hope he was right about this. "The rabbis would disagree that Islam is the only way."

"Rabbis know there can only be one truth. One God. One true path. All the rest are misinterpretations or bastardizations of God's will. Whether the rabbis hold to what is incorrect innocently or not I cannot say. But the wisest men know the truth: that Mohammad (may peace be upon him) was God's last prophet. Only in wickedness do men choose not to recognize it."

Beatríz considered what he said about rabbis. Rabbis had their own motivations for what they did and said. They were just men, after all. If they admitted they were wrong, they would be obsolete. Had she seen any evidence that rabbis knew more than other men? She had been unimpressed with those men and their wisdom on the whole, but were the men Ibrahim trusted any more trustworthy or wise? Wickedness seemed rampant regardless of one's professed beliefs.

"Tell me, Ibrahim, how is what you believe different from what I believe?"

"There is one God who took as his prophets Abraham and Moses. To them he revealed the will of God, the straight path."

"That is in the Torah."

Samira interrupted and told them to eat. They each broke a piece of flatbread and put it in their mouths.

After swallowing, Ibrahim continued, "Yes. And then God sent Jesus."

Beatríz forgot her mouth was full. "You believe in Jesus?"

"That he was a great prophet sent by God, yes."

She put down the bread wiping the crumbs off of her hands as if that would help her understand. "You believe in Jesus?" she asked again.

Ibrahim laughed. "Yes. And I believe the Christians embarrass him with their worship. What truth could there be in a religion that worships the infinite and ineffable God in the form of an idol made of stone and wood?"

Beatríz considered the peaceful and the pained Jesuses hanging in the church and in the barracks. Depicting God or any stories was strictly forbidden in the Torah and she had struggled with having images in front of her during prayer. But idol worship? Was that what the Christians were doing?

Ibrahim continued, "How could The Eternal be a man of human flesh? How could The Eternal perish like a common man? How can this be if there is one all-powerful infinite God who is everywhere, not fixed in any one place or time? Does this make sense to you?"

Beatríz shook her head.

"After Jesus, God, in his mercy, sent Mohammad as his final prophet (may peace be upon him). 'Islam' means 'submission.' One must submit to the one true path –"

Samira had had enough. She pounded on the table and commanded them to eat. Ibrahim lifted the flatbread to his mouth with great flourish and then Beatríz did the same. Only when they were all eating and speaking Arabic again about the unexpected heat and who might be coming for Samira's help that night did Samira seem content.

The next evening, Ibrahim brought a package to Beatríz. He had never given her a gift before. "I thought all day about our conversation last night and I felt I owed you an apology. Your religion is important to you and by disrespecting it I disrespected you."

Beatríz leaned against the cutting block. "I thank you for your concern. I thought it was interesting, actually, what you had to say." She had considered his words all night, for, as usual, she hardly slept, and had not been sure what she thought of his opinions.

Ibrahim nodded, studying Beatríz's face. She was self-conscious, wondering what he saw there. "Open it."

She did. It was a wooden spoon.

"A small token," he said. "I know you and my grandmother share at times and I thought it would be more convenient for you to have your own."

Her own. She did not own anything. Not one thing. Everything had been left in Toledo, in Lisbon, on Onur's boat, on the pirate ship. Not her satchel with the wooden button, her ruby earrings, or even her dress had survived the journey. This spoon was the first thing she owned in her new life. The first evidence that she might have her own things again. That she might one day have a home. She studied its smooth beauty and thanked him without being able to look up.

"And I meant to tell you," he said, "there are Jews in Djerba. Would you like to meet them? Perhaps you will feel more at home in their company."

Beatríz thought about it, wondering if anyone she knew

might have landed on these shores. But the thought of seeing them actually troubled her. Not realizing her hands had drifted to cover her stomach, she said quietly, "This is my home. Those people and I share nothing but a religion. I will stay here. But I thank you."

She held the spoon against her chest for a moment before turning and dipping it into the pot. Her voice uncertain, she said, "Unless you are suggesting it because you wish for me to leave. I have been here much longer than –"

"No. We like the company. And my grandmother likes your help."

"Thank you again. It has been so long since...." She did not finish. She was unable to narrow down all of things she had gone without, all the things she was thankful for. She was aware that Ibrahim stood and waited for the conclusion of her thought, but she could not speak past the lump in her throat. She stirred away her sorrow and her longing with his gift and felt his eyes on her.

That night, she thought about Yusef, as she often did. Thorns of emotion stabbed at her when his face merely flickered through her mind, and recalling entire conversations fairly tore her apart. But she could not stop herself. She wanted to remember as much as she wanted to forget.

She recalled a night they had walked together, just before his departure. She had dragged him into the shadowy archway of an abandoned building and pulled him to her, their faces inches apart. Breathing deeply, she had taken in his intoxicating musk, her knees growing weak. And when he had kissed her neck and let his lips drift to her bosom, she had had to concentrate on not collapsing. She had wanted to pull him down to the ground and let him run his hands under her dress like he had the one time they had snuck to the riverside and found themselves alone on a grassy hill.

He pulled back and caught his breath, reaching for her ruby earrings.

"Why did you wear these?" he asked, his face darkening.

"I will not let the Venetian's hatred of us diminish this gift. The earrings are beautiful. And we do not live in Venice."

Yusef had frowned. "Where is there a place for us, Béa? A place for us to enjoy a life together? I want it more than anything in the world."

She stepped into him. "Right here in Lisbon." He had opened his mouth to argue, but she pressed her fingers to his lips. "And if not here, somewhere else. Earrings. No earrings. Laws or no laws. We will build a life and be happy just for being together."

His shoulders relaxed and he smiled. "The world might disappoint me, but you never do."

Lying awake in Samira's house, Beatríz touched her stomach and felt disappointment enough for them both.

The next evening Samira was called away during mealtime. Ibrahim protested that the emergency could wait, that it was not good for her to run out each time she was needed. She nodded and agreed all the way out the door.

Ibrahim sat back down and sighed. "She will run herself into the grave."

"This gives her pleasure and purpose. I wonder if this is what has allowed her to grow so old."

"You know, I began counting the other day and I believe she might be at least sixty-five."

Beatríz's mouth dropped open.

"I am fairly certain I am twenty-five and she says she was

fifteen when she had my mother. My mother was over twenty when I was born. So yes. Sixty-five. Can you imagine living to such an age?"

"No," answered Beatríz, thinking that if life continued as it had been going, she was not sure she would want such a fate.

They reached for their food and ate in silence for a bit. Then he asked, "Since my grandmother is not here, shall we pick up our discussion of religion?"

Beatríz shook her head. "Another time. I am very tired today. I try not to show Samira, but each day I feel more weary. Each day I think it cannot get worse and then it does."

The baby hung in the air between them, unspoken.

"Tell me, Ibrahim, about your family."

"What is there to tell?" he said, trying to shrug off the question. When Beatríz raised her eyebrows and offered no way out but to answer, he began, "I was born in a village near Tlemçen, which, as you might know, is rather near Oran on the Mediterranean coast. I was the second to last child of seven. My mother died with the last and my father remarried. But a plague came through when I was young and carried him and his new family away, along with most of my brothers and sisters. My grandmother took in my younger sister and me and raised us. I married a girl from another village. You know the rest."

She could tell that speaking of his family, particularly of his wife, pained him, so chose not to press. "How did you become a trader?"

"Before I was married," he said, and Beatríz noticed his eye twitch as he said the word, "I knew I had to help support my grandmother. I made my way to the coast and sailed for a few years learning how business worked, learning new languages. I came home when I could and brought her and my sister my earnings. But one trip back my grandmother begged me to stay, to settle and find a way to trade by land. And so I did. Until..." His voice trailed off and he ate in silence, though it seemed each bite scraped its way down his throat. "And what about you?" he said finally.

She told him about her life and her family, and how she did not know who was still alive. She told him about Yusef and tried not to weep. Mourning for him had been so wrapped up with her terrible journey that it almost felt as if she had not done it.

Ibrahim looked at her with unfettered sorrow. "People who have not lost those they love most to violence cannot understand. There are deaths every day, but when it is at the hands of men, there is something . . . irresolvable about that pain."

Ibrahim reached out and touched her hand. Without thinking, she clasped it back. And then her mind swirled. Yusef's fingers laced through hers. A sailor holding her wrists. Yusef's hand on the small of her back. Hands grabbing at her.

Beatríz shot to her feet, her breathing shallow. Ibrahim sat wide-eyed as she backed away and ran for her room, sliding down against the door. She pressed her palm against her lips – lips where Yusef's used to linger – and held in a scream.

For weeks, Beatríz's had tried to deny that her stomach was growing, pretended she did not notice the aches, and ignored the swelling of her fingers and feet.

Until.

One morning, she had finished helping Samira make dough when she felt a popping in her abdomen. Nothing strong. More like a tickling within her skin. The sensation repeated itself and she had frozen mid-step without realizing it. Samira came to her side and put a hand on Beatríz's wrist. Beatríz tore her focus away from the mystery and described it to Samira.

Samira's smile widened showing the gaps where her front teeth had once been. *"Tifil,"* she said. And when Beatríz did not react, she pointed at Beatríz's stomach and made a wiggling motion with her fingers.

"The baby is moving?" Beatríz asked, the blood draining from her head. If there was something moving, then it was real. It was not an idea to hate or ignore. It was in there and it was growing stronger. Why did this surprise her? She knew. She knew. And yet it was inconceivable. Moving. Inside. Beatríz did not know whether to marvel or be horrified. She wanted to scream.

Samira pulled Beatríz's wrist, which she was still holding, up to her own lips to kiss. The gesture was heartbreakingly kind and Beatríz forced herself to smile a little before excusing herself from the room.

She sat and stared out the window for a long time. This was real. The baby would come. She had to make a decision about her future. And the child's.

With sadness pressing upon her chest, she waited for Ibrahim to come home. When he did, she asked if he would mind speaking with her privately. She knew Samira would not understand their conversation, but still she could not speak as freely if she knew they were being watched. They stepped into her room, both careful not to close the door all the way.

"I have decided to leave," she began, her voice catching at the end.

Ibrahim crossed his arms and blew out a long breath before asking, "Why?"

"This baby is coming whether I like it or not. I cannot go

on living by your charity. I am not your family, so you —" Her voice broke off and she pressed her fingertips to her forehead.

"*We* could be your family," he said stepping closer. He took a deep breath. "I could be your husband." He paused to let the words sink in then added, "Would you be my wife?"

Beatríz's stomach tightened. The question she had been expecting and dreading had been asked at last. She found herself unable to respond, to even think of one of the answers she had practiced in her head in case her suspicion was right.

At her silence, he crossed his arms harder against his chest. "Tell me why you hesitate."

Beatríz's lip began to tremble. The reasons were so clear and yet, with this kind man in front of her, she could not bring herself to say any of them.

"You are waiting for him still," Ibrahim said, his voice even, his face passive. It was not a question.

Beatríz looked at her feet and tried to compose herself enough to speak. "I know," she began then paused to breathe. "I know it is foolish. He is dead . . . And yet in my heart . . ." A group of children ran along the street outside squealing with joy. Beatríz wished she could feel that unadulterated happiness once more. "I fear I can never be wholly yours while I think of him."

"Do you like me?"

Beatríz's looked into Ibrahim's warm, welcoming eyes. Noticed the beautiful curve of his nose, his strong hands. She felt, as she often did, a wave of peace wash over her. She nodded slowly.

The smallest of smiles softened his lips. "And I like you very much. With that we shall have more to begin with than most marriages, no?"

Beatríz nodded again, but her stomach tightened further. She had loved Yusef with a passion that stunned even her, and she had thought that when she married, she would be unlike everyone else she knew who married for convenience.

He continued tenderly, "I think if we help each other find even a little happiness in this world, it will be a success. To be alone is no good."

Beatríz thought about the years spread out before her. She knew Ibrahim was kind. She knew she was having a baby. She knew most of the people she loved were dead or missing. As far as she knew, this was home. And if this was home, she wanted Ibrahim to be part of her life.

She nodded. "I will marry you," she whispered, a mix of joy and pain whirling so fast within her she could not separate them.

His face cracked into a smile and he rushed to take her hand. "You have made me happy. I will try to be a good husband to you."

"And I," she said, her voice breaking, "will try to be a good wife to you." She blinked back tears, knowing it was true. She wanted to make Ibrahim's life better, to repay him for having improved hers. If she could return only a fraction of the security and peace that he provided, she would consider her life a success. And yet.

"I will tell my grandmother the news." He squeezed her hand and looked deep into her eyes. She smiled despite her confusion, and that was all that he needed to laugh with relief. "You make me so very happy, Beatríz. So happy."

He leaned in and kissed her cheek before backing sheepishly away. "I am sorry," he said, flushed. "I should have asked."

Beatríz stepped forward and kissed his cheek. "If we are to be husband and wife, we will kiss quite often, I should think."

"It is not the custom of my people to do such things, especially before a wedding."

Beatríz nodded. "You will have to teach me your customs, but sometimes we can act like my people. We like kisses. Even when they get us into trouble." She smiled a little wickedly, but then remembered her brother hitting her at the card party for kissing Yusef so passionately, and of the overwhelming desire she had felt for Yusef. Of stealing kisses the morning before Yusef left Lisbon for the last time, and wishing he would forget custom and take her right there under the arched sea wall.

Her smile pinched. "Tell your grandmother. I will be here," she said, backing toward the window.

As soon as he left, and Beatríz heard Samira squeal with delight, Beatríz covered her mouth with her hands and cried as quietly as she could.

It was so different from the first time. Yusef asking her on the banks of the river. Her parents' joy that the union would help their business. *Erusin.* Miriam holding Yusef's and Beatríz's hands together, saying a blessing. The betrothal party with its candelabras and green dresses.

A touch on her shoulder made her jump.

Ibrahim's knit brow cut through her. "This will not be easy for you," he said.

She shook her head. "It is no reflection on you, Ibrahim. I wish..."

"I know."

Forgetting all propriety, she threw her arms around him. At first he was stiff, but after a moment, he leaned into her, and she felt his hands on her back.

"Shhhh . . ." he whispered, and she melted further into his embrace.

CHAPTER 23

For a few days, all was bliss. Or at least as close to bliss as Beatríz had had in a long time. They had decided that it made the most sense to stay in Djerba, and Beatríz began to feel like she might once again have a home. Ibrahim smiled often and found reasons and ways to stand close to and sometimes touch her. She focused on not being afraid, of knowing that he cared for her and that, unlike most men, his intentions were good. Samira was even kinder, if that was possible, and looked at her stomach not with concern but as the home of her first great-grandchild. The fearful voices in Beatríz's head were quiet and she thought of the past less often.

The peace was broken, however, by one sentence.

"I spoke to the Imam and he can perform your conversion the day after tomorrow," Ibrahim said casually while reaching for a spoonful of eggplant at supper.

Beatríz swallowed hard. "My what?"

"You look pale," he said reaching out and stroking her cheek. "If you are afraid of a man you do not know, we can simply do it here with my grandmother and myself as your witnesses."

To Beatríz, he sounded as if he were speaking under water. She strained to make sense of his words. "Forgive me, but my witnesses for *what?*"

"Your conversion. You will, of course, become a Muslim before we are married."

Beatríz concentrated on not letting her mouth fall open any further. "Why?"

He squinted at her as if unsure whether he really needed to explain. Then speaking slowly, he said, "Because I cannot marry you unless you are."

Beatríz excused herself quickly from the table.

Standing in her room she reprimanded herself and marveled at her capacity to see only what she wanted to see.

Ibrahim knocked and she allowed him to enter. He did not say anything but pressed his lips together, a mild panic in his eyes.

"What if I want to remain a Jew?"

At this he furrowed his brow. "Then we cannot marry."

"Ibrahim, it is not illegal for us to –"

"Not illegal, no. We are both people of The Book. But it would not be accepted by our friends and neighbors. Or by me."

"But . . . " she said, her voice falling away.

Then he said, "I want to be with you, but I will not defile either one of us. We must be married before we...." He flushed at the thoughts in his own head and his fingers twitched a little. "Before the child is born. I want to raise that child, but I want to raise it properly. And the only way is for it to be Muslim. I will not have a wife or a child who are not following the true path."

"And I will not –" she began, puffing herself up, but

realized she did not know what she would or would not do anymore. She needed a husband. She needed a father for her baby. She knew she would agree to do as he wished. "You are asking a great deal of me, Ibrahim."

He pulled at his chin. "We are asking a great deal of each other. This marriage will not begin easily for either of us."

Beatríz's hands jumped to cover her stomach.

He walked toward her and moved her hands away, clasping them in his own. "This will be good for us both. And we discussed this before: our religions are not so very different."

Beatríz looked at their entwined hands and softened. It was all just words, was it not? She was a Jew because her parents had told her she was. She became a Christian in Lisbon because someone said so. She could be a Muslim here because her desire to be with Ibrahim, as well as common sense, told her she had to be. Would it change her life so very much? She thought not. Her faith had been shaken if not shattered and she needed to begin anew in every way. Taking this step with Ibrahim might even bring her closer to God, to understand what was expected of her. Keeping a pious Muslim home was not such a difficult thing to imagine. She already did.

However, each time she envisioned Ibrahim as the man in that home, she felt a mild shock. Ibrahim was not the problem. His not being Yusef was the problem. Could she marry Ibrahim knowing that every evening when the door opened, she would hope Yusef would walk through it? Would that feeling fade? Perhaps when she and Ibrahim had a child of their own – a child. Ibrahim was willing to be a father to the baby. Ibrahim was willing to take care of her. It was the right choice.

"All right. I will do it," she said. "But I want Anisa to be one of the witnesses."

His flash of relief vanished. "She —"

"No, Ibrahim. This is what I want. The past is past. If she is angry, I will make amends. If you are angry, you will put your feelings aside. She helped me when I needed it." She put up her hands to stop Ibrahim from interrupting. "I know you disagree with what she and I tried to do, but I must say I do not care at this moment."

His expression was hard. "Anisa and I said many things that night. I do not know if she will agree to come here."

"It is time to be a family again. You only have each other and I will not be the reason that that is lost." She reached out for him and he melted at her touch.

"Yes," he said. "Ask her tomorrow."

He took her hand from his arm and kissed her knuckles, a gesture she thought she might never tire of. Then he made to leave.

She stopped him with, "Ibrahim, what will people say to your marrying a convert expecting a child who is clearly not your own?"

Unexpectedly, his face lit up with amusement. "Well, Beatríz, as the saying goes, 'Dogs bark but the caravan moves on.'"

Beatríz took a moment to sort out the meaning and then started to smile. They would be the topic of gossip at some tables for a while, but he was right. It truly did not matter what anyone else said or thought.

Anisa was not at home when Beatríz knocked and so Beatríz went looking for her at the marketplace. Beatríz spotted Anisa first, but once their eyes met, Anisa turned the other direction. Beatríz gave chase and finally caught up with her.

Anisa wheeled around and asked sharply, "What do you want?"

Beatríz hesitated a moment wondering if she ought to simply let the matter go, but she drew in a breath reminding herself that Anisa's sharp tongue was not only used to hurt others but also to protect herself. "Anisa, Ibrahim has asked me to marry him."

Anisa's eyes danced, but she said nothing.

"I am becoming a Muslim. Samira and Ibrahim will be my witnesses, and I would like you there, too."

Anisa still said nothing. She just twisted the strap of her bag around her hand.

"And before the wedding, I would like you to be my, uh . . ." She searched for the word for the woman who would help her prepare for the ceremony. "My *negaffa*."

Anisa's face twitched. Beatríz braced herself for rejection, had prepared for it. But waiting for the answer, she realized she would be quite hurt if Anisa refused.

"Yes," Anisa said, "I will help you." Beatríz exhaled audibly, but Anisa's eyes narrowed. "If you were not expecting a baby, would you be marrying my cousin?"

Beatríz looked down. "I do not know." Then she looked up at Anisa through her lashes. "But I am. And he asked. And I want to be his wife."

Anisa did not smile, but nodded pensively. "He needs a wife. It has been too long since he had happiness."

Ibrahim's first wife and Yusef haunted the space between them. "When will this all take place?" Anisa asked.

"Tomorrow is the conversion and the wedding will be next week. Samira is arranging the ceremonies and feast. I thought it ought to be quick, but she does not want to rush too much. I am at her mercy."

The women exchanged knowing smiles and said they would see each other in the morning.

Beatríz had not wanted to go to the Imam for her conversion. It reminded her too much of the priests taking people and forcing them into the baptismal fonts. She did not think that the Imam would be cruel or rough with her, especially with Ibrahim present, but she hesitated nevertheless.

Beatríz began by washing and putting on new clothes. Anisa had given a pale blue cotton robe with swirls of gold embroidery on the collar and cuffs to Beatríz as a present, and Beatríz admired the softness of the fabric against her sensitive skin. She marveled at how such a small thing made her so happy. In Lisbon, and Toledo before that, she had always liked when her mother gave her new dresses, but she could not say that their fine fabrics and delicate lace pleased her as much as this simple robe. She had never appreciated how much work it took to save for something new, or thought that clothes could be given out of love and not because they would make her more attractive in the eyes of the neighbors, or a more valuable catch in marriage.

After she washed, Anisa came in. Beatríz was as ready as she could be, and so they joined Samira and Ibrahim in the common room of their house. Samira stood next to the plain wooden table, palms pressed together, smiling wide. Anisa stepped to Samira's side and turned to face Beatríz, who felt uncomfortably on display. The dry, still heat of the morning pressed on her as much as her conscience, and she began to sweat. While the others stared at her, she tugged haplessly at her yellow veil and wiggled her newly washed bare feet, wishing someone would say something. Beatríz would have liked Ibrahim to have held her hand or offered some gesture of affection as she readied herself., but he was all solemnity and purpose.

"You will memorize the prayers over time," Ibrahim said to her, "but for now, repeat after me."

Beatríz breathed deeply. They were just words, after all. She would say them and try to believe.

She repeated, *"Ash-hadu anna laa ilaha illa llah wa-sh-hadu anna muhammadan rasoul llah,"* recalling the translation: "I bear witness that there is no deity but Allah and I bear witness that Muhammad is the Messenger of Allah."

And so it was done. Those eleven words were all it took to change her life. Samira pulled her into a hug stronger than Beatríz could imagine the old woman had the strength for, and Ibrahim kissed her cheek and backed away bowing his head. Beatríz basked in their affection and tried not to imagine what her mother and father might say if they had been present.

Anisa folded her arms, "So, no lightning bolts have come through the ceiling. Are you all right?"

Beatríz nodded. "Thank you for being here."

Ibrahim said, "It is custom to change your name to a Muslim name upon a conversion."

"Change my name?

Shyly he said, "I was thinking of *Hadiya*, which is 'gift.'"

Beatríz shook her head. "That is a lovely name, but my name is…my name. It is me. I cannot suddenly become someone else. This is all I can change for today."

"Hadiya," Samira said as she came forward to hug Beatríz again.

Beatríz shook her head, and said, "*Laa*, Samira." She pointed to herself and repeated, "Beatríz."

Samira patted Beatríz's cheeks and looked at her indulgently before calling her Hadiya again. Beatríz's helpless eyes met Ibrahim's and he proposed that they take a walk – chaperoned, of course, by Anisa.

They walked to the marketplace, Beatríz caught Ibrahim looking at her with sparkling fondness, and she felt awash in serenity.

The market itself was teeming, and Anisa, Beatríz, and Ibrahim took their time going from stall to stall. They passed a jewelry merchant and stopped to look at his wares. The table was sparsely laid out, but the work was fine. Beatríz's hands brushed across a pair of gold earrings designed with swirls. Ibrahim picked them up, held them to her ears and said, "Beautiful. I will get them for you. A bride is meant to have gold for a wedding present."

Beatríz's serenity shattered. "No, Ibrahim, please."

"I can pay for it. I have more than you think."

She put her hand on his and the merchant eyed them disapprovingly. "It is not the cost," she began, but could not finish. How to explain without hurting him that Yusef had given her earrings that she had treasured above all other belongings? That those earrings had been the last possession she had let go. That she did not believe she could marry him and not think of Yusef every day.

"You have given me everything. Let me give you these," he insisted.

Beatríz bit at her lips and watched him take coins from his purse. It would do no good to explain because it was not just the earrings.

"Thank you," she said softly.

"Put them on," Anisa suggested.

With shaking hands, Beatríz took them from Ibrahim. It had been so long since she had worn earrings that she had to push them hard through the closed up flesh of her lobes. She winced and found the pain was a relief. At least it gave her an excuse to wipe at her eyes.

When they reached the house again, Beatríz, restless, said she wished to keep walking and refused Ibrahim's offer for company. She wandered the streets only flinching occasionally at loud noises and low voices, not sure where she was headed, but needing to get away.

"*Ve con el diablo! Mala landre te mate!*" someone shouted.

Beatríz's head snapped to the side and she searched for the source of these familiar words. A turbaned man was lifting a fallen crate with olives spilling out, and was still muttering curses. He spoke Aragonese, which was so close to Castilian that Beatríz was suddenly transported to the land of her birth, to workingmen jostling goods and shouting in the streets. Beatríz gaped at the man gathering the rogue olives back into their crate. When he stopped to stretch, he startled at the sight of a woman staring at him.

Beatríz felt the need to say something. "You are from Aragon?" she asked.

"Yes. Teruel."

She lowered her *niqab*, as she was still unaccustomed to talking through it, and said, "I was from Toledo."

He squinted at her and said, "Then you are a *renegada*."

Beatríz gasped. Back in Castile before her family had left, Beatríz had heard the term used in impolite conversation for someone who reneged on his faith. A traitor. There were many whom she knew that converted and became New Christians, much to the frustration of their community, and were smeared with this term. But it was so long ago. Times had changed and circumstances had forced many to decide to do the same thing or die refusing. She did not think the same people would slander their neighbors these days for their choices. But maybe they would.

"I do not think that *renegados* fits us," she said.

"Us?"

She gestured at the turban covering his hair. "We are the same, I think."

The man let his eyes drift to her veil. "You were also forced to become a Muslim?"

"No."

"Then you are not like me," he said bitterly, sitting on a low wall. "I was converted against my will."

Beatríz walked to the wall and sat close enough to talk, but not suggestively near. "What happened to you?"

"Twenty years ago I was captured in battle. I was not wealthy enough to be ransomed and so I have been kept here all this time as a slave."

"For twenty years?"

"Yes," he said. Then he straightened up and added, "But I will escape someday. I will once again find my way to the mountains of Teruel and hunt in the forests of Aragon. I will feel the cool breezes and see the peaks rise above me. Not like this place. This flat, dusty island where no one cooks as my mother did, or thinks as I do. Where there is little to hunt, and the air is like an oven."

Beatríz shielded her eyes and was suddenly aware of the sun beating on her covered head. She looked around to see if anyone was listening to their conversation and asked quietly, "Can you not escape?"

"If we were not on an island, it might be possible. I have

tried. I will try again. At least I was not a galley slave. Then there would have been little hope."

Beatríz flinched.

"Did I upset you?"

Beatríz blinked rapidly and said no. She did not want to reveal anything to this stranger.

"How have you come here to Djerba?" he asked.

She watched the townspeople bustling by and said simply, "I left my home and landed here." She could feel him studying her, but did not turn to face him.

"And why are you a Muslim?" the man asked.

At this, Beatríz looked at him again. "I am to marry a man from Djerba."

"So you will never go home?"

She tugged at a corner of her veil. "I have no other home now."

"But you have people. Surely somewhere you have people. If you marry here, you will never see them again."

She cleared her throat and felt flames of longing lick up within her. "Everyone scattered. Some are dead."

"But not all?"

"In truth, I do not know what has happened to my family."

"And your friends? Tell me you do not miss those who understand you better than the people you know here! Who see colors the way you do. Who dream in your mother tongue. Who laugh at the same things that you find funny. That is more than religion. That is who you are."

"I do not know who I am," she said, folding her hands in her lap. "I have lost everything."

The man took a small knife and a stick out of a satchel on his belt and began scraping at the bark. "When you wake up in the morning, what do you feel you are?"

"Castilian."

"And?"

"A Jew."

He raised one eyebrow. "Then that is what you are."

She stood, frustrated by the conversation. This life in Djerba was the only chance she had. She could not doubt it now. It had to work. "I can change. I have only been Muslim for a few hours. I was a Jew for my entire life."

A wicked smile crept across the man's face. "You can change the language and how you dress and even what you say, but you are what you are. Why do you think they are burning people in Castile? They know there are liars among them just as I am a liar. Are you a liar, too?"

Beatríz wanted to rise in outrage, but the truth pressed down too heavily. "Yes."

"That is fine. We lie to save ourselves and to find happiness. Have you found happiness here?"

Beatríz did not answer, though she knew she ought to.

"Safety at least?"

She realized her head was nodding. She did not wish to answer any more of this man's questions, yet she could not make herself stop.

He shaved more bits of stick onto the dirt underfoot. "Safety is not to be underestimated. If you have someone to care for you, that is enough reason to change. As for me, safety is not such a concern, which is why I will escape to Aragon if I can."

"So even after all this time, you would try?"

"I would risk my life even if it was only for one decent slice of *jamon* and a bottle of wine."

Beatríz had not missed *jamon*, for her family, like

Ibrahim's, never ate pork. But the wine she had not realized she missed until the man mentioned it. And once he had, the thought consumed her.

Self-awareness pricked at her spine and she wished to speak more to the man, but a shout came from down the street and the man rose. A younger man came close and began talking quickly about olives and time, and something else Beatríz could not follow.

The man with whom Beatríz had been talking lifted the crate, bidding her farewell as he walked away. Beatríz gave a perfunctory wave as she was swept away by thought.

CHAPTER 24

On the day before the wedding, neighbor women hurried about Anisa's house, chattering and laughing. Beatríz understood few of their words, but took pleasure in their joy even though she herself had been consumed by doubt for days and had endured many sleepless nights. Samira laughed more heartily than usual and looked younger than her years. Even her limp seemed to have faded.

Beatríz tried very hard not to think of Yusef, of how this day was meant to be theirs. She tried not to think of the *chuppah* – the canopy – their brothers should have been holding over the couple during the ceremony, the dress her sisters should have been buttoning, the smiles her mother should have been smiling. She pushed away each thought with such force that she was exhausted before the sun shone strongly on the rooftops. The women, seeing Beatríz fade, brought her tea and began to dance. It was unexpected and thrilling to watch them twirl and laugh and sing.

Samira took Beatríz's hands and said, "Hadiya, you make Ibrahim happy. I never thought I would see him happy again.

I thank you."

Beatríz dropped her head, feeling unworthy of such love when misgivings seeped into every moment. But it was right. Ibrahim was good. And she wanted to be with him. Didn't she?

She squeezed Samira's hands in hers, and took a moment to marvel again at the hennaed floral and geometric patterns that had been painted on her hands and feet an hour earlier. Not reading Arabic, Anisa had had to show her where Ibrahim's name had been worked into the henna design during the *beberiska* ceremony. Beatríz smiled and felt comforted. She took her hands out of Samira's and once again traced her fingers across Ibrahim's name as she had countless times since the henna had dried.

Before the *beberiska,* Anisa and Samira, acting as Beatríz's *negaffa,* had given her a purifying milk bath – the *hammam.* Beatríz had hesitated to take part in the ceremony, but reminded herself that it was like a *mikvah,* a ritual bath she had taken monthly since she had begun to menstruate, and which she would have taken on her wedding day, if…. The milk had cooled her thoughts and her body, though her embarrassment flared when they changed her into her white *caftan.* She knew they could see her swelling belly. How could they let their man marry a woman so sullied? But they had all been through so much too, and so it seemed they understood that there is the ideal and there is the real, and that sometimes there must be a looking past to see what is necessary.

Colorfully painted platters of food were brought out for the crowd. Vegetables of greens, purples, and whites-turned-yellow were stewed and spiced. Olives, dates, fish, and even meat were set on low tables and on the floor in the middle of circles of silky cushions. But Beatríz could eat none of it. She sat, her body tense, and watched the women dance, wondering what she looked like with kohl around her eyes, in a veil, and laden with bracelets loaned to her by Anisa and neighbors to make her an acceptably dressed bride. Would her own mother recognize her? Pain stabbed across her head and she gripped her cup.

Without realizing it, she was on her feet, practically running for the door.

"Are you all right?" asked Anisa.

Beatríz froze and scanned the room, looking at the near-strangers now staring at her. The music had ceased, as had all conversation. Without a word, Beatríz hurried out.

"Beatríz, stop!" Anisa shouted, and Beatríz did. Anisa was standing half way down the stairs, her angular features made sharper by irritation. "Where are you going?"

"I —" She was not sure. She simply knew there was not enough air inside. "A walk."

"A walk?"

"Yes. I need . . . I'll be back. The party can go on."

"There are guests here for you."

Beatríz realized something. "They are here for you. And Ibrahim and your grandmother. They do not know me." And the power of that truth nearly knocked her to the ground. No one here knew her. No one shared her history. Knew how she had misbehaved as a child. Knew that her brother, Solomon, had been her best friend for most of her life. Knew that she hated *bacalhau*, Portugal's most commonly eaten fish, with a passion. Knew that she had seen a man threaten to drown his own child rather than allow it to be converted.

The slave had been right. She did not belong here.

"Anisa," Beatríz began, taking a step back up the stairs but then going no further. She thought of explaining herself. But she could not. "I want to speak with Ibrahim. Is he at the docks?"

Anisa narrowed her eyes, studying Beatríz. She nodded and then said, her voice full of warning, "You should return soon. It will embarrass him if you do not."

Beatríz winced. The last thing she wanted to do was cause harm or hurt the one person who had helped her the most. And yet, she could not go through with the wedding before spending a few minutes speaking with him. Or even better, spending a few minutes alone. She needed to think.

Beatríz wandered and found herself at the edge of the Jewish quarter – a place she had known of but, in her effort to build a new life, had chosen not to see. She hesitated. Was it wrong to want to be there?

From where she stood on the edge, she could see that the sand buildings looked the same as the others in Djerba, the smells of burning wood and sea salt were the same, and the people were focused on their business just the same. She had expected to feel differently when she passed through the arch that separated this section from the others, but she felt nothing. Relieved and disappointed that standing among other Jews did not give her any answers, she made to leave, but first stopped at the fountain, to cool her hands and face. She studied the faces of the passersby looking to see if any were familiar, but none were.

A woman came and put her hands in the water. Her ruby red gown was thick brocade, and her *camisa* puffed through gaps in the ribbons of her tied-on sleeves. This detail of fashion from a life seemingly so far away and long ago shocked her. Beatríz twisted the cotton of her loose robe in her fingers, feeling caught between relief and longing.

The woman pulled her black curly hair off her neck and

splashed water on her face and neck, sighing at the coolness. She caught Beatríz staring and asked if Beatríz wanted something.

"No," Beatríz said before rising and walking away. Then it occurred to Beatríz that the woman had spoken Portuguese and she turned back. "Are there others from Portugal here?"

The woman regarded her strangely and said, "Of course."

"Do you know Yusef?"

"Which one?"

Beatríz's heart began beating quickly. There was more than one. "Yusef of Lisbon."

"Which one?"

Beatríz's mouth felt dry and her headscarf hot. "A merchant. Son of Dom Abrão."

The woman looked around and Beatríz thought he might walk out of one of the buildings just for their speaking of him. "Not Dom Manuel?"

"No. Dom Abrão."

"Very short? With a sister in tow?"

"No," Beatríz answered, her voice shaking. "No sister. Tall. He was set to marry…a girl named Beatríz."

"No one of that description has come through."

The smashed hope made her wish she had not come at all. She covered her face, pressing the tears back. Feeling the woman's eyes on her, she lowered her hands. She was barely able to fill her lungs to thank the woman for her time.

Pointing at the henna designs, the woman said, "That is beautiful. When is the wedding?"

Beatríz stumbled away without answering.

Her mind hummed as she made her way to the waterfront. When she passed through the city walls, she did not allow herself to look around or to think about anything except finding Ibrahim.

When she finally found him, he was hard at work. Nothing about his actions or activities said that he was a man about to be married. It was so different for a woman, for she had to be cleansed and painted and fed and entertained.

He spotted her and let the bundle on his back slide to the ground. "What is wrong?"

"Nothing," she said, not quite managing the lie.

He stepped away from Fadil, his brow lowered as he regarded her. "You left the celebration at Anisa's house?"

"Yes."

"Why?"

"I needed to speak with you," she said swallowing hard. "About our marriage."

He cocked his head, letting his eyes take in her hennaed hands and feet.

She knew if she wavered for even a moment, she would be tempted to change her mind again. "I cannot marry you."

He stared at her with his light brown eyes and pushed an anxious smile into the corners of his mouth. "You are nervous. That is natural."

"No, Ibrahim. This is not from nerves. I have been thinking about this."

With clenched teeth, he asked, "For how long?"

"Since the moment you asked me to marry you. Before, actually."

His head snapped back as if someone had slapped him. "But I thought . . . I thought we discussed this. I thought you were changing your – Why n – Why?" He blinked rapidly and pulled at his chin.

"Because I feel – I feel wrong. Out of place. I do not belong in your world."

Ibrahim squinted at her as if this had never occurred to him.

To say what she needed to say, she had to look away from the thick full lips she wanted to kiss and from the strong hands she wanted to hold. Staring at the sea, peaceful that day and dotted only by a two masted ship that seemed to stand perfectly still despite having its sails open full, she explained, "Words come to my mind first in Portuguese. I dream in Castilian. I pray in Hebrew. When I speak in Arabic, it sounds strange. I do not know what I am saying or doing when I am here. I feel like a purse that has been turned inside out." Her eyes drifted to meet his.

He looked completely bewildered. "But you have been safe with us. Safe and content for the first time in many months. This is the right path. How can you doubt that this is what is meant to be?"

Confusion surged within her. He was right, of course. What madness to leave. To walk away from security. From a man such as Ibrahim. Kind. Patient. Loving. But she felt she had to finish what she had begun, for if she let it go another day, it would be too late. She would be married to a wonderful man who was not the man she truly wanted, and living in a place she did not like and without a community of her own. "I cannot stay."

He rubbed at his face and then his temples. He opened his mouth as if to speak, and then closed it again. He turned suddenly and began to walk away. She swallowed hard, wondering if those would be the last words they would ever exchange, yet she said nothing.

Then he turned back. "You care for me?"

"Yes."

His voice rose. "Then why is that not enough?"

"I do not know."

"You will change your mind."

"No." She reached for the edge of a discarded crate to steady herself.

He ripped the crate from under her hands and threw it against the sea wall sending bits of wood flying. She ducked as splinters rained down on her head and he let out a roar from the depths of his soul. Others turned to look at them.

He knelt next to her and growled, "I love you and you act as if you do not care."

"That is not true. I care."

He snatched her hands into his own and turned them over, revealing the design the women had put on her palms just that morning. "This is my name," he told her, pointing too roughly. "Put there because you said you would be my partner in life. Our wedding is tomorrow! How can you do this to me? To my grandmother?"

Unable to speak past her guilt, she merely looked away.

He grabbed her chin and made her face him. "That is not an answer."

"Because I am still waiting for Yusef."

Ibrahim looked at her hard. "He is dead."

"I know."

"You are ridiculous!" he exploded and leapt to his feet. "I have given you everything! I drew you from the sea and protected you from others who might do you harm. I fed you. I cared for you. Who else would do this? Who?"

Beatríz shut her eyes as if that could erase the pain she had caused

Breaking all social rules, he took hold of her in public. "Do you think there is another man who would want you the way you are? I was willing to forget that, but most men would not be."

She stepped back, pulling her shoulders out of his grip. "I know." Determination, fear, and regret split her soul evenly.

"So what will you do?" he asked, his nostrils flaring. "Live on charity? You told me your people were letting their women starve. Those are people you want to go back to? Then you are a bigger fool than I thought."

Beatríz's frustration began to bubble. Frustration with herself more than with him. "I *am* a fool," she said. "I am a fool not to marry you. I am a fool to even think of leaving this island. But it seems I do nothing but foolish things anymore. I was a fool to follow Yusef's family rather than my own. A fool to run from Oran when I learned of Yusef's death. A fool to let the pirates take me rather than let Onur kill me." When he opened his mouth to argue, she insisted in a voice far stronger than she believed she had, "I would have been better on the bottom of the sea. But after all of this, I do not wish to make the most foolish decision of all: promising to be your wife while thinking of another."

She did not wish to see his face crumple as it did. Did not wish to see him run his sleeve over his face as despair overwhelmed him. Did not wish to stand another moment watching his heart break. But she would bear witness to the pain she was causing. Pain he did not deserve.

He walked away from her, and this time he did not turn back. He stopped in front of a man loading a ship. They must have been friends, for the man squeezed Ibrahim's shoulder in greeting. This man had seen the argument, and who knew what he had heard? Beatríz waited as the men spoke quickly and in hushed tones.

After a while, Ibrahim walked back over to Beatríz. "This man's name is Amin. He is going to Gabés, which is just across the water, and will take you that far. You can decide where to go next."

"Oran, I suppose."

Ibrahim's face was stone. "It does not matter to me."

His coldness made her flinch, but she knew she could expect no more kindness. She did not deserve it. "But how will I pay?"

"My friend does not expect payment. It is a favor." He looked her up and down as if compelled to memorize her. His gaze lingered on her hennaed hand, and she made a fist as if blocking his view of his name could protect him from the pain. Looking away, he said, "You can sell the earrings if you wish."

Her fingertips grabbed at the wedding present he had bought for her. "You should take them back."

"No. I do not want them. It was a gift, Hadiya." Wistfulness filled his voice as he said her Arabic name.

Her heart squeezed. "These bracelets are borrowed from neighbors, though," she said, pulling the golden circles off of both arms and pressing them into his hands.

He gritted his teeth and explained, "Amin leaves in the morning and says you can sleep on the boat tonight."

"On the – but –"

His angry eyes slashed at her.

She took a step back. "But my things."

"You have nothing at my house." His voice was cold as he emphasized the word "my."

It was true. She had no possessions but a spoon and an old dress of Samira's that hardly fit. And it was not her house. It never would be since she had chosen to hurt them both by leaving it.

"I would like to thank Samira. To say goodbye."

"No," he answered quickly, leaning dangerously close. "I will explain. It will cause her grief and seeing you will make it worse." And with that, he turned away.

"Ibrahim!" she called out.

His step hitched, but he did not turn around.

In that fleeting moment, she stared at his strong shoulders, tense and hunched. The dark, perfect hairs sticking out from the bottom of his turban. His fists clenching and unclenching. What could she say? That she was sorry? That she loved him? That she would be forever in his debt? All true. But she could not say what he wanted to hear and so she simply said, "Goodbye."

Body stiff, he walked not back to work, but through the city gates to tell his family what she had done. Her chin quivered as she pictured Samira's face, lined with sorrow, and Anisa's, angry. Closing her eyes for a moment, she said a prayer for forgiveness and turned to Amin, blood rushing loud enough in her ears to drown out the sounds of the men at the waterfront who had gone back to work.

Ibrahim was his friend, so she expected him to be cold or rude to her. But his face was blank as he escorted her to his boat and pointed to a place on the deck where she assumed she was meant to sleep. He spent the afternoon in preparation for his journey, paying little attention to her, which suited her fine. He loaded food and water onboard, tied the last of his goods down, and spent the early evening talking to friends in a circle of torchlight by the brick and stucco city wall.

That night, she did not sleep fearing the travel ahead. After spending her life wishing to be on the sea, two of her three journeys had ended in violence beyond comprehension. She shook and shivered, unable to rest, fighting the urge to run to Ibrahim and stay on dry land forever.

Before leaving Djerba, she wrote a letter to Rebecca and Rabbi Aharon and asked Amin to send it with another ship. Her hope was that, if something happened to her on the journey, her friends would at least be able to inform anyone interested that she had been alive. She gave few details of the past months, knowing that there was no way to put it in writing. And if she did reach them, the evidence of her ordeal would be clear.

As promised, once Amin left her in Gabés, it was up to her to find food, housing and passage. Gabés was not nearly as crowded, so she was able to find a small room to rent, and paid the woman in charge by doing light housework. Beatríz went to the water's edge with trepidation every day searching for a boat going to Oran. While she waited, she earned money by writing letters, and, with relief and sadness, watched the henna fade from her body.

Eventually, she found a captain of a mid-sized ship who claimed to be bound for Oran. She knew perfectly well that he might steal her belongings or worse, but any man of the sea might do the same, so she braced herself and gave him more money than she had intended to spend on travel.

He told Beatríz that Oran would take a week or two to reach – if they were lucky. They had to go north toward Sicily and then, just past Tunis, would curve around the coast and travel west for a number of days.

Beatríz tried to keep her back to the rail and face the crew at all times. She squeezed the handle of the small knife – the first purchase she had made in Gabés, which she carried around constantly. She had it tucked in her hand, ready to prevent anyone from touching her, understanding that she would likely be thrown overboard for the offense but preferring it to the alternative.

The journey was without incident. Oran finally came into view and Beatríz prepared to disembark. The first mate came toward her just as they were about to drop anchor and asked for more money. Beatríz explained that she had already paid, but the man insisted more was needed. Beatríz clutched the knife handle in one hand and her purse in the other, wondering which would help her most. She decided on the money. After untying the leather thong and pulling out two coins, the man asked for more.

"I will have nothing left if I give you those."

"And there will be nothing left of *you* if you do not," he answered evenly, a knife, far larger than hers suddenly gleaming in the midday sun.

Beatríz handed him what he asked for and backed away, praying that that would be all he required.

Soon she was walking down the gangplank. The first time Beatríz had made this journey, she was being escorted to the sultan's palace for the arranging of terms for the new Jews' stay in Oran. She fleetingly wondered if there had been an upset in power in her absence, and if so, were her people still allowed to reside here? But the city seemed at peace, for that moment at least, and Beatríz was grateful.

At last she followed a bend in the street and saw the house from which she had fled so many months earlier, inconsolable at the loss of Yusef. Who could have imagined the turns her life would take and how much better off she would have been if only she had heeded Rebecca's pleas to stay?

A line had formed, as usual, outside of the rabbi's house. Beatríz wondered if she ought to join the line or simply enter as she had so many times before. She decided to go in, ignoring the irritated comments of the waiting men and women as she pushed the door open.

"We will call for you when —" Rabbi Aharon began to scold, but then he stopped and rose quickly. "Beatríz, you are here. Rebecca, she is here!"

Before he was able to make it around the table, Rebecca had sprinted out of the kitchen. "I did not believe it when I read your letter," Rebecca exclaimed. "But you are here. Actually here." Rebecca held her hands against her own cheeks, her full eyes gleaming.

Beatríz felt like laughing and crying, too, to see her old friend, but words would not come.

"Safe and here. I can hardly believe it myself," Aharon added.

"Come into the kitchen," Rebecca suggested. "We can have a drink, and Aharon, have Yoshuah help the women waiting outside as best he can for now."

After Aharon left, Rebecca whispered, "Since you convinced him to help the lost and widowed wives, the *agunah* line up ceaselessly. He hardly has time for any other business." She threw her hands up and looked to the ceiling for mercy. "But," she conceded, "it pays well and he helps them in their situations, though few end as yours have."

A stinging began behind Beatríz's eyes. "I imagine many end as mine have," she replied.

"With the man being found alive?" Rebecca asked bewildered. "I think not."

The words came to Beatríz as if spoken through wool.

"What do you mean?" Beatríz asked.

"You received my reply to your letter, did you not?"

"No," she said steadily, though the veins in her neck began

to throb with hesitant anticipation.

Rebecca's eyes widened and her fingers touched her lips. "Of course not. There was not enough time." Rebecca's face pinked at once. "Yusef is alive."

Beatríz felt as if the air had been sucked out of the room. She tried to hold on to the world as it melted away.

"Alive?" Beatríz heard herself say.

"Yes. I cannot believe you did not – He and your brother arrived here months ago looking for you."

"My brother? Which brother?"

"Solomon."

"Oh God," Beatríz gasped, pressing her palms to her temples unable to keep her thoughts clear enough to ask anything more. Rebecca brought her a cup of wine and Beatríz finally managed, "But...but how?"

Aharon had entered the room at some point and he explained, "The women who told us of his fate were right. He was captured and fought but he was not killed. He was chained to two other slaves and rowed for weeks. Then a storm came, a terrible unexpected storm. Remember those women mentioned that many ships were wrecked? Well, his ship broke apart as they said, but by some miracle, on his bench was one other man who could swim and they survived. They were shackled to another slave who was not so lucky, so Yusef and the other man swam dragging the dead man between them until a small vessel pulled them aboard and unlocked them."

Beatríz stared wide-eyed at Aharon.

"The sailors made it clear that when they reached shore they would sell Yusef and the other man again, so Yusef..." Aharon looked at his wife who nodded solemnly for Aharon to continue. "Yusef did not allow that to happen." Aharon looked away and let silence settle over them.

Beatríz shuddered to think of what her gentle love had done to regain his freedom.

"And so he will come and you can finally be together," Rebecca exclaimed.

Beatríz shook her head. "No. He will not want me." The words came out of Beatríz's mouth before she realized that she was speaking the truth. He would not. And even if he did, she did not deserve happiness. Did not deserve him. It was better to let him go, to let him think she was dead or lost to him. She dropped her head and forced herself not to picture his beautiful face. She wanted to find him. To touch him. But she was a whore carrying another man's child. And so Yusef, her dear Yusef, would have to find another. It was only right.

"What are you saying? He has been searching for you. And why are you sad?" Rebecca asked. "I thought you would be overjoyed to know Yusef was alive."

"I would be, but for this," Beatríz said, holding her bulging belly.

Rebecca gasped. In all the excitement and with Beatríz sitting behind the table, Rebecca truly had not noticed. Rebecca and Aharon exchanged glances, and Rebecca ventured, "What happened?"

And so Beatríz explained, the memories raw enough to make her wince now and then. Aharon sat stone-faced and Rebecca wept as the tale unfolded. When the story was finished, Beatríz looked around the table, grateful that at least she was among friends once more.

"So you see," Beatríz said, "I do not want Yusef to know that I am even alive."

"I already wrote to Yusef," Aharon told her, his face grim and gray.

Rebecca looked at him with dismayed recognition, then back at Beatríz. "After we received your letter, I told him to write so Yusef could meet you here as soon as possible. I did not know."

The day had already held too many surprises, so Beatríz took hold of her cup and finished her wine.

"He must be on his way already, but in case he is not, should we write to him again?" Rebecca asked.

Beatríz shrugged unable to make a decision.

The call for *Salat* floated faintly into the room and Beatríz rose suddenly, relieved to have something to do. "Would you excuse me for a little?"

"For what?" Rebecca asked.

Aharon clenched his jaw as he looked over Beatríz. "To pray," he told his wife.

Beatríz ignored his tension and added, "I also need a small basin of water."

Rebecca pointed to the corner, completely bewildered, before her husband pulled her from the room, saying, "You can stay here. We will leave."

On her journey Beatríz had continued to say the prayers Ibrahim had taught her, at first feeling it might help her blend in, and then liking the routine of it. And the painful reminder of all she had given up.

Beatríz chanted, *"Bismillah ar-Rahman ar-Raheem."* She struggled a bit as she washed her feet, an act not yet rote but oddly reassuring. Then she said, *"Ash-hadu anna laa ilaha illa llah wahdahu laa shareeka lahu wa-sh-hadu anna muhammadan 'abduhu wa rasouluhu."*

When she tried to put her forehead on the floor, her stomach stopped her, leaving her like a dog on all fours. She lowered her head and wondered why she was doomed not to fit anywhere. Beatríz knelt and continued. Her voice faded in and out as she found herself wondering what Rebecca and Aharon thought of this and how long she would continue.

Beatríz rose and opened the door for Rebecca to reenter. Rebecca's face was hard, but Beatríz ignored that and offered to assist in preparing food. Rebecca nodded, but once they were inside, Rebecca made no move to cook. She crossed her arms and asked, "So are you a Muslim now?"

Beatríz hesitated and then answered, "Yes."

"Why?"

"Because I had no choice. I was going to marry Ibrahim."

"But now you are not, so change back."

The words punched Beatríz. "I might," she said with a shaking voice.

"But you must."

"No, Rebecca, there is little I must do anymore. Having this baby is the only thing I must do."

Rebecca looked her over. "Would you at least change your clothes? What happened to your gown?"

Beatríz swallowed hard. "It was ruined." She tried not to think of how.

"The style is so…foreign."

"Foreign to who?" Beatríz wondered but did not ask. It was comfortable, practical, and had become more familiar to her than the heavy cloth of the gowns she had sweated in growing up. But she was living with Rebecca now and at the mercy of her and Aharon. She would change what she could to make herself pleasing to them, but she did not know what she was willing to give up.

"I doubt you have anything that will fit," Beatríz conceded.

A shadow passed over Rebecca's face as her eyes glanced

at Beatríz's middle. "I have a dress from when I was with ch–" She could not bring herself to finish the sentence, which only deepened Beatríz's shame. "Let me get it."

Soon the women were working Beatríz into the thick fabric and tying laces. Beatríz felt constricted and recalled the restlessness that had plagued her as a child, the need to escape. The dress hung so heavily on her, but she could not fight it. Could not fight anything anymore.

"There. Much better," cooed Rebecca. "I will not likely need it until after you have gone back to your own size." She smiled conspiratorially and touched her own middle.

Beatríz took a moment to understand what Rebecca was saying, and when she did, she felt jealous of her friend's serenity and joy. "How wonderful for you," Beatríz said, trying to sound pleased.

Just then Rebecca's son, Adan, toddled in and Rebecca wrapped her arms around the child.

Beatríz picked up a knife and began chopping herbs that Rebecca had laid out, wondering if she would cradle her own child so lovingly.

When she was nearly done, Rebecca said, "You are so changed, Beatríz. You used to chatter with me, ask for the latest gossip, begin arguments. You have hardly said a word without being prompted since you arrived."

Beatríz wiped her hands on a towel and bit at her lips. "I am sorry if I disappoint you."

"No," said Rebecca quickly. "It is just . . . if I had not seen it myself I would not have believed it."

Beatríz did not know how to reply.

Rebecca took the pile of herbs and dropped them into the pot of meat, which was boiling noisily. "Remember how you argued with the Sultan on our first day here?" Both women began to laugh, breaking the veil of tension that hung between them. "That man reprimanded Aharon for letting a woman speak. I thought for sure he would kill you or ask us all to leave. His face was so red!" Tears rolled down both of their cheeks as they bent double with laughter. "You – You told him he was indecent for not helping the man who had been robbed."

Beatríz sobered immediately. She had forgotten that part of the conversation. "Yes, the man's wife was raped and the Sultan did nothing about it."

Rebecca dabbed at her face, her expression changing quickly. "But there was nothing he could have done."

"I'm sure," Beatríz said, and she went back to chopping.

Arrangements were made for the rabbi's assistant, Yoshuah, to move to a neighbor's so Beatríz would have somewhere to stay. Beatríz could not sleep again that night, for her mind was full of the future and the past. The next day, Beatríz took a slow walk through the city. She wandered past the mosque, but chose not to go in. She went to the tanner's to say hello, and made a special effort not to wrinkle her nose as she entered her old home. She went to the square where she had once set up her letter-writing business and found abandoned women, the *agunot*, still looking lost and hungry. Beatríz could not bring herself to engage in conversation, and continued strolling, looking at Oran with eyes both clear and confused. This city would serve her needs and the people were kind enough. At the same time, she did not know where she belonged.

She stood outside the synagogue listening to the men pray. They did not, as the Christians did, chant at the same time. No one led them. At some services Jews prayed all together, but the morning ritual was done when a man could arrive, and he would join a small group that dictated their own pace. The familiar rise and fall of the words brought her back to happier times and the people she loved. And when she saw the artifacts of the place – the torah scrolls, the Star of David, the screen she once hated that separated men from women – she felt a comfort and a longing that took her by surprise. But she was not ready to make any decisions, so she walked on.

The days passed and they all waited without speaking of the waiting. Beatríz tried not to think about Yusef arriving, but he was always in her mind. She tried not to dream of him. Tried not looking for him on the street. Tried not to go to the water's edge to find if a new boat had arrived. Tried not to think she heard his voice coming through the window. She waited. And waited.

CHAPTER 25

On a non-descript morning, Beatríz wandered back from the market, taking her time since, back at the house, obligations and watchful eyes constantly weighed on her soul.

But as Beatríz turned the bend in Rabbi Aharon's road, she saw him. Yusef.

She blinked a few times. Could it be? She had wished for him for nearly two years. Could he truly be so close?

Standing very still, jostled by the passing crowd, she studied the figure. The slope of his shoulder. The curve of his leg. He turned his head, searching, and she saw the fullness of his lips. The thick brows. The piercing gray eyes.

Her heart quickened, and old feelings rushed back at her. Love. Relief. Lust. Joy. He was perfect. Thinner and more worn, but perfect. Suppressing a squeal, she started to walk faster, the distance seeming too great, the moments passing too long.

He recognized her, and his hand shot up to wave. Elbowing past the masses to reach her, he cried, "Béa! My God, Béa!" As the distance closed between them, she noticed his bottom lip trembling and his eyes filling.

He reached for her, and she could practically taste him on her lips. As if the past months had never happened, she was transported to the docks of Lisbon. To a time when the world melted away, and it was him and her and their love, no matter the struggles of the world.

He took hold of her face, pulling her toward him for a kiss.

Then they bumped awkwardly.

Yusef straightened and looked down at her protruding stomach. The color left his cheeks. He blinked and his lips moved wordlessly. Finally he asked, "Are – are you married?"

She shook her head and tears spilled over the lids. "No," she said, her voice trembling.

He turned his head away. For the first time, she could see the right side of his face – a scar, raised and reddish purple, ran from his forehead, over one eyebrow, and down his jaw. Instinctively, she reached her hand to touch his cheek. He grabbed her wrist hard and pulled it sharply away. Her heart broke through her chest and smashed to the ground.

They stood in frozen silence before he stepped away and let go of her throbbing arm. He said, "I looked everywhere for you, waited for this moment." He stopped to compose himself. Then he looked down at her belly and his face twitched into an expression of pure agony.

She spread her fingers across her stomach to shield it from his scrutiny and judgment.

"There is so much to –" He ran his fingers through his hair and she saw scars around his wrists, too. "This is too much." He turned on his heels and sprinted away.

Her head swam and she was keenly aware of being alone, of the passers by studying the motionless girl who stared at nothing. In shock, she walked down the street and opened the door to the rabbi's house.

Solomon stood in the entryway and Beatríz hardly felt the joy she ought to have at the sight of the brother she thought was lost to her forever.

"Beatríz!" he shouted then covered his face, lost in tearful relief.

She would not allow herself to weep, could not let feeling find a home within. She held her basket of goods in front of her, still as stone.

Solomon moved forward and wiped his face roughly. "Beatríz, I was sure when we said our goodbyes that was truly the last time I would ever see you."

"I know." She shivered recalling that night, and worked to hold emotion at bay.

Then Solomon's gaze drifted over her shoulder. "Beatríz, where is Yusef?"

She clenched her teeth. "He left."

"Where did he go?"

"I do not know."

"I nearly had to tie him down to keep him from running to the market – but I was afraid you would take different streets. He could not wait for you to – Did he run to find a place for you to live? The rabbi said he could marry you today."

Beatríz winced at the words, her mind flashing past memories and hopes a hundred times crushed and resurrected then dashed again. "No."

"Then what?"

She dropped the shopping basket to her side.

Solomon's eyes widened. "Beatríz."

Beatríz stared at him, waiting.

His eyes narrowed. "I always knew –"

"Knew what?" she asked sharply.

"You always had trouble hiding your passions when it came to men."

Her teeth ached with fury. "Not *men*. Only when it came to Yusef. And I never – You think this –" She opened her mouth but found herself unable to fight or to explain. If Solomon thought this was her fault, then Yusef certainly did. And they knew her better than anyone. Her legs began to melt, but she would not let her brother see her weak. "Leave, Solomon. You know nothing."

"Beatríz."

She walked into the house where she met Rebecca's expectant gaze with anger and went into her room. Beatríz could do nothing but grab a pillow and press it to her face.

If there was one thing Beatríz had learned, it was that grief came and grief went, but food preparation was a constant. She eventually went to the kitchen, though she did not look at Rebecca as she entered. She simply picked up a chicken, slapped it on the cutting block, and began to hack at it.

Rebecca said nothing.

Just as they were about to put the pot on the fire, Yoshuah entered and cleared his throat. "Beatríz, your brother is back."

Beatríz leaned hard against the table. "Is he?" she asked coolly.

"What should I tell him?"

Beatríz looked at Rebecca.

Rebecca asked, "Would you like Aharon to explain things to him?"

Beatríz shook her head, tamping down her rage. "Can you finish without me?" she asked Rebecca.

Rebecca nodded.

Beatríz turned to the boy and said, "Tell him to wait outside." She brushed her hands together and asked Rebecca, "May I live with you for a while more?"

"Of course," Rebecca said nervously. "But that will not be necessary, I suspect."

Beatríz sighed as she walked out. Rebecca's optimism was sometimes foolish, but was a trait Beatríz wished she still had.

The sunlight blinded Beatríz momentarily and her pause at the door gave Solomon time to come close. Before he could say anything, she began walking and said, "Let us go to the water's edge. It is a place I no longer take pleasure in, but at least it is more private." The hardness of her voice surprised even her, and her brother walked at her side speechless. Solomon put out an elbow to escort her, but she ignored it.

They wended their way outside the city gates and found a place to sit. Solomon began to speak but Beatríz cut him off. "No Solomon, I will talk. I will tell you everything and then I will leave. You and Yusef can decide what you want to do with the information," she said, the harsh word slicing the air between them. "But let me be clear. The way you behaved makes me almost hate you. These many months, I have learned that I can survive without you both. I do not want to but I can. And if you plan to scorn me, living without you is precisely what I will continue doing." Emotions rose within her, but she stabbed them into submission.

And so she looked out to sea and told Solomon every detail of her journey, from her first conversion at the hands of the priest to Miriam's murder, then Safi and Davíd, the plague and her journey to Oran, living at the tanner's, writing letters at the rabbi's, learning of Yusef's death, paying her way onto the first boat to leave this very harbor. She told him of the pirates and spared no detail, then did the same for her life in Djerba. She explained her second conversion and her near marriage. As she spoke, she never looked at her brother. Not when he gasped or murmured, not when he put a hand on her arm. She looked away and kept speaking, creating a space that allowed her to tell it all. And when she was finished, she stared at the sea and let the silence break over them both.

"Oh Beatríz."

"No. Do not say a word about it," she said, turning fire-filled eyes on him. But the pain in his face quelled her temper and she asked with a voice less sure, "What of your journey? Where is your family?"

"It was, as you can imagine," he said, "trying, but my wife and children are safely in Fez with her parents, who made it there themselves just a before we arrived. After we snuck out of Portugal, our ship was captured and brought to Malaga. We were forced to remain in the port and priests came aboard daily in an effort to convert us. When that did not work, the local bishop commanded that food be kept from us until we accepted baptism. At that point, a large number of passengers acquiesced. The rest of us...." He stopped to rub his forehead. "My wife would not hear of it. I argued that our babies were dying, but she refused. She said that I did not do... what I had done to get them back only to cave at the next challenge. After five days, the bishop relented and allowed us to receive food. By then my little ones were weak, but we gave them bread sopped in milk and, thank God, they survived. I thought I would lose them again."

He stopped to sob relief into his hands, and this time, Beatríz let herself reach out to him and touch his back. The warmth penetrated her skin and the shield she had put up to protect herself. She leaned against her brother's back, so glad to have someone she loved with her again, and waited for him to continue.

"Our ship remained in port for two more months before it was allowed to sail again with those of us who still resisted. No one would take us in any city. The ship had no supplies and no one would give or sell us any. But we survived. The little ones are... well, changed. They are so serious, as is my wife. But they are alive."

He turned to face her. "I ran off in the night forsaking you." He pointed at her stomach. "I should have helped you."

"You did what you knew was right. You had to save your children."

"If I had been with you instead, you would have been spared having –" He blushed.

"That is madness. Your children are far more important than anything else," Beatríz said. "Would you have been able to live without them? Would you have just sailed away from Portugal as if they were a table or a spoon that could not be packed?"

He shook his head.

"You are blessed to have them back. And I...." She let the thought hang in the air unspoken. "How did you find Yusef?"

"An incredible coincidence. My family and I made our way to Fez, and Yusef had come there hoping to find you. Yusef had gone to the rabbi's house and was told they had never heard of you. And then I went to the same rabbi. He said it was odd, that a man had just come and asked about the same woman not two days earlier – a man looking for the woman he was to marry. I ran through the streets asking for Yusef, and, though it is a large city, the Jewish quarter is still a place where a person can be found. Yusef was holed up in a terrible room with no windows, drunk and cursing the day he was born. I dragged him out of there and got him sobered up.

"He said he was giving up hope of finding you or anyone alive. But there I was, and that made him feel like he could go on looking. In the meantime, I had begun working with a man I had known in Lisbon. With my wife and children secure with her family, and all of us in need of income, I felt I could go out to trade once again. Yusef, having no obligations and still wanting to find you, decided to join. We searched methodically in every port along the coast of the Maghreb leaving messages whenever we could. In Safi people knew you and sent us here, but Rabbi Aharon told us that you had run off when you learned of Yusef's supposed fate. It nearly broke him to know that he had caused you such pain and that you were missing because of false news. We had to return to Fez with our goods, but Rebecca promised to tell us if you landed here. And when we got word, we loaded another ship and made this our destination."

Beatríz said quietly, "All of that searching only to find me like this." She hesitated, but made herself ask, "Will Yusef come for me?"

Solomon ran his fingers through his hair roughly. "I do not know. It is a lot to bear."

Beatríz snapped her tongue. "I am aware that it is a lot to bear," she said, pushing her fingers into her flesh and wishing once again that she could rip the thing out.

"But he loves you, Beatríz. Never have I seen a man so in love. I cannot believe that he will want to live without you."

Beatríz shrugged away his words and her hope.

As they walked quietly back to the rabbi's house, she heard the call to prayer coming from the minaret. Her step hitched, and her hand drifted to her veil as they sauntered uphill.

"So you are a Muslim now?" he asked.

"I am everything and nothing," she said with a sigh.

When they reached Aharon's home, she told Solomon, "If he does not come tomorrow, I will have my answer. But I do not want you to leave without saying goodbye."

"I can bring you to Fez with me no matter what he decides."

"My time is getting close, and I do not wish to travel more than necessary in my condition. I have friends here. I will come when and if I can."

He nodded and hugged her hard. "I will not leave without saying goodbye."

She pinched her eyes shut and wished she could stop feeling.

Beatríz slept fitfully that night. She had told all to Rebecca and Aharon, and they seemed sure that Yusef would come for her, but only Beatríz had seen his face and she was not so certain. She rose before dawn and sat looking out the window at nothing but the changing light. As the bricks turned from pink to orange, a knock at the door startled Beatríz. With an unsteady gait, she crossed the room and reached for the knob. When she opened it, she first saw Solomon and then Yusef.

Solomon hugged her and whispered, "I will be inside."

Beatríz pulled the door shut behind her and reminded herself to breathe. She and Yusef took a few steps away from the door and faced one another. They said nothing at first, just marveled at each other, at the changes they saw. She again studied his scars, his sunken cheeks, his hollow eyes. Beatríz resisted the urge to reach out and to speak.

Still he said nothing. He looked at her stomach. Then he took her hand in his, but dropped it. Finally, he touched the scar on her neck and asked, "What is that?"

"How I escaped," she said simply.

His shoulders slumped and his face went white. "This is my fault. I should have stayed."

"How could you have known? You warned me, Yusef. You told me the world was on fire and I could not imagine what that meant."

He shook his head and looked at her stomach again, letting out a long breath as he did. "I want to be with you, but I…. When I think of it, I feel sick."

"How do you think I feel, Yusef?" she said, her own outrage growing. "I tried to get rid of it. I did. But it grows stronger every day and it will be born and I will be its mother."

He frowned. "Would you give it away?"

Her insides roiled. "If we were in Lisbon and there was someone like Dom Carlo whose wife was barren, then perhaps. But here there is no one to care for it. I am sorry, Yusef, but I will not be responsible for another death or another ruined life. You should not want to be, either."

His jaw clenched and he said bitterly, "I am afraid that every time I look at it I will think of those men."

"As am I! Yet the child and the . . . events will be with us as surely as our scars. We cannot pretend all of it did not happen."

"No," he said with curled lips. "We cannot."

They stood in silence for a time and when her anger subsided, she resigned herself. "Yusef, there are girls, many other girls who need men. Girls who are untouched. Rescue one of them. I will find my way."

"But Béa, I do not want another girl."

"You do. You want the girl you left in Lisbon. Well, that is not me. I am changed in every way." Before she could stop herself, she said, "But I love you." She pulled in a deep breath and continued, "And I want you. Yet I understand if you cannot be with me."

Rebecca came out of the house just then. With uncharacteristic determination, she asked, "When will the wedding be?"

A hundred knives stabbed Beatríz when she looked back and noticed Yusef's gaze had dropped. "Excuse me," Beatríz said as she walked back into the house.

After closing the door, she did not have the strength to cross the room, so she sank down against the nearest wall and cradled her head in her hands. Beatríz was close enough to hear Rebecca murmuring angrily outside the door, but she did not move to stop the conversation. Nor did she look up, though she knew Solomon and Aharon were staring at her from just a few feet away.

The door opened and Rebecca walked in alone. "Go outside," she instructed Beatríz.

"He does not want me," Beatríz argued.

"He does."

"Did he say that?" Beatríz asked, allowing a hope to pierce her fear.

"No, but I can see it in his face."

Beatríz groaned in exasperation and hit the back of her head on the wall. "It is impossible."

Rebecca crossed her arms and waited impatiently.

"He cannot see past this," Beatríz argued, holding her stomach. "I will not ask him to."

"You do not know for certain what he can and cannot do."

Beatríz did not answer.

"You left here in despair when you thought you lost him

once, and look what happened. Then you nearly married Ibrahim, but you stopped yourself because you could not let go of Yusef's memory. And after surviving so much, you will allow fear to come between you?"

Beatríz rose tentatively and was relieved to see Yusef still waiting outside.

"Did you hear all of that?" Beatríz asked, half ashamed, half hoping he had.

Yusef tugged at this tunic but did not answer the question. "You almost married someone else?"

"You were dead. And I cared for him. He was a good man." Beatríz bit back her feelings. "He was willing to accept what had happened to me. He did not blame me for what happened."

"I do not blame you, Béa."

"But you will punish me for it."

Yusef stared at her. Then he reached out and traced his finger along the scar on her neck again. She shivered.

"I will punish myself if I walk away," he said, "but I am afraid I will punish you as much if I stay. I am rougher now and quick to anger. I cannot sleep. I want to harm any who crosses me. I am so different than before, and I fear you will hate me."

She pulled his hand away from her neck and pressed it to her stomach. "This is the only problem we have."

The baby thumped under his palm and his eyes met hers. But he did not leave.

She brushed away a tear as her resolve cracked. She wept in front of him against her will and when he folded her in his arms, she cried harder. She could not make herself push him away, could not stop wanting him to hold her tighter.

He murmured, "The world has used us both roughly." She

heard him pull in a jagged breath before he continued, "But when I think of my life without you, it is more painful than when I think of that baby or your trials or my many sins."

He broke his embrace and her heart sank. But then he reached into his purse and pulled out a coin of far less value than the one he handed her at the betrothal ceremony in front of his mother and father, her mother and father, their siblings and all of their neighbors. Now, with one brother and the strangers that had become family looking on from the doorway, he continued, "When I gave you a coin all those years ago, it was a promise. I want to keep that promise."

"Do not feel obliged to –"

He pressed the coin into her hand. "This is what I want. The wedding is a formality. You have been mine since the day we met, since I saw you in your nightshirt on the landing of my parents' house, when you spoke no Portuguese and blushed to have me look at you across the table. I endured imprisonment by thinking of you. I escaped slavery to get to you. How can I finally have you this close and let you go? It would be a sin worse than all others. Beatríz, marry me. Be with me. The rest we will face as we have faced so much else."

Beatríz heard sniffling behind her and knew it was Rebecca. Beatríz enclosed the coin along with his hand in hers and stepped forward. She leaned into Yusef, their stance awkward. But his arms tightened around her once more, and in that moment she stopped being afraid and listened to the beating of his heart.

CHAPTER 26

"**I** can marry you today," Rabbi Aharon said, beaming. But when he saw Beatríz and Yusef glance at each other hesitantly, he added, "If . . . that is what you wish, of course."

Yusef kept his eyes on Beatríz's cautious expression as he answered the rabbi's question. "Today is best, I think," he said, and only relaxed once Beatríz nodded. "Yes. Today."

Beatriz was so overwhelmed with joy she nearly collapsed.

"Beatríz," Rebecca said, swooping forward, "there are preparations we must do."

Beatríz could not think what she meant. There was no party to plan, no food to make, nothing to pack. But then the remembered the *mikvah*. Since beginning her courses, she had gone monthly to the ritual baths, and, as custom dictated, a bride went before the ceremony to the *mikvah* to purify her body. "Of course," she said, doubting there was enough water to purify her. But it needed to be done and so she would go.

Solomon said to Yusef, "We will go to the *mikvah* for you, too, my friend. A bridegroom always goes."

He straightened up proudly at the words. "Yes, of course. Though I need to get my clean clothes from the boat." A smile crept across Yusef's face. "You ladies will not spend too much time talking and lounging?"

The idea of their lingering now was absurd. How could she tarry when Yusef was waiting for her?

Rebecca chattered most of the way to the baths. Beatríz listened just enough to nod at the appropriate moments. But then silence fell between them and Rebecca stopped walking. "This is what you want, no? Marrying Yusef."

"Of course," she answered. "But I am nervous. An hour ago, I thought he did not want me at all, and now I am to be his wife in just as short a time." Beatríz began walking again and Rebecca followed. "I lost hope so long ago that this day would come."

"It is God's will that brought you back together."

Beatríz tried to turn her shrug into something less doubtful, but did not quite manage it in time and Rebecca saw.

Rebecca grimaced. "You do not believe in God now?"

"I do not know what to believe."

Rebecca looked at Beatríz's veil and pressed her lips together. "The idea of your accepting your conversion is absurd," she finally said.

Beatríz thought of standing before Ibrahim and Anisa and Samira, saying the words that would have changed her fortune and wondered what she believed of them. Ibrahim sounded as sure of his path when he had spoken of his religion as Rebecca sounded when she spoke of hers.

"What year is it?" Rebecca asked.

"1499."

"No. 5259, according to the Hebrew calendar. The true

calendar of our people. *Our* people. God chose *us* among other nations, and our covenant is older than theirs. Our ancestors were chosen by God at Sinai. Only *we* can truly serve God."

"Everyone says that, Rebecca. Everyone believes they are right!"

"God does not accept your conversion. The laws of our people – of *halakha* and *kashrut*—are binding upon you. You cannot turn your back on thousands of years of history. On your ancestors. On the lives given to hold onto a faith under attack. You cannot do it."

They had reached the *mikvah*, and Beatríz leaned a hand against the stone doorway. "Rebecca, it is too much to consider today. I am here. At the *mikvah*. I will marry Yusef under a *chuppah*. Let this be enough for now."

Rebecca, her color high, paused and then nodded.

They took the few steps down into the dank entry for the women's side of the *mikvah* and stood for a moment as their eyes adjusted to the flickering light of the oil lamps in the corners. Beatríz was comforted by the familiar scent of wet stone. The baths of Oran were not as grand as those in Lisbon, but Beatríz thought their simplicity fitting. No chandeliers here. No colorful designs. No draped cloth or padded cushions. The walls were covered in whitewashed stucco, but done so lightly that the stones beneath poked out.

An attendant stepped forward and held out her hand for payment. Rebecca thrust coins into the woman's hand and whispered to Beatríz, "My present to you."

Beatríz squeezed Rebecca's elbow in thanks, and the women moved deeper into the building. The floor was slick in spots, so they walked carefully across it. The dim rooms echoed with the hushed high voices of other women, but

Beatríz could not see them. Some *mikvahs* had large changing and sitting areas, which might serve as a place for friends and neighbors to congregate, but this one had just a few small rooms for individual baths and a space for disrobing directly next to each. The only sources of light were small slits where the ceiling met the walls, providing some air and much privacy.

They found their area and turned the corner. There were no doors, but each opening faced away from the others. Beatríz sat on the wobbly wooden bench to take off her shoes and stockings. When Rebecca reached to untie Beatríz's bodice, Beatríz suddenly thought of Anisa acting as Beatríz's *negaffa* in preparation for her wedding to Ibrahim, and a wave of regret and sadness passed over her.

She wanted to tell herself that this reunion with Yusef was meant to be. Fated. But it was an accident, was it not? A lucky one, certainly, but unexpected. When she sailed away from Djerba, she had not known such a miracle would happen.

She reminded herself that it was not the hope of finding Yusef that had sent her away from Ibrahim. It was the conversation with the slave, the one that had called her a *renegado* — a traitor — that had changed her mind. He had spoken of the value of being among one's own people, part of one's own traditions. He had made her remember how much she missed the familiar, missed the rituals. And here she was participating in one of the most comforting rituals of all: entering the *mikvah*, washing as an act of beginning anew.

And perhaps Rebecca was correct. Perhaps God did not accept either of her conversions. Perhaps the pull she felt over and over to be with her people was, in fact, God's doing. She did not know. But she wanted to believe that this was right. That she was making the best choice, and that maybe, just maybe, she could find peace again.

With these thoughts in her head, Beatríz removed the veil she had worn for many months, and folded it carefully before laying it on top of her gown.

"Your hair is so short!" Rebecca exclaimed, pulling at strands that brushed the top of Beatríz's shoulders.

Beatríz nodded, but offered no explanation.

She walked to the water, a sunken square not wide enough to stretch out in, though that was not its purpose. The water of the pool had to, by law, flow naturally, though she was unsure of its source. The stucco stopped two steps down, revealing roughly cut stone, and Beatríz descended the last few steps until the water reached just above her waist. She said, "*Baruch ata adonai eloheinu melech ha-olam asher kid-shanu b'mitzvo-tav v'tzi-vanu al ha-tevilah.* Blessed are You, Adonai, King of the Universe, Who has sanctified us with the mitzvot and commanded us concerning immersion."

Then, arms and legs wide, she submerged herself. She stayed under longer than she was supposed to, until her lungs began to sting, hoping the pain would clear her mind. She could never make up for what she did to Ibrahim and his family, but Yusef was what she had sacrificed everything for and she would finally have him. She would be his.

When she burst from the water, she cut off Rebecca's exclamation of concern by going under for a second time and then a third, as custom dictates. She did, however, switch to what was expected: dunking just below the surface enough to wet to the top of her hair and reemerging quickly.

Before she was finished, she added a prayer for significant first events, the prayer she had held in her heart in anticipation of her marriage to Yusef. *"Baruch ata Adonai, Elonheinu Melek Ha-olam sheheheyanu vikiamanu vihigianu lazman hazeh.*" As she considered these words, "Blessed are You, Lord our God, Ruler of the Universe, who kept us alive and preserved us and enabled us to reach this season," Beatríz could not help but bow under the weight of her thanks. It was, indeed, a wonder that they were both alive and on the threshold of joining their lives together.

Rebecca's glance swept over Beatríz's body as Beatríz rose from the water, and both women reddened. It was not that they were unaccustomed to seeing other women nude, for that was a given at the baths, but Beatríz's condition made for an awkward pre-wedding moment.

Beatríz dried herself and reached for her *camisa.* To make light of it, she said, "So, shall we go get me a husband? It seems I am in need of one."

When Beatríz and Rebecca returned to the house, they found Yusef and the other men with drinks in their hands. Rabbi Aharon set his down and called out a greeting. Yusef, his hair still damp from the *mikvah,* tipped the cup high and finished the contents.

Solomon waved her to him and whispered in her ear, "This is what you truly want? To marry Yusef?"

"Yes," she said quietly.

"Good." He squeezed her hand. "I wish our father and mother could see this wedding."

"As do I," she said, pushing the words past the lump in her throat. "But perhaps we will tell Papá about it in person one day."

"God willing. Constantinople is not so far," he said, his forehead wrinkling.

"Solomon, let us make this moment one of joy. How astonishing that after all that has happened, you are here to bring me to the *chuppah*."

He nodded and escorted her to Yusef. "Be good to her, my friend. I know this is not as you expected, but you will do right by my sister, will you not?"

Yusef nodded. "I will. I love her, Solomon. I will protect her and care for her as long as I live."

A smile started in the middle of Beatríz's chest. He loved her. And she wanted to be his. Officially. Forever.

"Shall we go to the square to begin?" asked Rabbi Aharon.

"Yes," Beatríz blurted out to the amusement of everyone in the room. She turned her face into Yusef's shoulder to hide her embarrassment, and relished his unique smell of sweat and sea that lingered in the cloth.

Rabbi Aharon waved them out to the street and they processed to the far corner of the square. The wedding had to take place outside, though Beatríz wished it was not so. She did not like being conspicuous anymore.

Aharon's assistants carried a prayer shawl, opened this *tallit*, and held it over Yusef's head. Once each of the corners of the *talit* were aloft, creating a kind of roof for the ceremony, they were ready to begin. Solomon and Beatríz walked forward, and just outside of the *chuppah*, Beatríz stopped to stoop as a bride was meant to do. Yusef emerged from the canopy, took her by the arm, and brought her under the covering. Solomon took one corner of the *talit* from Yoshuah and held it high, winking at Beatríz as he did so. A second *talit* was draped over both Yusef and Beatríz, and then the blessings began. Yusef and Beatríz shared a cup of wine and then Rabbi Aharon hesitated, looking confused.

"A ring. Yusef, is there are ring?"

Yusef's grip on Beatríz slackened. "No. There was one in Lisbon, but. . . ."

"Or a gift. A coin, perhaps?"

Yusef's face reddened. "I do not have . . . What I have is of so little value. Not befitting a wedding." He opened his purse and began to root around.

Beatríz thought again of their elaborate betrothal ceremony with the candelabras, the flowers, and the shining gold coin that was passed without thought. Who knew where that coin was now? Or if they would ever hold something of such value again. Oh that night, that beautiful night. Beatríz had been so sure of everything then. So pure of heart and body. Yusef had held her tight and there had been no trace of doubt in his heart or eyes.

Rebecca called out, "Take mine. My ring."

"We cannot," said Beatríz.

Rebecca pressed it into Yusef's hand as she said to Beatríz, "You cannot start with nothing. It is not my wedding ring." She exchanged glances with Aharon, who nodded his agreement with her act of generosity. "Aharon gave it to me before we left *Sepharad*. It is good luck."

Yusef put the ring on the tip of Beatríz's forefinger, and looked at her with his soulful eyes. She thought she might fall into them and be lost forever, and trembled with joy as he repeated the rabbi's words, "*Harei At Mekudeshet Li B'taba'at Zo Kedat Moshe V'Yisrael.*" Behold, you are consecrated to me with this ring according to the laws of Moses and Israel.

And with that, the couple was married.

Rabbi Aharon rolled out a parchment. "Beatríz," he said, "Yusef and I wrote this *ketubah* while you were preparing for the wedding."

"What could be in this marriage agreement?" Beatríz asked. "We have nothing." She did not say it with anger or bitterness, but with amusement. She had once blanched at these legal documents outlining what the bride's family would give to the groom's, and, an unthinkable thought to Beatríz, the *ketubah* sometimes spelled out the terms of payment in case of a divorce.

Beatríz shook her head suddenly wanting to laugh at the absurdity of the years lost while they waited for Beatríz's father to gather enough to pay Yusef's family, only to end up as she was – penniless and ruined.

Solomon came forward to sign as a representative of her family, and Yusef signed for his side. Then the rabbi's assistants also signed. It was awkwardly done, for unlike the ceremony Yusef and Beatríz ought to have had, no table had been set up just for this part of the ceremony. The men leaned down and used the dirt underfoot as their writing surface.

Aharon handed Beatríz the *ketubah* and Yusef a glass of wine for him to share with her and said another prayer. Beatríz drank deeply, and the alcohol made her dizzy, so when Rabbi Aharon said the traditional seven blessings, she took hold of Yusef even more tightly.

Finally, Yusef took the emptied glass and placed it underfoot. After getting an encouraging nod from Aharon, Yusef smashed the glass, the traditional end to the ceremony, and cheers rose up from their few friends and their many neighbors who had gathered to watch. Yusef leaned over and passionately kissed Beatríz, who nearly swooned at the shock of it all. She was his and his alone. The day had finally come.

The prayer shawl that had covered them was removed, and the one that had been held overhead was lowered. The young assistants folded both carefully while Solomon came forward to kiss his sister's cheek and pat his now-brother-in-law on the back. Over his shoulder, Beatríz studied the rather large crowd surrounding them. When she was back in Lisbon, she had wanted the entire city to celebrate her union with Yusef. Now she wanted to slink away unnoticed if possible. If she had learned nothing else in these past months, it was that attention was dangerous.

As if to prove her right, a man said loudly in Arabic, "By looking at the bride, it seems they could not wait for the wedding."

In an even bigger voice, his friend said, "It cannot be the groom's baby."

Beatríz hoped Yusef, whose Arabic was far better than hers, was not hearing any of it.

"No? Then who do you think is the father?" asked the first man.

Beatríz felt Yusef turn, and she pulled at his arm, hoping to draw his attention away.

The second man straightened his turban and said to his friend, "*I* am the father."

Beatríz cringed and tugged harder at Yusef, whose body was tense like a cat ready to pounce.

"No," said the first man. "*I* am the father."

At this, Yusef slipped from Beatríz's grasp and launched himself at the man who had begun the conversation, landing a solid blow. His friend yanked Yusef away, but Yusef knocked him to the ground and punched his face again and again with a fierceness Beatríz did not think him capable of. People cried out and Beatríz screamed. Members of the crowd leaped in to separate the men. Yusef shoved and dodged, trying to get back into the fight.

Beatríz pulled at Yusef and cried out, "Stop! Please Yusef!" Solomon was pushing hard against Yusef to get him to leave, and Beatríz was finally able to take Yusef's face between her hands. She turned his head so their eyes met. "Yusef, no more!"

His angry eyes darted around as he huffed and sniffed.

"Please," she said again, and something in her voice seemed to make him listen at last.

"If you kill him," Beatríz continued, gripping his cheeks so hard the skin of her fingertips turned white, "guards might take you away from me. I cannot be alone again. I could not bear it."

Yusef's breath slowed bit by bit until the man she knew and loved seemed to inhabit his gaze once again. He nodded and took her hands in his, continuing to calm himself, though his eyes darted now and again to the man still lying on the ground. The Jews of their quarter kept back, but the man's friend, whose nose was swollen and turning purple, leaned over and pressed the corner of his shirt to a gash on the other man's cheek.

"Let us leave this place," Rabbi Aharon urged, leading Rebecca toward their house.

Beatríz found herself unable to move from where she stood staring at the damage done by Yusef, a man she had loved for his gentle nature and soft touch. The last time Yusef had returned to Lisbon, men on the docks had suggested lewd things, but Beatríz had been able to move Yusef away quickly and avoided a confrontation. But there was no quieting this anger. For the first time, she found herself afraid of him.

"Do not pity that man," Yusef said. "He would have done worse to me if I had not hit so hard. If nothing else, I have learned *that* from my travels."

Beatríz took note of the jagged scars running down his face and nodded weakly.

"You did not expect me to let what they said go unanswered, did you?" Yusef asked, bitterness bubbling among his words.

Beatríz stared at the wounded man and then at her own body, misshapen for a bride. She opened her mouth to speak, but was unsure of what words to say, fearful of angering Yusef further. And dismayed by that thought.

Solomon saved her by saying, "The rabbi is right. Let us go."

At Rabbi Aharon's, they feasted modestly and spoke of everything but the fight, though Beatríz stole glances at Yusef's ripped knuckles. As night fell, Solomon excused himself saying he would come by in the morning to bid them farewell. He would be sailing back to his wife. Goods were loaded and Solomon felt confident he would make a bit of money from the journey. He and Yusef had decided that they would remain partners, with Yusef procuring goods in Oran, and Solomon being the one to travel back and forth. For now.

Dishes were cleared and Beatríz began to clean. Rebecca looked at her with an expression that told her that this night there was other business to take care of. Beatríz nearly dropped the plate she held. She had successfully put this out of her mind. Long ago, she could hardly wait to touch Yusef each time he came home from trading, and fought every urge that pushed her to be with him before they were wed. Had she and Yusef been married in Lisbon, she never would have stayed after the ceremony to help tidy up. And yet, nothing had gone as planned.

When Beatríz made no move, Rebecca came close to Beatríz, smiling conspiratorially, and said just above a whisper, "It will be fine. The first —" But then she stopped herself and her face fell.

Beatríz felt quite dizzy as flashes of the pirates entered her head. The light haired captain with his tidy shirt, the old men and their wrinkled bodies, the young ones with energy and bluster.

Unable to breathe, she turned away. Feeling Rebecca's arm around her shoulder, Beatríz murmured, "I cannot. I –"

"You must."

Beatríz lifted her fingers to her lips and pressed hard to keep from whimpering.

"Beatríz," she whispered, "the marriage must be consummated."

Sensing something amiss or just having poor timing, Rabbi Aharon took that moment to say, "It is late. We ought to leave this couple alone."

Rebecca did not move, but Beatríz straightened up and turned to face the men. Her husband – yes, husband – sat there and she had a duty. And so she stepped forward hoping not to look as if she were holding her breath. Which she was.

Yusef rose and thanked Rabbi Aharon for performing the ceremony and Rebecca for the food, and reached a hand out for Beatríz. Beatríz shuffled forward, aware of each muscle moving in her body. He led her to the room she had been sleeping in alone and shut the door. She began to shake, and when he stood close and his lips touched her cheek, she flinched.

Yusef stepped away. "Beatríz, you are shivering. And crying? What –" At the moment of recognition, he kicked over a wooden chair that sat in a corner. "Even *this* moment is ruined by those bastards!"

His anger only made Beatríz cry harder.

"Béa, please do not. I cannot stand to see you like this."

He wrapped his arms around her, but tensed as their bodies adjusted around her stomach.

"How will we move past this? How?" she asked in frustration.

He did not speak but held her as she calmed herself.

"Time. Time will help us heal. Of this I am confident." He caressed her face with his wounded knuckles. "May I at least kiss you?"

She nodded and he did, making her feel like she was sixteen again, in love and innocent. He reached behind and untied the laces of her bodice, pulling until her shoulders were exposed. He kissed her bare skin, letting his lips trace the curve up to her neck and then behind her ear. Her legs were weak, and when he moved his tongue under her chin and down her throat, she sank onto the mattress with a sigh.

He followed her down and kept kissing, easing the material lower and lower, exposing more of her flesh. As the air hit her breasts, terrible memories began to resurface, but she fought mightily to remember where she was and that the man touching her was the one she had loved forever and waited even longer for.

Yusef lifted her skirt up slowly, eyes locked on hers, awaiting a signal that it was too much. But she helped him pull the material higher, controlling her breathing and her thoughts and losing herself in the moment.

But then he froze. Hovering over her, he ran his fingertips along the scar on Beatríz's inner thigh. A scar she had nearly forgotten about. Samira had tended the wound with such care that infection had not spread, but despite her healing balms, it still looked like teeth marks.

Yusef fell back as if punched and then turned away. Running his fingers roughly through his hair, he stood. "What did they do to you? No. Do not tell me." He began to pace. "But how – how did you endure – how can you now –" He fell at her feet. "Béa, I need to see it all. So I know what to expect."

And so she undressed and sat, letting him look her over, feeling like an animal at the marketplace. The difference, however, was that when he saw a cut or a scar, he would kiss it, melting her shame and fear.

When he had finished, she took hold of one of his hands and lifted his scarred wrist to her lips. Then she did the same to the other wrist. His face crumpled and she leaned forward, kissing where the red slash began at his brow and down his cheek to his once-perfect neck. He swallowed hard and lifted his shirt, turning so she could see where the lash had torn apart his back. She gasped and remembered the woman telling of Yusef fighting against his imprisonment. But to see the welts made her want to scream. Instead, she ran her fingers along the lines and kissed the back of his neck.

"We have both endured so much," she said at last. "But we will get past it."

He turned to face her and laid his hands on her stomach. "Yet this," he said, "this is hard to get past."

She nodded. "You do not want me. I understand."

"Béa, I do. I do want to be with you. In every way. I love you. But . . ." He sat back a little and regarded her shape. Smiling awkwardly, he added, "In truth, I do not even know how to . . . how we would . . . It is daunting. I expected – I do not know what I expected."

She took his hands in hers and squeezed, becoming the strength they needed. "Then tonight, we should simply lie together and let that be enough. It has been a long day for us both."

He kissed her once more and looked at her with admiration and awe before blowing out the candle next to their bed.

Waking up with Yusef's body pressed against her back, the word that filled Beatríz's mind was "beautiful." The morning light streamed in, and even though she had spent much of the night marveling at the reversals of her life and remembering things she wished to forget, she had also spent it listening to him breathe jagged sleeping breaths that sounded to her like music. At one point, he had woken with a start, apparently recalled who was in bed with him and rolled his body so his knees fit into the back of hers. He had put an arm around her middle, and after some adjustment, had found a comfortable place to rest it. That was when she had finally fallen asleep.

Now with sunshine creeping across the wall, he kissed her shoulder blade and the nape of her neck then scooted a little closer.

"Good morning," she said.

He leaned up on an elbow and bade her a good morning. "It is unfair," he said, "that you are so beautiful. It must make other women tremendously jealous."

She smiled, relieved that the new day was starting off so well. "What will you do today?"

"Find work. I will gather goods for my next trade with Solomon, but I need to earn money until he returns with profits from the last shipment. There must be someone who needs help loading a boat." He kissed her again and asked, "And you?"

"I thought I would help Rebecca and Aharon as I have been. But Yusef, if we need money, I can write –"

"No. I will take care of us now. Work with Rebecca while

we live here, which I hope will not be too much longer. Aharon and Rebecca are, of course, generous to have us here, but living under another man's roof is no way to begin a marriage. Besides, eventually we will want privacy." He winked and rose to dress, but not before kissing her pinking cheeks.

CHAPTER 27

Less than two months later, Beatríz's labor began. Yusef and Beatríz, who were still living with Rebecca and Aharon because lodgings were so scarce, had just finished eating their morning bread when a squeezing across her middle stopped her short.

"*Amor*, are you ill?"

Turning her focus inward, she heard herself say, "I think the baby is coming."

Yusef jumped to his feet. "Let me wake Rebecca."

"No. Let her sleep." Yusef rose earlier than Aharon to work at the docks, leaving the new couple to begin each day together quietly. She assured him, "This will take time."

"Shall I stay home with you?"

"No, Yusef. Birth is women's work. You have your own business to tend to. Rebecca will send for the midwife, and I will be in their care. What more is to be done?"

Beatríz moved gingerly across the room and wrapped a piece of bread and some meat for Yusef to bring to the water's edge. Another pain, sharper this time, took her breath away.

"I am getting Rebecca," said Yusef.

Beatríz wanted to stop him, but could not get the words out.

Yusef nearly bumped into Rebecca, who was walking through the door. He was too flustered to tell he what was happening, but Rebecca only needed to see Beatríz's stance and red face to understand.

"How long have you been feeling like this?"

"Since last night."

"Last night?" gasped Yusef. "You did not tell me."

"Why worry you?" Beatríz answered. "You would never have slept."

He rushed back to her side. "Of course not."

"Then I was right not to tell you," she said. "Go do your work. Perhaps this will all be over before you come home."

Like a schoolboy being pushed toward his lessons, he dragged his feet and walked out the door. Then he stopped and turned to Rebecca, his face drawn. "You will not allow anything to happen to her?"

Rebecca shook her head, smiling indulgently. "Women have babies every day."

"And die from it."

"Shush, Yusef!" Rebecca snapped, her body tense. "Do not bring evil into this house with such talk. Go now."

Beatríz was not upset by his words. Women did die every day in childbirth. But somehow she knew she would not be one of them.

Hours passed and evening came, and still the baby had not arrived. Yusef came to check on Beatríz, but she was too exhausted to speak to him. She could sense his worry, but another pain came and she gritted her teeth and cried out, unable to pretend to be better than she was. He fell to his knees, clutching at her balled fist.

Rebecca hovered over him. "This is why men stay away from laboring wives." Escorting him to the door, she said, "You look faint, Yusef. Walk or drink or talk to Aharon, but do not come in here again."

Candles were lit, and still Beatríz panted and gasped, trying not to hate the baby for hurting her so, or to think about the men who caused her to be in this pain. But as soon as the infant shrieked its greeting to the world, all terrible thoughts fell away, and Beatríz marveled that this person had come from within her body. It was impossibly small and yet so perfect. She held it to her chest and laughed tears onto the child's still-wet hair.

"A girl. A healthy girl," said the midwife as she continued to work. "And no damage to you, so you can bear more children. Many blessings."

Beatríz felt great relief that the baby was not harmed by the tea she had taken to end the pregnancy. Thinking of Djerba pricked Beatríz with pain. She wished Samira could see the baby but knew it could never be.

Soon Rebecca was trying to show Beatríz how to put the child to her breast, and it was a good thing the baby understood what to do because Beatríz did not. All grew quiet and Rebecca paid the midwife with the coins Yusef had left. Then she settled down beside Beatríz.

"You should go to bed," Beatríz croaked.

"No. A first night with a baby is terrifying. You have no mother or sister to care for you or teach you what to do. I will rest later. And you should sleep."

Beatríz tried, but could not rest completely. All she wanted to do was look at the child and kiss her and never let her go.

And yet, the truth was, she feared what Yusef would say. The baby's hair was light brown, and her intense eyes were green. Yusef would ask if she knew where those features came from, and Beatríz would lie and say no, even though she recognized them from the captain. Beatríz had thought such certainty would make her hate the child, and while it was unsettling, Beatríz knew there was no changing what had happened.

Yusef knocked on the door just after dawn, and stood hesitantly until Rebecca invited him in. Rebecca then went to the kitchen so the couple could be alone.

"You are well?" he asked.

Beatríz said she was and held the child out for him to see.

"It is a beautiful baby," he said from across the room.

"Yusef, she will not bite you. Come closer."

He crept forward. "A girl?"

"Yes. Healthy." She gestured for Yusef to sit beside her, and with a slight grimace, he did.

"You are well?"

She smiled. "I already said I am."

He rubbed the child's light hair between his fingers. "She has your chin," he said, leaving the other traits unmentioned and the other questions unasked. "She is very pretty." Then he cleared his throat and stood. "I should go."

"What shall we name her?"

Yusef said stiffly, "I had not considered it."

Beatríz cringed, knowing that he probably did have names in mind, but only for children he could claim as his own. "I thought to call her Reyna."

"As you wish," he said, rising quickly and reaching for the door. Just as Beatríz registered the slight, he added in a gentler voice, "A lovely thing to honor your sister like that. Perhaps the child will have Reyna's enthusiasm and joy." And with that, he backed out of the room. "I must return to work, but I am glad to see you so well, my love."

Beatríz held Reyna to her lips and pressed them to the child's forehead. "He cannot hate you forever. He is a good man. A very good man. And you are too special for him to keep at a distance."

Those first days with Reyna were tumultuous while Beatríz grew accustomed to being a mother. Yusef seemed to accept the change in their lives, but Beatríz stood at the ready for any signs of anger or rejection. So one night when his frustration bubbled over at Reyna, who would not stop crying, Beatríz was ready to attack.

"I need to sleep."

"I know," Beatríz said, standing and rocking Reyna.

"I have to work in just a few hours."

"I have tried to feed her, but she does not want to eat," said Beatríz, who was already feeling miserable about not being able to soothe her child. "She is dry. I am not sure –"

Reyna began shrieking at this point, sending Yusef out of bed and onto his feet.

"Can't you make it be quiet?"

To hear him call her child "it" broke her heart. The tenuous peace she had created in her mind shattered under the weight of that word.

"*It* has a name, Yusef. Her name is Reyna." Then fury bubbled over and she continued, "She is *my* child. *Our* child now. And if that is not how you see her, then we cannot be together."

He opened his mouth to speak, but she cut him off, anger forcing words out of her mouth she did not know were in her mind. "Leave, Yusef. Leave this house. I will care for her myself. Go on."

"Are you mad?" Yusef shouted. "You cannot be alone. I have accepted what is, and –"

"I do not want you to accept her. I want you to love her."

Yusef grabbed his pants and pulled them on. "You want more than is possible. Give me time, Béa."

"Time? You have had months to grow accustomed to this."

"Believe me, it will take more than that. But I love *you* and –"

"Out, Yusef!"

His eyes searched her face to see if she was serious, and when he saw no wavering, he grabbed his shoes and headed out the door, slamming it hard. Impossibly, Reyna began to wail even louder. Beatríz put the baby on their mattress and covered her ears.

Just when Beatríz thought she might lose her mind, Rebecca walked in tentatively. "Beatríz, what has happened?"

"Yusef left us."

Rebecca picked up Reyna and began to bounce her. "It sounded to me like you forced him out."

Beatríz had forgotten how thin the walls were. Even so, she was unwilling to admit to her part in the fight.

"Aharon is speaking with him now. It is not easy in the early days –"

"He does not want Reyna."

"Did you?"

Beatríz's stomach sank.

"You have had more time to grow accustomed to this, and the child is part of you. Yusef has no reason to care for her, and yet he has handled himself quite well, I think."

Beatríz's pulse was slowing and the rage she felt was

diminishing. She realized that Reyna had quieted down, which was part of what allowed her tension to melt away. With no more than a little bounce, Rebecca had done what she had not been able to do: calm the child. Beatríz felt great despair at the thought of never being able to soothe her own baby. Or to make her husband happy.

As if reading her mind, Rebecca said, "Do not push him away. He belongs with you, and will grow to love her, too. I have no doubt." After a moment, she said, "I will bring him in." It was a question rather than a decision, and so Beatríz agreed, taking Reyna back.

Yusef stood in the doorway waving his white kerchief, twisting his mouth to keep from smiling.

"I just told you to go from me forever," Beatríz said. "How can you laugh?"

"Because you did not mean it any more than I would were I to say those same words."

"I would believe it."

"Then you are too sensitive. And insane if you think I would leave you. Béa, I survived a shipwreck to get to you. Do you think a baby's crying is going to chase me away?"

She shook her head, even though she truly had thought it might.

"If you are both done shouting," he said, tapping a now content Reyna on the nose, "we should try to sleep."

Beatríz stood stunned for a moment, amazed by his capacity to forgive.

"Goodnight, Aharon," he called out the door. "Thank you, Rebecca."

Beatríz heard their murmured replies and watched as Yusef undressed and curled up in bed as if none of it had happened. If only she had that talent, she thought, and settled into bed next to her husband and now completely peaceful child.

One afternoon, the women were preparing a *mulahwaj*, a hasty dish, when Beatríz took the opportunity to ask Rebecca a question she had been pondering for days. "Rebecca, was your bleeding regular after you gave birth to Adan?"

"After a few weeks, yes. By the second month, all was back to normal."

"I thought mine was, but it has stopped again."

Rebecca turned to her, and when their eyes met, Rebecca brought her hand to her mouth.

"It cannot be already," said Beatríz. "Reyna is only three months. I thought – It cannot be."

"Are there any other signs?"

Beatríz set down the pestle and admitted, "I want to sleep all the time, but I thought Reyna's keeping us up nights might explain my fatigue."

"Are you sick to your stomach?"

Beatríz sank to a chair and nodded.

Rebecca's eyes lit up. "I am not certain, of course. But would it not be wonderful if you were expecting again?"

Beatríz considered this. To have Yusef's child would be a relief. But so soon?

Rebecca smiled conspiratorially at Beatríz, and Beatríz found it so odd. Reyna had been brought from such heartache, and had elicited both pity and anger, while this child was already being treated so differently. As a blessing. A joy. Telling Yusef only confirmed this.

No sooner had she explained than he had shouted with joy and lifted her off her feet. "A father. I'm going to be a father?" He laughed and kissed her. "I should be careful with you," he said, setting her down gently.

Beatríz's skin prickled with awareness as her other child lay on a blanket nearby, but her anxiety was lessened when Yusef swooped over to Reyna and nuzzled her. "Did you hear? A baby is coming. Your *mamá* is making another baby." He tickled her tummy and Reyna giggled, winning his smile and another nuzzle.

Around this time, good news began coming fast. Letters from friends and relatives were making their way to Beatríz and Yusef. Some had survived great ordeals. Others had fared better but had simply not known where to send word. There was still no news of Yusef's father, Dom Abrão, but they did not entirely lose hope. Yusef and Beatríz were finding greater peace and joy, and Reyna was thriving. Solomon did as he promised and arrived in Oran with a shipload of goods that would generate a sizeable profit. Beatríz glowed to see her husband and her brother, both of whom had not spent much time together in Lisbon, laughing and working happily in each other's company.

But one evening, she walked into the kitchen where Solomon and Yusef were having an intense conversation. She heard, "And then to Constantinople," before Solomon caught sight of her and nudged Yusef into silence.

"What is in Constantinople?" Beatríz asked.

Solomon shifted in his seat. "Now that our father is settled there, he is ready to trade. And Yusef's brother has been successful in Venice. He wants to begin working with us, as well."

Beatríz pressed her lips together. "Does this mean we will leave Oran?" Beatríz asked Yusef.

He sat and pulled her onto his lap. "Someday I think we

will. We will want to live nearer to family, wherever things seem most peaceful. The Ottomans have been welcoming to our people." Yusef kissed her cheek. "But having a post here in the Maghreb is good, too. So for now, we will stay where we have friends. The sultan has firm control of this city, so I believe this to be a safe place to leave you. And the children," he said, putting his hand on her stomach.

She rose quickly. "Did you say leave me and the children?"

Yusef swiveled in his seat to face her. "Yes, *amor*."

The blood left Beatríz's head and legs, leaving her feeling like jelly. "When?" she asked, almost inaudibly.

Yusef looked at Solomon, who answered instead. "Within the year. I will come back with another shipment and Yusef will bring it the rest of the way."

"Why can you not be the one to go? Why must it be Yusef?"

Solomon began to explain, but Yusef interrupted. "Your brother has been at sea constantly these past months. He and I are partners and it is my turn."

"I will not let you!" she shouted, despite her desire to stay calm. Stepping to him, she gestured to his face. "Look at what they did to you last time. What will they do next?"

"Béa," he said, holding her hands as much to keep her from hitting him as to soothe her. "I have stayed with you for months now because of all that happened, but I am a trader. I must sail. You knew this would be our life–"

"I thought it would stop after – I thought –" She yanked her hands back and covered her face with them, pressing until she saw red.

Yusef wrapped his arms around her and spoke softly in her ear. "We are using the same ship now for each journey with the same captain. He is a good man with a family in Safi.

He wants to make money honestly. All will be well. You will see."

With his warm body pressed to hers and his breath tickling her neck, she found it hard to remember her anger and fear. Her breathing slowed and she put her arms around him, tucking her head under his chin. "I could not live if anything happened to you."

"No matter what, I will come back to you Béa," he said, seducing her with his calm certainty. "It is a promise."

Clearing his throat, Solomon said, "This is wrong. I will go instead." He held up his hands when Yusef began to interrupt. "Yusef, you were the one to say that, out of fairness, you should go. Yet I do not feel burdened by the idea of a journey."

"But your wife?" asked Beatríz.

"She does not mind my being at sea. She has grown accustomed to it. I rather think she likes being the commander of our house when I am away." He chuckled. "And with your baby coming, and all the rest . . . Since I do not mind, I do not want to force Yusef away from you."

Yusef fidgeted as if ready to hop on a boat that moment or at least to argue further, but then his eyes met Beatríz's, hopeful and pleading, and he sighed. "For now. But eventually I will go. Solomon cannot be away from his home and children indefinitely."

"Someday you will go," said Solomon, "but not yet." He winked at his sister who mouthed her thanks.

Five months later, Solomon returned with a partially loaded ship. The men added the goods Solomon had procured, and Beatríz included a letter to her father telling him of her marriage and her children, leaving out the rest.

At dawn on Solomon's last day in Oran, Beatríz went to the docks where Yusef had spent the better part of the night helping Solomon prepare to continue on to Constantinople. Reyna, now a year old and wanting to crawl rather than be held, wriggled in Beatríz's grasp, making it more difficult for Beatríz and Solomon to say goodbye.

"Stay safe," Beatríz said, standing on her toes so she could kiss his cheek.

"Take care of my sister and those babies," Solomon said to Yusef, who was holding their contentedly sleeping son, Ishaq. Solomon reached out to caress Ishaq's dark hair and Beatríz smiled.

The men shook hands and Solomon ran up the gangplank. He turned to wave and disappeared into the hold. After standing for a moment to see if he would return for a last word, Beatríz and Yusef took hands and, holding their children in their arms, turned their backs to the sea.

AUTHOR'S NOTE

While the characters in this story are entirely fictional, the events surrounding them are based on fact. The places they lived, the way they socialized and marked special events, the reasons they left their homes, and the difficulties they faced once they did come directly from history books and articles on the era.

Growing up, I knew Jews who called themselves *Sephardic*, meaning from Spain, though their families had immigrated to the U.S. from Iran, Turkey and even Israel. I never thought much about what happened to their ancestors between being expelled from Spain in 1492 and eventually finding stable homes. The intervening period (centuries, in many cases) was a mystery, even to my friends, and one on which I was excited to focus for this novel.

My husband, a scholar of medieval Iberian Jewry, wrote *After Expulsion: 1492 and the Making of Sephardic Jewry* (NYU Press, 2013), a history of the fate of the Jews after their expulsion from Spain in 1492, with an emphasis on those who then left Portugal in 1497. One night at a dinner party, I listened to him explaining his research to some friends, and by the time he got to plagues and pirates, I was hooked. I began asking him questions. Why did the Jews go to North Africa rather than Northern Europe? How did family members find one another? How did anyone get released from prison? What if pirates captured a person? How were letters carried? He had the answers to these questions (and sent me to his scholar friends when in doubt), and then proceeded to recount stories so incredible I could hardly believe they were true.

In fact, I had to tone down some of the true stories to make them seem believable to readers. For instance, Yusef's fate is taken in part from a document about a galley slave whose ship capsized. In real life, the man was caught in an air pocket, and a monkey (yes, a monkey) crawled upon his shoulders and the monkey's tapping on the hull is what brought rescuers to the man. This former slave went on to become a much-feared pirate. Stranger than fiction.

The possibility of a girl like Clara, however, escaping the slave island, São Tomé, was slim to none. But the island did exist, and having Clara in the story offers readers an opportunity to hear more about the fate of the children who were taken from their families. São Tomé, off the coast of West Africa, was an early Portuguese plantation island in need of a workforce. It was one place where Jewish children living in Portugal were sent when their parents refused conversion. There were rumors that the island was infested with poisonous snakes and giant lizards, conjuring up fears that fantastic beasts were devouring the children.

Many of the smaller details and anecdotes in this story also come from accounts of the time. Wild card games *were* held for the amusement of young people. Girls *were* accidentally betrothed after accepting an object, even one of no value. A would-be crusader *did* enter a church on horseback – though in reality, the priest was beheaded when he refused to grant absolution.

When I decided to make the protagonist of the story female, I asked my husband what would have happened to woman traveling alone. His response was, "Oh, that wouldn't go well for her at all." I could not, therefore, spare dear Beatríz lots of danger and heartbreak. Perhaps one woman would not have endured this many traumas. In fact, when I inquired about outcomes for various events, my husband would say, "She would very likely have had her throat cut and been thrown overboard." Throwing people overboard was apparently a rather popular solution to problems at sea. But while an individual might not have survived all that Beatríz did – plagues and sieges, pirates and sultan's advances – real women and men who found themselves on the move absolutely faced some combination of the difficulties presented in this story.

A reader might wonder why a woman like Beatríz would not have gone to places in Northern Europe, places that more closely resembled her life in Portugal. As was explained in an early conversation between Beatríz and Yusef, expulsions had begun in England in 1290, and Jews were systematically expelled from nearly every European country and kingdom from that point forward, straight through to France in the 1390s. During that era, the majority of Europe's Jews moved eastward into the undeveloped lands of Poland, Lithuania, and Russia. Of the group that, instead, made their way south, some settled in Spain and Italy, while others moved on to Muslim lands in Northwest Africa (known as the Maghreb, for modern nations such as Morocco and Tunisia did not exist), Egypt, and the Holy Land, and other parts of the Ottoman Empire. By the time the Jews had to leave Spain and Portugal, all routes to get to Eastern Europe were blocked by lands in which they were no longer welcome, forcing them to fan out across the Mediterranean to places already populated by earlier refugees.

When we meet Beatríz, we learn that she had grown up happily in a part of Spain known as Castile, but left her home for Portugal in 1492. In this year (not coincidentally when Columbus set sail), King Ferdinand and Queen Isabella, signed an edict forcing all who would not convert to leave, and tens of thousands fled into Portugal. But because it was just over the border, many maintained business and familial ties to those left behind. The Spanish king and queen then pressured their daughter's suitor, King Manuel of Portugal, to carry out an expulsion of his own. He decided to try conversions first. There were a variety of attempts to convince the Jews to acquiesce (including taking their children), culminating in calling all Jews to Lisbon promising them that they would be able to depart, and then closing the ports and forcibly converting them. There is little known of the actual process of the forced conversions of 1497 in Portugal, so I used records of other forced conversions elsewhere to try to paint a picture of what it might have been like.

As is shown in the novel, families split up and spread out across the Mediterranean. Boats were held in ports and the Jews kept aboard until they agreed to convert. Jews without permission to enter cities were jailed and held for ransom. So many people needed room, board, and ransom money that charity often dried up. People slept in garbage heaps in order to stay warm, while others slept in open areas where they were vulnerable to attacks. Rabbis argued amongst themselves. Unscrupulous captains robbed merchants and passengers. Pirates attacked. Spouses were separated. Women left alone suffered and sometimes starved if they could not prove their husbands were dead, a legality that would allow them to remarry. Plagues of all sorts swept through the region. Cities were constantly under siege by invading armies. And people protected themselves by adopting varied religions. It was a stunningly difficult time to be displaced, and not just for the Jews.

After the story ends, what would have happened to a family like Beatríz's? Some stayed in North Africa or continued on to the Ottoman Empire. Some abandoned hope of living Jewish lives, went back to Spain or Portugal and accepted baptism. But those who returned, and even those who never left, had struggles of their own. There was great suspicion that the "New Christians" were secretly practicing Judaism. In both Spain and Portugal, this mistrust gave rise to the Inquisition. This tension between "New" and "Old" Christians sometimes erupted into violence, as in the case of the massacre of *conversos* in Lisbon in 1506.

While this story of struggle focused on a Jewish protagonist and her plight, the struggles of the era were not limited to the Jews. What struck me was how difficult life was for so many people of different origins and religions throughout the region at this time. Families of all backgrounds faced disease, attack, and kidnapping. I, who am most put out by long airport security lines and insufficient air conditioning, marveled constantly at the fortitude of these people. People routinely set out from their homelands and built lives in new lands, only to be forced to start again and again. Their bravery and strength are humbling, and I hope this book has given you a taste of the challenges these people faced.

ABOUT THE AUTHOR

Michelle Ray is a writer, middle school teacher and Shakespeare fan. She lives in Silver Spring, MD, with her husband and daughters. Her first novel, *Falling for Hamlet*, was published by Little, Brown and inspired the E! TV show *The Royals,* which ran for four season. Her *Mac/Beth* & *Much Ado About Something* inspired no TV shows, but her friends started to think she has a twisted imagination. With this one, that suspicion might be confirmed.

CONTACT

Website: www.michelleraybooks.com
Facebook: Michelle Ray writer
Email: michelleraywriter@gmail.com
Twitter: @mraywriter

Made in the USA
Middletown, DE
07 April 2019